T0294242

SONG OF OUR SWAMPLAND

ALSO BY MANZU ISLAM

Fiction
The Mapmakers of Spitalfields
Burrow

Non-fiction
The Ethics of Travel: from Marco Polo to Kafka

ACKNOWLEDGEMENTS

I would like to thank the Arts Council of England and the Department of Humanities, University of Gloucestershire for supporting this project. I remember the late Ines Aguirre who has been my guide and inspiration and the first reader of the manuscript.

SONG OF OUR SWAMPLAND

MANZU ISLAM

P E E P A L   T R E E

First published in Great Britain in 2011
Peepal Tree Press Ltd
17 King's Avenue
Leeds LS6 1QS
England

ISBN13: 9781845231705

Supported by
**ARTS COUNCIL
ENGLAND**

I do not know your language, but I hear your melody
(Rabindranath Thakur)

For my brothers and sisters
Ashraf, Shafayet, Sharif, Lipi & Rupa

PROLOGUE

She came with a bundle of ledgers covered in blue. She was a hollow-eyed skeleton of a baby who was so silent that they thought she was a mute.

The childless English couple who adopted her weren't keen on the ledgers, but the woman at the adoption agency in Dhaka insisted. "The father wants them to go with her. It's his only condition. He had nothing else to give her."

So the couple brought them back to their cottage in Gloucestershire and in a fit of curiosity and perhaps guilt they had them translated. Then they burnt the ledgers and put the box-file of papers in the loft to gather dust.

When the last of her adoptive parents died, she inherited the cottage. There she found a letter addressed to her that led her to the box-file. She had driven down to the cottage to pick up the few things she wanted to keep. She hadn't planned to stay long, but the rain caught her.

It goes on and on, drumming the cottage with the fury of a tropical downpour. She has never seen rain like this in England. She goes upstairs to her old room and looks out through the window. Usually she would see the placid river, then the tall, rectangular mass of the Abbey Mill, and just beyond that the Bloody Meadow fringed with oaks and willows, and last the distant blue lines of the Malvern Hills. Today nothing is visible in the rain.

She sits in the rocking chair by the window, listening to the rain. Rain, rain, like the drumming fury of the gods. She begins to read the papers in the file and suddenly she sees the mouth, its huge gaping hole right in front of her face. From deep inside the mouth issues a gust of breath and memories, but she doesn't feel the slightest inclination to turn her face and look away. She gives her full face to them and feels as though they are calling her: Moni Banu, my daughter, you are the song of our swampland.

7

HOMESTEAD

"If the murder of my people does not cease, I call upon you to turn every home into a fortress against their onslaught."

Bangabandhu Sheikh Mujibur Rahman

CHAPTER 1

I have a hole for a mouth.

When people stare at me I often see a look of disgust, if not horror, in their eyes. Sometimes they display pity. Obviously it is not something that one can easily ignore, but I have learnt not to think much about it. I was born that way: with my lips, front half of my jaws and tongue missing. The rest of my body is well formed.

Naturally, I don't have the gift of speech but I more than make up for it by telling myself stories. Come to think of it, I have been very lucky in my life. I rarely forget anything. If people really knew me they would say: look, there goes the elephant's memory. When I see a thing, even for the briefest moment, its details never escape me. Years later, I can see every speck of its colours as vividly as when I first laid my eyes on it. I have a similar way with sounds and smells. And once they are all caught in the web of my mind they provide me with the threads with which I can spin the stories. Who wouldn't feel lucky with such spidery gifts? Sometimes my stories are so long that before I know it I'm flowing down a river, carried down its long meanders through numerous tributaries until, finally, I am offered up to the sea.

My name is Kamal. In Arabic it means the beautiful, the perfect one. Abbas Mia, the teacher in whose homestead I grew up, gave me that name. I was only two years old when I came to live with his family. If I had a name before that time, no one remembered it, but it never bothered me. I was happy being called Kamal, because I knew that the teacher had put in a great deal of thought and care when he named me. I like to believe that he named me with love.

It pains me to say so, but the truth is that in Abbas Mia's household my status was uncertain: I was neither an adopted son, nor a servant. In the beginning both the teacher and his wife, Ata

Banu, had wanted to adopt me. You see, they were a childless couple in their late thirties, which is considered quite old in our part of the world. Certainly no one ever heard of a woman bearing a child at that great age. When I came along they thought I was always meant to be theirs.

I was told that I'd been left alone in the market on the darkest night of the month. Despite my elephant's memory I don't recall that part of my life. Perhaps I was asleep when my parents left me under the banyan in the middle of the market, where the vendors – opening their stalls in the morning – found me. No one dared to touch me: they looked at the hole in my face and decided that I was a bad omen out to bring ruin to the village. People speculated who my birth parents were and why I'd been left in the market. Obviously they found the second part easy to answer. Who'd want a deformed child like this, who could only be a burden on his family? Allah, have mercy on those poor parents. As for the nature of my parentage ideas were limited by what was imaginable in our part of the world.

Some speculated that I was born in a poor Hindu family – perhaps an untouchable. Yes, yes, he looks like he is from the stock of latrine cleaners. No, he has the caste of hide cleaners written all over his face. Maybe, for all we know, his father is a blacksmith. Others thought that my parents were Muslim aristocrats who couldn't bear the shame of having me – or that I could only have come from a Muslim, landless peasant family; maybe even the abominable product of a liaison between a Hindu and a Muslim, or a Christian and a Hindu. No, he has the air of a Buddhist. We bet, said a few, he is a tribal – perhaps a Garo or a Chantal. You know, the people whose women take many husbands and rule their men folks. Whatever, he's hideous – a strange one for sure.

Apparently, as the day wore on, more and more villagers gathered around me, sat down cross-legged with their hookahs, watching me out of the corners of their eyes, but they didn't know what to do with me until the teacher arrived. When he brought me home, people talked behind his back: that foolish teacher doesn't know what a mess he's getting into. He must be desperate to take this ugly thing home. Oh, well, if you've a barren wife, what else can you do?

I suppose I would have been adopted if Ata Banu hadn't become pregnant with Moni Banu within a year of my arrival. I have, though, never resented Moni Banu's birth. In fact, she was the nicest thing that could have happened to me. She called me – when in front of other people – Kamal, but when we were alone – ever since her father had explained the meaning of my name – she called me Beautiful One. It might sound as though she was addressing a girl, but I loved it.

I did many household chores but I was not treated exactly like a servant. I tended to their cows, worked on their land, but I was not paid like a day labourer. I'm not complaining. I was very fortunate to be living in the teacher's homestead. Indeed, I consider myself one of the luckiest people alive.

When we were growing up, Moni Banu was the little one to me, hanging around me as if I could protect her from any danger that life might throw at her thin small frame and dark bright eyes. It was just as much a shock to her as it was to me when she became a woman.

Even before Moni Banu was thirteen her mother had decided that she shouldn't roam around with me any more.

"She thinks she's a boy," Ata Banu let out in one of her dramatic shrieks when she saw her entering the inner courtyard one afternoon, after a disappearance of some hours from the homestead. "What have I done to deserve such a curse?" At that moment Moni Banu paused by the lime tree, her face hidden behind the corner of her sari; then she searched for my eyes to exchange a conspiratorial wink before slinking away.

As it happened, a few days after her thirteenth birthday, the largest annual country-fair in the swampland was taking place – always a time of happiness for Moni Banu and I. Since we were little, we'd always gone there with the teacher. I'm not sure from what age it had become my job, but after the fair I'd carry home on my head the sack containing the purchases. These would be things like date-palm sweets, rice cereal and cooking utensils. At the fair, I was allowed to go around with Moni Banu to help her spend her money and show her the sights. She was fond of clay dolls and sweets. I know people saw me as the little servant boy taking care of his master's daughter. They weren't wholly wrong, but Moni Banu never treated me that way. Sometimes she gave me half of her spending money, shared her sweets and held my hand – especially when the tiger came in to the circus ring. "Beautiful One, look at the teeth," she'd say. "I'm scared."

She'd hide under my shawl and take tentative peeks at the tiger. On the way home at night her father would carry her on his shoulders, but if I fell behind she'd call out, "Where are you, Kamal? Bring the lantern closer."

From the time I was about ten and she eight, we were allowed to go ahead on our own. Side by side, but always running, we reached the fair. We thought it would go on like this forever, but Ata Banu had other ideas. For her, thirteen was already too old for a girl to be seen beyond the inner courtyard, let alone flaunting her face at the fair.

"Look at the girl, she has no shame," Ata Banu would scream. "Doesn't she know she's becoming a woman?"

Moni Banu would do things like kick the brass pitcher, spilling water on the dry clay yard, and storm off to her hut to sulk.

So that year I set off on my own, in the soft morning sun with two ducks and a sack of mustard that the teacher wanted me to sell. He wasn't able to come that year as he was away in town on school business. I was feeling sad about leaving Moni Banu behind, though coming to understand that it had to happen sooner or later. But I'd only just rounded the bamboo grove, and was about to climb down to the path on the swamp-plains when she came running.

"Wait for me, Beautiful One! How come you're going to the fair without me?" I stopped and smiled with my eyes.

It didn't take long to sell the ducks and the mustard. From the proceeds, the teacher wanted me to buy – apart from the usual date-palm sweets and rice cereal – a mortar and pestle and a spade from the blacksmith. Moni Banu had other ideas. She dragged me along to the snake-gypsy's stalls. While I waited impatiently to make my purchases, she skipped from stall to stall and tried on bracelets, earrings and studs for her nose. She was taking so long that I pretended I was going ahead without her, hoping that she would fall for my bluff and follow me. For twenty minutes, I made my way through a narrow passage dense with crowds, past pottery stalls, then weavers' stalls, pausing every so often to check if she was following. But there was no sign of her giving in, so I traced my way back. She was still there, looking at the trinkets in the same self-indulgent way as before. I was about to attract her attention and show my displeasure when she turned to face me with a smile. Her wrists were covered with glass bracelets; from her ears dangled two long beaded earrings; on her nose stood a stud with a red stone.

"How do they look, Beautiful One?"

Not wishing to encourage her, I looked away. She extended her arms towards me, jingling the glass bracelets. She cocked her head and held my gaze with her large, dark eyes. I knew that the teacher would be cross with me, but what else could I do but give in? When I paid for her purchases, I realised there wouldn't be enough money to buy everything the teacher had asked for. I suppose I could just about have got away with not purchasing the date-palm sweets and rice cereal. It would be harder to explain why I hadn't bought the mortar and the pestle – the old one needed replacing urgently – and I wasn't to come home, the teacher had insisted, without the spade.

On our way to the mortar and pestle stall, I made another fatal mistake: instead of hurrying past the amusement area, I slowed to Moni Banu's leisurely pace. She came to a halt as we approached the circus tent and stood watching the fire-eater on stilts who was advertising the spectacle inside. She insisted that we should see the show but I was determined not to give in again, and hurried on. She came running behind me.

"Ma won't let me come to the fair again," she said, as if about to burst out crying – in public. "How can you be so heartless, Beautiful One?" That girl really knew how to blackmail me.

We laughed at the clowns and admired the daring trapeze acts and the acrobats, but what we were waiting for was the old tiger. Moni Banu had lost her fear of him some time ago and no longer needed to hold my hand. Instead, when he came into the ring, she shuffled in her seat and seemed to be trying to catch his eyes. I don't know what she wanted to communicate, but when the ringmaster put his head into his mouth, she whispered in my ear: "I hope the tiger bites his head off."

To Moni Banu's disappointment, the ringmaster's head came

out intact, but I was in even deeper trouble. Now I didn't have enough to buy the mortar and pestle, or even the spade. I made her understand that I was scared of what her father might do to me. "You know Baba never gets angry with any of us," she said. "He'll never beat us, especially not you."

I knew that, but I was still worried. On our way to the blacksmith's, a voice halted us from the sweet shop. It belonged to Lal Mia the lazy, who lived in a village across the swamp. He never worked, lived off the few acres of land his father had left him, and read books. Apart from the teacher, he was the only other book-reading person I knew. Often he would come to visit the teacher, exchange books, and stay the night discussing them. I would crawl quietly close, sit leaning against the timber wall of the outer bungalow, and listen to them. Later, when I read the same books, I would try to judge if my views about them coincided with theirs.

Now Lal Mia beckoned Moni Banu to come and sit by him on the bench inside the sweet shop. While she did so I squatted on the raised mud flooring that formed the veranda to the shop. Lal Mia then called out to the vendor of sweets: "Give my young guests some *cha* and *rashgollas*." I knew it was generous and high-minded of Lal Mia to treat me like this, but I was scared of his hospitality. How could I drink tea with a mouth like mine? It surprised me that Lal Mia should be so lacking in common sense, especially considering his vast learning and progressive views. Moni Banu sensed my unease and told Lal Mia that we weren't in the habit of drinking tea. "That's fine," he said. "You can always have sherbet instead."

I could drink sherbet the way I drank water, but the prospect of doing so in public still worried me. I was not used to eating in the presence of others, even at home. Usually Ata Banu served my food in the kitchen, and I took it back to my hut, and ate alone. Sometimes Moni Banu came in to sit by me while I ate, but her presence never bothered me. When she was little, paying no heed to my manner of eating, she played with her clay dolls in a game that always involved some dramatic story in which I would be assigned a role, but never had to play it. She played my role herself with the diligence of a professional actor. Although the roles had variations, they always amounted to my being a brave traveller coming to the aid of a damsel in distress. For instance, if her clay dolly, in her role as an adventurous maiden, ventured to explore beyond the limits of our flat swampland, she would invariably be captured by the monsters that lay hidden in the dark depths of the border zone. As she was about to be devoured, my character would make his heroic appearance. "It's your go now, Beautiful One," she would say, as a prompt for playing the role herself.

She evidently felt that she needed to align her posture with mine as I ate, as if without doing that she couldn't get into my role. She tilted her head backwards until her face came parallel to the ceiling, and then she opened her mouth wide. Now transformed, she would engage the monsters in some serious swordplay, in which my superior strength and cunning would never fail to vanquish them and rescue the damsel from the jaws of death. Afterwards, she would treat me as though I was really the person in the play. "You are so brave, Beautiful One," she would say.

Later, she still accompanied me, but now doing household tasks like grating coconuts, slicing beans, or doing embroidery. I loved her doing the embroidery because I found watching her fingers dance among a tangle of colourful threads very soothing and mysterious. In those moments she told me about her day, relayed the gossip from the world of women, or sometimes, if the mood took her, sang a little song.

It wasn't always possible, though, to eat at home because I worked on the land and tended the animals. At lunchtime, the farm labourers and herdsmen would sit together in little groups, mostly under the shade of an umbrella tree, to eat their food. I took my lunch behind a rattan bush, but sometimes the herdsboys sought me out. "Look at the broken mouth," they would roar with laughter, "he's eating up the sky."

Now I was about to turn into a freak-show in the sweet shop, but the vendor, without intending it, came to my rescue. He served Moni Banu on the table with the rashgollas gleaming on clean china and the sherbet in a clear glass. He pushed a broken dirty clay pot and an equally dirty mug towards me on the mud floor. He stood over me, rubbing his hands.

"Give us a show, Kamal. Show us what your mouth can do. I bet it can swallow the whole lot in one go."

Moni Banu stood up. "We're not eating at your place," she said to the vendor. Then to me: "Let's get out of this stinky place. It's making me sick."

We hurried along down the path with Lal Mia running behind us. "I'm really sorry for the vendor's ignorance," he said. "Now you know why I talk so much about the need for enlightenment."

When we got to the shade of a mango tree, he asked us to stop there for a while because he had something for the teacher. He sat cross-legged on the dry, brown grass, his shoulder bag on his lap. Moni Banu stood behind him, looking impatient to get away, and I squatted in front of him. He took a book from his shoulder bag and handed it over to me. I opened it and flicked through the pages.

"Sorry, Kamal, there are no pictures," he said, "just words."

Moni Banu bit her lip and gave me a conspiratorial smile. Although Lal Mia was a trusted friend of the teacher, he didn't know that I could read. In fact, reading was a secret between the teacher, Moni Banu and I. Ata Banu knew about it but pretended that she didn't. For me, it began quite by chance when I was about seven years old and Moni Banu five. Since there was no school for girls in the swampland, the teacher had decided to instruct her at home. On the day of her first lesson it was raining heavily. I escorted her under my umbrella to the outer bungalow where her schooling was to take place. She sat wrapped in a shawl on the rattan mattress opposite the teacher, across a low desk. I squatted by the door and watched. First, he gave her a slate with a wooden frame and a number of writing sticks to go with it; then he opened the Bengali alphabet book with pictures of fruits, trees and animals.

"Herein lies the key to the universe," the teacher said, to the utter bewilderment of Moni Banu and myself, "its infinite wisdom and riches."

Although it would be many years before words such as "universe", "infinite", and "wisdom" had any meaning for us, Moni Banu then said something that took the teacher by surprise. "Can Kamal have some of those riches too?"

The teacher rubbed his chin with his hand, stared at the pages with misty eyes, and then cleared his throat. "You want to learn book-reading, Kamal?"

I didn't know how to respond; I stayed where I was by the door.

"Come over here," the teacher beckoned me. "Come, look at the book. I will teach both of you together."

From then on the three of us met in the outer bungalow, behind closed doors. When I was little, I tended the cows, ran errands and did some of the boy-servant's tasks around the homestead, but the evenings were reserved for our appointment with the teacher. When I grew older, I mostly worked on the land during day hours, but my routine for the evening never changed, at least not until I was sixteen. I don't know how things are in the distant parts of the world, but I am sure I was the only mouthless one who could read and write in the lowlands. I have, indeed, been a very lucky person.

From day one, the teacher meticulously followed the school curriculum: from primary to the end of lower secondary education. He taught us all the subjects – Maths, Bengali, English, History, Geography, Religious Studies, Physics, Chemistry, Biology, Social Science, etc. – and we had to conduct ourselves with the utmost diligence – except that I was exempted from recitations and oral presentations. I was happy to do my work on the slate, which the teacher presented me with at our second lesson.

"Treasure it well, Kamal," he said. "It could be your window to the world."

I had no idea then what he was on about, and I lay awake in bed wondering: how can this tiny slate be the window to the world? What am I supposed to see through this window?

I became very good at using the slate. For instance, if Moni Banu was asked by the teacher to recite a poem, I could jot it down as fast as it took her to finish it. "This writing speed is truly unbelievable," the teacher told me many times. "You're a real prodigy, Kamal."

Each year, we completed the school curriculum and progressed to the next class. Although each of us had our own favourite subject, we excelled in all of them.

Yet he made us promise to keep my education a secret. He feared for me if my learning became known, because people might feel uneasy at having to deal with someone in my condition – who was supposed to be both unfortunate and stupid, but was in fact wiser than themselves. Apart from the teacher and Lal Mia, there were only a handful of people in the swamplands who could read or write – which left a vast number of people who could take offence at my education. We kept it a secret.

However, during one of our learning sessions, many years after we had begun, I wrote on my slate: "What's the point of my learning, then?"

The teacher stayed quiet for a long time, screwed his eyebrows as though trying to illuminate some wisdom from the dark. "With books you can always amuse yourself," he said at last. "You'll never get bored, Kamal."

"I'm never bored, Sir," I wrote.

"Perhaps not now, but in your condition there will be times in the future."

"I'll always work hard. When I'm not at work I can always tell myself stories."

"Of course, you can. But we humans need our conversation with other intelligent beings."

"This is true, Sir. But in my condition I can't do much about that."

"There you're wrong, Kamal. If you treat them the right way, books can be your partners, with whom you can engage in infinite conversations."

At the time, I didn't really appreciate the teacher's argument, but came to see its value when some of the books I read kept appearing in my thoughts with their distinctive ways of seeing and feeling about things. Sometimes I found a character in a book whom I could regard as a friend and engage in long conversations.

Although I discontinued formal education at sixteen, I never stopped reading. I became, indeed, an even more prolific reader. And the teacher made sure that I never went short of books; almost every week he brought home one or two new ones. He was just as fond of those that came from the Arabic and Persian worlds as those that belonged to our Bengali and Indian traditions. He also borrowed for us many that came from various parts of Europe – from ancient times and modern. He liked books on most subjects, but he was particularly fond of literature, politics, history and philosophy. It was his privilege to have the first go, but once he had finished reading them Moni Banu and I drew straws to decide who had the next turn. Since I'm a very lucky person, I almost always won. He also brought home daily newspapers, which Moni Banu didn't like much, but I loved them as much as the books.

Now I took the book from Lal Mia and put it in the basket in which I'd brought the ducks. As Moni Banu and I set off on our way to the blacksmith's, Lal Mia shouted from under the mango tree: "Tell the teacher that I'll come to discuss the book on Thursday evening."

When we arrived at the forge, we found the blacksmith working on a blade for a plough. He was nearly bald with silvery fringes and a large belly hung over his dhoti. Moni Banu tried attract his attention as we squatted on the mud floor to his left: "Kamarji, we've an order for you." He grunted without lifting his eyes from the burning coal in the middle of the forge. We waited listening to the whoosh of the bellows as he pumped it by pulling a string with his left hand. Underneath a pile of sizzling coal a block of iron was glowing red and yellow. I'd seen the blacksmith work in his customary place at the entrance to the market many times before, but now at this temporary forge in the fair, I was drawn to his work in a way that really surprised me. Perhaps I hadn't really attended to the whoosh of the bellow before: now it made me feel wonder at the way we had learnt to harness the power of the wind.

My eyes followed the blacksmith as he brought the burning red iron out from the forge with a pair of tongs. It glowed and throbbed on the anvil as if some fire-eating creature was about to give birth to a new body for itself. Snatching a hammer with his right hand, the blacksmith began to beat it. Instead of killing it, he helped it to fashion its new body. I could already see its new teeth mimicking the blade of a plough. I was so astonished that my hands began to tingle as if the blood of the blacksmith was running through them.

"Don't bother me," he boomed as he placed the iron under the burning coal again. "Just go away." Moni Banu told him again that we wanted to place an order. "Come back another day," he said, without even looking at us.

It was late afternoon by then and we set off to return home. Moni Banu was happy with her glass bracelets, earrings and nose-stud, and I was no longer worrying about the money which should have been used to buy the things the teacher wanted. All my thoughts were on how to acquire the blacksmith's art. We weren't alone on the road. Clouds of dust rose from the feet of the people returning home after a day spent at the fair, and drifted across the dry swamp-plains. "Did you buy something nice for yourself?" people asked me. I shrugged my shoulders.

Already the winter chill had set in and I was hurrying to reach our homestead before it became dark because I wasn't carrying a hurricane lamp. Besides, we still needed to cross the river and the forest. Soon we left the column of people and turned right. Now Moni Banu and I were walking alone over jagged fields littered with jute roots.

"Don't walk so fast, Beautiful One," she begged. "I'm having stomach ache." I didn't pay her any attention and carried on. But when I looked back, she really was lagging behind. I stopped but she didn't make much effort to catch up. I went back and she said, "Believe me, Beautiful One. I'm having a bad stomach pain."

I believed her this time and held her hand as we crossed the narrow bamboo-bridge to the other side of the river. Across the river lay a long stretch of mustard fields, their yellow catching the last rays of orange from the sun. I knew that it would be dark soon. The bats were already flying across the sky, but Moni Banu sat on a mound of earth by the mustard fields. "It's so painful, Beautiful One," she said. "I need to take some rest."

I sat by her and watched the yellow of the mustard fading into the darkness. I lifted her to her feet and almost dragged her along as we entered the forest. Suddenly it was dark and fireflies were out in large numbers to dance their short lives away.

"I'm bleeding, Beautiful One," she said faintly.

I sat on the root of a tree and she put her head on my lap and lay on the ground. She groaned with pain, I stroked her hair, and then she didn't make any more noise. We stayed like this for a long time.

"I think I'm becoming a woman, Beautiful One," she said at last. I knew what that meant but I didn't know what to communicate to her. "If I'm becoming a woman and you're already a man," she said after a long pause, "then what am I to you?"

The strangeness of the question threw me, but I wanted to let her know that it would please me if she called me brother. But it wasn't as simple as this because there had been times when I looked at her with the feelings that a man feels towards a woman. And how about her little games? Sometimes, when we were alone in the inner bungalow, she would wrap the hole in my face with a red scarf, and ask me to walk around her.

"You look like a mysterious prince," she would say, giggling. "If the girls in the village saw you now, they'd fall in love with you."

Although I felt uncomfortable in those moments, I played along with her, but her mood could change suddenly. She would go serious on me and look me in the eyes without holding anything back. Then, head down, she would walk back to her hut.

Now, I tried to lift her to her feet. She said she wanted to stay here a bit longer. I knew that the teacher and Ata Banu would be worried; soon a search party would be out looking for us. But I let her stay on my lap, I stroked her hair and together we listened to the crickets, until we saw the lamps streaking through the trees and approaching us.

CHAPTER 2

Moni Banu was married off on 24th March 1971.

The wedding had been arranged long before the troubles began. Since Moni Banu was his only daughter, the teacher wanted the occasion to be memorable, but by then the war was almost upon us. For weeks now the whole country, on Sheik Mujib's instructions, had stopped cooperating with the central government: banks didn't open their doors, railways didn't run, offices stayed locked up. Across the country millions of people, their voices clamouring to end the long days and nights of captivity, marched through the towns and cities. Some, mainly youths and students, were learning the ways of armed resistance. Despite the secrecy and subterfuge, everyone knew that the Pakistani army was amassing a huge number of troops in its east wing to do away with the Bengalis once and for all. Our village was remote, far away from the places of power and politics, but we had been following the news. We were worried, but on that day, our villagers had decided to shut the outside world out. Nothing would stop them from observing the rituals as they had always done. Although I myself was not in a position to enjoy the occasion, those who could were adamant about doing so.

I busied myself at the back of the homestead, helping the cooks.

"Kamal," Moni Banu's mother told me, "don't go to the front of the house today. You understand me? You might scare the guests."

I helped the cooks dig holes in the ground for the giant pots, where the meat from the bull, which Ala Mullah had slaughtered earlier, would be curried. I peeled onions, garlic and ginger, cut them and piled them into mounds. Then I made several trips to and from the village tube-well, about a mile away, to fill the giant clay pitchers. When I had done this, the head cook said, "Kamal, you have done enough already. Go and enjoy the wedding a bit."

I went to the cowshed to check on the new calf. It seemed unsettled; perhaps it sensed the bull's death. I stroked its head for a while, then brought its mother in, and once she began to suckle it I made my way to the front of the homestead where we'd pitched a large tent for the occasion. Inside it we had laid rugs on the ground, on which many of the guests were already sitting. Outside the tent, under the open sky, there was a scattering of chairs, also occupied by guests. Hanging from the poles at regular intervals were flambeaux spreading bright white light, but there were no loudspeakers to blare out songs. In normal times, not to have them would have been unthinkable, but now people accepted it without thinking that the teacher was miserly. I checked the raised platform, laid out like a peacock throne for the groom, to see if he had arrived. He hadn't. I spotted the teacher with three guests not far from the platform, and tiptoed to sit behind them. There was Bilal Khan, the largest landowner in the village with the only brick-built house, and his son, Asad Khan. The third was Sona Mia, a farmer, who, when our regular muezzin was away, called to prayers.

"You're so lucky to have a dumb servant-boy like him, Abbas Mia. Certainly he's rather unpleasant to look at, but at least he can't talk back at you," Bilal Khan was saying to the teacher. "You can't believe the problem I'm having with my talking servants. They're getting so uppity and demanding all sorts of privileges."

I couldn't see the teacher's face, but I knew that he would be upset by Bilal Khan's words. Perhaps he would be tempted to reveal my secret and tell Bilal Khan that I was widely read and infinitely wiser than him. I don't want to brag, but this would have been absolutely true. But he couldn't do this because he didn't want to put me at risk, especially among people who considered themselves my social superiors – which included just about everyone in the village. I knew that the teacher would be thinking of something to say to divert attention away from me. In other situations talk about the imminent war and the political situation would have been his best ploy, but he couldn't risk souring the atmosphere at his daughter's marriage. Bilal Khan, like his son, sympathised with the central authorities of Pakistan and their Islamic ideology. Since 1947, most other people in our village had regarded the government in the West as the agent of their oppression.

"Kamal is an excellent worker. I leave the care of my lands and livestock to him. I trust him completely," said the teacher, which unfortunately put the focus back on me. Sometimes he could be so clumsy in the way he dealt with things.

"If you trust him too much you'll spoil him, Abbas Mia," said Asad Khan. "You have to show him who's the boss. Otherwise, he'll be given to treachery. Or worse, he'll entertain the notion that he's your equal."

"You don't know Kamal," said the teacher. "If you knew him you wouldn't say such things."

"With due respect, what is there to know about him, Abbas Mia? Hasn't Allah written it plainly on his face? I look at him and I know he's a brute."

I had learnt to ignore idiots like Asad Khan, but I knew that the teacher was getting very angry. But all he was able to do was repeat a meaningless, commonplace saying: "You can't judge a man by his face."

"Yes, it's true, Abbas Mia, but there are exceptions. I'd say your servant boy is one of them," said Asad Khan. Up until then Sona Mia had been listening to the conversation with his head down. He lifted his head and cleared his throat.

"Have you really, really looked at him, sir?" Sona Mia asked Asad Khan. "If you had, you'd have known what I've seen. Only goodness and wisdom. I tell you, sir, he's Allah's chosen one."

"What? Have you lost all your senses, Sona Mia? How can he be Allah's chosen one with a face like that? More like he's Allah's curse. For all we know, he could have been born a wretched, untouchable Hindu. Or the bastard son of a pig-eating Christian. Do you think Allah cares for those types?"

The teacher was puffing at his hookah with such fury that dense smoke was spewing out of his nostrils. If he continued like that, I thought, he would soon faint.

"With due respect, sir, Allah loves all his creatures." Sona Mia turned to face me. "Look at his eyes, sir. Do you see any hatred? No. Have you wondered why not, sir?"

I couldn't take this discussion any more; so I got up and moved away as quickly as possible without breaking into a run.

I headed towards the ceremonial gate at the front where the public road meets the boundary of our homestead. On the way, I bumped into Big Suban, the woodcutter.

"Kamal, where have you been?" he asked. "I've been looking for you everywhere." I gave him a smile – I suppose because I was very tense; usually I try not to smile, for it only widens the hole in my mouth and scares people off. But Big Suban wasn't bothered. In fact, I never bothered him. I wanted to look around a bit, so I gave his arm a squeeze to let him know that I would see him later, and continued walking.

When I reached the ceremonial gate, the boys manning it turned their torches on me. If I had known of their presence I would have avoided it. Now they had me at their mercy.

One of the boys pulled at my shirt. "Look at his face. A bottomless hole there," he said. "Full of slime and rotten fish."

I lowered my head.

"Hey, mouthless one, how are you enjoying your mistress' wedding?" asked another boy.

I stood with my head lowered and with my legs shaking.

"Why don't you say something, eh?" said the same boy. "Have you vomited all your brains out of that hole of yours?"

From behind, someone poked at me with a stick. "Can't you see the cripple's sad. Perhaps he wanted to marry Moni Banu himself."

Amidst mocking laughter the boys surrounded me with their torches, the naked flames almost burning the hole in my face. I shielded my face with my hands and slumped to the ground.

As always, the teacher was keeping an eye on me; he came tearing through the crowd and shouted at the boys. "Leave him alone. Get out of here, you rascals." The boys were stunned; they couldn't believe that the teacher would react so strongly on my account. He was shaking and breathing so hard that I feared he was about to have a heart attack. The boys were still standing by the gate, but he started to push them and scream at them.

"If you bother our Kamal again, I'll have you rascals beaten to pulp." I was shocked by the teacher's conduct; I hadn't heard him express such violence before. When the boys dispersed, the teacher pulled me up from the ground. "Sorry, Kamal," he said. "I wish I could tell these idiots about your book reading. That would put them in their place."

I ran to the inner courtyard, out past the backyard and towards the forest. I climbed the jham-berry tree that I used to climb with Moni Banu when we were children. Then it struck me that I hadn't seen Moni Banu at all that day, and that had rarely happened since the time she'd been born nineteen years before.

While I was looking at the stars through the branches of the tree and remembering our years growing up together, I heard fireworks going off with a loud bang. It was the signal that the groom and his party had arrived. I knew the women attending Moni Banu would rush to the fence separating the inner from the outer part of the homestead to peek at the groom. I jumped down from the tree because it would be my only chance to get a glimpse of Moni Banu in her bridal dress. I ran through the dark as fast as possible, but I was too late. The women had already come back and were surrounding her like the Great Wall of China. I gave up on the idea of seeing her and was heading for the front yard when Ata Banu spotted me. She said, "I hope you haven't been showing your face in the front yard. If you scare my guests, I'll chase you out of this homestead like a dog. You understand me? Now, go and sit in the kitchen. I'll come and feed you."

I pretended to head for the kitchen, glancing back to check if Ata Banu was still watching me. I couldn't see her, but had to make sure that she wasn't trying to catch me out. I hid behind the pomegranate bush and waited for a minute or two. A large frog was sitting there so quietly that I thought it was dead. I nudged it with my toe; it croaked and jumped off. No, Ata Banu wouldn't have time to watch me on a day like this. She'd have so many things to do, so many guests to look after. I went around the back of the homestead, cut across the dry jute fields and, edging the pond, arrived at the front. The guests were already seated under the tent, waiting to be served with their meals. I saw the teacher shaking his head. When he saw me, he sidled up and said, "What to do, Kamal? They've brought the brothers Ajud and Majud Ali with them. They'll put us to shame for sure."

The teacher had good reason to be worried; the brothers were legendary eaters throughout the swampland. Each of them could eat as much as ten people and they were regularly hired for weddings. Oh, the unfortunate families they'd put to shame! Not long before, at the beginning of the winter season when Gulab Ali was giving a feast for his son's marriage, the bride's family brought along the brothers as guests. They ate so much that Gulab Ali went short of food. Some of his guests went home with empty stomachs. Imagine the shame of it. For months, poor Gulab Ali didn't dare show his face in the bazaar. When he finally emerged, he couldn't meet people's eyes, and walked head down like a hunchback.

In view of these hard times – about which everyone agreed – there'd been no problem convincing the groom's family that they should bring only fifty guests. From the teacher's side of the family and friends there would be about thirty; in addition he needed to feed some of the village poor and wandering beggars.

So the teacher had arranged a feast for about a hundred people. Although the bull was large and healthy, it would provide only just enough meat for that number. I thought it a pity that the guests never had a chance to see the bull, except as meat. He was pretty with his large horns, black sheen of his skin and hump that swayed as he swaggered through the swamp bed. I'd delivered him myself from his mother's womb and reared him. He looked fierce to other people, but I knew how gentle he was. When I went to the field to work, I took him along. He would munch grass all day and in the evening we would come home together. During the dry season, I took him across the dusty swamp bed to the river's edge to feed him. He loved being in the water so much that I had to drag him out.

One evening, a few days before the feast, when I was returning home with him, Moni Banu was sitting alone by the pond and watching the sun go down. When I stopped by her she looked up and said, "You must be angry with me, Beautiful One." I shrugged my shoulders, but she continued. "It's the truth, isn't it? The bull will be slaughtered because of me." But even if I could speak, I wouldn't have said anything to her. I walked on with the bull and settled him for the night in the shed.

Now I approached a cluster of guests around the tent. Luckily, the boys who'd bothered me earlier hadn't come back. When Big Suban saw me, he said, "Kamal, come and see the sight. Oh, such sights! Brothers Ajud Ali and Majud Ali are on top form tonight." He made some room for me and I squatted to observe them.

They sat with their heads down, hunched over their plates, their shirts off, their guts hanging like ripe jackfruits. Already they'd gone through several plates of rice and ladles of bull curry scooped from the giant pot. When they wiped their plates clean, they looked up and belched. Ala Mullah, who was serving them, said, "I suppose you're still very hungry, gentlemen. Shall I serve you another round?" The brothers smiled and grunted, "No, no. We're exceedingly full. We don't want any more. Thank you."

But everyone knew that if they really didn't mean to have any more they would have covered their plates with the palms of their hands. Instead, they merely cupped their plates around the edges, leaving the inner areas of the plates exposed. People smiled because they knew what it meant. Yes, they wanted more. Besides, their eyes were cast forlornly on the empty surface of their plates as though they hadn't eaten a grain of rice for a long time. Poor starving brothers. As soon as Ala Mullah refilled their plates, the brothers sprung into action. Heads down, they plunged their hands into the rice, kneaded large portions with bull curry and green chillies and salt, then shoved them into their mouths. They sweated profusely, globules dropping on their plates, but that didn't interrupt the rhythm of their eating. Within minutes they wiped clean the plates and belched. Once more Ala Mullah served them – the same way and the same amount. People said, "Wah, wah such eating! Brothers are real champs."

I wanted to enjoy the spectacle, but was getting nervous seeing the brothers in such good form. The teacher peeked through the cluster, looking very tense. When he moved away, I followed him.

"They'll put us to shame, Kamal," he said. "We are fast running out of food. What should we do, Kamal? What to do?" I showed him through gestures, which he always understood, that I wasn't going to eat myself.

"Good idea, Kamal," he said. "None of us must eat until the groom's party has finished. We don't want to be shamed, do we?" I tagged along with him as he went around telling his relatives and friends not to eat.

"Groom's family lack sense. I hope I haven't made a mistake by giving our Moni to them," he said. "What do you think, Kamal?" I gestured to him that I thought they were good people.

"May be. But how can they go for such silly, backward tricks? Especially at a time like this. It's just stupid."

He then headed for the inner courtyard to tell our women folk not to eat until the groom's guests had finished. I was following him, but he told me to go and keep an eye on the brothers.

They were still eating but had slowed down slightly. "I hear the big pot is nearly empty," Big Suban whispered in my ear. "Oh, poor Abbas Mia. Allah have mercy on him."

Now the brothers were almost totally drenched with sweat. Beside them lay the bull's bones piled high on a rag. Perhaps they were near the end. They had already eaten as much as nine people's portions. Ala Mullah had been told that only ten more portions were left. But even if the brothers matched their previous best – ten portions – the teacher would be spared his shame. When the brothers finished their tenth portions, they wobbled as if drunk, and leaned back on their elbows. Majud Ali even gagged a bit. We thought he was about to throw up. The teacher was standing behind a group to my right. He looked very pleased, thinking that the brothers had had enough. Ala Mullah bent over the brothers and asked, "Are you still hungry, gentlemen?"

They pulled themselves up on their buttocks and said, "No, no. We don't want any more." Yet, to our astonishment, they weren't covering their plates with their palms. When Mullah served them again, the teacher looked as if his honour had already been lost. He was sweating as profusely as the brothers. He hurried away; he couldn't take it any more. But after the twelfth portion it was all over. Suddenly the brothers fell sideways and started to snore. Some of the groom's guests looked decidedly disappointed. I was relieved because there were still three portions left and the teacher's honour had been saved.

I went to look for him. He wasn't among the guests, so I ran to the pond where I knew he'd be and communicated the good news. He didn't say anything for a while, then asked me to fetch his hookah. I went to the inner courtyard and prepared it. As I was about to return to the pond, Ata Banu caught sight of me. I thought she was going to give me a real telling-off for not waiting for her in the kitchen, but she didn't. She said softly, "Have you eaten anything, Kamal?" I made her understand that she shouldn't worry, that I would eat something later, and I made my way back to the pond.

The teacher hardly reacted when I offered him the hookah. He was looking at the darkened plains beyond the pond. "Are you all right, Kamal?" he asked. I nodded. He took a puff and said, "Don't take any notice of Bilal Khan and his ignorant son. You're far superior to them in knowledge and intelligence. And a far better human being. I wish I could tell them to their faces. Ignorant fools."

I sat down beside him.

"Now that Moni is leaving us," he said, and put a hand on my shoulder, "we're going to miss her, aren't we, Kamal?" I made a little noise from the back of my throat, and told myself: Yes, I will miss her. More than anyone can imagine. Under the half moon the ripples were barely visible on the pond, but together we widened our eyes and watched them. I was still thinking of Moni Banu when he spoke again, "War is coming, Kamal. I can sense a catastrophe. How can we survive it?"

We went back to the front yard. While the teacher mingled with the guests, I went to see the champion eaters. They were still snoring where they'd fallen. No one was looking at them now. Flies crawled on their faces and buzzed as though they were having the feast. I wondered how the brothers were going to get home – surely they wouldn't be able to walk for quite a while – then remembered I'd seen two odd contraptions brought along by the groom's party. They looked like stretchers, made with bamboo poles and jute canvas – evidently to carry the brothers home.

I went back to help the cooks. "Have you seen the groom?" the head cook asked. "I hear he's a handsome fellow." I shrugged. "You are not jealous, are you, Kamal?" He laughed, but I turned my back on him so that he couldn't see my eyes.

The giant clay pitcher was empty and the head cook wanted me to fill it up again. I made several trips to the tube-well to fetch water in large kerosene cans, which I balanced from a pole on my shoulder. After that I washed the plates, the serving bowls and the huge pot in which the bull curry had been cooked. As I was sweeping up, Abul – the boy who helps me to look after the cows – came for me. I followed him to the inner courtyard, to the hut where Moni Banu was waiting, all dressed up to be married.

Abul left me at the door. I was surprised to see that she was alone and wondered where the women and the girls were. They couldn't have gone to see the groom, because he was still sitting on the raised platform in the tent in the outer courtyard.

"Come and sit by me, Beautiful One," Moni Banu said, sobbing. She looked beautiful in the flaming red sari, her face painted with dots of henna, with a gold leaf dangling over her forehead.

I sat by her, but facing away. I couldn't bear to look at her straight on.

"You don't want to see me, Beautiful One?" She sounded hurt. "Am I already becoming so distant from you?"

I purred from the back of my throat and touched her hand, but stayed where I was.

"Have you eaten anything the whole day?"

I shook my head to make her understand that I had eaten.

"Don't lie to me, Beautiful One," she said, rather crossly. "You know you can never lie to me."

She was sobbing again. I stayed motionless, smelling her scent. Yes, they'd put rose scent on her, but that didn't drown her sweat. Her tang of blackberries.

"Look at me. I want to see your eyes."

When I turned, she lifted the huge cone-shaped lid that lay at her feet. Under it there was a plate of rice, a bowl of bull curry, green chillies, and rice pudding.

"I saved these for you," she said. "I'm not hungry."

I made her see that I wasn't hungry either.

"I want you to eat for me, Beautiful One," she begged, her eyes watery. "You can't deny me this now."

I showed her that I would have some of the rice pudding. Before I could reach for the bowl, she picked it up.

"Tilt your head back."

I did and she scooped a good portion of rice pudding with her fingers and put it inside my mouth. I looked at the corrugations on the tin roof and tasted the cream and sugar. Neither the fact that half of my tongue is missing, nor the lack of the front parts of my jaws, nor having to do without lips, ever spoiled my enjoyment of good food. Perhaps I've never tasted the full range of flavours, but I was compensated by the very sensitive half of my tongue, my palate and throat; with the back of my jaws and teeth I could chew anything.

When the bowl of pudding was finished, she put her fingers onto the stump of my tongue. I licked them clean. "You are not going to forget me, Beautiful One, are you?"

I don't know what I communicated to her then. In any case, she was about to say something more when we heard the laughter of the women. I jumped off the bed and Moni Banu wiped her fingers on the inner creases of her sari.

I didn't watch the ceremony in which Moni Banu said *Yes* to be married and the groom lifted her veil and fed her sweets. I kept myself busy. I went to check on the cows – the calf still looked nervous; then I went back to the cooking area to sweep and help the cooks gather up their things.

Abul called me again to load up the bullock cart with the dowries and other presents. Since the bride and the groom and some of the elderly relatives were to travel on the bullock cart, there was not enough room for all the presents. The groom waited nervously, head down, to take Moni Banu away from the place where she'd grown up and lived for nineteen years, from the people she knew and loved. Then, in a tumult of crying and sobbing, Moni Banu, held by her mother and women relatives, made her way to the bullock cart. The whole thing was getting too much for me, so I decided to head for the pond, but was met by the teacher who said, "Someone needs to carry the trunk with her dowry, Kamal. Go with Moni."

First to set off were the people with torches and flambeaux, then the stretchers and the eight pole-bearers carrying Ajud and Majud Ali, who were still snoring. Amidst all the wailing, the bullock cart began to move. With Big Suban's help, I put the trunk on my head and followed the procession out of our homestead, along the mud road, then on to the vast dry and dusty swamp-plains. Through the night, we walked and walked under the half-moon. Apart from the thumping of our feet on the ground and the rustling of our bodies, there was no noise, except from time to time some jackals howled far off in the dark. I didn't pay much heed to anyone walking alongside me. I was alone with my load and the rhythm of my feet on the ground. I was thinking of Moni Banu, her new life, and that she wouldn't be there any more to tell me: "Beautiful One, I'll take care of you."

CHAPTER 3

We walked the whole night across the vast stretches of the swamp-bed.

In the morning, with the red glow of the sun throbbing through the haze above the bamboo grove, we arrived at the Alams's homestead. From now on it would be Moni Banu's home. Situated on higher ground than the surrounding area, it had several well-built tin bungalows and, like our homestead, a wall separated the inner from the outer part. They put me up in the outer bungalow, which was spacious with cane recliners and chairs. Several palm trees rose and drooped over it. Soon after my arrival, they served me with breakfast, which I didn't touch. I couldn't eat in front of strangers. Judging that I was tired and in need of a nap, they made me a bed, but my mind was restless.

Instead of falling asleep, I went out for a walk around the homestead. It had two large ponds, their muddy green waters teeming with fish. Along their banks there were lines of mature date palms and large native olive trees. In their banana grove, apart from the local varieties, there were imported trees from across the seas. Right around the homestead I saw fine mango trees, budding with green fruits, and lean, tall papaya trees with mopped branches. The low-lying land around the compound, which I presumed to belong to the Alam family, was also of good quality. Although the earth looked parched and bone-dry under the early summer sun, I knew that with the coming of the monsoon rain, perhaps in a few weeks' time, it would turn into fertile beds for paddies. I could almost see their fresh green fluttering in the wind, and then turning gold and drooping under the weight of their heavily laden sheaves. All in all, my exploration had convinced me that the Alam family was pretty well off, and that Moni Banu would be well provided for. If there was one thing I couldn't bear it was the thought that Moni Banu would suffer hardship in her life. Now at least I didn't have to worry about her on that score. I was still worried, though, about her husband, Zafar Alam. Was he a good man? Would he be kind to her? If he dared be cruel, I swore by Allah that I would kill him.

Soon after I returned to the bungalow, Moni Banu's father-in-law, Kabir Alam, came to visit me. He was a large, clean-shaven man, and appeared very dignified. He sat on a recliner some distance away, not facing me, looking at the palm trees through the open door, and the bush beyond. He didn't speak for a long time.

"What are you to Moni Banu? She seems very fond of you," he asked at last. Since I couldn't respond to him in sound I didn't know what to do.

"My parents had a servant boy. His name was Bulbul. I used to call him Singing Bird. You see, he and I grew up together. I regarded him as my own brother," he went on, still not looking at me. "And what did Singing Bird do in return? He betrayed me."

I wanted to know in what way Bulbul had betrayed him, but he was still staring out at the palm trees through the open door, and the bush beyond. Why had he chosen to tell me this story? Did he suspect that I might betray Moni Banu? This was hurtful. I would rather die than betray her.

Suddenly he said, "You must be hungry. I'm sending you lunch," and left me. I was glad that he left because he was beginning to annoy me. Soon two boys brought in my lunch and closed the door behind them as they left. I was alone in the bungalow. I waited for a while before I began eating, but then realised that Moni Banu must have said something about my eating habits. Otherwise, it wouldn't have occurred to them to leave me alone with my food. I was pleased that she was still thinking of me.

After lunch I was dozing off, but woke up with a start when Moni Banu's husband, Zafar Alam, opened the door. He sat on the same recliner as his father and also looked out through the open door in the direction of the palm trees and the bush beyond. I suppose both father and son preferred that position because they didn't have to look at me straight on. Zafar Alam offered me a cigarette, which I declined. He was short and stocky, had a round face, and a thick black mop of hair on his rather large head. You wouldn't have said he was handsome, but neither would people say: Look at the mismatch! Such an ugly husband for such a beauty. Yes, Moni Banu was so beautiful that my words can never describe her properly. I always thought Allah must have been so happy, so full of joy when he made her.

Zafar Alam fretted restlessly in his recliner, lit a cigarette and said, "Moni tells me that you're like a brother to her. You can regard me as a brother too."

I was pleased. It couldn't have been easy to introduce me to her husband in such terms. I began to feel good about Zafar Alam; he didn't seem prejudiced and this made me feel that he would take good care of Moni Banu.

"I hear you're a book-reading man," Zafar Alam said. "I love reading books too."

This time I wasn't so pleased to hear what he had to say. In fact, I was annoyed with Moni Banu for giving away our secret. He looked at me as though I should make some gesture in response to his words, but I kept my eyes cast firmly on the floor. He turned and looked again at the palm trees and the bush beyond. "Don't worry, Brother Kamal. Your secret is safe with me."

He stayed silent for a while, smoked his cigarette, then suddenly said, "I don't know how to put it, Brother Kamal. I feel I've always known Moni. I think I love her, you know." I was taken aback by his frankness – and annoyed and puzzled. How could he love her already, since he'd only known her for a few hours? Was he just indicating that his first encounter with Moni Banu had been a pleasant one, and that it promised a good relationship to come? Perhaps. Or was it that I didn't know much about the mystery of love? Who knows. Perhaps he was jealous and wanted to hurt me. Could he suspect from the way Moni Banu talked about me that there was something between us, something that could never be spoken in words?

"Yes, books. They can be an instrument of war too, especially people's war, can't they, Brother Kamal?" he said. "I wanted to ask you what you thought about Che Guevara. I've been reading his *Guerrilla Warfare*, you know. Now that war is coming, I feel all of us should read him. Did you know that he was a great lover too? Now that I have Moni to love, I can become a revolutionary too."

Of course, I had read Che Guevara. About two months ago the teacher had brought home a copy in Bengali translation, which I read with care, and was much impressed by it. I thought the methods of warfare outlined in it would be very useful if we had to fight against a powerful enemy like the Pakistani military. He looked in my direction, but I turned my eyes downwards, because I couldn't communicate any of this to him; I had that facility only with Moni Banu and the teacher. Besides, what could you say to such adolescent, romantic nonsense?

He got up, looking a bit frustrated. "I'll come back later in the evening with pen and paper," he said. "We've a lot to talk about, I believe."

That night the two boys brought in my dinner and left me alone as before. As I wasn't very hungry, I didn't try any of the fish and meat curries, and ate only a small portion of rice with potato and aubergine bhaji. I was so tired that all I wanted to do was to fall asleep, but I had to wait for the boys to come and clear up. As I was getting ready to sleep, Kabir Alam came in, sat on the recliner and began smoking his hookah. Although he looked out through the door, the view of the palm trees and the bush beyond was now lost in the dark. Next to him, on a table, stood a hurricane lamp. Despite being turned up to its highest flame, it barely illuminated more than a small circle around it. I could just about see him. My bed was near the left wall, far beyond the reach of the light. I preferred it that way because, even if he wanted, he couldn't possibly have seen me.

"I wonder why, of all people, Abbas Mia has sent you. Is he sending me a message?" he said, his face now turned towards me. Since he couldn't see me, and I had no particular desire to engage with him, I stayed as still as possible.

"I hear Abbas Mia is a stubborn man. Apparently he considers himself better than anyone else. I tell you, this is a dangerous trait in a man. The vanity of self-righteousness," he went on as though he was talking to himself. I supposed he'd had a run-in with the teacher on the wedding day, and the teacher must have put him in his place, and now he needed to get it off his chest. He got up and took a stride towards the door, then stopped to say, "I hope Moni Banu is free of such traits. They are even more dangerous in a woman. My son is a good boy, but he has a wild streak in him. I wanted a daughter-in-law to tame him. Not to add fuel to the flames."

As soon as he left, I laid my head on the pillow. My eyes were fast closing on me but I kept them open, because I remembered that Zafar Alam had promised he would visit me in the evening with pen and paper. We were to have a proper conversation. I sat up, walked the room, looked through the window, but he never came. I suppose it was unreasonable of me to expect him to leave Moni Banu on her own on their first night as a married couple.

I lay on the bed again, but my mind was whipping up a storm of great ferocity that circled round and round the bridal bed, decked with fresh petals and garlands, where Moni Banu and Zafar Alam were to spend their first night together as husband and wife. Had he prepared himself for the bed with a good portion of sparrows' eggs mixed with honey, milk and liquorice, as Vatsyayana instructed for such occasions? Was he whispering sweet words in her ears, perhaps even humming a film song, rubbing his nose on the back of her neck, then putting his tongue to her lips? He would be going wild at Moni Banu's smell, her sweat, ah always mingling with attar, and her hair cascading fire over him, then his fingers travelling along her hips and loosening the knots of her undergarment. Stop. I mustn't allow these obscene thoughts. Oh Allah have pity on me, give me strength to stop it. I swear I had meant to let her go because it was best for both of us, and to be happy about the moments we'd had together, and to see her from now on as no more than a sister. But was she cooing to his advances, clinging around his body like a creeper, and licking his tongue with her tongue? How were you explaining, Moni, the token of our remembrance on the day of the first summer storm? What were you saying about the marks I made with my nails on your breast? No. Stop. Stop. I hit my head hard against the floor to make those thoughts disappear, but they kept coming back. In desperation I got up and began whirling and whirling like a dervish, on and on until I was floating like a leaf caught in a whirlwind. Then everything was blank.

In the morning I heard uproar and thought I was dreaming.

When I opened the door I saw Zafar Alam standing before me as if he had gone mad. For a brief moment I thought something terrible had happened to Moni Banu.

"You haven't heard the news?"

I must have looked dazed.

"It began last night. You know, the operation *Search Light*. Already they've slaughtered thousands in Dhaka."

Zafar Alam was so agitated that his red eyes almost popped out of their sockets and he was gasping for air. My first response was one of relief, because whatever had happened had nothing to do with Moni Banu. She was safe. Zafar Alam must have thought I hadn't quite grasped the enormity of what he'd said.

"Yes, the Pakistani army declared war on us last night. Now that they've made Dhaka a graveyard, they're spreading out to the provinces."

Finally I awoke.

"They're coming for us, Brother Kamal. It'll be doomsday for us Bengalis."

He was shaking so much I thought he was about to break into pieces. I moved forward to hold him, but he was already among the crowd that had gathered in front of the bungalow. The elders were tense and subdued, their eyes spoke just fear, but the youth had worked themselves up like Zafar Alam, and they were about to explode. Almost all of them were carrying spears, knives and bamboo sticks. Zafar Alam shouted with all his strength; the whole gathering went quiet. I don't know how the others felt, but I felt as though I was screaming through him.

"We will not let them pass," he said. "We will fight them in the swamps, in the rivers, and in the paddy fields. *Joi Bangla*."

Across the yard, the youth, like a ripple, waved their weapons above their heads and joined him in the chorus. It throbbed in the air: *Joi Bangla*. It took Kabir Alam quite a while to gain the attention of the crowd.

"Do you know what you're saying? How can you fight a modern army with only sticks and knives?"

There was a hushed silence for a while, then one of the youths, his voice cracking with emotion, said that there were millions of them, and that, "Surely, they couldn't kill us all."

"You fools. Your bravery and your millions are nothing before fighter-planes, tanks, gunboats and machine guns," said Kabir Alam. "You've no idea what they'll do to you. They'll mow you down from miles away. With just the press of a button."

They looked baffled.

"I'd rather die fighting with what we have," said Zafar Alam. "I don't want to die like a dog."

The youths waved their weapons and roared like thunder: *Joi Bangla.*

I could understand Zafar Alam's sentiments, but I couldn't help being alarmed by his willingness to die. It was all very well for him to fancy himself as a dead hero, but what would happen to Moni Banu? Over the years I'd seen many widows in our village, wrapped in their white saris. I tell you, they all counted beads and waited for death to deliver them from their misery. My misfortune to be born mouthless was nothing compared to theirs. How could he wish something like this on Moni Banu? I felt his declaration of love for her was just empty talk, that the fool didn't know the first thing about love. If you love someone, no matter how bad it gets, you cling to life for her sake.

In the crowd someone had turned on a transistor radio. Everyone stopped to listen. When we heard the station announcing itself as the radio of independent Bangladesh, everyone cheered. I was very happy too. We listened solemnly to the report on the massacre of thousands of unarmed civilians and students in Dhaka, but cheered again when we heard that Bangabandhu had formally declared the independence of Bangladesh. "*Joi Bangla*" shouted the youths. All of a sudden the broadcast ended with what was to become our national anthem. A soft, mellow song by Rabindranath Thakur that Abbas Mia had encouraged Moni Banu and I to memorise many years ago.

> My Bengal of gold, I love you
> Forever your skies, your air set my heart in tune
> As if it were a flute…

I didn't know that a song could do such things, but I was trembling as though a tornado was whipping up inside me. It couldn't have been the words, because familiarity had numbed me to their meaning as I drilled them over and over again on my slate. What was unmistakable, though, were the tears in my eyes, but I didn't know whether they had to do with the gratitude I felt for the land that had given me a place on earth, or with the sadness I felt for those who'd been killed in Dhaka, or with the horror that awaited us. Or, something else altogether. Whatever it was, I wasn't alone: I had the strange thought that our bodies had melted in a forge and been sculpted into a giant flute. And that the flute had gathered the wind from the sky to play itself. I wonder what would have happened to us if the crackle of the radio hadn't jarred us back to our separate bodies.

Someone shouted that we needed a flag. How else could we have shown that we had a nation of our own now? Zafar Alam ran to the inner part of their homestead and came back with a green sari and a red blouse. They looked new to me. I was sure that they were Moni Banu's wedding presents. It made me doubt even more his declaration of love. How could he rip up her wedding presents to make a flag?

And it was clear he had very little idea about how to make a flag. It took a tailor's suggestion, who happened to be there among the crowd, to send him running to fetch a pair of scissors, needles and thread. When the tailor set to work, people surrounded and encouraged him. "Look at the tailor. Ah, such mastery of the craft. He's the best, isn't he? Bah, bah, the magician at work." Paying no attention to the crowd, he cut a yard-long piece from the green sari, shaped the back of the red blouse into a map of Bangladesh and sewed the map on the middle of the sari piece. As soon as it was done, one of the youths snatched it off the tailor and mounted it on the blade of his spear. He ran with it and the others followed. They ran round and round the yard screaming their hearts out. *Joi Bangla.* I would have added my voice to theirs.

Someone shouted, "To the town. We'll face the army there," and the crowd thrust their weapons into the air, broke into a run and veered off out of the yard and down onto the dry swamp-plains. When Kabir Alam saw Zafar Alam moving with the crowd he ran after him. I don't know what he said, but both the father and the son came back together.

43

It was already late morning; I needed to set off to be back at our homestead before dark. I wondered how the teacher and Ata Banu were taking the news. I indicated to Zafar Alam my wish to go.

"Have some breakfast first," he said. "I suppose you want to see Moni before you leave."

I nodded.

When the boys came to clear up after my breakfast, they asked me to follow them to the inner courtyard. They took me to a tin-roofed hut with paved flooring. In the deep recess of it, Moni Banu and Zafar Alam were sitting side by side on the bed. I sat on a floor-stool. I was surprised to see Moni Banu looking so radiant. I thought she would be burdened by the news of the massacre. Her manner was bashful, and from time to time she glanced at her husband as though he were the most enchanting creature. Zafar Alam was moved to repeat the same changing moods and the gestures as his bride. It seemed that they were already bound together by a secret complicity. Was this, I wondered, what a couple in love looked like? Perhaps I was wrong to dismiss Zafar Alam's declaration as empty talk. Would Moni Banu be so silly as to say the same thing about Zafar Alam? I didn't know what to believe any more.

"You're going back then, Kamal," she said.

I nodded.

She got off the bed, came over to me, and handed me a bundle, wrapped with a piece of cotton. When our hands touched she looked me in the eyes. I thought she was about to say something, but her trembling lips couldn't form any words. Was she trying to address me as Beautiful One? I don't know, but she had tears in her eyes. She covered her face with the corner of her sari and hurried behind the bamboo screen that stood to the left of the bed. Zafar Alam looked a bit uncomfortable, but cleared his throat and said that the bundle was for my journey; it contained rice-cereal and date-palm sweet. "From our own palm trees. The best in the swampland."

Moni Banu came back to sit beside her husband on the bed. When I stood up to take my leave she stayed with her eyes downcast. "Kamal," was all she said. Zafar Alam accompanied me up to the road.

"We never had that conversation, Brother Kamal. I don't know whether we'll get the chance again. But one thing I know for sure. Even if we live through this war, nothing will remain the same for us."

From here to our village took me about five hours. I had to walk the dusty swamp-plains, wade through the muddy waters of the scattered pools, balance on narrow ridges between the paddies, and cross the rivers on bamboo bridges. I heard the buzzing of people from the start, but it was only when I crossed the first stretch of the plains, and went around a bush to take the second stretch that I saw them. There were thousands of people, armed with spears, knives and sticks, marching to town to face the Pakistani army.

People asked me: "Aren't you joining us to kill the enemy?"

I kept my head down and walked on as fast as I could. At one of the crossroads when someone asked the same question, his companion said:

"Can't you see his face? He can't possibly understand the meaning of such things."

I walked and walked, wondering what Moni Banu wanted to say when she looked at me. Then I heard the tune again:

My Bengal of gold, I love you
Forever your skies, your air set my heart in tune
As if it were a flute…

And I became the flute to play in the sky again.

CHAPTER 4

The days following my return from the Alams' homestead were
desperately lonely and I kept myself busy with household chores.
Ata Banu seemed deeply affected by her daughter's absence: if she
wasn't praying, she was counting beads. I'd see her in the inner
courtyard, circling between the pomegranate and the lime tree,
her thumb shuffling the beads at a furious pace. During the late
afternoon, when the wrath of the sun had mellowed a bit, she
added Koranic verses to her walks. Sometimes, if I were engaged
in some task inside one of the inner huts, I would mistake her
recitations for the coming of the rain. I would flare my nostrils to
catch that delicious smell that rose at the first drop on the baking
earth, cock my head to the tin roof for that unmistakable sound:
dull, liquid pattering that brought music from the open sky. But
there was no rain. The humidity and the heat kept rising. I would
try to avoid Ata Banu, but if her eyes caught me she would say,
"Doomsday has arrived, Kamal," before going back to her beads
and the verses.

I usually got up when I heard the morning call to prayer, but
since my return I'd slept through it. It was different, though, on
the day that Sona Mia called for prayer. When our regular
muezzin was away, which happened several times a year, people
called on him to do azan. It was not that I disliked our regular
muezzin, but Sona Mia's voice had a particular appeal for me, and
I looked forward to hearing it. He was a farmer and a devout
Muslim with a long white beard. He drove a bullock cart during
the dry winter months. Every time I heard his azan I would sit up
on my bed and feel his deep, resonant voice reaching me from the
depths of his soul. I never made it to the mosque, but when I
heard him I'd remember Allah and be grateful to him.

When I was young, Sona Mia had often given me rides on his bullock cart. "Don't you forget that you're one of Allah's chosen creatures, Kamal," he'd say. "Allah must have sent you to this earth for a very particular purpose." I loved to listen to him talk to me like this, but later, when I grew up, I would ask him, in my manner, which he understood, what was that particular purpose?

"I don't know, Kamal. It's between you and Allah. All I know is that Allah loves you." And he would put his hand on my head, brushing my hair, and say: "It doesn't matter that no one knows your origin, Kamal. Hindu, Buddhist or Christian, Allah doesn't care for such things."

Now, hearing Sona Mia's azan, I sat up on my bed, feeling that Allah's love was washing over me. I got up to perform my morning duties – fed the cows, cleaned the shed, and after fetching several buckets of water from the tube-well, went out with a cotton bundle slung across my shoulder, containing a clay pot of gruel and a small water carrier. I wished the bull was alive and coming with me; he was such good company. If reincarnation is true, I hoped he'd be back as a human. Anyway, I headed towards the lake because the teacher had a few rice fields by its southern edge. By now the lake had become a tiny pool after a long dry season. Some of the saplings had lost their usual pale green and had turned yellow. I feared for them because I knew that in a few more days the lake would dry up completely. If the rain didn't come soon, we would lose the entire crop. Even in the midst of war we couldn't do without rice. I stepped on the canoe-chute to lift water to feed the saplings. Even after hours of labouring, the land looked as dry as before, but I wasn't going to give up. Soon I was stepping on and off the stem of the canoe-chute at such a speed that I lost track of time. Besides, it was helping me to stop thinking of Moni Banu.

I hadn't noticed that Big Suban had been watching me for some time. "Slow down, Kamal," he shouted, "you want to kill yourself or what?"

I stopped and looked up. He was sitting under the spreading branches of the kapok tree and puffing on his hookah. I climbed up to join him.

"What's the point of tending the rice fields?" Big Suban said with a sigh. "Soon the Pakistani army will come and burn everything to ashes."

I shrugged my shoulders. Such possibilities would not stop me.

"You're a fool, Kamal," he said. "You don't know the ways of the world." I arched my eyebrows as if to say what did he know. Although our communication was rather limited, Big Subhan considered me as his best friend. I likewise. At times I regretted that he could not read and write – we could have communicated much better – but he never had the opportunity to acquire such skills. He was also thought to be a bit simple, but I never found him so.

Big Suban was a large man with a small head. He went around the village with his axe offering his services as a woodcutter. I'd often meet him in the forest, felling trees. Although we had some chance meetings, most of the time I sought him out. When I heard the unmistakable thwacking of his axe, I couldn't resist the temptation to look for him. I would follow the sound, but wouldn't reveal myself to him immediately. I would stand behind a tree some distance away and observe him at one with his axe, as though it were an extension of him. In regular swift movements, his body and the axe arched back and fell deep into the trunk. He felled trees faster than anyone I knew in the swampland, but I never sensed any aggression in his work. What I saw was more a game of passion between his muscles, the wood and the metal than anything else. He was always happy to see me, and each time he would immediately take a break to puff on his hookah, and tell me things that mattered to him, but sometimes I was content just to observe him for a while and leave.

What he talked about most often was taking a wife. "When I cut wood I think about women all the time, Kamal," he would say. "Your life is a big hole without them." He would then look at me, at my mouth, and go quiet for a while. I would cast my eyes downward and laugh inside. Rubbing his chin, he would begin again.

"Don't you want a wife for yourself, Kamal?" he would ask. Again I would do nothing to communicate a response. "As soon as I get some money together, I will get a nice wife, and you will be the chief witness. My best man." When he used to say this, I'd show him my pleasure by laughing with my eyes. Anything for you, Big Suban, you're my friend. He would place his hand on my shoulder and say, with his voice cracking, "I feel Allah has sent you for me. You know, to be my friend. If I could give my mouth to you, I would."

Years went by and still Big Suban didn't have a wife. Who would give a daughter to him? He had no land, no cows, no brothers, only the axe and his muscles. But these failures never stopped his talk.

Whenever Big Suban wanted to go on an adventure, he came for me, and I was happy to go along with him. Sometimes Moni Banu, when she was little, came along with us. One day, about two years before, long after Moni Banu had stopped following me beyond the fence that divided the inner from the outer courtyard, I met Big Suban in the forest. It was about midday and, with a mischievous smile on his face, he asked me to follow him.

"I will show you the most amazing thing you have ever seen, Kamal."

I followed him, curious, but a bit apprehensive that he might be leading me into some risky situation. We walked through the forest, then past long stretches of sugar cane, and finally arrived in dense bush. I tapped on his shoulder to ask where he was leading me. He smiled and said, "Trust me. I'll show you something very special."

Halfway through the bush, we came to a slope. He began to crawl up it and motioned me to do the same. When we reached the top I turned my eyes away in panic. He had taken me to where we could get a full view of the secluded pond in which the village women bathed.

"Don't worry, Kamal," Big Suban said. "No one will know. Just feast your eyes."

Although the women weren't naked, they were careless about their modesty, revealing some of their skin when they climbed in and out of the pond, or changed into dry clothes. I must admit I was enjoying what I saw, but was becoming very nervous too. I tapped Big Suban on the shoulder and indicated my desire to leave.

"You're a strange one, Kamal," he said. "You don't like looking at women?"

When I got back to our homestead, I rushed towards my hut. I was near my door when Moni Banu, who was grating coconut under the shade of the lime tree, called out, "Come and listen to me, Kamal."

I was afraid to face her eyes and went inside as if I hadn't heard her. Later, when she came to ask me what was wrong, I didn't open the door. She went away rather cross. After a few minutes she was back again. This time I pushed my slate under the door. I'd written on it that I was very tired and wanted to rest a bit. I sensed that she wasn't convinced by my explanation.

"You're not ill, are you, Beautiful One?" She pushed the slate back for me to write my answer, but I didn't return it. Reluctantly she left again. For the following few days I avoided her. I don't know whether it was out of shame, or because I could never lie to her face-to-face, or because I had become aware of the strangeness of her kind. I spent many sleepless nights worrying about it, but I also took pleasure in replaying the images by the pond, especially just before falling asleep.

Now under the kapok tree Big Suban said, "You're missing Moni Banu, aren't you? I wish I knew some magic to make your pain disappear. Oh, Kamal, my friend, I don't understand the cruel way Allah sometimes plays with us." As he puffed on his hookah, hot wind blew among the kapok branches, then the last of the crimson flowers, dark and shrivelled now, landed on us. I don't know how long had passed before Big Suban suddenly asked me, "Are you joining the liberation forces?"

I shrugged, to tell him I hadn't given the matter much thought.

"I might join up," he said. When I raised my eyes in question, he said, "I want the war to finish quickly so that I can get back to cutting wood. How can I get a wife with the war going on?"

When Big Suban left me I didn't feel like watering the saplings any more. I cut some grass for the cows and decided to go back to our homestead. As I passed in front of the mosque I met Sona Mia. He asked me how I was and I made him understand that I was scared.

"Allah will not abandon us, Kamal. He will look after us, especially you, His chosen one." Whilst I had taken this for granted as a child, now I didn't really understand how it could be true. I never prayed or called his name. Still, I was, as always, happy to hear these things from Sona Mia.

"I've made a special prayer for you, Kamal. You see, someone has to survive the war to remember us all."

I must have looked surprised, because I didn't really grasp the meaning of what he'd said.

"You see, Kamal, many, many of us, probably millions of us will die in this war. If you ask me how I know I couldn't say anything that would make sense, but I know you will survive. Then we'll be your memories. I'm glad that it will be you."

That evening in my hut I didn't light my lamp. If Sona Mia's voice wasn't going round and round in my head, I was thinking of Moni Banu. It was getting too much for me; I wanted to escape from both of them. In the past, if I needed to escape, all I had to do was open a book. I would be drawn so deep into its world that there was nothing beyond its pages and I'd forget what was bothering me. Moni Banu used to tease me, "Books are like drugs to you, aren't they? As soon as you open a page, you become a zombie. I could be dying of pain before you and still you wouldn't lift your face up. It's a terrible habit, you know."

Perhaps it was, but how I wished for a new book just then. It had been some time since the teacher had brought anything new.

Before the troubles the teacher used to go to town for new books. He told me he borrowed them from the Muslim Institute library, where his mentor, the legendary scholar Zomir Ali, was in charge. In fact, it was Zomir Ali who had founded the library way back during the British time.

Before he became a librarian, Zomir Ali was an official in the British Indian civil service. I never knew why he had chosen to give up such a prestigious position to become a lowly librarian in a provincial town where there were very few serious readers and scholars. Was it to atone for serving the colonial masters with his considerable learning and skills? Perhaps not. People who suffered from such guilt usually turned to religion: Hindus became sadhus and wandered from village to village with their begging bowls, and the Muslims went on hajj and built mosques. Zomir Ali wasn't a man of religion at all; he was against all religious traditions. I think it was under his influence that the teacher became a man of modern and progressive ideas.

Although I had been reading his books for years, I had met Zomir Ali only a year ago. I remember the occasion very well. At short notice the teacher needed to go to town to buy a blackboard for his school. Since it was during the season of water, he asked me to take him there in our dinghy. We set off in the morning; I paddled and punted until we reached the town in the afternoon. He bought the blackboard and I carried it on my head, then he asked me to take it to the dinghy and rest there for a while. He wanted to go to a restaurant for supper and buy a takeaway meal for me; we would return after I had eaten. It would be the early hours of the morning before we got back, but the night was moonlit. I waited and waited for him. In the meantime, clouds had gathered, the wind blew, and rain came. It seemed the downpour would go on for the whole night.

At last the teacher came and told me that he'd been delayed because after the meal he'd gone to see Zomir Ali to borrow a book.

"The wind is too strong and we wouldn't see anything in this rain. We can't return tonight, Kamal," he said. "Zomir Ali has kindly invited us to his house."

While the teacher held his umbrella over me I gobbled the meal in double-quick time. With the blackboard over my head, I arrived with the teacher at Zomir Ali's house. On the way the teacher told me that Zomir Ali was a bachelor who lived alone. He wasn't sure of his age, but it was at least eighty.

To our surprise we found the door open. Cautiously we entered the large, brick-built house, room after room dark and silent. Wherever I looked there were books, on the floors and on the walls – rows and rows right up to the ceiling. A house of books, I said to myself. We entered a room with a damp and musty smell, and there on a recliner by a dim hurricane lamp was Zomir Ali. He had long white hair and an equally long white beard; he looked rather frail.

"Is it you, Abbas Mia?" he asked. It was only then I realised that Zomir Ali was blind. When the teacher said "Yes", Zomir Ali asked again, "Who's that with you?"

"He's the boy who lives with us."

"What's your name, boy?" Zomir Ali asked. The teacher told him that I couldn't speak.

"But he can read and write," he said. "In fact, he has read all the books that I borrowed from you."

"Including my translation of Darwin's *The Origin of Species* and the *Quran*?" said Zomir Ali.

"Yes, Venerable Scholar. He read them end to end and several times."

"Is that so? Interesting."

It was the first time I'd heard the teacher telling anyone about my ability to read and write, and it felt very strange because I was not in the habit of seeing myself, in my dealings with other people, in those terms. They were my private affairs, confined to my inner world. Well, except to Moni Banu and the teacher.

"Come here, boy." Zomir Ali beckoned me with his stick. When I went and sat by him, he put his hand on my head, slid it down on my forehead, then on my nose. He was about to say something but stopped. I could feel his salty fingers deep inside my mouth. He withdrew them abruptly.

"He doesn't have a mouth," the teacher said.

Zomir Ali stayed silent for a while, then he put his hand on my head again and rubbed it gently. "Forgive this blind old man. You see, I never met anyone like you. If I were told that there lives a man without a mouth and yet he has read Darwin and the Quran, I never would have believed it. In fact, I would've regarded it preposterous. A bizarre fantasy. Yet, you're here. How extraordinary. I'm indeed honoured to meet you. What do they call…"

"Kamal, Venerable Scholar. We call him Kamal."

"Ah, the Beautiful One. The Perfect One," said Zomir Ali and then he turned to speak to me.

"I want to talk to you so much. For instance, if I say that you and I stand here, with our respective forms, as a result of millions of years of random mutations and selections, what would you say to that, Kamal? I'd love to hear your views, but how do we communicate? You don't have a mouth to speak and I do not have eyes to see. Perhaps our meeting is the most improbable and random of all events."

Then he turned to the teacher: "Abbas Mia, did I hear you right? Did you say that Kamal lives with you?"

"Yes, Venerable Scholar."

"What is this supposed to mean, Abbas Mia? Do you take him as your servant boy?"

"He looks after my land and my livestock. And sometimes he helps around the house, but we do not regard him as our servant."

"Do you pay him wages for his services?"

"I don't pay him, Venerable Scholar. He's part of my household."

"What is that supposed to mean? I take it that he's not your slave. What then? Have you recognised him as your son?"

I held my breath hoping the teacher would say *yes* and then everything would be fine and I'd be the happiest person on earth. The teacher lowered his head, scratched his ear, but said nothing.

"What's this, Abbas Mia? Do you regard him as your son or not?"

"It's a complicated story, Venerable Scholar. There's no easy way of answering this."

"Of course, these matters are always complicated, but I'm really disappointed in you, Abbas Mia. Are you ashamed of him? Or is it something to do with our stupid hang-ups about the so-called highborn and lowborn? I expected you to be above such things."

"I'm very fond of Kamal. In fact, my whole family is fond of him."

"Yes, I heard you. But that wasn't what I was asking, Abbas Mia. I'm really disappointed in you."

Zomir Ali then turned to me.

"You're indeed a perfect one. Don't take any notice of people if they tell you otherwise. I'm really honoured to meet you."

I was pleased with how he regarded me, but a bit upset by the way he treated the teacher. Of course, I would have loved nothing more than hearing the teacher call me his son, but only I knew how much he had done for me.

Suddenly Zomir Ali stood up and asked me to follow him.

"I'll show you the books. It's not every day that I receive a reader like you."

I followed him, the teacher behind us with the hurricane lamp. Zomir Ali took us around the rooms without even groping with his stick to find his way and stopped briefly before each of the walls before moving on. When he stopped he tapped the shelves with his stick and told me what kind of books they were. Apart from the vast collection of Bengali books on numerous subjects, he had many foreign books. Later, the teacher told me that Zomir Ali had spent his considerable inheritance, and his savings from the days when he served the British Empire, acquiring books.

Turning and twisting through the rooms, going along the dark, damp corridors, he took us to a small room clogged with large books. I immediately recognised these books from their red canvas binding; these were some the teacher had borrowed for us to read. The teacher was, I later learned, a member of a very small group to whom Zomir Ali had lent some of these books. One had to be a member of the Muslim Institute library for many years before becoming a part of this small group. Unknown to the members, Zomir Ali kept a record of their borrowing habits. If he approved of the range of books members borrowed over the years, and the frequency with which they did so, he invited them to his home. He would then engage them in lengthy discussions to find out what they thought of these books. If he was satisfied by their answers, they were allowed to borrow from his private collection. Even then they had to wait a few more years before Zomir Ali let them have some of the books in red canvas.

Sliding his stick over them, Zomir Ali told me: "If you want you can borrow any of these books, I'll be honoured if you do so."

The teacher looked at me with amazement, because Zomir Ali had never before made an exception to his rigorous vetting procedure. He'd even denied a visiting close relative the privilege of browsing through the books in red canvas. Moreover, he had never granted anyone the unconditional right of access to all of his special collection as he did to me. I was indeed a lucky person.

The books in red canvas binding were handwritten by Zomir Ali himself. They were Bengali translations of books in foreign languages that he had made over the past fifty years of his life. Even with failing eyesight he had continued this work; he had stopped only a year or so before he went completely blind. He had translated from Sanskrit, Persian, Arabic, English and some other European languages.

I stood before him, baffled. He picked a book from one of the lower shelves and handed it to me. "Take this book. But come and tell me what you think."

Then remembering that I didn't have the faculty of speech, and that he was blind, he said: "Perhaps you, Abbas Mia, could read to me the thoughts that my young friend might write."

The book he picked up for me was a Bengali translation of *Hayy ibn Yaqzan*, written by an Arabic physician called Ibn Tufayl, who lived in Granada in the twelfth century. I remember enjoying the adventures of Hayy, who was stranded alone for many years on a desert island, and who in his solitude re-imagined the world. As I read the book I wondered why Zomir Ali had chosen it for me. Did he feel that I would find solace in it because my deformity and my lack of speech had thrown me, like Hayy, into a life of solitude? Or, did he give me the book merely to find out whether I, like Hayy, had re-imagined the world in a particular way? Did he think that my solitary pondering had led me to conceive life and its meaning in such an original way that he had to get it out of me? Perhaps he was just testing me: had I fallen for Hayy's seductive reasoning in denying the sensuality of existence in order to achieve spiritual unity with the divine? In the event, I didn't get the opportunity to communicate with Zomir Ali about the books I borrowed from his library. Although he asked after me many times, and sent me more of those books with red canvas bindings, a year had gone by and I, for one reason or another, hadn't been able to make it to the town. Now that the war was on us I doubted whether I would get the chance of seeing him again.

Now Ata Banu called me from my dark hut to pick up my dinner. I took it back there as I always did. There was no sign of the heat and the humidity abating. Not even a breeze to offer momentary relief. If only Moni Banu was there, keeping me company, telling me stories or embroidering as I ate. I wondered what she was doing now. Perhaps she was with her husband, serving him the dishes that she had cooked, fussing over him. What kind of stories would she tell him? Would she ever sing him those sweet little songs that she used to sing to me?

I couldn't eat much. I went to the kitchen, washed the plates, and came back to my hut. I was sweating so much that I thought I would take a bath in the pond. On the way there, I came across Ata Banu going round and round in the dark inner courtyard. It was only when I heard her muttering that I knew it was her. When she heard my footsteps she said, "Is that you, Kamal? Doomsday is near. The war and the heat are the same thing. Do you follow me? The sign of Allah's anger." I stood there, immobile in the dark.

"How did you find Moni, in her husband's homestead?" she asked. "Do you think her in-laws are going to treat her nice? They seemed very bad types to me." I wanted to show her with gestures that Moni Banu was fine and that her husband and in-laws were very nice people, but in the dark I couldn't do so. So, instead I made a noise from the back of my throat – as sweet as I could muster. "Why you making that ugly noise?" she screamed. "You evil one. Get your ugly face out of my sight." I don't know why she always spoke so harshly to me; it seems my face brought out the worst in her.

It felt nice in the pond. I stayed submerged up to my neck in the water and from time to time, closing the hole of my mouth with one hand, I took dips under. When I surfaced from one of the dips, I saw a light by the steps of the ghat. I wondered who it could be. I climbed up the steps cautiously, but before I reached the top, realised it was the teacher. He was smoking his hookah. I dried myself and sat beside him. Except for the hookah's gurgles we stayed silent. I had been out of the water for only a few minutes and was already feeling hot. Everything was still: not a blade of grass moved. When at last teacher began to speak, he told me how rapidly the war was spreading; already the Pakistani army had captured most of the district towns.

"Yes, Kamal, they have butchered thousands of innocent people. Just as they did in Dhaka. All you need to incur their wrath is to speak Bengali, eat rice or just wear a lungi. Now they are heading our way. You know my views. I don't want to lower myself to their level and become a beast. What should we do?" He took a long drag on his hookah. I didn't know what to say.

"Perhaps we should build a giant boat and wait for the land to flood," he continued. "It won't be long before the monsoon rain comes and everything's under water. We could launch our boat then and spend the rest of the war wandering about in it. We know the layout of the swamps, the extent of the floodplains, the bends of the canals, the zigzags of the tributaries, the directions of the wind and the currents. No one could catch us and we would be safe. This must be our best option, Kamal. What do you think?"

I was listening to the hookah's gurgling and thinking that perhaps the teacher was right, but before I could indicate this, we saw a line of lights on the plains. A sudden shiver ran up my spine and I opened my eyes wide and looked hard at them. Somehow they didn't look like fireflies dancing in bright loops in the dark. Nor did they look like the swamp flames which had scared Moni Banu and I in our childhood, believing they were made by watery phantoms. These lights, the teacher and I were sure, belonged to humans. But who were they, and why were they coming our way? Was it the Pakistani army or their armed collaborators? The teacher was puffing on his hookah so rapidly I thought he was going to choke. I found my breathing becoming erratic. Our first impulse was to run and hide, but then we remembered Ata Banu. She was on her own in the inner courtyard. While the teacher went inside to fetch her, I stayed with my head down behind one of the banks of the pond, cocking my ear in the direction of the plains. My sense of hearing is more acute than most people's. "You're like a whale, Beautiful One," Moni Banu used to say.

The bearers of torches were a noisy lot and although they were still very far away I could just about hear them. It was enough for me to realise that they were only our villagers. I was so relieved that I lay on my back and stared at the sky. It was full of stars. I could get carried away looking at them, but I got up, remembering the teacher and Ata Banu. They were by the fence dividing the inner from the outer courtyard. They were ready to make a run for a hiding place, but when I told them the torchbearers were only our villagers, the teacher sighed with relief. Ata Banu looked at me fiercely, but didn't say anything harsh. She usually left me alone when the teacher was present. She went back to the inner courtyard; the teacher and I went to meet the torchbearers by the pond. They were ex-students who had come to take their leave.

"We're going to join the freedom fighters," said one of the young men. "We want your blessing, sir."

"Where are you going?" asked the teacher.

"We'll cross the border into India. From there we'll go to a training camp. If everything goes well, we'll be back in the swampland within a month to fight," said the same young man.

"Don't take it lightly, boys. In war, people get killed."

"We know the risk, sir," said another young man. "But if we stay around they will come and kill us anyway. We might as well die fighting."

"Shouldn't we do everything to survive as well?" said the teacher. The young men remained silent.

I could sense something of Zafar Alam in them. So eager to die. One by one they knelt down to touch the teacher's feet for his blessing, then disappeared down into the dark plains.

"We have to build a boat, Kamal," said the teacher again. "This is the only way. Fighting is not our thing, but survival is." Although I wasn't sure how he planned to build a large boat in a time like this, I nodded. He sent me to fetch a dry lungi from the inner homestead and went into the pond for a quick dip. While he dried himself, he said, "I wish Moni was here." I looked at him and he knew this was my wish too. "Do you think she'll be safe in her husband's household?" I nodded enthusiastically and he smiled as if an inner joy had slipped through his skin. Seeing him happy made me happy too.

I lay on my bed and fanned myself with a palm leaf. Hot, humid air brushed my skin. I was sweating more than before I took a dip in the pond. There was a distant thunder echoing through the sky and I thought it might rain, but the heat and humidity just became more unbearable. I went out, walked around the perimeter of the homestead, then along the rows of palm trees, but there wasn't even a whiff of a wind to promise a respite. I came back to the pond, washed my face, and sat down by the ghat for a while. It was a bit cooler there and I fell asleep.

I woke up when someone placed a lamp in front of my face and whistled. For a moment I thought that the demons who were chasing me in my dreams were for real. It took me a while to recognise the men. They looked agitated and asked me to wake the teacher up. They had something urgent to tell him. While they waited by the ghat I went inside to call him. He wasn't sleeping. He had already sensed the arrival of the messengers and was making his way out to meet them.

One of the messengers said that they had found an old man in the market. He lay curled up under a banyan and was barely alive. Earlier they had seen a group of refugees passing through; they must have left him there to die.

"When we poked him, he mumbled something very faintly. We couldn't make out what he said," the other messenger told the teacher. "But we were sure that he called your name." We lit two lamps and went with the messengers, who walked side by side in front of us. No one spoke for a long time, but as we climbed from a long stretch of paddy ridge to the road, one of the messengers broke his silence to say that the day before the Pakistani army had massacred a lot of people in our district town.

"They say it's hell in the town. Refugees told us that bodies are everywhere. Dogs, vultures and crows are feasting on them. If they hadn't left they would have died of disease or the stench. I don't know how that old man managed to escape." His voice seemed to be coming from a far distance, from somewhere beyond the dark, but I was thinking: who was this old man? And why would he be calling the teacher's name?

I looked at the messengers' lanterns swaying about their knees. They looked like feet without bodies, walking on their own. I shivered and the teacher coughed as though he was choking. It was so dark that we didn't realise when we reached the market. Then we heard the dogs bickering among themselves. As we came nearer, we expected them to scatter. They didn't. One of the messengers shouted at them, and still they didn't budge. Now, instead of bickering among themselves they started to bark at us. They looked mad, mean and hungry for human flesh. We sensed an imminent attack and backed off, taking refuge in a nearby tea stall. I didn't relish the prospect of facing the dogs again, but one of the messengers said that if we didn't go out soon the old man would be eaten alive. At his suggestion we lit large torches that we found in the stall and came out to face the dogs. Four of us, forming a line, swung our torches together. The dogs barked and finally disappeared into the darkness.

We thought he was dead. He was naked except for a torn piece of cloth wrapped around his loins. He lay curled up, face down. One of the messengers turned him over. I didn't recognise him at first, but the teacher rushed to him. He wasn't dead, only unconscious. The dogs came back and started to bark at us again. They must have been waiting for the man to die. We took him to the tea stall. While one of the messengers wetted his head with cold water, the teacher massaged his feet. After a while the man began to come to his senses. He opened his eyes to tiny slits and made a faint gurgling noise.

"You, Venerable Scholar…" said the teacher, barely able to contain his need to cry. I felt bad for not recognising Zomir Ali immediately, but he looked so different with his long hair and beard shaved off. I went with one of messengers to the bamboo grove and came back with a straight pole. To it we secured an old rattan mat that we found at the back of the tea stall. It wasn't a perfect stretcher, but it would do the job. We placed Zomir Ali in the pouch it made. He didn't make any noise. I am not sure whether he lost consciousness again or just fell asleep. I was at the front and the teacher at the back. We lifted him up and carried him to our homestead.

CHAPTER 5

Zomir Ali lay, barely alive, in the outer bungalow.

For days the teacher and I nursed him. I kept vigil over him during the nights and only slept in the early hours, on the floor next to his bed. When he didn't respond to us, we opened his mouth to feed him. That was Ata Banu's idea. She churned a pail of milk at dawn and prepared a large glass of buttermilk for him, mixing in salt and palm sugar. We dripped tiny drops into his mouth from a spoon. Nothing happened at first: the drops simply formed a pool in the hollow of his mouth. I was afraid that he might choke, but to my relief, he twitched his nose and began to swallow. In the early morning of the third day, as I was about to close my eyes, I heard him scream: "Fire! Fire!"

I got up to check on him. Since he was blind, I couldn't quite decide whether he was still asleep. I opened his mouth and dropped in a spoonful of buttermilk. He spat it out. "Who is it?" he demanded. I gurgled from the back of my throat and touched his hand. He didn't recognise me. I took his hand and slid it over my face. Still he didn't recognise me. I bunched his fingers and put them inside my mouth. They lay motionless for a while, then he yanked them away.

"Kamal, is it you?"

I squeezed his hand to say *yes*.

"Are we all dead now?" he asked.

Zomir Ali made a quick recovery, but his feelings about what had happened to his books were still very raw. His entire collection had been thrown onto a bonfire. When he spoke to me about it, he was so upset that I feared he might lapse into a coma again.

"When you see books burning, you know Fascists and Nazis are about. Yes, Kamal, it's as simple as that. It doesn't make any difference whether they don the uniform of the Pakistani army or come proclaiming the purity of Islam. You see, more than anything else they fear ideas and rational thought. All of them are Fascists. Bloody Nazis."

When he finished he sobbed as though he had lost his children. I didn't know what else to do other than put my hand on his shoulder.

"I'm so lucky I've found you, Kamal. It's just as well that I can't see you. This way I can imagine what you really are. The perfect one, the beautiful one."

We spent long hours together. If not in the outer bungalow, I would sit with him by the pond, or go out with him for walks around the village. When people saw us they would say, "Look. There goes a blind and a dumb. What a fine couple they make."

One day, as I was leading him along the rows of palm trees, he said, "Perhaps, you could rebuild the library."

That would, indeed, be an honour. But I was baffled he should say it, because someone like me would never have the means to buy books, or even be allowed to enter a library, let alone work in it. I would be chased away as soon as I went anywhere near it: "How dare you show your nasty face here. Don't you know that it's a place of learning? You must be too stupid to even know that. You're disturbing our readers. Piss off!"

Zomir Ali must have read my thoughts because he said, "Sorry, Kamal. What I meant to say is that you and I could build it together. Don't you think we'd make a fine team?"

Another afternoon, as we set off for our walk, Zomir Ali was complaining before we'd even crossed the compound. He had good reason to because it was very hot and humid. We sat on a mound, under a kapok tree. A cool breeze would have sent our hearts leaping up to dangle from the quivering red of kapok branches, but only the hot wind blew from the dusty plains and the flowers spat their boiling red venom at us. I was thinking of moving on to look for a cooler place when Big Suban thumped his way across the plains to join us. Now at least I would have a mouth to speak with. Zomir Ali asked him who he was.

"I'm the woodcutter. But the trees are laughing now," said Big Suban.

"What a strange thing to say," replied Zomir Ali.

"Now that war is on, no one hires me to fell trees."

"Yes, I understand that. But surely they don't laugh?"

"You'd be surprised what the trees are like. I've had so many conversations with them."

"What nonsense you are talking. Do you have any proof of that?"

"Ah, proof!" Big Suban laughed out loud. "It's something secret between me and the trees."

"Come on," said Zomir Ali with a sarcastic tone. "Share some of those secrets with us."

"I promised the trees not to give away our secrets, but I can tell you that they are wise and full of meaning."

"Yes, yes," said Zomir Ali with exasperation. "No doubt the trees have found in you a most rational interlocutor. I bet it's like two wise friends exchanging deep thoughts, eh?"

Big Suban scratched his head and looked at me for support. I smiled with my eyes to show that I was with him.

Zomir Ali gasped for air as if he was drowning in a still, dark pond. "Talking trees, my foot. How can we form an independent republic with dimwit citizens like you? Full of irrational, superstitious nonsense," he said, pointing his finger to where Big Suban had been sitting. He hadn't noticed that Big Suban had already stood up and moved away to get a closer look at the man who was running towards us. Zomir's finger was now pointing at the dunghill from which hot steam rose as though the sun fell deep inside it. Still pointing his finger, he continued, "It'll be more like an empire of fools. Talking trees, my arse."

My eyes followed Subhan. Dense clouds were gathering low in the east. Soon after, thunder ripped the sky and a gust of wind blew across the palm trees. It gave me shivers. Was it the sign of an early summer storm? For a moment I'd forgotten the running man. Suddenly he was only a few yards away. I was shocked. Never before had I seen Lal Mia the lazy running. Physical exertion, even just moving, wasn't his thing at all. He preferred to stay glued for hours on end to a nice, comfortable spot, preferably leaning against a pillow, gossiping, reading books, smoking his hookah. He even preferred to have his food served to him where he lay. The man was really lazy. Now he stood before Zomir Ali, his lips trembling, having trouble releasing his words.

His breath broke the barrier at last, "I saw them floating in the river."

Big Subhan was the first to leap to his feet; he ran on ahead without looking back. Lal Mia was almost dragging Zomir Ali along; I was behind them. From the distance I could see a crowd by the river bank. As we came near, the teacher broke from the crowd and stood before Zomir Ali.

"I wish I were blind too, you Venerable Scholar," he said. "No human eyes should see this."

I wish I hadn't seen them, but I saw them. Face down, bobbing among the hyacinths and lilies, were the bodies. Hundreds of them. We had no idea where they came from. All we knew was that the river had brought them the way it brought driftwood and debris from all over the country.

"We need to bury the bodies," said the teacher.

By now clouds had almost completely darkened the sky, but the river gleamed when now and again lightning flashed. The wind was gathering speed as it whistled past us, making our lungis and shirts billow. The early summer storm was upon us.

"We must bring in the bodies before the wind carries them away," said the teacher.

Down the mudbank, followed by a group of villagers, he waded into the water.

"What's happening?" Zomir Ali shouted to me.

Since both Big Suban and Lal Mia were in the water, I had no mouth to answer him with. Finally the storm had done what it had come to do: unleashed its demons. Huge waves leapt over the mass of hyacinths and drove their way up the mudbank. If I hadn't been alert we would have been dragged down into the river. I grabbed Zomir Ali and pulled him further up the slope. When I looked back I saw the tangled bodies were loosening from their cocoon among the lilies and the hyacinths, about to be carried away by the wild, murky currents.

I knew the danger, so I feared for those who went into the water to gather the bodies. No one could withstand the river in such a terrible mood. When the next lightning struck I saw our men clambering onto the shore. I was much relieved, but where was the teacher? Oh Allah, he was still in the water. In the next flash of lightning I saw his fragile frame clinging desperately to a fishing pole, but he wouldn't let go of the body he held. I knew he wouldn't be able to hold on for much longer as the storm galloped in at breakneck speed. Oh Allah, save the teacher. But before I could free myself from Zomir Ali, who was clinging on to me, Big Suban ran down the slope and jumped back into the river. He snatched the body from the teacher's clasp and let it drift into the waves, and then dragged him up the mud bank to the shore.

Broken branches, sheets of tin, planks of wood, and all sorts of other debris from the houses were flying all around us. We needed to find shelter quickly. I put Zomir Ali over my shoulder and ran with the others through the sheets of rain and wind. We didn't know where we were going. Suddenly we found ourselves in front of a big house, high above the riverbank. It belonged to Dinesh Babu, the fish merchant. We knew that it was empty because he and his family had already fled to the refugee camps in India. We took shelter in the large outer bungalow. Fierce winds lashed the gables and the windows but the bungalow, with its tall bamboo beams, was strong enough to withstand it. We groped along the floor and found a hurricane lamp in a corner. We lit it and waited for the storm to leave.

"I shouldn't have let the little girl go," said the teacher.

"Why not?" asked Zomir Ali.

"The least I could do was to give her a burial."

"How do you know that she needed a burial? Was she a Muslim?"

"I don't know that, Venerable Scholar."

"For all we know, she could have been a Hindu."

"Yes, Venerable Scholar."

"So it is the best that the river has taken her."

The teacher didn't seem to have taken in the sense of Zomir's argument. He sat slumped on the floor, looking like a dead frog in the dim flutter of the lamp. With time the whoosh of the wind had lost its demon's breath. Loud banging on the hinges settled into gentle creaks. The rain, though, kept on pattering on the tin roof.

Now we were more at our ease. Big Suban found a hookah, lit

it, and passed it around. "I never thought the Pakistanis would go this far," said Lal Mia the lazy, between puffs on the hookah. "You know, plucking us as though we were weeds?"

"In a land of pure Islam nothing is too far, my friend," said Zomir Ali. "All they need is to imagine a tiny stain on you. Even a faded one gets these purewallas going. After that they're only too happy to clean you out. Or pluck you, as you prefer to say. It doesn't make any difference if they modelled themselves on laundrywallas or gardeners. Or the gasman when the Nazis called on the Jews."

"I thought this cleaning business had died a long time ago, with Hitler," said Lal Mia.

"Yes, but if you fill your ears with the pure melodies of Islam, the news doesn't reach you, does it?"

When we couldn't hear the rain any more, we came out of the bungalow. I was guiding Zomir Ali through the puddles and broken branches along the slippery path; the teacher went ahead with Big Suban. I expected to see them when we climbed the high ridge along the riverbank, but they weren't there, so I climbed down again with Zomir Ali. There behind a badly damaged cowshed I spotted them; they appeared to be looking at a large fallen tree. When I came nearer I realised that they weren't looking at the tree, but the boat that lay underneath it. It looked smashed up as the massive trunk had gone through its cabin and the ribs of planking that supported the decks. I recognised it as one of Dinesh Babu's cargo-boats. It must have been brought ashore for repair before the war began.

The teacher went around the boat, stooped beneath the branches to examine the hull, and stopped at the stern. He prodded the broken rudder and turned to face us.

"I think we've found our boat."

"What?" said Zomir Ali.

"We can repair the boat and wait for the monsoon rain and the flood."

"What for?"

"You know what'll happen, Venerable Scholar. The Pakistani army is bound to arrive here sooner or later. So we should be prepared."

"Yes, I know that. But you are not thinking of naval warfare, are you?"

"I've no intention of fighting, you Venerable Scholar. All I want to do is wait for the flood, then sail the boat and see out the war."

"So all your book reading comes to this. Just the desire to save your own skin."

"This is a large cargo-boat, you Venerable Scholar. I can save quite a few people. Ideally I'd love to take one from each family."

The teacher looked around the boat one more time and set off ahead of us. I made my way slowly up the slippery path with Zomir Ali; Big Suban was behind us. Zomir Ali was muttering to himself: "Now the fool wants to play Noah. Building ark, my arse."

Big Suban laughed out loud at this.

"What's so funny?" Zomir Ali asked.

"Ah, this is good news, you Venerable Scholar. You see, I'm the only one left in my family. So the teacher is bound to take me on board."

"Maybe, but that's not funny."

"I'm not a book-reading person, you Venerable Scholar."

"Yes, yes, I can see that. But what's your point?"

"Doesn't everything that goes in Noah's boat, go in pairs?"

"It's all nonsense, but still I don't see what's so funny about it."

"If he takes me on board, he has to find me a woman, doesn't he?"

Zomir Ali turned around and flailed his hands, and screamed, "You lecherous fool. If I were him I'd pair you with a hog!"

Big Suban cowered as if to fend off a blow but he kept on smiling. We lost track of the teacher when instead of going around the bend of the river we took a short cut through the mango grove.

As happens every year, the storm had caused havoc among the mango trees, felling thousands of young fruits. Their smooth, green skins covered almost the entire grove floor. We couldn't move without stepping on them. As soon as I saw them I planned to gather some. I knew that Ata Banu would be pleased with me. She would cook sour dahl, flavour the fishes with them, and, above all, she would make jars and jars of pickle.

I persuaded Big Suban to escort Zomir Ali back to our home-stead, promising him a share of my picking. Then I ran to Dinesh

Babu's granary, now empty and taken over by the bats, and came back with a gunnysack. I was then alone, on all fours on the slippery ground full of puddles, among the smell of green mangoes, torn leaves and branches. As I was about to pick my first mango, drops of rainwater, caught in the folds of leaves, fell on my back. Oh yes, how could I not remember the last year when Moni Banu and I came to pick mangoes together. She had just reached eighteen then. Since that day when we returned from the fair late, when she turned a woman, she had been stopped from going out with me beyond the outer fences of our homestead. That had been five years before. From that time on I had to go into the inner courtyard to meet her, though she still kept me company while I ate in my hut.

It was terrible. Even before she reached eighteen, families across the swampland started to visit our homestead. They would bring sweet yogurt, coconut bread or pots of thick milk as presents. Sometimes even a large catfish or several dozen duck eggs. Unlike my secret education, people knew of Moni Banu's, though not the extent of it. They had no idea that she read things like Thakur's *Charulata*, Tolstoy's *Anna Karenina*, Omar Khayyam's *Rubaiyat* – or Che Guevara's *Guerrilla Warfare*. Mind you, few of them would even have heard of these authors, let alone known the contents of their books. They thought she could just about read and write. Even that was a source of unease to many of the families. But the fame of her beauty was such that they all wanted to have her as a bride for their sons. Once they had arrived they would be taken to the outer bungalow where the teacher would question them. I would listen in, hiding behind the bungalow.

The teacher would always begin his questioning with the subject of education. He would ask them about the level of education achieved not only by the prospective groom but also by their families. In most cases the meeting would end at this point. He would say: My daughter is not feeling well today. So sorry that she won't able to come here to show her respect. The families would take this as the sign of rejection and leave. If he liked what he had heard, he would throw in the names of some authors or books, and observe their faces. If they looked baffled, which was nearly always the case, he would repeat the routine. Only those very few who passed the education test would then be engaged in religious discussion. If he found any sign of blind faith or religious intolerance in their views, he would end the meeting in the same way. Moni Banu was frequently "unwell". Days and weeks would go by without any family passing either test. If they were lucky enough to pass, they got to see Moni Banu. She would be called in to serve paan to the guests, who would inspect not only her figure and her face, but also her every gesture and movement. I can assure you that she never failed to impress them. The teacher, though, would still be far from convinced of their suitability. He would wait to see if they raised the matter of dowry, which they invariably did. "Thank you for visiting our homestead," he would say abruptly. "I'll get in touch with you soon." He never did.

"Primitives," he would later mumble, "how dare they demand a dowry for our Moni." At this rate he would never find anyone suitable for her. But I was happy. I knew she should be married – it was really the best thing for her – but I didn't want to lose her. During the nights such thoughts would play on my mind: I would feel guilty for being so selfish.

Since she had turned eighteen at the beginning of the previous summer, families in pursuit of Moni kicked up a permanent dust cloud across the plains. I would sit by the pond and watch them approach our homestead. However, as soon as they climbed the slope onto the road by the palm tree, which led to the gate at the outer fence, I would disappear. Ata Banu had told me, very harshly, to keep a low profile when prospective grooms and their families visited us.

Something unusual had happened a few days before the early summer storm that year. Ata Banu, who for years hadn't left the inner courtyard, went to visit her father's homestead. It had something to do with her inheritance. On the afternoon when the storm came I was lying in my hut. I felt protected by the dense line of betel palms at the back that screened it. I was listening to the wind and the rain and felt light in the cool air. I wrapped myself with the bed sheet and was drifting into the mood in which I always told myself stories.

I heard a rattling. At first I thought it was the wind that had suddenly changed course and was lashing the door. Then I heard a voice. I got up to open the door, but Moni Banu wouldn't come in. "Are you coming to the grove, Beautiful One?" she asked.

I hesitated and stood holding onto the panels as the wind funnelled in. "Let's go and pick green mangoes," she said.

It had been one of our favourite activities, and each year at the beginning of summer we would look for the signs of the coming storm, and be ready to reach the grove before anyone else. How I'd missed it for the past five years! Now Moni Banu wanted to take me on a childhood adventure again. I knew that in Ata Banu's absence we could take the risk and get away with it. I don't know how the teacher would have taken it, but he was away too. I was still hesitating. I wasn't sure whether it was the right thing to do.

Moni Banu giggled. Not like a child, but a shameless woman. "You're not scared, are you?"

Suddenly Moni Banu grabbed me and pulled me out. Within seconds I was as drenched as she was. Then she ran out of the inner courtyard. What was I to do but follow her? Out of the protective enclosure of the homestead we felt the full force of the wind. We staggered from side to side, pushing through the wind like tacking boats. The rain had dimmed the landscape so much that it looked like the picture of the island from the end of the world that I once saw in a book.

We entered the grove. It was much darker there than it had been on the path by the plains. But I could just about make out the shapes of things in the remaining light. Fearsome wind with a demonic whistle lashed the trees, tossing and turning their canopies so hard that I felt the grove was about to cave in on us. No one else would dare to come out there in weather like this. It was far too dangerous. I was relieved that no prying eyes could spread gossip about us in the village. A scandal would ruin Moni Banu. She would be shamed, a fallen woman.

I was still scared by the force of the wind and the sound that it was making. Several trees had already fallen and branches were flying everywhere. I took shelter between the buttress-like roots of a giant kapok tree, but Moni spread her arms and whirled around as though she'd become one with the storm. Then she went down on all fours, picking green mangoes. "It's not the time to be scared, Beautiful One. Let's become sorcerers. Really wicked ones," she said, and giggled. I had no idea what she was on about, but began to crawl beside her, looking for mangoes. When I felt the smooth coldness of the first mango in my hand I realised we hadn't brought a sack for our pickings. I tried to communicate this to her, but she seemed unconcerned. Then she looked at me and I was taken aback by the gleam in her eyes. The gloom had not dimmed them, but made them brighter. Like the burning orbs of a jackal.

She knelt down and gathered some mangoes in the fold of her sari, and then threw them in the air. She hadn't come to pick mangoes. What was she playing then? Was she going mad at the coming of the rain after the long dry season?

She loosed her hair, circled around me and sang a song. It was barely an echo among the roar of the wind and the drumbeats of the rain on the leaves, but I felt caught up in the madness of the moment too. I couldn't help noticing her figure, wrapped tightly in her sari. Yes, it was the full figure of a grown woman and my man-eyes crawled up her curves shamelessly. She held my gaze, not to challenge my desire, but flame it further.

"What are you looking at? I knew it, you're a wicked sorcerer," she said and ran.

She hadn't gone far when a branch flew from one of the trees and hit her in the face. She lay face up among green mangoes, leaves and branches, her eyes closed. She seemed to have fainted. I ran to her and saw that one of her cheeks was bleeding slightly. When I touched the wound with the tip of my finger she groaned. No, she hadn't fainted. Beneath her blouse, red, thin and wet, her breasts rode the rapid waves of her breath. What was I to feel? I don't know, but I felt a current rushing through my veins, blinding me. Was I being a wicked sorcerer? She breathed hard and rapidly and opened her mouth. I slid my bloodstained finger over her lips. She bit it, at first gently, then harder. I didn't withdraw my finger but slid it deeper in her throat. She kept on biting me until I bled in her mouth. Then she grabbed my hand and withdrew it from her mouth and opened her eyes. She licked her lips and looked at me and entered my eyes through the gloom and the rain. Still holding onto my hand, she turned sideways and curled up. She pressed my hand against her breasts and moaned. I felt like breaking through my skin and exploding like the rain that pelted down on us from the gaps in the canopy. "Wicked sorcerer, mark me," she said. I dug my nails into her and ploughed them through her breasts. She didn't cry in pain, but moaned with pleasure. This is how we created our token of remembrance.

We didn't talk about it afterwards. We carried on as if nothing had happened. Nor did I touch her again until on her marriage day when she fed me rice pudding.

Now I filled the gunnysack with green mangoes and headed home. What was Moni Banu doing now? Was she preparing puffed rice with mustard and green chillies, as wives do on rainy days, for their husbands? Or was she thinking, like me, of the moment in the mango grove during the storm? I wondered what lies she would tell her husband about our token of remembrance.

CHAPTER 6

Heat waves returned after the storm.

I got up early when I heard Sona Mia from the minaret. His voice seemed more enchanting as the war progressed. I felt that he was singing to coax Allah to ward off its impending horror.

It was still dark when I went to see Zomir Ali in the outer bungalow. He was already up and waiting for me to take him to the toilet in the bush behind the palm trees. As soon as he sensed my presence he said, "I wish that idiotic Sona Mia wouldn't bray like a donkey so early in the morning. Bloody moron."

He annoyed me so much that I wanted to leave him in the bungalow to soil his clothes and shame himself, but I came back because it was my duty to take him out to toilet. He whined and gave out little coughs as he cleaned his bowels. "Are you there, Kamal?" he said. I was in no mood to answer, but he kept on asking. "Are you angry with me, my friend? Ah, I see. You didn't like what I said about Sona Mia. I thought a book-reading man like you – I mean, a man of reason like you – would have no truck with the likes of Sona Mia. Sorry if I have upset you."

At last I kicked a lump of mud and broke a twig from the low branch of a lychee tree to indicate my presence.

"I wish you were my eyes. All I have are the memories of books. Even before I went blind I saw the world as a reflection of books. I didn't see things, Kamal. I didn't see things."

I was counting time for him to finish. He stayed quiet for a while, then began again. "I know I could see things again if you were to describe them to me. For instance, how does a tree look like in the morning mist? Perhaps, you're seeing a tree right now. Does it feel solitary? Or does the mist gather all of them up into a community of whispering souls?"

I looked up at the hazy lines of palm trees, but didn't see any whispering souls. To me they were just trees: leaves, branches and trunks. Or just mouths waiting to feed on the sunlight. I must say I was surprised to hear Zomir Ali speak of such things as whispering souls. I thought a man who took such pride in being so rational would consider such talk nonsensical, even downright idiotic. I wondered what made him say such things.

Once he'd finished I took him to the pond where he brushed his teeth. Then I led him back to the bungalow and fetched his breakfast. While he ate his soaked, soft rice cereal with brown sugar lumps, I squatted on the floor. Not too near. I was still annoyed with him.

I was always surprised by his manner of eating. I thought a learned and refined man like him would show more restraint in the way he took his food. He scooped large handfuls and shoved them inside his mouth and slurped loudly – like a hog.

After his cereal, he became more restrained with the tea. He took a sip and paused. "It's so frustrating, Kamal, not to be able to talk to you. I've so much to say to you. For instance, I wanted to ask you what you thought of *Hayy ibn Yaqzan*."

Of course, I'd thought a lot about *Hayy ibn Yaqzan*, but I wasn't going to play his game. I knew he wanted me to be his little clone. Was it the idea that someone disfigured like me – whom the world had decided was a potato head – could be an intellectual that excited him? How could I explain that I was happy the way I was. Besides, I'd never really opened a book to gather knowledge, but to nourish my inner world with a particular way of seeing things. I suppose for Zomir Ali I was an enigma: a deformed farm labourer, if not a servant, who mainly went about performing the simplest of tasks, but was at the same time exposed to the ideas that he regarded as the fruits of humankind's highest pursuits. Maybe he thought of me as riven with contradictions – a hopelessly split soul. Perhaps I was, but I never felt that way. I would never be his clone. And nothing would ever make me look down on Big Suban and Sona Mia.

I gathered the empty breakfast bowl and the teacup and left him. In the kitchen, Ata Banu was muttering her usual Arabic verses. I was about to leave when she addressed me.

"The day I saw your mouth I knew that evil was coming," she said. "You're an omen of badness."

I was getting irritated by her constant abuse, but I ignored her and continued on my way. Already the early morning mist had lifted and the red glow of the sun trailed the plains to the pond. I was so absorbed thinking about Moni Banu, wishing she was there to lift me from my gloom, that I didn't notice the teacher coming down until he was just a step behind me.

"I hope I haven't given Moni away to a wrong family. I'd never forgive myself if she suffers. Oh, how I miss her," he said with a sigh. Then he turned to look at me. "Now we need to look out for each other more."

I met his eyes and he understood my feelings.

"What do you think of the boat?" he asked.

I had seen it before its present sorry state, squashed under the tree. I'd thought it a fine boat and communicated as much.

"Yes, yes, it's a fine boat," he said. "But it needs a lot of work." I nodded.

"Once it's fixed we could sail in it and stay safe for the rest of the war. I know it will work, Kamal."

I'd heard him say this many times in recent days.

"It has to work. Otherwise, we're doomed. Some of us have to survive the war to build the nation afterwards. What do you think?"

I wanted to ask, Why us? Were we the chosen ones? Who decided that? But I kept looking at the yellow ripples on the pond.

"I don't know why I feel like this. Do you think I'm being irrational?" Then he changed tack. "It's not time for abstract discussion. We must be practical and act now. You know the blacksmith's craft, don't you?"

He knew very well that I'd been dabbling in it for some time, so I made no response.

"I think we need some blacksmith's work to repair the boat. You know, nails and things. I heard the old blacksmith has already joined the ranks of the refugees. So we'll have to make do with you."

It pleased me to hear that the teacher needed my services as a blacksmith. I smiled with my eyes and purred softly. He put his hand on my head and lightly brushed my hair.

"We should be ready by the start of the monsoon. If we delay we give the war the chance to swallow us up." He climbed up the stairs, but turned back.

"Go and check on the boat. Big Suban is working there. Then meet me at the market. Alright?"

It was already hot and humid. I needed to take a quick dip in the pond to cool myself before going to check on the boat. I covered my mouth, held my breath, and let myself sink to the bottom of the pond. My feet dug into the soft mud bed and I felt cool. I'd always enjoyed being in the depths because the silence there, undisturbed even by my own breath, made me feel that I was at the beginning of the universe. Perhaps it was then that time had set in motion the chain of events – probably due to no more than a speck of dust blown slightly off course – that resulted in my being born mouthless. If time were to begin again, maybe another dice-throw of creation would have made me the man who lifted Moni Banu's bridal veil to feed her with sweets. But then again, I could have been the bull whose sole purpose in life was to have its throat cut and reach a meatiness of such perfection that it propelled the brothers Ajud Ali and Majud Ali into establishing a record-breaking feat at Moni's wedding. So, when I surfaced from the depths I felt, as I always did, lucky for the ways things turned out for me.

Long before I reached the boat I heard the unmistakable thwacking of Big Suban's axe. When he saw me he stopped.

"The teacher roped me into it, Kamal," he said. "You know, I don't like cutting dead trees."

We sat in the shade, leaning against the boat's hull. He prepared his coconut chillum and began to smoke. Heat was still burning the ground. I could see a shimmer running over the dry, dusty fields to the river. Big Suban didn't speak for a while; all I could hear was the gurgle of water inside his chillum as he took his customary vigorous drags.

"You must be missing Moni Banu."

Only Big Suban really knew how I felt about her.

"You must be sad, Kamal. But at least you have someone to feel sad about. I've never found anyone to have those feelings for."

I put a hand on his shoulder.

"I'll find myself a wife after the war. What do you think, Kamal?"

I slapped his shoulder, grunted from the back of my throat, and smiled with my eyes. He looked happy, too, his eyes glistening.

"Do you know what I'll tell my wife when I'm married? I'll tell her: 'Cook a nice fish curry for Kamal. He's my best friend.'"

He got up and went back to his work. I watched as he struck the huge girth of the trunk with his axe. Yes, his muscles, as always, tensed up and eased in harmony with the metal and the wood. Yet the passion wasn't there. I would never really understand what went on between Big Suban and living trees. I made a dumb show of chopping with an axe to ask if he needed any help. He said not until he'd cut through the trunk; that would take an hour or so. Only then did I remember that I'd come to check on the boat. The boat's hull and the cabin were broken in many places, so they would need a large number of rivets and nails to put them together again.

I was on my way to the market to meet the teacher when I came across Sona Mia. I asked, in my fashion, where he was going.

"To the paddy fields, Kamal. The saplings need watering. They are Allah's bounty to us. We can't let them die."

I asked him if we would be able to gather the harvest this year.

"Perhaps not. But I'm a rice farmer. My work is to sow, care for and reap rice. No matter how bad it gets, I should do my work. As long as Allah keeps me on earth."

I asked him if he was scared.

"I am scared, Kamal. Like everyone else."

Would he consider coming onto the teacher's boat?

"The teacher is a wise man. I know he doesn't believe in Allah, but he is still doing his good work. These things are very mysterious, you know. But I don't see myself going in the boat."

Why not?

"As I said, I've got to water the saplings and wait for the harvest. And the azan. Someone has to do the azan."

But if no one is left in the village, then what's the point of azan? Who would he be calling to prayer?

"Perhaps no one. But this will turn into a ghost village if no one does it. And don't forget that our ancestors are buried here. I can't desert them."

78

But if my ancestors were Hindus or Buddhists, who would give succour to their souls?

"Don't worry, Kamal. You see, Allah doesn't make any difference between Muslims, Hindus or Buddhists. He loves them equally. When I call out for prayer, they all hear me. Do you know why? Because I remember them all."

When I was about to take my leave, he said again, "Don't forget that you're Allah's chosen one. You'll remember us all."

There was no sign of the teacher in the market. It looked deserted. Then I noticed the dogs; they seemed to be asleep under the banyan, but I was scared. My heart was pounding so hard that I thought it would wake them up. I went on tiptoe, hoping to reach the tea stall unnoticed, but the dogs had already sensed me. First a little skinny one lifted its head and looked at me. When it began to growl, the others lifted their heads up too. I knew they were hungry and would chase me. I made a run for the tea stall; luckily its door was open and I managed to secure it before the pack came. They milled around outside the door, turning restlessly in small circles, sniffing the door, whining and barking. They were pleading with me to open the door. I shuddered to think what they'd do if I did. Normally they lived off the scraps of rotten meat, fish and human faeces that littered the market. Now they were starving. I supposed that the men who'd owned and worked the tea-stall had left like so many others for the refugee camps in India.

I didn't want to be meat for the dogs. If I could light a torch, I'd have a fighting chance against them, but there was none in the stall. All I could do was wait and listen to their growling and barking. Perhaps a group of refugees would pass by the market. But if that happened, how could I draw their attention? I had no mouth to scream. I looked around the stall again and there was a drum – hidden in a heap of junk under the platform on which the owner sat. I was surprised; the owner was not known for any interest in music. Perhaps it belonged to one of the workers who joined in the meetings of the Bauls. Anyway, it occurred to me that I could draw the attention of passers-by with the sound of the drum.

So I began tapping the drum with my fingers. To my surprise the dogs started to let out soft, mellow barks. Then they went into prolonged whining as though the drum was speaking to them – what it was saying to them I don't know, but I, too, found the sound soothing. I was beginning to forget the dogs, then quite by accident I hit the drum hard. Immediately the dogs howled as though frightened, and then they scattered. When I stopped drumming the dogs came back to growl and bark again. Now all I could hear was their hunger and desperation. I waited for an hour or so but no one passed through the market and the dogs stayed where they were. I knew I had to get out before night fell. I would stand no chance against them in the dark.

I made up my mind that I would hit the drum hard and when the dogs scattered I would take the risk and run for it. I hung the drum round my neck and came out hitting it as hard as I could. The dogs were pacing about nervously by the banyan. Seeing me they stopped, then began barking fiercely. I hit the drum with all of my force and ran. I knew that if I made it to the bamboo bridge over the canal I would be safe. When I had nearly passed the market stalls and come within sight of the slope, on the other side of which lay the canal, the dogs gave chase. I stopped hitting the drum and ran. Then I rolled down the slope and scampered onto the narrow bridge. The dogs came down to the slope and whined and barked so sadly that I felt sorry for them. I was their last chance to stay alive.

On my way back to the boat I met the teacher. He had forgotten about our meeting in the market. It was just as well, otherwise he might have been eaten by the dogs.

"What are you doing with the drum?"

I tried to explain to him what had happened.

"I don't understand what the dogs have to do with the drum. I sometimes don't understand you, Kamal. Is it a story you're making up?"

I just shook my head. Anyway, we went off together to see Big Suban. On the way, he told me that he hadn't been able to find any proper boat-builders, but had persuaded two carpenters to come and repair the boat. "They'll be here first thing tomorrow," he said. "I want you to wait for them with breakfast."

When Big Suban saw me with the drum he said, "You want to make music, Kamal?"

The teacher explained that the drum had something to do with the dogs.

"You want to make them dogs dance, Kamal?" said Big Suban. "Oh I'd love watching dancing dogs. I bet they'd make a nicer show than dancing bears."

I was having one of those days when no one understood me. I wished Moni Banu had been there to straighten them out. When I shook my head to show that he was completely wrong, Big Suban smiled and said, "I see it now, Kamal. You want to use the drum to make conversation with the dogs and win them to our side. Yes?"

"You do speak such nonsense, Big Suban. I don't understand what goes inside the head of yours. Count your lucky stars that Venerable Scholar is not here. He would've thought you a..." said the teacher.

Big Suban wasn't put out at all. He looked very serious, as though he was thinking something profound.

"I can see Kamal playing the drum and the dogs responding to his bidding," he said. "He can send them after the Pakistani soldiers and make them bite their bottoms. It'd be real good, no?"

On our way back to the homestead I walked on ahead of them. I couldn't stand listening to them any more. Near the outer bungalow I heard the crackle of a radio. I had no idea who'd brought it. I left the drum outside, as I didn't fancy another round of wild speculation about it and the dogs.

No one paid me any attention when I came in; they were all engrossed in the radio. I knew them all, except two who were sitting on chairs. Zomir Ali and Lal Mia the lazy were on the bed, leaning against pillows, the rest were on the floor. I took my place on the floor. When the teacher came in he sat beside Zomir Ali on the bed; Big Suban sat next to me. The light had already faded, but the lamp wasn't lit.

The broadcast was crackling, fading in and out. It was the radio of independent Bangladesh. Every freedom fighter is a grenade, said the radio, but in eternal recurrence. Exploding among the enemy only to be born again to explode anew.

"Bah, bah. Our fellows are genuine supermen," said Zomir Ali. "General Yahya must be shitting in his khaki pants."

The two men in the chairs looked quizzically at the blind, frail figure of Zomir Ali. Even if you knew him well it was hard to tell whether he was being serious or sarcastic.

Invading beasts are killing humans, let us kill the beasts, said the radio again.

"Hunting beasts, very good," said Zomir Ali, "It should be a piece of cake for the humans. I wonder what kind of beasts are they? Hyenas or buffalos?"

I wished Zomir Ali didn't try to be clever all the time. One of the men in the chairs looked annoyed.

"Would you shut up. We're trying to listen to something important."

Then there was a song about saving a flower. Everyone knew what it meant and quite a few, including Zomir Ali, moved their lips to sing along with it. I had no lips to give to the song, but then it was followed by:

> My Bengal of gold, I love you
> Forever your skies, your air set my heart in tune
> As if it were a flute…

As soon as that tune drifted into me, I became, as always, the flute to play in the sky.

The radio crackled uncontrollably and then went dead. One of the strangers stood up to speak. He and his companion belonged to the liberation forces.

"We are leaving your village tomorrow but will stop by on our way back. In three days' time. Anyone who wants to join us can come along. We still need many more volunteers."

Two young men from the floor raised their hands.

"You two want to volunteer?"

"Yes, but we don't know how to read and write. We're just peasants," said one of them.

"You don't need to read and write to join the liberation forces. Some of our best fighters come from backgrounds such as yours."

Big Suban's eyes lit up when he heard this. He raised his hand.

"I'm a woodcutter. Can I be a fighter too?"

"Of course you can," said the man.

"Count me in then," said Big Suban.

Was this what he really wanted to do? I tried to catch his eye, but before I could do so the teacher got up and asked me to follow him outside. He wanted me to slaughter some chickens for the guests. I went to the coop with the hurricane lamp and caught three chickens, wrung their necks and took them to Ata Banu in the kitchen. She asked me to fetch Datla Nuri to help her pluck them.

Big Suban came with me. Datla Nuri lived by the old grave-yard which lay several fields and a patch of bush away from our homestead. Big Suban didn't speak for a while, but I could feel that he was very excited.

"What do you think, Kamal – me becoming a liberation fighter?"

I held the hurricane lamp in front of me so that he could read my gestures: I thought you wanted to sail in the teacher's boat.

"What would I do in the teacher's boat?" he said. "I can't cut trees. Perhaps some dead wood to feed the cooking stove. Most of the time there'd be nothing to do. You know I don't like to be idle. To be honest with you, I saw myself just doing servantly tasks for higher-up people on board, and I didn't fancy that, Kamal. I'm happy being my own man and cutting trees."

I touched his hand to show that I understood his sentiments.

"If I join the liberation forces, I'll be somebody, no?"

We crossed the bush and the graveyard in silence, but as soon as we reached the bamboo grove, behind which lay Datla Nuri's hut, Big Suban laughed and said, "Some woman might even want to marry me after the war."

No one lived on this side of the bush, facing the graveyard, except Datla Nuri. The land on which she'd built her hut belonged to the teacher; she was landless. She was known as a beggar woman, but I'd never seen her begging. In fact, she was the hardest working person I knew. She did laundry for the landown-ing families, fetched water for them, collected firewood during the winter months. She delivered babies. She also worked as a labourer on the road-building project, breaking bricks and carrying loads like any man. Her usual job, though, was husking rice. No one did it better. She could pound rice in a giant mortar for hours on end. The rhythm and the sound she made were beautiful. I loved them as much as I loved the thwacking of Big Suban's axe. She always had a smile on her face and spoke her mind. She made people laugh too and loved telling rude jokes. For that, some of the more pious village men regarded her as a shameless, fallen woman.

"That's why she's so ugly. And that's why no one married her," they would say. But I knew that women in their private gatherings – except Ata Banu – let themselves laugh until they were in stitches at her jokes.

Datla Nuri was cooking. As always, she lifted her buckteeth and laughed. "How come I don't see you no more, Nephew? I thought you'd gone to war with them boys."

She left her cooking to come back with us. She would often do odd jobs for Ata Banu for free – returning the favour the teacher had done her in letting her build her hut on his land.

As we walked through the bush, Big Suban asked her, "You not scared to live here, Big Sister Nuri?"

"What do you mean, Suban?" she said. "All them old ghosts and demons never dare to show up before me. When the young ones come all cocky, I just show them my teeth and hiss. They can't disappear quick enough."

"I wish you could frighten the Pakistani army. But they have large moustaches and are very fond of calling Allah's name. They'll shoot you dead from miles away," said Big Suban.

"I'm not scared of them," she said. "I'll just sneak up on them and cut their throats."

"You don't understand their machines, Big Sister Nuri. Just one of them is more powerful than all the swords and spears put together. To defeat them we have to acquire the ways of the gun."

"You joining them boys in the liberation forces, Suban?"

"Yes, Big Sister. I'll come back here after my training and drive the Pakistani army out of our swampland."

"And then, Suban?"

"I want to get back to cutting my trees in peace."

"Don't you try to fool me, Suban, I know you well. You want to make a name for yourself in the war. So that some silly girl will marry you. No?" And she cackled loudly.

We left Datla Nuri in the kitchen with Ata Banu and joined the men in the outer bungalow. Zomir Ali, Lal Mia and the teacher were still on the bed, and the liberation fighters in their chairs. As soon as I came in the teacher sent me out to fetch some paan for the guests and his hookah. I went back to the kitchen to fetch them. Datla Nuri had already set herself to cleaning the chickens. Ata Banu was chopping a gourd.

"Tell me, Nephew, what do the liberation fighters look like? Are they tasty looking?" Datla Nuri asked, laughing. "Do you think they'll sweep me off my feet?"

"You two are all nasty mouths," snapped Ata Banu.

Datla Nuri gave me a sly look and laughed mischievously.

"From now on I'll just call Allah's name like you respectable ladies," said Datla Nuri. "And like them Pakistani army," she added after a pause.

I didn't want to be caught up in their quarrel, so I made a quick getaway. I handed the hookah to the teacher, placed the paan box in front of the liberation fighters and sat down on the floor. It seemed they were discussing the teacher's idea of spending the duration of the war in the boat.

"Now that the war is on, you can't opt out of it. We are all involved," said one of the liberation fighters.

"I'm not denying this. I know that it will come to us soon. That's why I want to prepare the boat," said the teacher.

"If everyone runs away, then who will resist the mass murderers and the rapists?"

"You are fighting. And many others like you will fight. I can't see myself fighting. I'll be happy if I can just save a few lives."

"You want us to die, so that you can enjoy the fruits of the liberation afterwards."

"I'm not thinking about afterwards. All I'm concerned with is getting away from the war until it blows over. It doesn't suit me. It brings out our dark passions too much. I just can't bear it."

"So, you want to stay pure while we die."

"I don't want you to die. I'd like to save everyone."

"I don't know what universe you're living in. Besides, there's no hiding place. Sooner or later the Pakistani army will come to kill you. Would you not take up arms then?"

"I don't know what I'd do then. But at this moment I don't want to consider that option."

"Don't you want to see a free and independent Bangladesh? Don't you love your land and your language?"

"Of course I love my land and my language. And of course I want a free country, but I worry about what this nation business will do to us."

"We'll worry about it when it comes. Now the only way we can be free is by becoming an independent country. Otherwise, we face rape, pillage and genocide at the hands of the Pakistanis and the followers of Islamic purity."

Taking the opportunity of a pause in the exchanges between the teacher and the liberation fighters, Zomir Ali leaned sideways, as if trying to catch the attention of the people sitting on the floor, and said, "What does Kamal think about all this?"

All faces turned in my direction, all looking rather puzzled.

"How do you expect him to speak?" said one of the liberation fighters.

"I don't expect him to speak, but he can write," said Zomir Ali.

"Write! What do you mean?" asked Lal Mia.

"Ask Abbas Mia about it. He'll tell you," said Zomir Ali.

At first the teacher hesitated, then he looked at me rather apologetically and told them the story of my life, and how he had taught me to read and write, the books that I read, and why he'd kept my education a secret.

Big Suban looked at me with astonishment. "What's happening, Kamal? You a book-reading fella?"

I had dreaded this moment for many years. The way they had seen me was about to fall apart. Would they suddenly begin to hate me?

Lal Mia came and sat in front of me and touched my hand. "Sorry, Kamal. Please forgive me. All these years I've treated you wrongly. I treated you as just a body with a hole. I had no idea that you had a mind swimming in a sea of words. If I had known your truth, we could have become two lovers of the written word."

This rather curious way of putting it made me feel uneasy.

"There you go again, Lal Mia," said Zomir Ali. "If you talk like this you'll scare the young man away."

"I'm just expressing my regrets to the young man. I don't know how my speech was inappropriate, you Venerable Scholar."

"You'll work it out the day you understand the difference between knowledge and wisdom," said Zomir Ali.

Lal Mia touched my hand again and looked at me rather forlornly. With my eyes I thanked him for treating me in such a kind way. He got up and went back to sit on the bed. The teacher passed him the hookah and he began to puff away absent-mindedly, as though Zomir Ali's words were still running around in his head.

Big Suban nudged me with his elbow and whispered in my ear, "Now that you're a learned fella, will you still be my friend? Or do you intend to keep company with only learned gentlemen?"

He knew very well that we would always be friends, so I didn't respond. He was about to say more, but Zomir interrupted.

"I still don't quite understand, Abbas Mia; why have you felt the need to keep Kamal's education a secret?"

"As I told you before, you Venerable Scholar, I feared that it might incite people's jealousy and hostility towards him. He has enough to cope with as it is."

"Does anyone here feel jealous and hostile towards Kamal?"

"Of course not," said one of the freedom fighters and the others nodded in agreement.

"There you are, Abbas Mia. No one is jealous of him," said Zomir Ali. "I don't think you got it right. I wonder if there is more to it than what you've said."

"Here we are among friends and enlightened people. But out there it's a different story," said the teacher.

"To be honest, I'm not convinced by your argument. Could it be that you yourself are not clear why you kept Kamal's education a secret? If the knowledge had been public he could have reached a higher position than his present station in life, by becoming a scribe or a letter writer. Had that happened, perhaps you'd have been compelled to consider him more as a son than a servant."

The teacher tightened his mouth and looked down. I was feeling increasingly uneasy. I needed some fresh air. When I got up, Zomir Ali said, "Would you please bring your slate."

I didn't want to do this. All I wanted was to get away – to take a dip in the pond, but I didn't feel I could disobey Zomir Ali. I went to my hut and returned with the slate.

"Write something," he said, more as an order than a request.

I stood there for a long time looking at the black space of the slate. Then I remembered the teacher telling me years ago that the

87

slate was a window to the world. Even now I was no more sure than I'd been when I first heard this what I was meant to see through it.

"Have you written something, Kamal?" asked Zomir Ali.

"I'm Kamal," I wrote.

"Lal Mia, would you read to me what Kamal has written?"

"He has only written: 'I'm Kamal'."

"That's good, Kamal," said Zomir Ali. "Now add: 'I'm a man of letters'. And make sure that you always carry your slate with you and never erase what you've just written."

After the meal, the liberation fighters and Lal Mia slept with Zomir Ali in the outer bungalow. Despite her protests, Big Suban and I escorted Datla Nuri to her hut. Neither of them spoke on the way. Now that my secret was out, it was as if they weren't sure how to treat me. Datla Nuri hesitated at the door, then turned around to say, "I hear my nephew is a learned fella now. Can you become a policeman? I hear they make big money."

"How can Kamal become a policeman with the war on?" said Big Suban. "You don't know anything, Big Sister."

"Don't *you* pretend to be a learned fella with me, Suban. You're as foolish as they come. I bet no one will give their daughters to you even if you come back from the war as a big fella."

Big Suban didn't mind; he just laughed because he knew Datla Nuri's ways.

"Nephew, your mother must have prayed real good for you. Fancy having a learned fella for a son," she said as we were about to leave.

Big Suban didn't go back to his hut that night, but stayed with me. We laid rush mats by the pond to sleep. It was much less oppressive there than in my hut. We lay under a dark sky. Not a single star was visible, but fireflies traced a fluttering line across the pond.

"Let's eat a jackfruit," Big Suban said.

I got up to follow him. We found a ripe jackfruit by its smell and brought it back to the ghat. Although it was sweet, I only managed a little. Big Suban ate most of it. We washed our hands and faces in the pond and went to lie on the mat once more. There was a slight breeze now.

"I'm really going to be a liberation fighter. Do you find that surprising, Kamal?"

I made a noise to say that I wasn't surprised, but I was still wondering what had really made up his mind. Only a few days ago he'd been keen to go in the teacher's boat.

"I'm happy that you still want to be my friend, Kamal. I can't do any book-reading talk with you. Just the old talk as we used to do. War or no war, I'm still a woodcutter. No?"

I looked up at the sky and still there was no sign of a star.

"I suppose now that I'll be away with the liberation fighters, I won't see you for a long time. But I'll think of you, Kamal."

I touched Big Suban's hand. He stayed quiet for a while. Perhaps, like me, he was trying to look through the dark.

"I promise you, Kamal, I'll get myself a wife after the war. Will you still be my chief-witness, my best man?"

I grabbed his hand and shook it to tell him that of course I would.

"Fancy having a book-reading man as my chief-witness and best man. I'm so lucky, Kamal."

CHAPTER 7

When I heard Sona Mia's azan I opened my eyes.

His voice draped over me the way the early morning mist drapes the ponds and the plains. I didn't, as ever, feel like rushing to the mosque, but I was happy to let Allah's breath enter me through the hole of my mouth. I wanted to linger on the joy that I felt, but the discovery that Big Suban had left without waking me changed my mood. His axe lay on the rush mat on which he'd slept. He never went anywhere without it. It was unlikely that he'd forgotten it, but then why would he leave it? What was I to do with it? Had he left it as a gift, as a token of friendship? Or, had he just left it in my safekeeping until the end of the war? It dawned on me that I wasn't going to see him for a long time. Perhaps I'd never see him again. It made me feel very sad. I had always felt fortunate, but now it seemed that the lucky stars had dimmed on me. First Moni Banu, now Big Suban. But I understood why he hadn't woken me up. Neither of us liked the fuss of goodbyes. I'd thought that he wasn't going to leave the village for another three days.

When the mist, washed with a pink glow, thinned slightly, I sat up and looked towards the plains. I saw a blurred figure moving fast and in a straight line. I felt sure it was someone riding a bicycle on the ridges between the rice paddies – and doing so with the consummate skill of a tightrope dancer. I stood up for a better view. He was much closer now. Who else could it have been but Ala Mullah? No one rode a bicycle like him. I hadn't seen him since he served that record-breaking meal to brothers Ajud and Majud Ali on Moni Banu's marriage.

I gathered the rush mats and Big Suban's axe and ran. I didn't want Ala Mullah to see the axe and ask questions. I hid the axe behind the water pitcher in my hut, next to the drum, and then went to greet Ala Mullah. Zomir Ali, Lal Mia and the freedom fighters were still asleep.

"What's wrong with Big Suban?" said Ala Mullah. "He passed me by like he didn't see me. That's not like him."

I shrugged my shoulders and brought him out a floor-stool.

"A cup of tea and some biscuits would be nice."

I went to the kitchen where Datla Nuri was helping Ata Banu prepare breakfast. When I mentioned that Ala Mullah wanted tea and biscuits, Ata Banu gave me a disagreeable look.

"He's a greedy dog, that Mullah," said Datla. "I tell you, it's not Allah's name but the smell of food that itches him day and night."

Ata Banu made the tea but said that she had no biscuits. I brought the tea to Ala Mullah, who took a sip from the cup and said, "The war is very bad for my business. No one is having religious ceremonies any more. I haven't had an invitation since Moni Banu's marriage. What is a mullah to do during wartime? If it goes on like this for too long, I'll starve."

I patted him on the shoulder and smiled encouragingly as if to say it wouldn't come to that.

"I hear you have some liberation fighters here. Do you think they'll be able to do something for me? Oh Allah, don't forget your devout worshippers," he said, and started to recite some Koranic verses loudly. I could hear movement from inside the bungalow. "Who's that idiot spoiling our morning?" yelled Zomir Ali. "We don't want some donkey braying at this hour."

Ala Mullah stopped and bit his lips. I went inside to see if Zomir Ali needed to be taken to the toilet. He did. When Ala Mullah saw us, he stood up from the stool.

"Assalamualikum, you Venerable Scholar."

"Do you know the meaning of the words that you have just recited?' asked Zomir Ali.

"I'm just a poor mullah, you Venerable Scholar. How would I know the meaning of these Arabic words? I just recite them."

"I thought so," said Zomir Ali and then addressed me.

"Where's your slate, Kamal?"

I wasn't carrying it. He ordered me to fetch it. When I came back with it, he said, "I hope you haven't erased what I asked you to write on it last time. I want all these idiots to know that you're a book-reading individual."

I hadn't erased: I'm Kamal. I'm a man of letters.

Ala Mullah looked baffled. He stuttered and said, "Kamal, a book-reader? I never knew that."

"Now you know. So, show your proper respect to him."

"Yes, you Venerable Scholar. But I still don't understand how. Neither the teacher nor Kamal ever gave me any inkling of it."

"There must have been clues. You're just too dim to catch them. Anyway, it doesn't matter now, does it? Can you read and write?"

"Just a little, you Venerable Scholar. I attended religious school."

"I bet in those places they didn't even give you a proper religious education, did they? Talk to Kamal, he can teach you a lot. He read the Koran in Bengali translation, you know. So, unlike you, he understands its meaning."

Ala Mullah was still staring at me, perplexed, but Zomir Ali hadn't finished with him yet.

"In fact, Kamal can teach you about other religions too. You see, he read *Bible, Torah, Bhagavadgita, Tripitakas, Avesta*. The writings of Chinese sages like Confucius and Lao-tzu. Also the Greeks like Plato. Everything in Bengali translation. So, learn from him."

Yes, I had read those books over the years: they were Zomir Ali's own translations – part of his collection bound with red canvas. I'm sure Ala Mullah hadn't even heard of most of these books. He looked on with astonishment as I escorted Zomir Ali to his toilet in the bush behind the palm trees.

"Sorry to have taken the liberty of revealing your education. I still can't work out what made Abbas Mia keep it a secret. It doesn't make any sense. Well, past is past. Now you can look forward to the future as an educated man."

I was angry with him for putting Ala Mullah down so harshly. What had education done to Zomir Ali? How could he have such vanity and be so cruel? I had no intention of seeing myself as an educated man if that was what it meant. Besides, he had no right to take liberties with my life.

"You need to express yourself in words and with learning to

live meaningfully. Otherwise, what's the difference between us and cows?"

I made no response, still fuming with him and thinking that I'd rather be a cow than his kind of educated man. Besides, you don't need to have read books to engage in meaningful conversation. You don't even need words at all. For instance, I'd had some wonderful conversations with Moni Banu and Big Suban where no sound passed between us. I began to feel that there was a huge difference between the vanity of knowledge and wisdom.

I brought breakfast to the outer bungalow. For troubled times, it wasn't a bad breakfast, consisting of steamed rice breads, scrambled eggs with green coriander, and jackfruit with thick milk. Ala Mullah sat with Zomir Ali, Lal Mia, the teacher and the two liberation fighters on a rush mat laid on the floor.

"Don't the liberation forces require the services of a mullah?" asked Ala Mullah.

"I don't know about that," said one of the liberation fighters. "But if you want to join us as a fighter then you're welcome."

"I wouldn't ask for much. Some rice twice a day would be enough. I know the holy verses that can protect you boys against bullets."

Before the liberation fighter could answer, Zomir Ali said, "How long will you go on peddling this nonsense? Can't you think of anything else to make a living? If I had anything to do with this war, I'd make sure that we got rid of the ways of unreason once and for all. Like Kamal Ataturk did in Turkey."

I suspected that Zomir Ali had brought in Kamal Ataturk's name deliberately to implicate me in his scheme of things.

"Kamal, are you there?" he shouted.

I had no intention of responding to him, so I hurried out of the bungalow. From the kitchen I picked up the carpenters' breakfast and set off for the boat. Instead of taking the short cut through the mango grove, I went around the school yard, which is situated on much higher ground than the rest of the village. Usually this was the only area in the village that remained dry during flooding. On it – apart from the school building and the playing fields – there were, at the fringes, some jute fields. From the middle of the playing field I looked around and saw no one.

Neither did I hear anything. It was late morning by now and the sun was already hot and glared on the school's tin roof. There was no wind to ruffle the dust that heaped between patches of dried-up grass. When I looked at the jute fields, their stalks reaching higher than my height, at the dense mass of their green leaves speckled with tiny yellow flowers, I felt a strange sensation. I had no reason to feel that I was looking at dead, petrified plants, but that's how they appeared to me. My stomach tightened and I was gasping for breath. I was thinking: I must flee this cursed place. My fear increased when I noticed a movement in the jute field. Without waiting to see what it was I broke into a run and hid behind the school building. I had to recover my breath before I could look at the jute field. Then Sona Mia emerged from it and sat down, though I had to blink several times to be sure that I wasn't seeing a ghost.

He was smoking his hookah when I approached him.

"Oh, it's you. I hear you are a learned man," he said. "I suppose that's why you've taken to carrying the slate. But I can't read. So, we have to communicate the way we used to. Is that all right with you?"

I'd lived my life in a way that conformed to people's expectations when they saw my face. A simpleton. It had become my second nature. I supposed it was too late for me to change that.

"I'm not surprised, Kamal. I've always known that you're a wise one. But you don't need book reading for that. It's Allah's gift."

I felt uncomfortable being talked about in these terms. Desperate to change the subject, I pointed to the jute.

"Yes, I was just inspecting the jute stalks. As you can see they have flowered. So, they should be ready for cutting in few weeks' time. But at a time like this, where can I find people to give me a hand?"

I made him understand that I'd help.

"Yes, I know you will, but that's not enough," he said. "They will rot this year."

He kept dragging on his hookah and staring at the jute stalks.

"I saw Big Suban. He's been acting very strange. I don't know what's the matter with him. When I asked him if he'd seen you, he just stared at me. I thought he would burst out crying."

"He's joining the liberation forces."

"Oh, I see. He must be finding it hard to leave you. You two have always been bosom friends."

I nodded and made him understand that Big Suban's leaving would be painful for me as well.

"But Allah will never abandon you, Kamal." He puffed on his hookah and then said, "We have difficult times ahead of us, Kamal. We will be seriously tested. You will find yourself in many situations where it would be easy to hate, but never let the feeling of love leave you. I know you won't, Kamal."

He got up, put his hand on my shoulder and said, "That's why it will be our privilege to be your memories," and disappeared among the jute stalks.

When I reached the boat, the carpenters still hadn't arrived. I inspected it to establish what blacksmith's work it needed. Obviously the carpenters would need iron spikes to fasten the planks to repair the hull. I could easily make them. I examined the wooden rudder and I realised that it would need a new metal brace. I could make that, too, without much difficulty. The problem was, how to set up a forge and find the iron to work with. There was the old blacksmith's forge in the market, but I was afraid of the dogs.

When the carpenters arrived, the first thing they noticed was my slate.

"What are you doing with that?" one of them asked. "What's written on it?"

I pretended that I had no idea what was written on it. Luckily neither of them could read.

They had a quick look around the boat before tucking into their breakfast. After the breakfast they were lolling around, smoking hookah because they couldn't begin their work until the logs were cleared off the boat. I knew that the teacher was dealing with the matter. He soon arrived with a group of villagers. I was surprised to see Zomir Ali, escorted by Ala Mullah, following behind. I supposed he'd come for the walk.

It didn't take us long to clear off the logs. The teacher went around the boat, inspecting it. To me he said, "You better start making the nails."

I was about to respond to him in gestures when Zomir Ali asked Ala Mullah if I was using my slate. When he said no, Zomir Ali said, "Use the slate, Kamal. It's a more efficient way of communicating than with your hands and eyes – and the little grunts that you make from the back of your throat."

My hand was trembling as I took the stick between my fingers to write on the slate. Apart from the teacher and Moni Banu no one had seen me write before. All I could think of was the dogs, so I wrote: "I'm scared of the dogs."

The people who'd helped to clear the logs had already gathered around me. They opened their eyes as if they were witnessing the strangest possible thing: a mouthless being who could write. Ala Mullah came forward from the group and took the slate from me. He looked at it very seriously for a while and then said, "Kamal has written that he's scared of the dogs."

Most of the people in the group broke into laughter.

"What's the point of writing, Kamal, if that's all you can write?" said someone from the crowd. "I can't write but I'm not scared of the dogs."

People broke into laughter again. Zomir Ali raised his voice and the people fell silent.

"You idiots are missing the point. Unlike you illiterates, Kamal can write. Think about it. Besides, he's a book-reading man."

"So what?" said one man. "Do you expect us to give him our salaam now? He's a stupid mouthless. And nothing will change that."

The teacher stood up and asked everyone to go home. Once they'd left, he asked me about the dogs. I explained to him in writing that I needed to visit the old blacksmith's shop in the market to see if I could find some of his instruments to set up a forge. I was simply afraid of the dogs that roamed the market.

Ala Mullah volunteered to come with me to the market. There was no sign of the dogs; their hunger must have driven them elsewhere. The forge was wrecked, but I could rescue enough of the instruments to set up a new one. I was particularly pleased to find the bellows and the anvil. I also found pieces of good quality iron to work with.

"Besides reading a lot of big books, you know so many things,

Kamal," said Ala Mullah. "Whereas I only know the words of Allah. How am I to survive with the war on? I suppose I could go with the Pakistani army and be their collaborator. I know they are very fond of Islam and they would like a mullah like me. But how can I rape and kill my own people? That's not me, Kamal, but how am I to survive?"

I wrote on the slate: "You can always go with the teacher in the boat."

"I suppose I would have something to eat in the boat. But would the teacher take me?"

"I don't see the teacher denying anyone. He wants to save as many people as possible," I wrote.

"But a boat of this size wouldn't be able to accommodate more than ten to fifteen people. How would he make his selection?"

"I don't know," I wrote. "But I suspect that the teacher has some scheme in mind."

"Are you going?"

"The teacher hasn't mentioned anything, but I'd love to go," I wrote.

"I'd love to go too," he said. "Especially considering how much I'd benefit from your learning. You're such a gifted one, Kamal."

We parted. Ala Mullah rode off to town and I returned to the boat. Then I dug a hole nearby to set up the forge. The carpenters would need the spikes and the brace in two days' time; I made them understand that I would have them ready by then. I worked the whole day, and by the late afternoon, I had the forge ready.

I was making my way through the mango grove when I heard that unmistakable thwacking of the axe. If Big Suban had left his axe with me, what was he cutting the tree with now? Maybe he had an old axe, but it wasn't easy to explain why he was cutting a tree at all. He wouldn't have accepted a new commission just as he was about to leave the village. Why was he doing this crazy thing?

I could hear distant thunder rumbling and see clouds drifting through the sky. I knew it would go on like this for a few more days before the monsoon came. I sat leaning against a mango tree and listened to Big Suban's axe. As ever the sound played with my senses and communed with my soul. Now I was sure it was Big Suban's way of being with me. He wanted to stay with me the best way he knew until he left the village with the liberation fighters.

"I'm not a man of words," he used to say; "my axe speaks for me." He must have shadowed me the whole day and only begun thwacking when he was sure that I was alone in the grove. He wanted to make me happy and I was happy. He stopped suddenly, just as the sun was about to go down below the horizon.

On my way from the kitchen with Zomir Ali's dinner I heard Sona Mia calling for the last prayer of the day. I stopped to listen to him. I knew he wanted to tell me of Allah's love, but he sounded as though demons were howling in his ears. It made me shiver and I hurried to the bungalow with the food. Zomir Ali was through his first plate of rice, slurping as usual, when I heard the tinkling of a cycle's bell. Why was Ala Mullah back so soon? I came out with the hurricane lamp to meet him. He looked very tense.

"What's the news from the town, Mullah?" asked Zomir Ali.

"The news is very bad, you Venerable Scholar. I'm told by a reliable source that the Pakistani army is on the move. But the really bad news is that they might come after us. You see, they suspect us of sheltering liberation fighters."

I heard a commotion in the dark, then the teacher's voice. Ala Mullah repeated his news.

"Then we can't sleep in our homestead tonight," teacher said. Both Zomir Ali and Ata Banu were reluctant to leave.

"I'm too old and tired of running. Let me be," said Zomir Ali.

"I hear the Pakistani army is made up of devout Muslims. They won't harm me. They're sure to recognise a pious woman. Besides, they have mothers too," said Ata Banu.

"Yes, they have mothers. But that doesn't mean they will regard you as one," snorted the teacher and almost dragged Ata Banu along. Zomir Ali, whom Ala Mullah was escorting, followed us. We went past the bush, Ata Banu muttering her Arabic verses. Datla Nuri came out from her hut as we were cutting the corner of the graveyard and took over from the teacher in guiding Ata Banu. The teacher had decided that we should pass the night in one of the dry ditches in the middle of our stretch of the swamp plains. It was a good choice as it would allow us to detect the movement of the army from any direction.

If we needed to run, we could take shelter in any of the nearby bamboo groves.

It was a dark and starless night. We went behind Datla Nuri's hut. There we saw that there were hundreds of lamps streaming into the plains from all sides. Other villages must also have heard the rumours of the coming of the army and were fleeing just as we were. We made our way to the ditch. I have no idea where the other people took shelter, but suddenly all the lamps disappeared and once more it was dark in the plains. It was decided that Ala Mullah, the teacher and myself would take turns to keep guard. We didn't see anything, but jumped every time thunder ripped the sky.

When my turn came to keep guard I sat on a mound above the ditch and opened my eyes and ears wide. In the pitch dark I could see nothing except fireflies gleaming like distant stars, looping and gliding. Everyone was sleeping; I could hear their breaths. Zomir Ali and Datla Nuri were snoring. I opened my ears even wider. At first I wasn't sure because it was like a faint echo from a far distance. As through from across the seas. But I wasn't imagining it; Big Suban was hacking away: the thwacking of metal on wood was unmistakable. He wanted to be with me and I with him. I would miss Big Suban, but I didn't feel sad. I followed the beating of his axe and drifted into sleep with a warm and happy feeling. When the teacher tapped me on my shoulder I was still asleep on the mound from which I was meant to keep guard.

The next morning the liberation fighters came back. Apparently the war in the swampland had taken a new turn and they had to return to their camp earlier than they'd planned. We fed them breakfast and they set off from the outer bungalow with the two volunteers who'd earlier expressed their interest to join the liberation forces. There was no sign of Big Suban.

I followed the passage of the group as they took to the plains. It was only when they crossed the river and took the dirt road that headed north that Big Suban emerged from a bamboo grove. I watched him join the liberation fighters and the two volunteers, and saw him disappear at the bend of the road. I wondered whether felling men with firearms – even though they were the enemy – would change him.

CHAPTER 8

The next day I was already working at the forge when the carpenters arrived. I got up to serve them breakfast.

"Are you a blacksmith by caste?" asked the taller of the two.

I shrugged my shoulders.

"I suppose you're at least a Hindu?" asked the shorter one.

Perhaps I was a Hindu, but again I shrugged.

"Who are you, then?" they asked together.

I pointed to myself and to the forge, but I don't think they understood what I was trying to tell them.

"You're a funny one. Everyone knows who he or she is. Otherwise, where would you belong and who would claim you? You'll be so lonely," said the tall carpenter.

I shook my head.

"I'm not an educated man. But I know that if you can't claim a place where you come from and where you belong, you'll be homeless. Not a nice place to find yourself. Hindu, Muslim, high caste, low caste – it doesn't matter, but you have to be something. If not, you're a rudderless boat. Just drifting. No human can live like that," said the short carpenter.

I gave them a polite nod and returned to the forge to work on the spikes. The carpenters brought their breakfasts and sat on a piece of the tree trunk that lay to the left of the bellows.

"Can you show us some of your writing, Kamal?" asked the tall one. "You see, we don't know how to read and write."

I had just put a slab of iron under the burning coal and was pumping the bellows. I paused, picked up my slate and wrote: "Brother Carpenters, if you don't mind, I'd rather get on with my work."

"What have you written? For us writing appears like rows of

100

rice plants. Some standing still, some moving with the wind," said the short carpenter.

I pointed to them both, to the words on the slate and smiled, hoping to assure them I had written something good and complimentary about them.

"Yes, yes, we know," said the tall one. "We're the best carpenters in the swampland. But thank you for writing it down. Now that it appears in writing, I suppose no one can deny the truth of it any more."

They went back to work to shape the planks to repair the hull. I continued to pump the bellows. After a while I pulled the red-hot lump of iron out with a pair of tongs, and placed it on the anvil. I cut the slab into long strips with the chisel and the hammer, beat their lower edges into sharp points and then dipped them into water. I continued making spikes until midday. I was happy transforming and moulding metals into useful shapes. Besides, the whoosh of the bellows and the clang, clang of the hammer were, as always, music to my ears. I could listen to those sounds for hours without getting bored. I wished Moni Banu had been there to see me. I bet she would have said, "I told you, Beautiful One, didn't I? One day you'll be a real blacksmith."

I went back to the homestead to bring lunch for the carpenters. While they were eating, the teacher came to inspect progress.

"We're the best carpenters in the swampland," said the tall one. "Now that Kamal has written it on his slate, the truth will be known."

The teacher smiled and came over to me in the forge. He took my slate, which I'd forgotten to wipe clean. He whispered in my ear, "Deviousness begins with writing, Kamal. So, be careful."

By late afternoon I'd finished the spikes and the brace. On my way back to the homestead I paused in the mango grove. I wanted to hear that unmistakable thwacking as Big Suban hacked away at the trees, but the grove was silent.

When I got back I saw a large crowd in front of the outer bungalow. They were passionately discussing the imminent arrival of the war to our village and what we must do. Some argued that we should move further to the east, to more remote villages, but it was clear that nowhere in Bangladesh was safe.

Local militias, drawn mainly from the Islamic parties, were springing up everywhere. They were often more fanatical and brutal than their Pakistani mentors. Others insisted that we should move, as many had already done, to the refugee camps in India. That didn't appear to be an attractive option because, apart from the long and arduous journey, the spread of disease was claiming many lives in the camps.

"Why not stay in the village and make friends with the Pakistani army?" said Bilal Khan. "Once they know that we are good Muslims, they won't harm us."

People looked down and stayed silent. They all knew that what Bilal Khan had said did not tally with what they'd heard was happening throughout the country. They couldn't imagine collaborating with a force that had already raped and killed thousands of their fellow Bengalis. Yet they couldn't quite bring themselves to say so to his face. Bilal Khan was the largest landowner in the village and many of the people present were sharecroppers on his land. Besides, he wasn't a bad man, despite his Islamicist and communalist views. He helped his sharecroppers in bad times and had never molested any of the minority communities living in the village. It was Zomir Ali who broke the silence.

"What about the Hindus? Surely you've some Hindus in this village?"

"Yes, we have Hindus. We just have to convince the Pakistani army that we haven't got any," said Bilal Khan.

"How would you do that? You can't change what lies hidden under our lungis and dhotis, can you?"

Before Bilal Khan could think of an answer, his son Asad Khan, who was sitting next to him, said, "Hindus are not our concern. All we care about is saving the village."

Zomir Ali was about to reply but the teacher held his hand to stop him.

"I still think that the boat is our best option," he said.

"It's a good idea, but how many can you take? We have about four hundred people still left in the village," said Asad Khan.

"The boat can take ten to fifteen people," said the teacher.

"It doesn't solve our problem, does it?" said Asad Khan. "Anyway, how would you make your selection?"

The teacher didn't have an answer to the question; he dragged on his hookah and shuffled on his floor-stool. I felt disappointed because I thought he had already worked out a good method of selection.

"Book-readers should have priority," said Lal Mia, "because without knowledge, the world would be a dark place."

"You have to eat, even in your lighter place," said one of the peasants, "so we rice growers should have more of a claim to a place in that boat."

"Of the four hundred people left in the village more than three hundred are rice growers. So your claim is absurd," said Lal Mia.

"We aristocrats and landowners should have the priority because it's the command of Allah and a law of nature," said Asad Khan. "We must respect it."

Zomir Ali was, no doubt, about to say something brutal to Asad Khan when the teacher stopped him again. He dispersed the gatherers by saying that he would find a just solution by the time the boat was ready to sail.

We spent the night again in the ditch in the plains. Zomir Ali and Ata Banu were again reluctant to come but the teacher persuaded them. The sky was dark and kept on rumbling, but there was no rain. From time to time Datla Nuri sang snatches of songs in her harsh, rasping voice. We bore it in silence, except for Ata Banu.

"Nuri, your voice blows the smell of shit in my face," she said.

Datla Nuri laughed and stayed silent for a while, but then began again. She fell asleep after midnight. In the absence of Ala Mullah, the teacher and I kept vigil. Every time the wind rustled the bamboo groves or thunder ripped the sky, I feared the worst. I felt the army had melted into the dark, was waiting and watching us. I became so fearful that I closed my eyes when lightning illuminated the plains because I didn't want to see them advancing on us. The teacher sensed my fear.

"Are you feeling alright, Kamal?"

I couldn't even grunt to answer him. He touched me to reassure me.

"The boat should be ready in few days' time," he said. "We'll be safe once we set sail."

I tilted my head but he couldn't have seen me in the dark.

"We should take Moni in the boat," he said. "What do you think, Kamal?"

This time I grunted from the back of my throat to say that it was a good idea.

"You should go to Moni's husband's village as soon as possible," he said. "Bring her with you. And, of course, her husband too. We mustn't sail without them."

I was pleased that he wanted to take Moni Banu on board, but I wondered what other people might make of his decision to put his own family first. I suspected they'd see it as selfish and unjust.

Towards dawn, the wind picked up and the clouds massed low in the sky. Dust blew in our faces and the bamboo groves whistled with the wind. Datla Nuri got up and said, "The rain is coming." Soon everyone was up. I could just about see the other people who had taken shelter in the plains for the night scattering away fast. They didn't want to be caught up in the rain in the middle of nowhere. We wanted to get away quickly too, but it wasn't easy with Zomir Ali. Datla Nuri broke into one of her songs about rain.

"Shut up your mouth, you devil woman," said Ata Banu. "Don't torment us further. We're already living in hell."

We hadn't made much progress when the sky broke. We were drenched within a minute. Datla Nuri was teasing Zomir Ali.

"I'm young and pretty. If you'd eyes you'd have chased me like a bull."

Zomir Ali kept his scholarly dignity and didn't say anything, but Ata Banu looked at Datla Nuri in disgust.

"Don't you have any shame, you ugly old hag? You're worse than a bitch-dog in the market."

Datla Nuri didn't pay her any notice and kept on teasing.

"I bet you want to have your way with me, don't you? I know quiet ones like you, all lusty inside. No?"

Only when the teacher raised his voice at her did she leave Zomir Ali alone. She was still in high spirits and hummed her songs, which, strangely, sounded quite good in the din of the rain. For some reason the first spell of monsoon rain had always made me feel happy, but it wasn't the same without Moni Banu.

Once we arrived back at the homestead, I went to see the carpenters. They kept working through the rain and finished repairing the hull before the dim of the day slid into the darkness of the evening. Only the wooden cabin needed more work on it; and the teacher had gone out to look for a sail and some boatmen.

The rain didn't relent, and we knew that it was going to go on for days on end. Already the inner courtyard had become muddy and pools formed in the depressions. I laid planks of wood between the huts and between the inner and the outer courtyard. I did that at the beginning of each monsoon; it somewhat eased the difficulties of walking on slippery mud. I went to see the cows in the shed; they looked miserable and thoroughly soaked as we hadn't re-thatched the roof after the storm. I took them out of their corral and tied them up in a corner over which the roof was more or less intact. I gave them some straw, dragged the dinghy out, and took it to the pond. In a few days' time the pond would merge with the plains, the plains with the river. Roads would disappear. Only in the dinghy would we be able to get to places.

The teacher had just arrived when I took dinner to Zomir Ali.

"I doubt the army will move on a rainy night like this. I think we can sleep in our beds tonight," he said. "But we must be vigilant."

The teacher wanted to eat with Zomir Ali, so I brought his dinner to the outer bungalow. The rain was relentless and, despite my straw and bamboo hat, every time I went out I got soaked.

"I've found a sail. Once the rain relents a bit, two boatmen will bring it to us," said the teacher. "But they are not keen to come along with us."

"It's all a crazy idea, Abbas Mia. If you want to escape the war, you'd better go to the refugee camps in India," said Zomir Ali. "Don't forget that after the flooding the plains will become war zones too.'

"I know the floodplains, you Venerable Scholar. I was born here," said the teacher. "They are vast, and their secrets are like the labyrinths of olden times of which you and I have read in books."

"Of course, we've read of such things. But here it's a matter of life and death. Not some bookish game."

"I completely agree with you, you Venerable Scholar. Because we know the floodplains and their watery mazes, we can stay safe from the army."

"If the Pakistani army brings along one of their collaborators who also grew up in the floodplains, then what would you do?"

The teacher stayed quiet for a while, puffed on his hookah and then addressed me.

"If we don't find a boatman, we'll have to make do with you, Kamal."

I had never sailed a large cargo boat; all I knew was how to paddle a small dinghy. The war was definitely changing my life: man of letters, blacksmith, and now the possibility of becoming a boatman.

Zomir Ali asked me to join them with my slate; the teacher would read out my writing.

"Now that we have no books," he asked, "do you miss reading them, Kamal?"

"Not much. Now I've more time to tell myself stories," I wrote.

"Is that so? May I ask, why did you read books in the first place?"

"I was taught to read. So, I read. Then it became a habit," I wrote.

"Is that all? I thought you would have seen some higher purpose in books."

"Some books amused me, but they have nothing to tell me," I wrote. "The words in books and the life I lead belong to two different worlds. The paths between them hardly ever cross."

"Hasn't reading made you a better man?"

"That is for others to judge, you Venerable Scholar. What I can tell is that words hardly capture the meaning of my feelings."

"Is that so? I'm really disappointed in you, Kamal," said Zomir Ali. "I thought the books connected you with the refinements of human civilisation."

"Sorry, you Venerable Scholar. As I said before, some of the books truly amused me."

"Perhaps I'll have a better idea of you – you know, what you really think – if you care to tell me about a particular book that you read. For instance, what did you think about *Hayy ibn Yaqzan*?"

"Hayy was suckled by a deer. I liked that. I also liked the stories of his life on a desert island. He was brave and clever to survive on his own," I wrote.

"Yes, yes, that's all very well, but what do you think about his philosophical system? You know, how he strove for a higher meaning of things? Was he right, for instance, to transcend sensual knowledge for a spiritual quest? Or aren't you intrigued by the similarities between Ibn Tufail's story and that of Daniel Defoe? Doesn't it make you wonder that *Hayy ibn Yaqzan* was written six hundred years before *Robinson Crusoe*?"

Of course, I had considered some of these questions when I read the book, but I wasn't going to engage with them now just because Zomir Ali wanted me to. I wanted to tell how I felt about the book rather than what I thought about its ideas. Besides, I was still angry with him and didn't want to play his games.

"I didn't care much about those things. I was just happy with the idea that a wild beast had it in her heart to give succour to infant Hayy. For his part, Hayy always pined for that beast," I wrote.

"It seems reading has done nothing for you, Kamal. I thought you would have seen beyond these silly sentimentalities," said Zomir Ali. "You seem as stupid as you look."

Yes, yes, you Venerable Scholar, you can call me any damn names that please you, but you can't force me to respond in the terms that you want. I will serve you, I will do my duties, but you will not dictate what goes on inside me.

Up until now the teacher was merely reading what I wrote on the slate. He now looked at Zomir Ali, annoyed.

"You don't understand Kamal, you Venerable Scholar," he said. "He has his own way of making sense of things."

I slobbered dollops of saliva on the slate, rubbed out the writing furiously, and then left. Rain was still falling. Now most of the inner courtyard was under water. I went to the kitchen to pick up my dinner. Since Ata Banu had already gone to bed, I ate there. Back in my hut, I was still scared that the sound of the rain would muffle the soldiers' boots, and that I wouldn't hear them until they had us surrounded. I listened for other sounds beyond the rain, but couldn't hear anything else, except occasional thunder. I thought I should at least keep my eyes open, but what can you do against monsoon rain? It has a way of speaking to your senses.

When I got up the next morning I had to strain my ears to catch Sona Mia's call to prayer. It was almost drowned out in the splashes of the downpour. When I caught it, it sounded more enchanting that ever: it was as if the music of the rain had added another layer to the purity and the passion of his voice. I was glad that the sadness and fear that I heard in his last azan had gone.

Now the water came up to the mud platform of my hut. I waded through the inner courtyard to the kitchen, then to the teacher's hut. He and Ata Banu were still sleeping. I went to the outer bungalow to see if Zomir Ali was up. He was sitting hunched up on his bed. When he sensed my coming he said, "You must be angry with me, Kamal. I didn't mean to be rude to you. I was a bit frustrated that you wouldn't engage with me. I know that you are highly intelligent, and that you thought a great deal about the books that you read. Yet I don't understand why you play the fool with me." He stood up and added, "Please forgive me, Kamal." How could I remain angry with him? He looked so fragile.

I took him to his toilet under an umbrella, to the bush behind the palm trees. The rain was so heavy that he was dripping before we got there. He sat holding the umbrella and I waited in my customary position. Even though this area was a bit higher than the surrounding fields and more protected by the canopy, it became as soggy as syrupy palm bread. Besides, streams of water were running through it.

"I wish you could describe the rain to me," he said. "I know I could see it again if you were to do so."

I stood there looking at the rain and wondered why he wanted to see things through my eyes.

"After the war I want you to come and live with me, Kamal. We'll run the library together. You see, I have no son to turn to."

I didn't know how to respond, so I kept looking at the rain.

Later that day I waited for the carpenters by the boat, wearing my straw and bamboo hat. I wasn't sure whether they would come on a day like this. They were late, but they came, and they worked through the rain. It didn't take them long to repair the cabin and put the brace on the rudder. In a few days' time the river would come over the banks and roll under the boat.

Except for occasional lulls, rain poured down on us for days on end. Besides this, torrents of water flowed into our stretch of the river all the way from the foothills of the Himalayas. By the third day the river had already topped its banks, claimed the lakes and the ponds and spread over the plains. Now, as far as the eye could see, there was just water. We were just a tiny island in it. We would live in this waterworld for the next four months.

If I hadn't left the dinghy in the pond, I could have paddled it from just outside my doors. Now I had to wade through knee-high water to get to it. No more than a few strokes of the paddle propelled me over the pond's submerged walls. Then I paddled the dinghy over the fields which, only a few days ago, had been dry and dusty. The rain was still falling as heavily as before. I guided the dinghy gently into the bush. There the low scrubs and the creeper bushes had vanished under water, but the tall trees, their lower trunks submerged, seemed as if they were bouncing off a mirror. I remembered coming here in the dinghy with Moni Banu, in between the downpours and with the sun out, and feeling that we were the first man and woman at the beginning of time, and she telling me, "Beautiful One, look at the water. It's kissing the canopy."

I paddled past the graveyard. At Datla Nuri's hut water lapped against its mud platform. I brought the dinghy right before her door and banged it with my paddle.

"Oh Nephew, thank Allah that you came by. I thought I'd die alone in my hut."

When she asked me where I was going, I made her understand that I was taking a trip in the dinghy to the floodplains.

"Are you going to catch some fish?"

As I didn't have my fishing spear with me, she went inside her hut and came back with one.

"Catch some fish for me, Nephew. Otherwise I'll starve."

I paddled into the plains, past the place where we had slept only a few days before in a dry ditch. Now waves were galloping over it as if it had always belonged to the realm of the water. I headed towards the half-submerged bamboo groves. The paddy fields there lay on slightly higher ground than the rest of the plains, making the water shallower. In our stretch of the floodplains there was no better place for spear-fishing than this. In past years at times of flood, Big Suban would spot me from the distance and race his dinghy towards me.

"What took you so long, Kamal? I've been on the lookout for you for ages," he'd say.

We loved to fish together. Sometimes we came here with our lamps in the night. Some fish couldn't resist light; they came and danced with joy until our spears found them.

Now I saw a shoal of large fish swimming in the shallows, their dorsal fins almost out of the water. I easily speared a few of them and went back to Datla Nuri's hut. I gave her half of the catch. She was pleased.

"Don't forget to come by and take me out. I don't want to be trapped in my own hut," she said as I was about to paddle away.

The teacher was in the kitchen when I arrived; he and Ata Banu were pleased to see the fish.

"Kamal, I want you to set off for Moni's husband's village as soon as possible. Perhaps tomorrow morning. We'll wait for you. Once you're back with them, we'll sail our boat."

CHAPTER 9

In the morning the rain had relented, but patches of dark clouds remained, hanging low in the sky. Ata Banu woke up before me and prepared my food for the journey. Using a piece of a torn lungi she made a bundle in which she put puffed rice, bars of palm-sweets, and a bunch of lychees. I remembered Datla Nuri all alone and stranded in her hut. I wanted to fetch her in my dinghy before I left. I thought she could stay in my shed until I came back from Moni Banu's husband's village.

"Oh Nephew, thank Allah that you came for me. I didn't sleep a wink the whole night," said Datla Nuri as soon as she saw me. "What's a poor woman to do against big, poisonous snakes? They were all trying to get into my hut."

I looked at her and she understood that I was sorry that I hadn't come to check on her the previous night. It didn't take her long to get into a teasing mood.

"Oh Nephew, I hear you're off to see Moni Banu. You must be laughing inside. If I were you, I'd be careful of the husband. Who knows, he might be a very jealous type."

I should have left early in the morning as the journey was long, but I couldn't go without completing some of the tasks around the homestead. I prepared a large container of jackfruit rinds mixed with water for the cows, and left them with enough hay to last for at least two days. Then I took Zomir Ali for his morning visit to the toilet. I assumed the teacher would take my place with him while I was away.

While I was packing my clothes for the journey I realised that the homestead would be left without a watercraft. I went to the back of the homestead, cut ten banana trees, and made a raft with them. I knew that the teacher would be hopeless with the raft, but

Datla Nuri could manoeuvre it as well as I could. By the time all these tasks were done, the early morning mist had lifted. The glow of the sun sneaked through the gaps in the clouds and fell on the inner courtyard's floodwater.

At the door of the kitchen, Ata Banu handed me the bundle.

"I don't want to see your face if you come back without Moni," she said. "And don't frighten her in-laws with it." Then she blessed me with a long recitation of Arabic verses. When I stepped into the water from the kitchen, she said, "I leave you in the care of Allah. He will take care of you for me."

From the outer bungalow the teacher waded through the water with Zomir Ali in tow. They came to see me off at the pond.

"Be careful, Kamal. Informers and collaborators are every-where," said the teacher. "Go and bring Moni as fast as you can. The quicker we set sail, the better. I don't know how much longer we'll be safe in the village."

I looked at the teacher to reassure him that I would be quick indeed.

"May wisdom guide you, son," said Zomir Ali. "I hope you're carrying your slate. You'll need it to make yourself understood among strangers."

Teacher, though, leaned on the stern of the dinghy and said, "Try to judge a man's character before you show him your slate. You never know if he'll take kindly to your learning."

"Don't worry about him, Abbas Mia," said Zomir Ali. "He has a wise head on his shoulders."

The teacher gave the dinghy a push and I began to paddle. Within minutes I was in the floodplains, heading west to Moni Banu's husband's village. If everything went well I would be there by late afternoon. I didn't want to paddle along the banks, in plain view of the villages. It felt safer to take a course through the middle of the floodplains. Already many familiar landmarks had disappeared. Clumps of hyacinths had floated in to colonise this watery expanse. My dinghy rose and fell with the waves. I knew the ways of the changing seasons, but in that moment it felt as though this had always been a waterworld.

In normal times many boats would have been plying these waters by now, carrying goods and passengers between the island villages that dotted the floodplains. From their dinghies, fisher-men would have been busy laying traps and nets. Now, with the war on, no one dared take to the waters. I paddled past the market where the dogs had chased me only a few weeks before. It looked like a jutting mass of clutter, marooned in the waterscape. I couldn't even tell where the lake that I crossed to save myself from the dogs had been.

At first the gaps between the clouds had allowed patches of sunlight to shimmer on the water. But I hadn't gone far before the thunder was back and the clouds closed the gaps in the sky. It began to rain again. I put on my straw and bamboo hat and paddled on; picking up speed between two half-submerged bamboo groves, I reached the next floodplain. The ground on which the annual fair took place, where Moni Banu and I had loved to come in our childhood, should have been on its left flank. The old banyan, its hanging roots dangling just above the water, was the only visible sign.

It became so gloomy it was hard to see further than a few yards in front of my prow. The wind picked up too, making the water choppier. Now it was more difficult to keep control of the dinghy, but I made good progress with the wind coming from behind me. But the dinghy was filling up with water, so I steered to a small island with a tall, pointed structure. It was a familiar landmark, a place where the Hindus brought their dead to burn, but now even the ghosts had left it to the winds. I pulled the dinghy onto the mud slope and got down to scooping out water with a calabash. I had to work fast to prevent the hull filling up again. I ate some of the palm-sweets to give me strength and pushed on. But as soon as I turned the bend around the island and took to the open waters, two long racing boats, their hulls painted black, came out of nowhere and surrounded me. My hands trembled and my grip on the oars slackened as it dawned on me that these were river bandits. I knew of their fearsome reputation and feared that my journey would end right there. They asked me who I was and where I was going. I stayed silent and smiled to draw their attention to the hole of my mouth. One of the bandits grabbed me by the hair and danced his machete before my face.

"He's a stupid cripple. Leave him alone," said the bandit chief.

They went through my things, and when they found nothing valuable, one of them kicked me. Then the bandit chief spotted my slate.

"What you doing with this?" he asked.

I smiled again.

"Don't show me your ugly mouth again," he screamed. "If you do, I'll throw my spear right in it."

I lowered my eyes.

"Maybe he can write," said one of the bandits.

"Don't be stupid. If he can write, I'm the king of England," said the chief. "Just give him two more kicks for wasting our time."

One of his followers grabbed me by the hair and executed his master's command. Then they left. My backside was bruised but it wasn't serious. I plunged my paddle into the water and cut through it with all of my strength. As I gained rhythm and speed, I couldn't help thinking that perhaps the teacher was right to keep my education a secret. Had the bandits found out about it, who knows what they would have done to me.

To reach the Alam homestead I needed to cross the mighty river Meghna. Although it looked much the same as the rest of the floodplains with which it had merged, the waves in it were larger and the currents more dangerous, particularly for a small dinghy like mine, but I had no other option. When a big wave hit me and tossed the dinghy up in the air, I realised that I had entered its course. I soon regained my balance and rode the waves with my paddle. Then I heard a rumbling sound. I was certain it wasn't thunder. My mouth became dry with fear, but I knew I mustn't panic. I had to do whatever it took to reach Moni Banu and bring her back. I began to pull the oars with all of my strength, and then it occurred to me that I stood no chance in the open water of the river. I stopped and changed direction, steering for shallower waters. Not far in the distance I spotted a dense patch of kash grass and reeds. I headed towards it.

The rumbling sound was getting closer. My heart pounded against my ribs, but I was determined not to let fear get the better of me. I paddled as fast as I could and was nearly thrown overboard as I hit the line of kash grass and reeds. I got off the dinghy, pulled it out of sight and waited. The water here came only up to my chest. Within minutes the gunboat passed in front of me. Between the grasses and the reeds I saw the Pakistani flag fluttering. Closing the hole of my mouth with my hand, I dipped under the dinghy, and held my breath for a long time. When I surfaced, I heard bullets screaming over the river, but I had no idea where they were aimed. I ducked again, then again, until the sound faded. I was still scared when I took to the river Meghna.

The rain stopped and the sun broke through the gaps in the sky. Once more the waves on the river were reflecting glimmers of light on their crests until they reached the shadowy patches under the clouds. Gliding on a fast, oblique current, I crossed the river and rowed along its left bank, marked only by floating trees. At the next bend, I would turn left and continue along the villages as far as the mosque with the white dome, then left again into the next stretch of the floodplains. Somewhere in there lay my destination.

Long before I turned the bend I saw smoke rising over the lines of trees. Dense smoke plugged the gaps between the clouds, making the sky darker than when it rained. Yet, I hadn't quite realised the enormity of it. When I got closer, it seemed as if the bonfires of doomsday were consuming the earth: row after row of homesteads, village after village along the river bank was burning. The fires no doubt had something to do with the gunboat. My muscles tensed with fear, but I paddled on. When I turned the bend to the left, I saw islands of fire raging across the floodplains. One of those islands was the Alams' village. A shiver ran through me, because I feared that something terrible had happened to Moni Banu.

I moored my boat by a bush under a fig tree and lay there hidden. After a while, amidst thunder, the downpour came again. I waited for the rain to settle to a steady drizzle before climbing up to the village. As it was situated on high sloping ground, the village escaped the flood and I had only to avoid little streams cascading down the slopes and the pools formed in small depressions. Here the rain had dampened the fires and all that was left were smouldering heaps of burnt-down homesteads. I didn't see a soul, nor did I hear a voice. I located the path that led to the Alams' homestead. Apart from the occasional hissing of fire, silence reigned. I didn't know whether the people had fled, or had perished, trapped in their burnt-down huts.

From the distance I saw something run across the road. I took cover behind a waterlogged creeper bush with sweet pink flowers and waited. From nowhere a boy came on the road, looked nervously around, and ran off again. I followed him into a patch of tall grasses. I saw the blood in a stream of rainwater. It seemed to be flowing from the ground beneath a large hayrick. I traced my way along it, and just behind the hayrick, saw the bodies. About fifteen of them. There were men and women of all ages, and children. Some were face up, some down.

For a long time I stared at the body of a young woman in a blue sari, face down and sunk in the mud. I didn't dare turn her in case my worst fears came true. I touched her hair, soaked in blood and rainwater. I cried, my tears fell on her hair and merged with the water. It couldn't be Moni Banu, not her. She couldn't die before me. Oh Allah, please, do not let this be.

All the huts in Alams' homestead were burnt and still smouldering. I looked around, relieved not to stumble on charred bodies, wondering what had happened to them all. I ran wildly through the fields and bushes. I was getting so desperate that I ran back to the body of the young woman and turned her face up. I still didn't know who it was as her face was covered with mud. I ran back to the Alams' homestead to fetch something to carry water in, found an aluminium cooking pot among the debris heaped in the yard, and filled it up with water from the stream. I washed her face. Her mouth was wide open and twisted as if she had died screaming. No one should have to die that way, but she wasn't Moni Banu.

I squatted on the soggy mud in the courtyard of the Alams' homestead, in front of the smouldering outer bungalow where I had slept the night after Moni Banu got married, wondering what to do next. A boy appeared from behind me and shouted, "Gone. Bang, bang." I jumped and slipped in the mud. By the time I could get up, the boy had run away. I followed him in the direction he had taken and ended up in jungle. I looked around for him, but saw only rain dripping from the leaves. Suddenly he appeared from behind a tree, looked at me, then moved on, rather slowly, as if he wanted me to follow him, which I did. After several twists and turns, we reached a group of people. All looked scared and confused.

I approached a lady to inquire after Moni Banu and her husband. She cringed back in horror. From the back of the group a man came forward; I tried to communicate with him in gestures, but he understood nothing. When I showed him my slate and made the movement of writing with my fingers, he took me to a young man, a student at the university in Dhaka who had returned to his village to escape the war. I asked him in writing if he knew what had happened to the Alam family. He told me that they had already left for the refugee camps in India; that they themselves were waiting for the guide to come back and take them. As I felt that I couldn't return to our homestead without at least talking to Moni Banu, I resolved to follow this group, if necessary, all the way to India.

We waited in the jungle. No one spoke of the calamities that had befallen them, of their relatives and friends recently butchered, of homesteads burnt to ashes. They spoke only to ask endless questions about when the guide would come. Night fell and we were still waiting. It was so dark that I couldn't make out the person next to me. Hindu and Muslim prayers buzzed through the rain and the wind. Sometimes a child complained or cried.

It was past midnight when the guide arrived. I approached him with the help of the student, who lit a torch to allow me to write, and then read out my question about the whereabouts of Moni Banu. The guide looked at me with suspicion but, being reassured by the student, told me in a whispering voice what he knew. It was he, indeed, who had guided Moni Banu and the Alam family, about four days ago, to India. When I expressed my wish to be taken there, he asked if I had any money. I wrote that I didn't have any. He told me a long story about the cost of the journey: bribes to be paid to collaborators, expenses for safe houses and food, and the sum required to hire boats, both for the initial stretch of the journey and then for crossing the river.

"How about your commission?" asked the student. "How come you forgot to mention that?"

The guide rubbed his neck and grinned, but said nothing. The

117

student told him it was really callous to ask for money from someone like me, especially since they had already given him everything they had. The guide said nothing and marched off to organise the journey, but came back after a while to say that I could be one of the pole-bearers for a sick, old man.

We set off after midnight. The guide led us with his torchlight; and two of us, situated somewhere in the middle, carried the old man. I took the rear end of the pole from which the old man, wrapped in a canvas sheet, was suspended; his son took the front. The student stayed close to us with his torchlight. It didn't take long to cross the village and arrive at the edge of the floodplains, where the boats, with their dim fluttering lights, were waiting for us. As soon as we got in, the boatmen dug in their poles and punted the boats out into deeper waters; then they took to their oars.

It was so dark that we knew of the presence of the other boats only by the sound of their oars cutting the water. It started to rain heavily again. As these boats didn't have cabins, we sat huddled on the open deck, and shivered. I must have dozed off because I did not notice when the boats reached the point where we needed to leave them.

One of the children cried out when she was woken abruptly from her sleep.

"Shut her up, woman," said the guide. "You want to have us all killed. This is a danger zone."

I don't know what the mother did to the child, for it was too dark to see. Whatever she did, from then on the child settled into a faint, echoing sob interrupted by violent drags of breath. We picked up the pole with the old man dangling from it. He made no sound when we jerked him up on our shoulders and I realised I hadn't heard him at all during the boat journey. We went up a ridge and then down to shallow floodplains where the water came up to my waist. Parents picked their small children up onto their shoulders, but older children had to make their way with the water to their necks.

We needed to go under a bridge over which some collaborators kept guard. The guide had bribed them to let us pass, but on the condition that we didn't do anything to betray our presence. Otherwise, they would be forced to shoot at us. I heard the collaborators joking and laughing among themselves above us as we passed under. As we emerged on the other side, some of them leaned over the railings and started to shout at us. "You motherfucking Hindus. We're going to cut your balls off. Perhaps we should cut your throats like we do your bloody cows. Allahu-akbar." Then they began throwing stones at us. Some of the people were hit and panic set in. We tried to run, but it wasn't easy to make progress with our feet sinking into the muddy swamp-bed, and with the water coming up to our waists. The guide tried to calm us by saying that the collaborators were just having fun, and that they wouldn't do us any real harm, but no one listened to him. Amidst a chorus of Allahu-akbar, the collaborators began firing in the air. Some of the adults and many of the children began screaming.

Somehow we managed to reach a waterlogged jute field. The son and I were completely exhausted and wanted to rest a bit. The guide insisted that we push on because we were still close to the bridge. Apparently a Pakistani army patrol was due there soon. Then the guide discovered that some of the people had got scattered in the dark. He went back with his torch, looking for them. We flattened some of the jute stalks to make a nest over the water and rested the old man on it. Still, he didn't make any noise. The guide came back with most of the people who'd got scattered, but a family of four was nowhere to be seen. He wanted to push on without them, but the student wouldn't move until they were found. He and the guide searched again, but came back empty handed. Reluctantly the student accepted that we couldn't wait, otherwise the safety of the whole party would be at risk.

"Don't forget that this is war. You save some idiots, you lose some idiots. That's the way it is," said the guide. "If you want to stay alive, get rid of those goody-goody no-good feelings. Do you understand me?"

We pulled the old man up and set off through knee-high water, through darkened jute fields, the stalks lashing us from all sides. We continued like this for about half an hour, until we emerged into paddy fields, just as waterlogged as the jute fields had been. Then after about twenty minutes we entered another patch of jute fields, and walked on until the sun appeared over the horizon. The jute fields seemed to stretch for miles; in the far distance, along a line of tall trees, I could just see the outline of a village. The guide told us to stay in hiding until the night. Apparently the village belonged to a hardcore Islamic fundamentalist group, the most feared of the collaborators, who couldn't be bribed, and would cut your throat without the slightest hesitation or pity, while reciting the name of All Merciful Allah.

It was still raining. We found a narrow ridge between two plots of jute fields, just above the water, and perched there like a line of wet crows on a tree branch. I, like the others, sat there plucking off the leeches, hundreds of them, from all over my body. When the son called the old man and he didn't respond, he unwrapped the canvas and looked at him, shook him, looked up to me with terrified eyes, then broke into a sob and shook him again. The guide came across and peered at the old man.

"He's bloody dead," he said. "Get rid of the body quick."

Who knows when he died? What was certain was that there wasn't enough dry ground for a grave – or anything with which we could dig. The son and I wrapped the body in the canvas, and accompanied by the student and the guide, took it to a jute field some distance away. We spread our palms in front of our faces, the guide muttered something that vaguely sounded like a prayer, and then we let the body sink in the shallow water. The son sobbed, saying that he didn't want his father to be eaten by foxes.

"Stop that nonsense," snapped the guide. "With the war on, foxes have better, juicier bodies to feed on than your bloody father."

We came back to perch on the ridge. I munched soggy puffed rice; no one was curious, no one looked at me. While the adults – men and women – walked a bit further into the jute field to relieve their bowels, the children did theirs where they were. We drank water from below the ridge, from the jute fields.

In the afternoon the rain stopped and the guide went on to survey the route ahead. We got worried as he was gone for a long time and the evening was approaching. Some thought that perhaps the collaborators had caught him, but the student kept saying that he'd most likely gone to sell us out. I couldn't see the student's face when, draped in the bright evening sun, the guide came running back. He told us, his voice crackling with fear, that some collaborators were heading our way. We ran deeper and deeper into the jute fields until we thought it safe to stop. Some of us crouched in the soggy mud with the water coming up to our chests, while the others remained stooped under the yellowing jute leaves. To my right a baby started to cry. The guide leapt from his crouching position and came over to the mother.

"Bloody woman. You want to have us all killed."

I don't know what happened, but the baby became quiet. Now we could hear the collaborators passing through the jute field to our left. We held our breaths, chattering our teeth, and perhaps others did it too, but I wasn't ashamed of wetting myself. When I felt the warmth between my thighs I wished that it would wrap me up in a cocoon, because all I wanted was the chance to float in warm liquid, breathe away my memories and fall asleep. If the student, who was crouching next to me, hadn't whispered I wouldn't have realised that the collaborators had moved on.

A commotion broke out to my right.

"You bloody woman," said the guide. "You allowed the master devil Shaitan, to enter you."

We hadn't heard the baby cry, and hadn't been given away to the collaborators because the woman had drowned him.

"Who's the father?" asked the guide.

"Oh the father," said someone. "He was killed when the gunboat came to our village."

The guide snatched the dead baby from the mother and ran through the jute field. When he came back it was dark and we started to move again. I wanted to keep an eye on the mother, but it wasn't possible. We followed the guide's dim, flickering light, walking and walking until we arrived at the river crossing at about midnight.

The boat wasn't large. One by one, the guide, focusing his torchlight on our faces, counted us before we went on board. The woman who had drowned the baby wasn't among us any more. We had no idea whether she'd got lost or whether she had decided to follow her baby.

"Bloody woman. Shaitan has taken her," said the guide. "She is better off with him."

The boat was so cramped that we had standing room only. It

began to rain again and the wind howled against the sail, but squashed between the bodies I fell asleep, upright as I was. I woke up only when the people I was leaning against shook themselves, ready for disembarking. We were escorted to a village where we were distributed between homesteads, and given cooked food and a place to sleep.

From then on we could move during the daytime. We weren't too far from the border: only a day's walk and we would be in India. Although the Pakistani army hadn't yet arrived in this area, they sporadically shelled it from a distance. It was quiet when we washed ourselves by the well and ate our food, but as I was preparing to sleep, the bombardment began and went on until morning. Some shells seemed to land nearby. I spent the rest of the night counting explosions.

We began again in the morning. It was raining, but we didn't have to wade through the water any more. In these parts the ground was much higher than the swampland in which we lived. From the village we took a narrow path to join the main road to India.

There were thousands of people on the main road. The line stretched for miles. The road, though not waterlogged, was slushy. No one seemed to mind, because it was far better than the killing fields they were leaving behind. Even the children, as if in a herd of animals, followed their elders without complaint. There were Hindus and Muslims of all ages. No one was bothered to know who was next to him or her as they trudged through the slush.

Between the student and me there was an old lady, doubled over her stick, with a bundle hanging from her neck. Every so often she asked if it was far to go; and the student told her each time that it wasn't far.

"Where are your people?" he asked.

"Collaborators killed them all," said the old lady.

"Did you know them?"

"Yes, some of them are my neighbours. I even fed them with sweets when they were little."

"How did you survive?"

"They hung the bodies of my sons, daughters and grandchildren from our jackfruit tree. Then they sat me under it and left. I suppose they wanted me to die of grief and hunger."

"Do you know where you're going?" asked the student.

"I'm going where everyone else is going," she said. "I heard no one would kill us there. And there would be food for us."

Suddenly the shelling began again. People, thousands of us, scattered in panic. The student and I picked up the old lady and took shelter in a ditch by the road. We thought we could wait for the bombardment to end, but it went on and on. When a small group, disregarding the danger, took to the road, many of us, after only a moment's hesitation, followed it.

The student offered to carry the old lady on his back, but she refused. We walked on and on through the rain, bombs falling all around us, but somehow no one was hit.

We arrived at a gorge, and through it reached a huge valley with fast-moving, shallow rivers. Bombs were falling on it from all sides.

"Have we arrived?" asked the old lady.

"We have. Just across the valley is India," said the student.

"I don't want to go to a foreign country. All I want is food and shelter. I don't want to die either, because if I do, who will remember my children and grandchildren?"

The student was getting impatient with the old lady; he just lifted her up on his back and marched on. It was almost night when we crossed the border and reached the refugee camp. Already there were thousands of white tents and people were busy setting up many more. It was a sea of mud; and the smell of human waste mingled with that of disinfectant. Every now and then dead bodies were brought out from the tents in stretchers to be burnt or buried.

I persuaded the student to help me look for Moni Banu. We went from tent to tent, but there was no sign of her. Then the student came across a man from his village, who told him that he knew the tent where the Alam family was placed. He volunteered to lead us there. As we passed tent after tent my heart was beating with the prospect of seeing Moni Banu again. Would she be pleased to see me, would she open her dark eyes wide for me, and say I missed you so much, Beautiful One? Perhaps she had become a different person in the last three months; perhaps she would talk to me with indifference, and without taking her eyes off her husband.

When we got to the Alams' tent I looked around, but couldn't see Moni Banu. Although Kabir Alam looked much thinner than when I had last seen him, and rather more withdrawn and dishevelled, I recognised him immediately. I gathered that the lady with a bandage around her head, who was breathing erratically in her sleep, was his wife. I hadn't met her when I visited their homestead.

Kabir Alam coughed all the time. He barely opened his eyes when I greeted him and his voice was so faint that I had to lower my ear to his face to hear him. He asked me about the teacher and Ata Banu, about our village, but he didn't look at me to receive my answers. Then, becoming agitated, he told me that Moni Banu and Zafar Alam weren't in the camp any more. They had gone to some secret location inside Bangladesh to be trained as liberation fighters.

"Zafar's wife is such a headstrong girl. I told her so many times not to go, but she wouldn't listen to me," he said. "Women aren't made to bear arms."

The effort of talking had sapped his energy; he collapsed like a rag-doll and closed his eyes. From time to time he coughed, but he didn't say any more, nor did he open his eyes. I stood by him for a while and then left.

No one would tell me the location of the training camp, so there was no point my staying any longer. I resolved to make my return journey the next day. I looked for the old lady everywhere, but couldn't find her. I hope she lived to remember her children and grandchildren. The student had already made contact to join the liberation forces. He came to see me off at the border zone and told me that he would tell Moni Banu, if he came across her, that I had come looking for her.

"See you in independent Bangladesh," he shouted as I was crossing the border.

CHAPTER 10

When I entered the flooded bush at the back of our homestead the first person I saw was Datla Nuri, about ten yards ahead of me, punting the raft. I paddled swiftly and caught up with her.

"Oh Nephew, you are back," she said. "Oh Allah, how worried I was for you. I thought the Pakistanis got you."

I smiled with my eyes to show her that I was fine.

"How come you're on you own? Where's Moni Banu?"

I indicated with open palms and a shake of my head that I hadn't found her.

"If Ata Banu sees you, she'll give you a real telling-off. Stay out of the inner courtyard. Understand?"

I moored the dinghy and went into the outer bungalow, where the teacher and Zomir Ali were sitting together, smoking hookah. The teacher jumped up as soon as he saw me.

"What took you so long? Where's Moni?"

He wanted a quick answer, but I paused to consider the best way of communicating my response. Even for the teacher, who seemed to have a sixth sense for what I wanted to say, the story of my journey was too complicated to be conveyed by mere gestures and signs.

"Tell me, Kamal. What's happened to Moni?" The furrows of his brow were deepening with anxiety at my silence.

"Hello, Kamal. I'm glad you're back safely. We were all so worried for you," said Zomir Ali. "Perhaps what you have to say can only be communicated in writing."

"It's not the time for playing games. If you need to use the slate, hurry up with it," said the teacher.

I wrote about where I had been and how I had gone as far as the refugee camps in India, looking for her, but to no avail. I told him what I had heard about her and Zafar Alam.

"That Zafar is a no-good idiot. Oh no, what a mistake I made giving Moni to him in marriage," said the teacher, looking anguished. "I bet he's bent on having her killed."

As the teacher hadn't bothered to read out what I'd written, Zomir Ali didn't know the reason for his outburst.

"Why should a young man want to have his newly married wife killed? It doesn't make any sense, Abbas Mia."

"That idiot is dragging her to war."

"Perhaps it was she who insisted on joining the liberation forces."

"Moni is too sensible to do anything like that."

"I thought you raised her to be a young woman of independent spirit," said Zomir Ali. "Even in wartime one mustn't forget the ways of reason and learning that one has cultivated. Otherwise, we'll be joining the ranks of the barbarians."

Instead of responding, the teacher slumped back into his chair, and started puffing his hookah. It was getting dark. When I got up to light the lamp, I heard Ata Banu. I was surprised to hear her because she rarely came anywhere near the outer bungalow. She must have persuaded Datla Nuri to bring her on the raft.

"Where's my daughter? What's happened to my daughter?" she wailed. "You, Kamal, you evil ungrateful one, you are worse than a treacherous snake. How dare you come back, all safe and sound, leaving my poor daughter to die?"

The teacher took the lamp and went to the door.

"Please be quiet, don't you know that Venerable Scholar is here. You're upsetting him."

The teacher laid the lamp down and went out. I could hear Ata Banu wailing again and the teacher rebuking Datla Nuri.

"Have you lost your senses to bring her here?"

"I didn't want to come, but she forced me," said Datla Nuri.

The teacher took Ata Banu back to the inner courtyard. Now I was alone with Zomir Ali.

"I know there is much more to your story than the meagre bits you've given us. You have been rather – as they say – economical with the truth. Am I right, Kamal?"

I brought the lamp back from where the teacher had left it and hung it from the hook in the middle of the room.

126

"I understand if you have kept things from us. Perhaps much of what you've seen in the course of your journey is unspeakable. Am I right, Kamal?"

I sat by the bed and tried to stay as still as possible.

"It must have been difficult for you, Kamal. I'm glad that I don't have to see horror any more."

I looked at Zomir Ali. He squeezed the lids over his blind eyes as though to make sure that a miracle had not returned his vision.

The teacher returned. "Sorry, you Venerable Scholar. Moni's mother is feeling a bit upset."

"You don't have to apologise for her. A mother's grief is perfectly understandable."

The teacher then turned to me and said, "Go and fetch the dinner for Venerable Scholar. I'll dine here too."

I went to the kitchen with trepidation, because I knew that Ata Banu would start on me again as soon as she saw me. I was relieved to see Datla Nuri alone there. She told me that she had prepared a sleeping brew for Ata Banu and settled her in bed.

"Tell me the truth, Nephew," she said. "Is it really true that Moni Banu will wear trousers like a man and shoot a gun?"

I did a comic pantomime of wrapping myself in a sari and picking up and firing a gun.

Datla Nuri, as always, joined in the fun. "I bet you want to see her in them trousers, no?"

I took the dinner for Zomir Ali and the teacher to the outer bungalow. While they ate on the bed, I squatted on the floor.

"We mustn't delay any more, Kamal. It's getting too dangerous," the teacher said. "We should set off as soon as possible."

I asked him if he had found the sail and the boatmen yet.

"You know, Harihar Majee and Bidudhar Majee, the brothers who keep otters," said the teacher. "They'll bring the sail tomorrow. I have also persuaded them to come along with us."

"So, who are you taking in your Noah's ark, then?" asked Zomir Ali.

"You, Venerable Scholar, of course. My wife, Kamal, myself, and the boatmen. The rest I don't know yet."

I was very pleased by the way the teacher had included me as though I was a member of his family.

"You don't want to take an old man like me, who has passed his time," said Zomir Ali. "I've nothing more to give."

"What are you saying, you Venerable Scholar? You are…" But the teacher was interrupted before he could finish his sentence.

"I know what you are going to say, Abbas Mia. Let us give these sentimentalities a rest. Instead, you must find a way of filling your fifteen places that is both rational and just. Of course, your immediate family is another matter."

The teacher kneaded a portion of rice with potato bhaji for a long time before scooping it into his mouth. I could see that he didn't know what to say to Zomir Ali.

"You know me, Abbas Mia. I've no time for religious myth, but Noah's pairing was perfectly logical and fair in its own terms. He wanted to reproduce God's creatures on earth."

"I am not Noah, you Venerable Scholar. I just want to survive with my family and a few others."

"Yes, yes I understand you, Abbas Mia, but the problem of choosing the 'few others' still remains, doesn't it? Unless you are clear on the purpose of your journey, you can't make a rational and just selection. You see, in terrible times like war one has to be more vigilant. One has to apply reason and justice with more rigour than ever. Otherwise, the worst excesses of our instincts take over and we end up committing more savage acts than any animal is capable of. You see, animals are driven only by the urge to preserve their lives and procreate. We, on the other hand, can increase by many fold the savage power of our drives by our cunning and intellect, which in the end bear no relation to the urge to preserve our lives. We can be brutes for the sheer pleasure of it. So, we need the constant vigilance of reason and justice, especially during the time of war."

The teacher looked more lost than ever. He was now kneading his rice aimlessly without bothering to scoop it up to his mouth. What Zomir Ali had said made sense, but I still didn't like him lecturing the teacher. Sometimes he sounded so self-righteous and pompous.

I heard a boat approaching and went to open the door. It was Ala Mullah; he moored his dinghy and came in without greeting me. He looked very agitated.

The teacher lifted his eyes from his plate. "What's the news, Mullah?"

"Very bad, you respectable teacher. It came to me from a reliable source that the Pakistani army is very angry with us. Someone has informed on us that many of our boys are leaving the village to join the liberation forces. There's a good chance that we might be raided tonight."

The teacher left his meal unfinished and got up.

"We must find a hiding place for tonight."

"You're panicking unnecessarily, Abbas Mia. We've already fled so many times and the Pakistani army never came. I doubt they would venture into the floodplains at night."

"We mustn't take any chances, you Venerable Scholar. Ala Mullah gets a lot of good information from his fellow mullahs. You know, the ones who have become collaborators. So, we can't take his information lightly."

The teacher then asked me to take him to the inner courtyard in the dinghy. I took him, but he failed to persuade Ata Banu to leave her hut. When we came back to the outer bungalow, Zomir Ali also refused to budge.

"I would rather have a nice sleep than suffer the bloody swamps and the jungles. Especially on the information of an unreliable mullah. Besides, it won't be a great loss if they burn me at the stake now."

The teacher tried blackmail.

"If you don't agree to come, I won't be able to persuade Moni's mother to leave her hut."

Reluctantly Zomir Ali agreed to come. Again I carried the teacher back to the inner courtyard; Ala Mullah followed with Zomir Ali in his dinghy. We stopped at Ata Banu's door; the teacher called her out.

"Oh Moni's mother – do you hear me? Venerable Scholar is here, and he refuses to go with us if you don't come out."

Ata Banu, accompanied by Datla Nuri, came gingerly out of her hut and stepped into my dinghy; Datla Nuri went into Mullah's. It was a dark, cloudy night, but at least it wasn't raining. We took the floodplain to our left, paddled through the forest of kapok trees, then over the submerged jute fields, heading for the bush surrounding the secluded pond, where once Big Suban had brought me to see the village women bathing.

We dug our punting-poles in the water between two tangled bushes and tethered our dinghies. Ata Banu kept muttering her Arabic verses. From time to time Ala Mullah joined in with her from his dinghy, his voice much louder. Zomir Ali was whining about being dragged out of his bed for the discomfort of perching on the narrow plank between the gunwales of the hull. He was quiet for a while, and then turned on Ala Mullah.

"How reliable are your so-called reliable sources, Mullah?"

"Very reliable, you Venerable Scholar. You see, they're proper collaborators of the Pakistanis, who never go anywhere without consulting them. In fact, it is the collaborators who tell them which village to raid."

"Yes, yes I know, but how come they let you have their secrets?"

"You know that they are my fellow mullahs and I attended the same religious school as they did. Besides, when I'm with them I speak very passionately about maintaining the purity of the Islamic State. I also tell them, in a very rousing fashion, how much I hate impures and heathens. I even pretend to choke with anger when I tell them how much I want to burn them alive or cut their throats. So, they believe that I'm like them; they tell me, Ala, you're a proper holy warrior."

"Am I to believe that it's all pretence, and that you don't believe any of those things?" asked Zomir Ali.

"What are you saying, you Venerable Scholar? Am I not here with you all? If I had gone to their side, I'd have done very well."

"You're not answering me, Mullah. I asked you if you believe any of the things that you say to them."

"Everyone here knows who I am. I don't have to answer this."

"But I don't know you. How am I to know that you are not acting with us, in a very rousing fashion, as you claim you do with them?"

Suddenly Datla Nuri raised her voice.

"Leave Mullah alone. We've known him since he was hanging from his mother's tits. He's a bit greedy for good food. Also a bit simple in his head, but he's all right,"

The rain that had been threatening all day finally came, heavy and slanting. Ata Banu asked me to take her back to the homestead. I didn't know what to do and waited for the teacher to say something, but he kept his mouth shut.

"Are you disobeying me, you ungrateful snake?' she screamed. "If you don't start paddling now I'll chase you out of our homestead like a dog."

Since I didn't hear anything from the teacher, I started paddling. Ala Mullah followed. As we made our way back to the homestead, Ata Banu was still fuming and venting her anger at the teacher.

"Don't ask me to hide like a shamed woman any more," she said. "Must we lose our honour because of the war?"

I lay on my bed for a long time with my eyes open, with the rain pouring down on my hut, waiting for the army's raid to come. When I woke up early next morning the rain had stopped so I heard Sona Mia's azan clearly. He was calling the faithful to prayer, but I couldn't help feeling that he was speaking to me, telling me how I was the chosen one, and how Allah loved me.

That morning there was hardly any cloud in the sky and the sun poured in on our homestead. While I was getting on with my morning task of feeding the cows the teacher came to me to say that he was going to a village some distance from ours, but he didn't tell me the nature of his business. I presumed that he wanted me to take him there in our dinghy, but instead he told me that Ala Mullah would give him a lift in his dinghy on his way to town, and that he would find someone to bring him back. "I want you to wait for the Majee brothers. If there is an army raid, you know what to do – don't you?"

I was waiting for Harihar and Bidudhar Majee to bring the sail, but by midday I decided to go out fishing. I wanted to take some lunch with me, so I went to the kitchen. I was surprised to see Ata Banu there, hunched over a curved-cutter, chopping a gourd.

"What do you want, Kamal?"

I bunched my fingers and gestured to my mouth, and she – stopping her cutting – said, "Shall I make you a bundle of gruel with molasses? You like that, don't you?"

I nodded and sat down by the door.

"I hear Moni is carrying a gun these days. Doesn't she know that it's an evil man's thing? She mustn't touch it. It's all her father's fault – teaching her book-reading and all them nonsense." I listened with my head down.

"Don't you go around thinking that you're a big man now. Do you understand me? I don't want you to go near a gun either. I need no book-reading to know that it's a sure way of getting killed. If you are gone, who will feed the cows?"

I rubbed the back of my neck and lowered my head further.

"Our homestead is already lonely without Moni. So, don't try to make it even lonelier by following that brainless Big Suban into fighting. I don't like it – you understand?"

I wanted to find an excuse to get away, but I had to wait until the gruel was ready. Luckily it didn't take long.

"I'm leaving you in the care of Allah. He will look after you for me," she said when she handed me the bundle.

I looked at her, surprised, because I wasn't going for long or far. She looked at me as though she was about to say something, her eyes becoming watery, but she turned her face quickly away from me, then she resumed her hunched posture over the curved-cutter, chopping the gourd.

I paddled my dinghy to Datla Nuri's hut to tell her to look out for the Majee brothers, and then made for my favourite fishing spot by the bamboo groves. It was a windless day and the sun was strong. Heat bounced off the water and crawled into the dinghy. No one was around. The bamboo trees were still and silent as if they were closing in upon themselves with the anticipation of danger. After paddling very quietly over the area, I stopped, planted the punt-pole deep into the mud bed and tethered the dinghy to it. Then I got into the water with the spear at the ready. I took several turns wading around, but there was no sign of any fish. Suddenly a fishing kite screamed overhead, shattering the silence. For some reason it made me feel uneasy, so I got into the dinghy and punted towards the homestead. When I was under the fig tree to the left of the bamboo groves, I stopped to eat my pot of gruel. It was very tasty. Yes, Ata Banu had indeed prepared it the way I liked it. The sky was still clear over the floodplains and I wanted to give fishing one more try, so I headed towards the mango grove by the river. Once there I decided not to stop, but instead, crossed it quickly so I could check out our cargo-boat. It looked impressive floating on the water. I was about to climb in to inspect it when I heard the noise. It was coming from the river and it sounded familiar.

Now I know what I should have done. At the first sign of their coming I should have raced back to the homestead. I know both Ata Banu and Zomir Ali would have been stubborn old mules, but I should have forced them, put ropes around their necks if necessary and dragged them into my dingy to take them to a place where they would never have been found. Sure, they would have unleashed their foul mouths at me, but they would have been safe. But everything was happening so fast and I couldn't think straight. In my panic I climbed into the cargo-boat and lay in the cabin's vast cavern, silent and full of swaying shadows. When I heard the gunboat stop in the river, I realised that the raiding soldiers wouldn't go past the cargo-boat without climbing in to check it. Was I too late? I rushed out of the cabin and jumped down into the dinghy and started paddling. Then I heard several smaller engines starting off. I had just time to reach the mango grove when the engines roared in my direction. I felt the angel of death was leaping towards me, but they stopped. I presume it was to inspect the cargo-boat. It was just as well because it gave me time to hide my dinghy behind the dense lines of floating trees tangled with coiling creepers. Within minutes, seven speedboats, full of soldiers and flying Pakistani flags, sped through, unleashing high waves against the trees. My dingy shuddered, but they didn't see me. There was no doubt they had come to raid our village. There would be death, only death. I prayed that somehow Datla Nuri had convinced Ata Banu and Zomir Ali to come along with her to a hiding place.

Once the engines stopped, there was silence for a long time, but then they started again. This time the speedboats seemed to be going around the village, broadcasting messages with loudspeakers. They seemed calm, reassuring voices, almost warm, spoken in good Bengali – perhaps they belonged to well-educated collaborators. They echoed over the floodplains: *Perhaps you heard rumours about us, but we swear in the name of Allah that they are all false and malicious. We come to you as friends and brothers, to bring you greetings in person, share a glass of water with you, and help you with all of our means. If we lie, be sure that we will burn in hell for eternity. Come brothers, come sisters, show your faces so that we can convey our respects to you.*

The more I heard the voices, the more I became afraid for Ata Banu and Zomir Ali. Even if they didn't trust them, they wouldn't be able to do anything about the danger slithering their way. Bringing poison, only poison. I became so desperate that I paddled through the mango groves, the open floodplains, and then the waterlogged jungle to arrive at the bush by the palm trees, where I used to take Zomir Ali for his toilet. But I was too late; a speedboat full of soldiers was stationed outside our outer bungalow. I couldn't help shivering and opening the hole of my mouth so wide I sucked in so much air I felt dizzy. I should have risked it, I should have tried to reach Zomir Ali and Ata Banu even if it meant committing suicide, but I turned back. Allah forgive me.

I turned the dinghy around and headed for the school yard – the highest point in the village and still free of floodwater. Instead of taking my dinghy all the way there I left it some distance away and swam on my back with a clump of hyacinth on my face, then waded through a patch of tall kash grass to reach the jute fields fringing the yard. I remembered meeting Sona Mia at this spot and wondered how he would respond to the voices with the loudspeakers.

It was only when I started to climb the tall jham-berry tree that I realised I had been heading towards it from the moment I heard the gunboat. Once in my childhood, when Ata Banu had told me off, I ran away from the homestead, and hid in its dense foliage. No one had found me for two days. I remember seeing the teacher under the tree, calling for me many times, but he never suspected that I was on top of him. In the end, hunger had made me climb down of my own accord.

I suppose deep down I sensed that I would be safe within the dense foliage of the jham-berry tree. It was as though my limbs made their own way to the tree and drew me up like a spider. Soon after I had settled on one of the high leafy branches, two speed-boats arrived. About twenty soldiers got off, marched through the clearing between the jute fields, and positioned themselves in front of the tin-roofed school building. Then I heard the loud-speakers again. They were asking people to gather in the school yard. Don't listen to them, don't come anywhere near the school yard, I wanted to shout, but all I was doing was gushing air through the hole of my mouth and ruffling the leaves in front of me. Nothing happened for a while, then the speedboats came again, but this time they arrived with some of our village men. One of them was Sona Mia.

I feared the worst for Sona Mia and the other villagers who were brought in with him, but I was puzzled to see them being treated well. Apart from being courteous, the soldiers offered them cigarettes. It was still bright and sunny. As I looked out on the floodplains I saw some dinghies, with about ten to fifteen of our village men on board, coming towards the school yard. They were also treated well by the soldiers. I was beginning to feel that perhaps I had been a bit hasty in thinking the worst. Perhaps these soldiers were different from the others whose handiwork I had seen earlier, on my way to the refugee camps. I was almost happy thinking that nothing terrible would happen to Ata Banu and Zomir Ali.

After unloading some large crates, one of the speedboats set off again, carrying Sona Mia and some of the villagers on board. Most of the soldiers, about fifty, remained in the school yard. From the crates they removed bayonets, a large number of clubs, and three machine guns. I didn't know what the clubs were for, but they fixed the bayonets to their guns, and positioned the machine guns around the school yard. About ten of them climbed on the tin roof of the school building. Half of them were facing one side, the rest the other. In the meantime, the speedboat carrying Sona Mia and the others went around the village. I could hear Sona Mia's deep, resonant voice, as if calling for prayer, appealing to our villagers to come out of their hiding and gather in the school yard. He was telling them how nice the Pakistani soldiers had been and how well they had been treated. My heart was pounding and I was finding it hard to breathe because it was becoming clear to me what awaited them, and I knew that very few would fail to respond to Sona Mia's summons.

Even before the speedboat returned, the floodplain – shimmering with midday sun – was teeming with dinghies. Our villagers had come out of hiding and were heading for the school yard. Among them there were men, women, and children of all ages. Normally about five thousand people lived in our village, but now with so many having fled to the refugee camps, there were between three and four hundred left. It seemed nearly all of them had now gathered in the school yard. They were nervous, but not unduly alarmed. I was confused. Seeing the positioning of the soldiers, the bayonets and the machine guns, I was gulping air again, and feeling dizzy, but still trying to convince myself that nothing terrible would happen.

It was now afternoon and clouds had gathered low in the sky. From nowhere a flock of crows flew into the jham-berry tree where I was hiding. They perched on the branches around me and started their harsh, loud cawing. One of the soldiers from the roof took a shot at them; the bullet whistled through a branch just above me. The crows cawed even louder as they flew off and disappeared over the floodplains.

I heard the officer in command giving instructions with a loudspeaker. He told his soldiers to separate the men, the women and the children, and line them up. Some of the elders seemed baffled. Sona Mia came forward as though to talk to the commanding officer, but two soldiers rushed him with their rifle butts. He fell to the ground and the soldiers pulled him up by his ears and dragged him back to his place in the line. Suddenly some of the children panicked and tried to run. From the rooftop the soldiers picked them off one by one with their rifles. For a few seconds an eerie silence descended on the field as though the shock of what they had witnessed had made them mouthless like me. Then some of the adults exploded into angry cries and rushed to reach the fallen children. They were also shot down by the soldiers from the rooftop. Waves of trembling swept through the villagers as though they were a forest of saplings lashed by a fearsome windstorm. Nothing could live through this. Nothing. Ata Banu had been right when she said that the doomsday was upon us.

"No one breaks the line," shouted the commanding officer.

No one broke the line, except Sona Mia, who came forward again. A soldier rushed towards him, but he had already lifted his hands to his ears and began to perform the afternoon azan.

Allahu akbar: Allah is the greatest, he called, his voice so pure and so perfectly modulated, with so much love in it that the soldier advancing on him suddenly stopped. The villagers, too, became quiet as though their mothers were humming them to sleep after a storm had passed.

He paused, before he called out the next line.

Ash-hadu alla ilaha illallah: I bear witness that there is no God except Allah.

He paused.

Yes, yes, but he was also asking Allah to bear witness to what was happening to his chosen creatures here on earth, in the school yard.

Ash-hadu anna Muhammadur rasulullah: I bear witness that Muhammad is the Messenger of God.

He paused.

Yes, yes, but he was also asking me to bear witness to what was happening.

Hayya alas-salat: Make haste towards prayer.

He paused.

Yes, I will always pray for my brothers and sisters. Every time I breathe it will be a prayer to your memories.

Hayya alal-falah: Make haste towards welfare.

He paused.

Yes, I ought to have taken my place in the line. Forgive me, my brothers and sisters, for not stepping in to receive your death in my own person.

Allahu akbar: Allah is the greatest.

He paused.

Yes, but look what great work the soldiers are doing to your own creatures in your own name. Please do something – have mercy on us.

La ilaha illallah: There is no God except Allah.

Yes, but there was nothing more to say.

When he'd finished the azan, Sona Mia began to pray, but even before he could take his first bow to Allah the soldier put his bayonet through him. Blood spurted out like a fountain as he fell to the ground. Why did you make me see this, Allah? Why didn't you make me eyeless and earless too?

For a while the villagers were silent again, then, as they began to pray, the buzzing of their voices rose as though swarms of bees were emerging from the depths of the earth. One of the machine guns unleashed a burst of fire over the heads of the people, but this didn't stop the buzzing. Perhaps it had been planned well in advance, but it was only then, over the buzzing of the prayer, that I heard the commanding officer order his men not to use bullets. He divided the soldiers into three groups. Each of these formed themselves into columns of pairs as they advanced on the three lines of the villagers. In each pair, one soldier carried a club, and the other a rifle with an open bayonet.

Suddenly the soldiers, in concert with their commanding officer, who was orchestrating them with a loud speaker, began to shout *Allahu akbar*. Slowly, and with drilled precision, they moved into the lines of villagers, clubbing and bayoneting them. My head was spinning so much that everything was becoming blurry, but I still heard the villagers as they were praying louder and louder as though they wanted to reach their Allah before the soldiers got to them. Why didn't you listen to them, Allah? I remember that the soldiers, despite the fervour with which they shouted *Allahu akbar*, soon looked exhausted. They should have known that it is not easy to kill a human with such methods. And so many of them. I still wonder why the commanding officer was against using bullets.

I remember gasping for air, then vomiting as if my insides were gushing out through the hole of my mouth. I desperately tried to hold onto the branches as they began trembling as if the tree itself had gone into a spasm.

It was evening now and the sky finally broke. At first lightly, then it became a downpour. Because the sky had turned so dark, and with my head spinning, I could barely see what was happening down below, but I knew the killing was still going on. I could feel each death as though it was mine. Now, lighting torches and flambeaux, the soldiers moved among the lines like glow-worms. Beating hard on the canopy above me and on the tin roofs, the rain had muffled all other sounds, but somehow the prayers still reached me. From time to time I also heard bullets tearing through the rain. No doubt the soldiers with machine guns were mowing down those who broke the line. How long it went on for

I don't know, but it seemed to last for hours. Then suddenly they stopped. Now and then the commanding officer gave instructions with his loudspeaker, and some of the soldiers talked among themselves, but no matter how hard I tried I couldn't catch the prayer. Not even a faint echo. Now there was only the rain.

At the commanding officer's instruction, some of the soldiers sent up flares. They illuminated the sky with a yellowish glow; I saw golden strips of rain falling but I didn't dare look down. I don't know what the soldiers were doing at this point; perhaps they were searching for survivors to finish them off.

Perhaps because I was trying so desperately to cling onto the tree's branches – it seemed to have gone into a spasm again – I was only vaguely aware of the gunboat engines starting up and the soldiers leaving the school yard. Now that their torches and flambeaux had gone, darkness was complete. For a long time I didn't dare climb down and remained clinging to the branches, telling myself that it was only the nightmarish dream that had been visiting me since the beginning of the war. When I finally climbed down and crawled on all fours, my hands and knees moving over a bridge of dead flesh, it became clear that this was as real as real could be. Allah, so many bodies. Like the mangoes that littered our grove after the early summer storm. I crawled through pools of liquid, not sure whether I was touching blood or rainwater. I was almost galloping over the bodies. I wanted to get away as fast and as far as possible from this killing field.

While going over a pile of bodies I thought I heard a noise. My first response was to ignore it, but when I heard it for the second time, I had to stop. How could I run, leaving someone alive among the dead? A man's voice was coming from beneath the pile; I shifted through the bodies to reach him.

"Who are you?" he asked.

I couldn't even make a little sound from the back of my throat.

"Who are you? How did you survive?" he asked me again.

I took his hand and put it on my face.

"Ah, they shot you through your face. But how come you are still alive?"

This time I put his fingers into my mouth and was able to grunt a little.

"Kamal, is it you?"

From his voice I knew that it was Ducktor Malek, a man of huge bulk with long curly hair and a thick, drooping moustache. He was a jatra actor and a big eater. With some effort I helped him to his feet. He took off his shirt and vest and stood under the rain.

"The smell of blood makes me sick," he said.

I was astonished by the calm and collected way he spoke. He didn't sound like a man who had just survived a massacre. We went to the edge of the field. I left him there, swam for the dinghy, and came back for him; then together we headed for our homestead.

"Perhaps you and I are the last two men standing," he said. "What do we do now, Kamal?"

JOURNEY

Once more I shall come back to… this Bengal
Perhaps not as a human, but a Brahminy kite or a shalik bird.

Jibananda Das

CHAPTER 11

Finally the teacher launched the cargo boat.

Unlike recent mornings it was misty. Everything was so still that when I opened my mouth my palate didn't feel the slightest flutter of wind. While Ala Mullah directed the rudder at the helm, the Majee brothers dug the punt-poles into the mud-bed and propelled us through the mist. Soon we were away from the flood fields and slid into the waters of the river. Here the mist was even denser. We could hardly see beyond the boat's prow. Joker the otter jumped off the cabin roof, gave a shrill cry as though he had seen something frightening, and scuttled across the deck to be near Harihar Majee, but he had no time for Joker as, like his brother Bidudhar, he had just put his punt-pole aside, and taken to his oar. Without the wind to assist them, they pulled the oars with all of their strength, and yet we hardly made any progress.

We were nine people on board – and Joker the otter. We were all men, except Datla Nuri. Six among us were Muslims, and the Majee brothers were Hindus. No one knew what I was. Ever since he had conceived the idea, the teacher must have spent many hours wondering who to include in his travelling party, but I am sure the likes of Ducktor Malek, Bosa Khuni or Asad Khan never came into his reckoning. Now, here they were on the foredeck, standing beside the teacher as though he would never have imagined travelling without them. Bosa Khuni was the most unexpected one. He was a professional cutthroat and the most feared man in the village. Even in the midst of this horror he made me feel scared as he staggered on board with his pockmarked face and bulging red eyes. I wondered what Zomir Ali would have made of the composition of our travelling party. Would he have pointed out to the teacher that destiny had let him off the hook?

In the event, he didn't have to decide who to select for the journey. It was death that had decided for him. We were simply the village's leftovers.

I went to sit near Ala Mullah at the helm.

"Do you think we'll see our village again, Kamal?" he asked.

I shrugged my shoulders.

"We don't have much to come back to, do we? We might as well be wanderers like the snake-gypsies."

I grunted from the back of my throat to say that I understood his sentiments.

"Do you think we can stay out of this war, Kamal? Especially now that the gunboats are patrolling the floodplains. I bet the liberation forces will also be more active around here soon."

Right then I didn't want to entertain such possibilities. All I wanted was to get away, as far as possible.

"What did you do with the bones of Ata Banu and the Venerable Scholar?" asked Ala Mullah.

I wrote on my slate that I'd dived with them to the bottom of the floodplains and buried them in the mud bed.

"What did you see in the school yard? Ducktor Malek wouldn't tell me anything. I know the teacher went to look for you there, but he wouldn't tell me anything either. What did you see, Kamal?"

I held my slate in front of me, but my hand wouldn't move. I felt as though Sona Mia's azan was climbing to my ears through the soles of my feet.

"Are you feeling all right, Kamal?"

I turned away from him. Luckily just then Datla Nuri called me from the cabin. She wanted me to draw some water from the river. I dropped the pail, attached to a rope, into the murky water. I pulled it up and took it to her. She was squatting in the rear corner of the cabin and was lighting a clay stove.

"Only gruel with salt and green chillies for breakfast, Nephew. If you want to eat something nice, you better start fishing."

We didn't have any nets or hooks for fishing, only spears. As the river was too deep for spear fishing, we needed to find shallower waters. Once the mist had lifted I would go out in my dinghy, which was tied to the stern of the boat, and explore for possible fishing grounds.

"Nephew, sleep by me in the night," said Datla Nuri. "I don't trust that Asad Khan. He has evil eyes. He's already looking me up in a funny, funny way."

I smiled with my eyes, went out, and climbed onto the cabin roof. The mist had lifted slightly, and the trees on the floodplain, their foliage tinged pastel-red, were now vaguely visible. It was still windless, but the boat had caught a current, and was moving fast. Taking a break from the oars, the Majee brothers sprawled out on the rear deck to smoke their hookah. Ala Mullah was guiding us with the rudder. I remembered Zomir Ali's request that I should be his eyes and describe for him the shifting moods of the rain, the trees, or the wind. I looked at the sun, its rays trailing a long line on the murky river water. I talked to myself as though I was talking to Zomir Ali: It's red, you Venerable Scholar, it's red I'm seeing. Perhaps you saw with your skin at your end, perhaps you saw red when they set fire to the bungalow. Sorry, you Venerable Scholar, that I couldn't be the custodian of your books, as you wished, but from time to time I will open my eyes to take in the world for you.

Joker jumped onto the cabin roof, circled me squeaking, and then came to sniff me. He gave a shrill cry and jumped off to be near the Majee brothers. Emerging from the cabin, Datla Nuri called us to breakfast. One of the Majee brothers took the helm from Ala Mullah, the other one pulled the oar. Together, they steered the boat off the river and into a floodplain. Then they punted the boat into a dense patch of high rice plants, which should have been harvested weeks before, since clusters of golden pods were now rotting on their stalks. They stopped the boat and came inside the cabin for breakfast; Joker followed behind. Ducktor Malek, Asad Khan, Bosa Khuni, Ala Mullah and the teacher sat together in the middle of the boat. The Majee brothers and I, being much lower in status, sat behind them, near the clay stove. Joker slunk around us, whimpering. When Bidudhar Majee opened the cabin's small window and whistled, Joker jumped out.

"He'll catch his breakfast now," said Harihar Majee.

Datla Nuri was standing over us with the pot of gruel.

"Can he catch fish for us too?"

"Oh yes," said Harihar Majee. "When he's fishing, Bidudhar just has to whistle and he will bring in whatever he catches."

"Did you hear that, Nephew?" said Datla Nuri. "You are not the only fish-catcher in the boat."

She served us the gruel, salt and fried chillies, and then she went back to serve herself a portion. I expected the teacher to take the lead and say something about how he saw the journey should proceed, where we should go, and what each of us needed to do, but he seemed locked into himself. His eyes sunken, he kept on kneading a handful of gruel, without caring to swallow it. But how could he have recovered from Ata Banu's death and what he had seen in the school yard? Perhaps he was having dark thoughts about Moni Banu, seeing her groping her way to where her mother had gone.

"Are you with us, Abbas Mia?" asked Ducktor Malek.

The teacher shook his shoulders as though waking up from sleep, looked at Ducktor Malek with startled eyes, and then swallowed his kneaded portion.

"Tell us how you are planning to take us to the Promised Land," said Ducktor.

"What Promised Land, Ducktor? If you are seeking the Promised Land, then you have to flow with this war," said the teacher. "This boat is sailing away from the war."

"So, this is a boat for runaways and cowards," said Bosa Khuni.

"I haven't forced you to come, Bosa. You are free to leave," said the teacher.

Bosa Khuni mumbled and stuffed himself with gruel like a hungry dog.

"As you well know, Abbas Mia," said Ducktor, "I'm not cut out for violence. My temperament is not suited to the rough and tumble of war. As a man of arts all I want is peace to practise my craft, but that doesn't mean that I'm neutral."

"*He's* definitely not a neutral. He's a collaborator of the Pakistani devils," said Bosa Khuni, pointing to Asad Khan. "He's our enemy. Let's cut his throat."

"No one is cutting any throats on this boat. You understand me?" declared the teacher. "If you want to cut throats, then go and join the war."

Asad Khan pressed his chin hard against his throat and tightened his face.

146

"He's too cowardly for that. All he does is cut people's throats while they sleep. Has he forgotten that he would have been hanged if it hadn't been for my father's help?"

"Don't forget that I've cut many throats for your father. I've simply done my job, but it's your father who employed me. So, if I were to walk to the gallows, you father should be ahead of me."

Asad Khan had tightened his face so much that he was finding it hard to breathe.

"If Bangladesh comes, aristocratic Muslim families like us will be pushed around. Lower classes, Hindus and the cutthroats like him will have the upper hand. And Allah's natural order of things will fall apart."

Bosa Khuni laughed.

"Now he's showing his true colours. Bloody collaborator."

The teacher had had enough; he raised his voice. I was pleased that he was at last taking charge of the situation.

"Enough of this bickering. If we don't stick together, we will all perish," he said. "I want this boat to sail through the war with everyone alive."

"We're waiting for your good counsel, Abbas Mia. You're in command of this blessed ark. You're our Noah," said Ducktor Malek. "Point your finger and we'll follow."

"Don't burden me with your theatrical language, Ducktor. I'm no one's Noah, but our best bet is to sail for the swampland in the north-east. Once there we will navigate its mazes and stay ahead of the war. It will be hard, but if we pull our resources together we may see ourselves safely through it."

"What's so special about that part of the swampland? If it's such a labyrinth, how come I've never heard of it? Besides, if it's a true labyrinth we might get lost in it and be fodder for the mighty Minotaur," said Ducktor Malek.

"Give it a rest, Ducktor. Just trust me."

The late morning sun was blazing on the patch of rice plants, making their leaves and their rotting grain pods appear much yellower than when we first saw them. Bidudhar Majee whistled and Joker surfaced from beneath the rice plants with a large catfish between his paws. He came on board with it and circled around the Majee brothers, whistling.

"Let's get going," said the teacher.

The Majee brothers dug in their punt-poles and pushed us out of the rice fields. The sky was getting darker and began to rumble. On the river the wind broke the calm surface of the water. Waves hit the hull. While Ala Mullah took charge at the helm, the Majee brothers rushed to hoist the sail. As soon as it was up, wind from the southwest rushed in, puffing it up like a swollen belly. The boat sped through the water, heading north.

Harihar Majee took the helm and the rest of us gathered on the foredeck. A few boats now appeared on the river, carrying goods such as earthen pots, jute fibres, or coconuts. A few fishermen were out in their dinghies, spreading their nets. About midday we faced our first gunboat. The panic among the other boats alerted us to its coming long before we heard its engine. We hid behind the nearest island village and let the gunboat pass. We followed the wind to the north again and by early afternoon left the river for the floodplains. Datla Nuri cooked the catfish and we stopped for lunch by a market which we were surprised to find open. A large group of men, armed with machetes and spears, surrounded us. They kept asking who we were and where we had come from, suspecting us of being either a group of bandits or collaborators. Then someone recognised Ala Mullah who, earlier in the year, had been in this market preaching at a religious gathering.

When they heard what had happened to our village, and the purpose of our journey, the people offered to shelter us. They said that gunboats on this stretch of the river hadn't dared enter the floodplains, but the teacher said that it was probably only a matter of time before they came. They looked at him with astonishment.

"Even during the British times no colonial official dared to come here to collect taxes," said an old market man.

"I know, but this war is very different. This is not just a war, but genocide. The Pakistani army is bent on wiping the entire race of Bengalis from the face of the earth. They will travel any length to carry it out," said the teacher.

The old man looked worried. "What should we do then?"

"You have to decide amongst yourselves, but I believe our best chance lies in the floodplains further north-east. That's where we are heading."

"If we're not safe here, I doubt that we'll be safe anywhere in Bangladesh. We'll wait a few more days to see what happens," said the old man.

"Don't wait long. We waited – and see what happened to us."

Before we left, the people from the market gave us rice, salt, spices, sweet potatoes, matches, kerosene, firewood, and cooking oil. They also gave us lungis and Punjabi shirts for the men, and two new saris for Datla Nuri.

Dark clouds continued to gather and from time to time the sky rumbled, but it didn't rain. As the floodplains here were clogged with hyacinths, water lilies and lotuses, we couldn't use the sail. Bosa Khuni, Ala Mullah and I took turns with the Majee brothers to punt the boat. It was only where the floodplains ran over lakes and small rivers, where the water was relatively free of vegetation, that we could use the sail or the oars.

We stopped in the late afternoon among a bed of hyacinths and lilies. Bosa Khuni and I went off in the dinghy to explore the area and look for a suitable shelter for the night and to do some spear fishing. At first I was doing the punting while he sat on the stempost.

"I never knew that you were a book-reading man, Kamal," he said. "Should I treat you with more respect from now on?"

I shook my head to say that it wouldn't be necessary, but he continued saying: "Yes, I'll treat you with respect, Kamal. It's right that an unlettered man like me should treat you with respect. Especially considering that you're one of us, and not some stinking landowner."

I kept on punting without looking at him. The wind was curling the hyacinth leaves and fluttering their purple flowers. Bosa Khuni kept talking.

"I bet you've heard things about me that make your hair stand on end. I don't blame you. To tell you the truth, when I remember what I've done I'm scared of myself."

I saw a shoal of fish near some flat, trembling water lily leaves. I punted towards it, but Bosa Khuni, who was supposed to be doing the spearing, stayed where he was. He seemed deep in thought. The dinghy went over the water lilies, scattering the shoal away.

"You know I'm not a talking man, Kamal. Talking messes up your mind and gives you bad dreams. If something crops up in my mind I just cut it off before it can take me down with its gibberish. But with the war on I've been thinking about things. I don't know why, but I feel I can talk to you. Do you mind?"

I lowered the punt into the water and moved my head.

"Perhaps because you don't have a mouth, I feel that you won't throw my own words back at me, so that they can carry on gibbering," said Bosa Khuni, looking very serious. Then he chuckled and said, "And let's be honest about something, Kamal: we look as ugly as each other, eh? So, there is something between us."

I didn't know how to respond, so I moved my head and bent my body to push the punt.

"Do you feel anything when you spear a fish?" he asked, looking serious again.

Once more I just moved my head.

"Exactly," he said. "I don't feel anything when I cut someone's throat. I do a job and I do it clean. What do you say to that?"

I was thinking that, surely, spearing a fish and cutting someone's throat weren't the same thing, but I had no means of communicating that to him.

"I tell you something, Kamal. You see, I know a fellow professional who started to go mad. Do you know what he told me? He said that things started to go wrong for him when he began looking into the eyes of his jobs. It's all rubbish, I told him. Do you know why?"

I wasn't looking for fish any more; just punting.

"When people die there is nothing in their eyes. I told him that it was the gibberish in his mind that was doing him in. You see, he was seeing himself in their eyes. You know, like in a bloody mirror. Am I talking sense, Kamal?"

Using the movements of punting I hid my eyes from him.

"I know you're not giving me back a whole load of gibberish to mess me up. But I bet you're talking quietly inside, aren't you, Kamal? I hope it's not gibberish."

I saw another shoal of fish and followed it. Suddenly Bosa Khuni stood up, arched his spear above his head, and let it rip through the water. It zeroed in on a large carp. We had a hard struggle dragging it on board. It was jumping and flapping its tail so violently that the dinghy tilted from side to side. From his gunny bag, which he always carried, Bosa Khuni took out his machete and, with a single blow, cut the carp's head off. Blood splashed all over the hull. A drop flew through the hole of my mouth and landed at the back of my tongue. Bosa Khuni smiled, his bulging red eyes popping out even more than usual in his huge pockmarked face. I bent over the gunwale to wash my mouth. Then the sky, with fearsome thunder, finally broke. We were drenched in seconds.

"But what I really wanted to say, Kamal, you know, with the war on, is that –" he stopped abruptly and put his face up to the rain.

"I can do what I do and still be part of something big. Do you follow me, Kamal?"

As I wasn't sure what he was trying to say, I shook my head.

"Until now I have cut throats for myself alone. You know, to make a living. Now I can cut enemy throats. Obviously, for free. It will do something towards our land becoming its own boss. No? And I can be, you know, what's the big word for the genuine fella-who-loves-his-country?"

I wanted to say, You mean a patriot? But there was no way that I could convey it to him in gestures, so I looked over his head to the rain.

"I want to show that I love my country. It doesn't mean I'm going all soft on gibberish like loving my people. You see, even a cutthroat needs a country. A place he can call home, and where he can speak his own tongue without feeling like a stray dog. Some people, even though I don't give a damn for their types, need a place to speak their own kind of gibberish, don't they? Anyway, am I wrong, Kamal, to feel that the best way I can be a genuine fella-who-loves-his-country is by practising my own craft? With the war on, aren't people cutting each other's throats anyway? The only difference is that they're mostly doing that with guns. And that they are giving themselves big names like army, freedom fighters. Am I right, Kamal?'

I had the feeling that it wasn't just the question of choice of weapons and names. There had to be something more, something noble, especially when a freedom fighter took up his or her gun, but

I couldn't figure out exactly what. Perhaps, it was a matter of intention, the willingness to die for your people as the freedom fighters had supposedly done, but how could I know it without getting into their heads? Besides, who could tell that Bosa Khuni didn't possess such intentions? I grunted from the back of my throat, and kept concentrating on the punting.

"Thank you, Kamal. You know, for not messing me up with gibberish."

In the distance I spotted a small island with a clump of trees. I punted towards it as I thought it might provide us with good shelter for the night.

When I came within about twenty feet of the island, I saw something move. At first I thought it was the wind shaking a creeper bush beneath the trees, but soon I was in no doubt that it was either an animal or a human on all fours. It lumbered between the bushes. Bosa Khuni saw it too. He jumped off the dinghy, waded through the waist-high water towards the island, and launched his spear. Instead of finding its target, the spear hit a tree trunk. He came back to the dinghy, grabbed his machete in a huff, and rushed towards the island once more.

When he came back he was grasping a woman. She made no sound as Bosa Khuni held his machete to her throat. She was trembling like a cornered prey, waiting for the inevitable to happen.

"Who are you? What the hell are you doing here?'

She didn't respond. She was covered by a black veil that was soaked in rainwater, and smeared with mud. When Bosa pulled back the veil she looked young – perhaps not more than twenty years old, like me.

"Where are you from? How did you get here?"

She gave a vacant look, but nothing came from her mouth.

"If you don't talk, I'll cut your throat. Understand?"

She made a little sound with her nose as though suppressing a sob, but still didn't speak.

"Perhaps she's like you, Kamal. She hasn't got a tongue with which to speak."

Bosa Khuni pulled her mouth open and looked inside. She had a tongue.

"Are you deaf and dumb?"

She lowered her eyes.

"Look at her face, Kamal. It's not a Bengali face, is it?"

She looked a bit different from the faces I knew, but I couldn't tell whether it was a Bengali face or not.

"Perhaps she's a Bihari. Our enemy."

Bosa Khuni then asked her in Urdu, the same questions that he had asked before in Bengali. She kept her eyes lowered and still she didn't say anything. He raised the machete to her throat.

"I have a feeling that she's Bihari, Kamal. Shall I cut her throat?"

I hit Bosa Khuni on the shoulder and grunted from the back of my throat.

Bosa Khuni lowered the machete.

"All right, Kamal," said Bosa Khuni. "But if she proves to be a Bihari, I promise you, I'll lift her severed head. No gibberish can save her."

We put her in the dinghy and took her to the boat. We were nine to begin with, now we were ten.

CHAPTER 12

Despite the rain, everyone had gathered on the foredeck, their hands roofing over their eyes, to see us bring aboard the strange veiled woman. As soon as she came on the deck, Joker came chattering, circled around and sniffed her, then scuttled away. No one said anything until Joker plopped into the water.

"Who is she?" boomed Ducktor Malek.

"I am not sure. She won't open her mouth," said Bosa Khuni. "But I think she's of the enemies. You know, a Bihari whore."

The veiled woman squatted on the foredeck, her head bent over her knees, her teeth chattering. She looked like a wet scarecrow.

"Let us not jump to conclusions. For all we know, she could be the daughter of someone like us. Perhaps her family has also been butchered by the Pakistani forces," said the teacher.

"Something in her face tells me she's a Bihari. Unlike Kamal, she has a perfect mouth and a complete tongue, and yet she doesn't speak. I wonder why?" said Bosa. "Perhaps because she's scared that her accent will reveal her for what she is. A Bihari whore."

The veiled woman didn't move at all. She seemed to have closed herself so tightly in the cage of her veil that nothing got through to her. For a moment I had the terrible feeling that she had stopped breathing. I wanted to go up to her and shake her, but I, too, was frozen and I did not dare walk in front of all these eyes and make a scene.

"People don't open their mouths for many different reasons, Bosa. Perhaps, she's deaf and dumb. Or, perhaps she has seen the face of hell as we did in the school yard. If some of us had sealed our mouths like her, it wouldn't have surprised me at all," said

Ducktor Malek. "What is there to talk about afterwards? Nothing, absolutely nothing."

"We may find out who she is if we take her veil off. We know that a Bengali woman of her age is likely to wear a sari. If she's a Bihari, she's more likely to wear salwar-kameez, isn't she?" said Bosa.

He stepped forward and leaned over the woman as though about to pluck off her veil. Datla Nuri pushed me aside to slap Bosa hard on his back.

"Don't you dare touch her, you ugly brute," she said in her harsh, rasping voice.

He looked shocked as Datla Nuri lifted the woman to her feet. She still had her head bent, her eyes closed and her face blank, but I was relieved that she was breathing. Datla Nuri bared her buckteeth as if to say if Bosa dared so much as twitch, she wouldn't hesitate to sink them into his neck. Then she led the woman inside the cabin. It took Bosa Khuni some time to regain his composure.

"Already we've a collaborator on board. Are we going to have a Bihari serpent among us too? Don't you know what their kind is capable of doing to us?"

"Don't be so paranoid, Bosa. She's just a poor girl. What harm can she do to us?" said the teacher.

"I don't trust her kind," said Bosa. "If it were up to me, I'd cut her throat. But at least we should get rid of her."

"For one thing, we don't know that she's a Bihari," said the teacher. "Even if she is, she's in our care now. No one should lift a finger to her or molest her. Is that understood?"

"With due respect, sir," said Bosa. "I heard some boys saying that the Pakistanis and the Biharis are squashing us like flies, because we Bengalis are full of soft gibberish. I tend to agree with them, sir."

"I'm not surprised that *you* agree with them, Bosa," said the teacher. "If we become beasts like them, then what's the point of having a country of our own? Aren't we trying to have something better?"

For a moment I thought I was hearing Zomir Ali, because the teacher sounded so much like him. I could see that Bosa Khuni was very annoyed at being lectured; he mumbled and walked away. It was still raining, but no one could bring himself to go inside the cabin to fetch out the straw and bamboo hats. When the teacher asked me to get them, I was upset. It was as if I was thought to be without manly feelings – that somehow it didn't matter if I came upon a young woman changing her clothes. But I didn't disobey the teacher and tiptoed my way inside the cabin. Already Datla Nuri had partitioned it by hanging jute sacks at the rear end. Now the part where the clay stove lay, and where Datla Nuri had done her cooking earlier, was blocked to view. I could hear gentle movements of feet on the wet cabin floor and the faint rustle of clothes.

"Is that you, Nephew?"

I grunted from the back of my throat to announce my presence.

"Fetch me a pail of water. Hurry up."

I brought the water and stood outside the curtain of jute sacks.

"Don't come in. This is a women's area now. Leave the pail outside."

I left the pail outside the partition, collected the straw and bamboo hats, and went to the foredeck. I handed a hat to everyone, but Asad Khan refused to take his, saying they were for peasants, and that he would rather get wet than look like a stupid bumpkin. Luckily for him, the rain stopped, and the sun came out. I was sent inside again to fetch dry clothes for everyone.

As soon as he'd changed his clothes, Ala Mullah placed a small rush mat towards the prow and began his evening prayer in silence. Asad Khan passed behind him to sit alone on the stem post. In the middle of the deck, Ducktor Malek and the teacher sat cross-legged on a rattan mat. Bosa Khuni squatted beside them as he prepared a hookah. I leaned over the gunwale, behind the praying Mullah. Everything was eerily quiet until a flock of wild geese flew low over us, quacking. My eyes were drawn to the water, to a clear patch between clusters of throbbing lily leaves, and there I looked at the reflection of the evening playing itself out in orange and purple.

I'd seen bubbles, but assumed that they were made by fish, and jumped and nearly fell backwards when Joker suddenly surfaced. He snorted and clambered on board, and then shook himself, spraying water all over me. Bosa Khuni laughed.

"He's a funny one. He even looks like a joker," he said.

I thumped my foot on the deck just inches away from Joker's wet, brown nose to show him that I was annoyed with him. He scuttled away to the Majee brothers on the rear deck. Asad Khan stayed where he was; Ala Mullah came and sat cross-legged with the teacher and Ducktor Malek; and I squatted beside Bosa Khuni. The teacher passed the hookah to Ducktor Malek, who puffed it vigorously, blowing out dense smoke through his nose. In the meantime, the Majee brothers had untethered the boat and started to punt through the bed of hyacinths and lilies.

Handing the hookah to Bosa Khuni, Ducktor Malek said, "We can't just idle away our days, smoking hookah and looking at the water."

"I agree, Ducktor. You are the man of jatra. Why don't you do something to keep us amused?" said the teacher.

"Yes, I was thinking that we should stage a jatra. Everyone will have a part in it. What do you think?"

Before the teacher could answer, Bosa Khuni said, "I don't know about the others, but I can't act or sing."

"Bosa, you surprise me. I never thought of you as a sissy-missy big baby," said Ducktor Malek.

"Say what you like, Ducktor, but I don't want to make a fool of myself."

"I assure you, Bosa, you wouldn't be making a fool of yourselves. I tell you, and I ought to know, everyone can act or sing in their own way. But if you don't feel comfortable with such traditional theatrical methods, no problem. You can just mime, dance or whatever. Besides, no one will be looking at us. We'll only be amusing ourselves."

Bosa Khuni shook his head; I was worried too. How could I be in a jatra without a mouth? I was hoping that the teacher would kill off the idea, but it wasn't to be.

"You're on, Ducktor," he said. "We'll have a go. What jatra do you have in mind?"

Half closing his eyes, Ducktor Malek played with his thick, drooping moustache.

"How about the *Ramayana*?" he said. "Have you read it, Abbas Mia?"

"Yes, I have. Kamal has read it too." Then he looked at me. "Haven't you, Kamal?"

Yes, I'd read it and indicated so with a nod of my head.

"That's wonderful. Perhaps, the three of us could work together to make a jatra out of it. You know, shape it in a way that suites all tastes."

"That sounds good, Ducktor," said the teacher.

It wasn't dark yet. All around the boat, the purple hyacinth flowers fluttered gently and consorted with the mauve of the evening. As far as the eye could see, there was nothing but the sky, water clogged with vegetation, and scattered clumps of trees, their canopies hanging over the water. Our boat, punted from both sides of the hull by the Majee brothers, was making slow progress towards the island, which still lay some distance away. Asad Khan lifted himself from the stem post and walked towards us.

"I don't want anything to do with the *Ramayana*. It's a Hindu book," he said. "You haven't got your Bangladesh yet. And already you want to turn us into kaffirs and infidels."

Bosa Khuni, who was puffing the hookah, popped his red, bulging eyes out at Asad Khan and snorted.

"Look, who's talking? A bloody collaborator," he said. "I don't know much about *Ramayana*, Ducktor. But count me in. Perhaps, I can play a silent part."

"You can't allow lower classes to talk to me like this, Abbas Mia."

Asad Khan bit his lips, pushed his chin hard against his throat, breathed heavily and waited for a response from the teacher.

"Everyone is equal within the boundary of this boat. All have the right to free speech too," said the teacher. "If we don't cherish these values, there is no point of having Bangladesh."

"Has everyone gone blind? Can't you see that the whole Bangladeshi thing is an Indian conspiracy? They want to turn us into Hindus and kaffirs. I thought you would've had more sense, Abbas Mia," Asad Khan said.

Ducktor Malek gave such a loud, sarcastic laugh it sounded like the thunder that had regularly exploded over us since the beginning of the rains. Asad Khan turned around and started to walk back towards the prow. Ducktor Malek called him back.

"Come, come here. I'd hate to lose a cast member on a matter of political or theological dispute. I'm sure Valmiki took a lot of poetical license when he composed the *Ramayana*. For instance, the *Puranas* say nothing about Sita's exile, and yet Valmiki did exile her. We can do the same. If you like, you can, perhaps, play the demon king Ravana. And, contrary to Valmiki's version, make him vanquish Rama. How does that sound to you?"

Asad Khan looked back, his chin still pressed hard against his throat. "You can't talk me into it with your fancy talk, Ducktor. Remember that I'm a pure Muslim of Arabian origin. If you think you can drag me into your polluting Hindu nonsense, you're in cloud-cuckoo-land."

In his haste to reach the prow Asad Khan nearly stepped on Joker, who gave a shrill cry, scuttled over the deck, and jumped into the water.

Ducktor Malek shook his head and turned to Ala Mullah. "Do you think I'm trying to pollute you, Mullah? My way of calling Allah may not be very conventional, but I am just as much a Muslim as anyone here. All I'm trying to do is entertain people, but what thanks do I get for it? Funny, how it's always us artists who get the blame."

Ala Mullah shrugged his shoulders as if he hadn't a clue what Ducktor was on about.

"I hope you're not thinking of burning me at the stake, Mullah."

" How can you say that Ducktor? I am only a poorly educated mullah, but I esteem your talent. You are the best actor in our swamplands."

"So, you will take a part in the *Ramayana*," said Ducktor Malek.

"I wish I could, Ducktor. It'd be an honour to play alongside a legendary actor such as yourself. But as a professional man of religion my position is rather sensitive."

Ducktor Malek received the hookah once more from the teacher. He shook his long, curly hair and took a puff.

"So, what are you saying, Mullah? You're also dumping me like chicken shit. Spare me your bloody flattery. I can see through you, you know. You are just as bad as Asad Khan. You are worried about appearing in a so-called Hindu play, aren't you?"

"Don't be unfair, Ducktor. If I were a communalist I'd have joined the ranks of the collaborators. It'd have made me rich and powerful. Instead, I'm in this boat with you," said the Mullah. "You must know that I've utmost respect for our Hindu brothers, but I'm an Islamic preacher."

"Forgive me, Mullah, for hurting your sensibilities. You are indeed the most open-minded mullah in our swampland. A beacon of hope for inter-faith harmony," said Ducktor Malek, rubbing his enormous belly. "Now the matter of the Jatra. If we are creative we can easily solve this little problem. Perhaps, you can take poetic licence with the story as well. Perhaps you can play Rajarishi Vishvamitra. You know, Rama's teacher. Perhaps, you can replace him with an Islamic saint of your choice. Think about that, eh?"

The teacher looked worried; he coughed and changed his posture.

"I don't want to interfere with your artistic decisions, Ducktor, but isn't the question of poetic licence getting a bit out of hand? After so many poetic licences, I wonder how much of the *Ramayana* would be left? Besides, it is a sacred text of the Hindus. We mustn't upset their religious sensibilities. We have to be extra careful in this regard, Ducktor, as we've two Hindus among us."

He was talking about the Majee brothers, but I'm sure it crossed his mind that my birth parents could have been Hindus, though in his household no one raised the subject. Not even Ata Banu had dared do so when she was angry with me. I was neither converted to Islam, nor was I circumcised. I have always been very careful about my privacy, but once after fishing, while changing my lungi, Big Suban saw my nakedness. He said, "How come you look like a Hindu, Kamal?" As soon as he said this he bit his tongue and never mentioned the subject again.

It was almost dark when we reached the island. I went inside the cabin. Datla Nuri and the veiled woman were still behind the curtain of jute sacks. I heard a scraping sound and realised that Datla Nuri was scaling the carp. I also heard her giving instructions – which must have been to the veiled woman – for turmeric roots to be ground to paste. The only noise I heard came from Datla. Was the veiled woman really, like me, without the gift of speech? Or, was she one of the Biharis who were going around with the Pakistani army and the collaborators, slaughtering us? I heard again the buzzing of the prayers in the school yard before the soldiers had gone through the lines with clubs and bayonets; and I trembled with rage. I felt like dragging her out by the hair to Bosa Khuni and screaming: she's all yours, Bosa, do as you please with this Bihari whore.

"Is that you, Nephew?" asked Datla Nuri. "What's wrong with you? Why are you breathing so hard?"

When she came from behind the curtain, I turned my back on her and set about filling the hurricane lamps with kerosene. She came around and looked at me.

"What's going on in your head, Nephew? Tell me the truth?"

One by one I lit the four hurricane lamps without meeting her eyes, and hung three from the hooks across the cabin. As I was about to go out with the remaining lamp, she said, "Is the girl bothering you, Nephew? You can trust me. I promised Ata Banu that I'd look out for you."

I went outside with the lamp. It was dark now and the Majee brothers, having secured the boat for the night, were joining the rest of the men on the foredeck; Joker, squeaking gently, followed them. I climbed onto the cabin roof and sat leaning against the mast pole. Despite the rumbling, the sky was clear. In the light of the half moon I could see the dark, bluish shadows of the island's clumps of trees. I could even see a few stars in the sky. People were talking on the foredeck, but I didn't want to listen to them, so I went to lie on the stem-post. Now their voices softened into murmurs, except when Ducktor Malek spoke. He sounded like distant thunder. I tried to listen to the lapping of the water against the hull, but couldn't prevent the memories from the last few days dragging me down in the floodplain full of clotted blood. I didn't want to drown, but how was I to surface with so many garlands of bones around my neck? How I wished for Moni Banu, for her to tell me: Take my hand, Beautiful One, I will lift you up.

I don't know what had happened then, but later Datla Nuri told me that I had started making terrible noises. Like the bull, she said, when he had his throat cut on Moni Banu's marriage. She and the men had restrained me and taken me inside the cabin where I fell asleep. It was not until supper time that Datla Nuri woke me. I didn't feel like eating, but couldn't go back to sleep.

Everyone was inside the cabin now. Three of the hurricane lamps, their flames throbbing gently, were still dangling from the same hooks on the roof where I'd hung them earlier. They'd moved the fourth one from outside to the mast post, which rose from the deck and went through the cabin. On the rattan mat sat Ducktor Malck, the teacher, Asad Khan and Ala Mullah in a circle; beside them on the bare planks of the deck squatted the Majee brothers and Bosa Khuni. Datla Nuri was serving them food.

"How's our visitor? Has she opened her mouth yet?" asked the teacher.

"She's fine, but she hasn't spoken yet," said Datla Nuri.

"What was she wearing under her veil?" asked Bosa Khuni.

Datla Nuri bared her buckteeth and hissed, "Why so interested in women's clothing, you ugly pervert?"

Ducktor gave one of his long, operatic laughs. Bosa Khuni lowered his head. Datla Nuri was about to go back behind the curtain, but Ducktor stopped her.

"Sister Nuri, we have a part for you in our jatra."

"You want me to dance shamelessly before you? I don't want you men ogling at me."

"No, no it's a serious jatra. Perhaps, you can play Sita. You know, she was the most virtuous woman of her time, who walked through fire to prove her chastity."

"She's too ugly and of shameful character to play Sita," said Bosa Khuni. "It'd be more appropriate for her to play one of the evil hags. Or one of the man-eating rakshasas."

Datla Nuri looked fiercely at Bosa Khuni, but the teacher stopped her before she could say anything.

"I'm fed up with you lot bickering all the time. We are doomed, you understand, doomed, if we don't get along with each other."

"Yes, yes, I agree. That's what the jatra is all about. Harmony," said Ducktor. He then turned to the Majee brothers.

"What parts do you two want to play?"

The Majee brothers looked at each other, terror-stricken.

"We are untouchables, you respectful Ducktor," said Harihar

162

Majee. "We are not allowed to recite the scriptures. If the Brahmans find out, we'll be in trouble, sir."

"There are no Brahmans on board. So, you should be all right. Besides, it's time that we do away with the matter of who's allowed and not allowed to read such and such books."

"We can't read, sir," said Bidudhar Majee.

"Yes, yes, I know. I didn't mean…"

Ala Mullah intervened before Ducktor could finish his sentence.

"*Ramayana* is a holy book of the Hindus, Ducktor," he said. "You can't just do what you please with it."

"Great art is born when you take risks with the stories of the past. I don't want to settle for a second-rate production of the *Ramayana*. Nothing short of originality will do."

Now quite a few people tried to speak at the same time, but they backed down when the teacher raised his voice.

"We are not getting anywhere with this discussion. We should thank Ducktor Malek for coming up with the idea of staging the *Ramayana*. It should bring us together rather than separate us." He then turned to Ducktor Malek. "You are the director. You decide who plays what role."

There was silence for a while until Bosa Khuni spoke.

"Will the Bihari woman be playing a role too?"

"We don't know that she's a Bihari, do we? So stop going on about it. Yes, everyone will play a role," said the teacher.

"What kind of jatra will it be? Kamal and the new woman don't speak. Bosa doesn't want a speaking part either. And the rest of us, apart from you, Ducktor, can't sing a note. Besides, I wonder how many of us are capable of speaking our lines," said Ala Mullah.

"This is not a problem, Mullah," said Ducktor. "Perhaps we should get rid of singing and speaking altogether. Perhaps, we should have a silent jatra. In fact, for some time now I've been thinking of doing such an experiment. It would be a wonderful and innovative jatra."

Then he said, "Oh, Sister Nuri, do you have some of your excellent rice and carp curry left? I haven't yet filled a quarter of my stomach. A man of my size requires a bit more food, you know."

"You greedy eater. You're worst than my ducks. Hasn't the school yard made any difference to you? All you're interested in is filling your huge sack of a stomach. You should be ashamed of yourself, Ducktor."

Datla Nuri then turned on Ala Mullah and Bosa Khuni who were licking their plates and waiting to see if Ducktor made any headway.

"Hey, you two. Stop licking your plates like skinny dogs! Go and wash your hands. I have only one portion left for my nephew."

"We're in a fine mess," Ducktor said. "Honestly, this war is nothing but a farcical theatre. It's even making a politician out of the likes of Datla Nuri. Fine mess."

"What? I don't understand what you're saying, Ducktor," said Bosa Khuni. "But what I say is that we can't starve ourselves to death because our enemies have done such a bad job on so many of our people. Even in hell a man's got to eat, isn't it?"

Ala Mullah was feeling uneasy at what both Ducktor Malek and Bosa Khuni were saying. He hurriedly got up with his plate and went out to the foredeck to wash it and his hand. Soon all of them went there; I was still pretending to be asleep. Datla Nuri left a plate of food by my side and withdrew behind the curtain.

Joker came in whimpering, made some birdlike squeaks, and frantically started to sniff around. He'd taken a liking to the left corner at the front of the cabin, where there was a heap of dry hay. He kept circling the area, chattering all the time. Suddenly a strong but sweetish smell wafted my way. At first I thought Joker was just peeing, then I realised that he was smearing his musk to carve out a little home for himself in this large cavern of a cabin. He then licked and nuzzled his fur for a while and became quiet.

I got up and looked at him. He was rolled into a ball and was sleeping. Up until now I hadn't been carrying my slate around, but for some reason after seeing Joker, I came back and hung it around my neck. I took one of the hurricane lamps from the roof and went out to the foredeck to join the men.

The night was much clearer than it had been during recent days. There were many stars in the sky. The half-moon throbbed in the clear patches of water between the vegetation. Everyone asked me how I was. I was fine, I wrote on the slate. Bosa Khuni asked what I'd written.

"He's fine," said Ducktor Malek in his theatrical way.

"Bloody hell," said Bosa, "he didn't need writing to say that."

"You illiterate brute," said Asad Khan, "you'll go to your grave like an ignorant cow."

"When I cut your throat we'll see who bawls like a cow."

Once again the teacher had to raise his voice to stop them bickering.

As there was no toilet facility on board, the Majee brothers had placed a gangplank to the island. First to go was Ducktor Malek. He carried a hurricane lamp in one hand, a spouted pot in the other. His enormous bulk went lumbering over the creaking gangplank. As soon as the flicker of his lamp disappeared behind the darkened line of trees, Asad Khan cleared his throat to speak.

"It's the likes of that no-good Ducktor that put us in this mess. If they hadn't dabbled in Hindu things, and hadn't tainted our pure Islam, we would be all right. It's the likes of him that gives the Pakistanis plenty reason to suspect all Bengalis. You know, as polluters of Islam."

Anticipating Bosa Khuni's response, the teacher intervened.

"I've told you, and I'm telling you again. No bickering, no backbiting in this boat. I don't want to hear these sorts of things again. Understood?"

Asad Khan trotted down the gangplank onto the island without a lamp. I presumed he just needed a pee. He came back shortly and, without exchanging a word with anyone, went inside the cabin. There was no sign of Ducktor coming back.

Ala Mullah pulled a pail of water from the side of the boat. While doing his ablutions for the night prayer, he kept muttering to himself: Islam is a religion of peace.

I went up to Ala Mullah and wrote on my slate, "Are you all right?"

"I'm not a learned person like you, Kamal. I don't even know much of what is written in our holy book, but I've followed Allah with my heart. How could Allah care for such things as pollution? He loves all, doesn't he, Kamal?"

I touched Ala Mullah on his shoulder and wrote, "Of course, He loves everyone."

"Thank you, Kamal. You must be very close to Allah."

I almost asked him, the way I used to ask Sona Mia: Would I be close to Allah even if I was a Hindu?

He finished his ablutions, placed his prayer mat in the same position as before, and began praying. From time to time he sobbed. After his prayer he looked fine, as though whatever was bothering him had disappeared.

Teacher began to worry that Ducktor Malek had not reappeared and asked me to go to look for him. I went into the cabin to fetch one of the lamps. Bosa Khuni was already waiting for me on the gangplank. We hadn't got far before we spotted a light.

"Is that you, Ducktor?" shouted Bosa Khuni.

"Can't a man have some peace and quiet while he relieves himself?"

"We were worried for you. So we came to look for you," said Bosa Khuni.

"I was just finalising the casting for the jatra. And thinking what adjustments I must make to stage it in silence. It's a big artistic challenge, you know."

Ducktor and I came back to the boat. Bosa Khuni stayed behind to settle his accounts with nature. Once he was back, the teacher, Ala Mullah and the Majee brothers paid their visits to the island. Soon most had gone inside the cabin to sleep; only Ducktor and I were left on the foredeck.

"I want you to play Hanuman, the monkey warrior."

"Why Hanuman?" I wrote.

"He's loyal and dutiful. He's righteous and brave. I think he has a lot of potential for conveying very serious moral lessons. His character also takes the lead in quite a few big action scenes. I thought you might enjoy them."

"Have you considered that I might simply be taken as a comic figure? When I do my monkey walk with bent legs and hanging hands, I'm sure to make people laugh. Whatever serious character motivation I might have would come to nothing. The same would happen with the action scenes. When I pretend to fly through the air, carry the mountain on my back, fight the demons in my monkey style, spy on Lanka to locate the whereabouts of Sita, or finally set fire to Lanka with my tail, I will just be a comic figure. People will laugh," I wrote.

"You can fashion the character in any way you like. I believe in giving my actors maximum freedom with their roles. Anyway, comedy has great merit. You know, you can expose a lot of serious stuff through laughter."

"Not, if the laughter is unintentional. Not if people laugh because the actor appears ridiculous when he might be trying to be serious," I wrote.

"Don't give me a hard time, Kamal. I was expecting trouble from the others, but not from you. Just sleep on the character. I'm sure you will find a way of playing it that agrees with your temperament."

We didn't speak for a while. I was listening to the crickets chirping from the island.

"I'm still very hungry, Kamal. That Datla Nuri woman doesn't understand the needs of large people."

I was still listening to the crickets.

"Are you going to eat your portion of rice and carp curry, Kamal? You know, I can't think creative thoughts with my stomach empty."

I went inside the cabin to fetch my portion of the supper. Ala Mullah, the teacher, and Asad Khan were sleeping in the middle of the cabin. The Majee brothers were asleep near Joker. The three of them were snoring gently as though echoing one another. There was light behind the curtains. I could hear the women moving, but they didn't speak.

Ducktor Malek almost snatched the plate from me, hunched over it, and plunged his hand into it. He made vigorous squelching noises and got through the plate within minutes. He then licked his fingers and belched.

"My stomach is not quite full yet, but you have given me some peace of mind, Kamal. Now at least I can have some good artistic thoughts about the jatra."

Ducktor Malek leaned against the side of the hull and lit the hookah. I was about to sit next to him when I heard Datla Nuri.

"Are you there, Nephew?" she said. "We want to do our nature visit before sleeping. The jungle here looks very evil type. Would you accompany us?"

Datla Nuri came to the foredeck, carrying the fish-cutter and a large bundle wrapped with straw. The new woman, who was no longer wearing a veil, came behind her with her head down. She was wearing one of Datla Nuri's new saris, but its corner was drawn in a way that I still couldn't see her face. She carried a lamp and the spouted pot.

Datla Nuri didn't see the plate on the deck. She kicked it as she came between Ducktor Malek and I.

"Have you just had your dinner now, Nephew?"

I nodded my head to say yes.

"I hope you are telling the truth, Nephew. If I find out that greedy Ducktor has gobbled it, I will split his stomach open." And she waved the fish-cutter at him.

"I promise you, Sister Nuri. I haven't eaten a single grain from Kamal's plate," said Ducktor, almost stuttering.

I went ahead with a lamp over the gangplank; Datla Nuri and the new woman followed behind. Datla Nuri asked me to wait behind a bush. She and the new woman went further on. I couldn't see their light, but after a while heard a scraping sound as though someone was moving earth. When they emerged, Datla Nuri wasn't carrying the bundle any more.

"Did you hear any noise, nephew?"

I nodded my head to say yes.

"But I'm telling you, you heard nothing. Understand?"

I wondered what she had done with the bundle. Perhaps, it contained the new woman's clothes, and she had just buried them. I suspected that Datla Nuri had found out that the new woman was a Bihari, and that she was trying to protect her. I didn't say anything as we walked back to the boat, but I was thinking of coming back later to check what Datla Nuri had buried.

The women had gone to sleep. Ducktor Malek was on the foredeck, humming a song.

"I can't sleep, Kamal. Would you take me out for a trip in the dinghy?"

I wasn't sleepy myself, so I agreed. I took one of the lamps, hung the slate round my neck and we set off.

There were more stars in the sky now. The floodplains looked greyish blue under the half-moon. The crickets were still chirping from the island, but as I punted the dinghy away from it, and beyond a dense patch of hyacinths and lilies, and paddled into a clearing, their sound became a faint echo in the night. In the distance I could see small fires spurting out of the floodplains. I knew that they were formed from the gases of rotting vegetation, and yet they still sent shivers up my spine. I wondered if Moni Banu was still as scared of them as we were in our childhood.

I paddled to the end of the clearing and stopped by a clump of kash grass. Ducktor Malek hadn't said a word since we had left the boat. I could only hear his heavy breathing. I dug the punt-pole into the mud-bed and tethered the dinghy to it. I then sat on a plank in front of him. He took the coconut hookah, lit it slowly, and began puffing on it.

"Why did you lie for me, Kamal?"

"I don't know," I gestured. Then I wrote, "I suppose I didn't want you to get into trouble with Datla Nuri."

"Is that so?" he asked, and kept on puffing on his hookah. After a while he said, "I'm so tired, Kamal. All I want is to sleep and sleep, but I'm scared of closing my eyes."

"You have to take some rest, Ducktor. You need a clear head for the jatra," I wrote.

"Yes, yes the jatra. It's been helping me to keep my eyes open, you know."

"It might help us to sleep as well," I wrote.

"Perhaps. Once we are drawn into the characters in a jatra, whose lives are very different from our own, we can perhaps forget ours. On the other hand, we might be prompted to see those characters as reflections of ours. Isn't that what's happening now, Kamal? Aren't we squabbling over the roles for precisely this reason?"

"Sorry, Ducktor. I merely raised questions about my role because I thought you had serious intentions with Hanuman. I believed that a monkey role with my appearance couldn't be anything but comical."

"I had no such serious intentions, Kamal. I jumped at the teacher's suggestion because I felt it would help me to keep my eyes open."

He was waiting for me to write something on the slate, but I looked out over the floodplains. I was trying to understand why he wanted to keep his eyes open.

"Anyway, what do I know about the *Ramayana*. I haven't even read the work," he said. "Someone told me the story once. For all I know it could be his own version. Perhaps, it had nothing to do with the original."

I could keep from the question no longer. "Why don't you want to close your eyes, Ducktor?" I wrote.

He puffed for a long time on the hookah.

"I don't know, Kamal,' he said at last. "Perhaps because I fear that if I close my eyes the things that I saw in the school yard will become real for me. Do you understand that, Kamal?"

"But you were there, Ducktor. Doesn't that make it real?"

"When they started to go through the lines with clubs and bayonets, people began to pray. But all the time I was thinking about the parts I played in the jatras over the years. You see, I was in the middle of the line and they were taking a very long time to reach me. You were there, weren't you, Kamal? So, you must have seen how long it was taking them."

He took a break and puffed on his hookah.

"For some reason a role I played in my youth suddenly came to me, and then I became stuck with it. It was going round and round in my mind. It was from the popular jatra, *Nabob Shirajudulla*. I wasn't playing the heroic Nabob, but his treacherous general Mir Jafar. I remembered having acted the role in a comic vein. You see, I used a very high-pitched, womanly voice for him. Besides, I rolled my eyes and did my silly walks as Mir Jafar went about his treachery and betrayal, selling our country to the English for two hundred years. I remembered the audience doubling over with laughter at my antics. Later, many of them complimented me, saying that they didn't know that villains could be so funny."

He stopped, puffed on the hookah, and tried to look into my eyes. "When the two soldiers who were doing the clubbing and bayoneting came to me, I was still chuckling. Just at that moment, as luck would have it, the commanding officer called one of the soldiers back. You know, the one who was doing the bayonet job. The commanding officer had found someone alive at the beginning of the line. He called the bayonet man back to finish him off. As a result, the one who was doing the club job faced me on his own. He didn't know what to make of me. So, he paused. He asked me in Urdu why I was laughing, and not praying like the rest. I kept on chuckling. He poked my stomach with his club and said, 'You must have grown this on swine fat, you motherfucking heathen.' I don't know what motivated him to act like this, but then he said he wanted to spare someone. Curiously he wanted that someone to be the most wicked and evil-looking heathen he came across. Apparently, I was that. 'You look like the bastard son of the devil himself,' he said. He spat in my face and asked me to move back to the line behind. You see, they had already gone through that line and the commanding officer had checked it out. He clubbed me on the head, kicked me to the ground and dragged a few bodies over me. I don't remember much afterwards. I must have fallen asleep. I only woke up just before you crawled over me."

He put new tobacco in his hookah and lit it.

"Now do you see why I don't want to close my eyes? It's strange, but real things happen to me when I close my eyes. Otherwise, I can pretend that I am just playing roles in some jatras."

He didn't say anything for a long time. I asked him if it would help if I paddled the dinghy a bit. He didn't even look at the slate. I pushed the dinghy away from the bed of hyacinths and lilies, and began paddling in the clearing. I stroked the water lightly and at an even pace. Within moments, the dinghy was gliding over the water as if carried downriver on a placid current. I went round and round the clearing, hoping that Ducktor Malek would fall asleep. He would stay quiet with his head down for a long time, but every now and then, as though from the verge of sleep, he would jerk his head up, and reach for his hookah.

Suddenly it went very dark and the wind picked up. I raced the dinghy, but was caught up in the rain before I could reach the boat. Everyone was asleep in the cabin. I dried myself and lay down to sleep between the curtain that marked the women's area and the group in the middle of the cabin. Despite there being a lot of empty room near the middle group, Ducktor Malek settled himself near the Majee brothers and Joker. Instead of lying down, he sat cross-legged as though getting ready for meditation. Sensing his presence, Joker whimpered and chattered for a while, but soon got back to his synchronised breathing with the brothers. I wanted to fall asleep listening to the rain, but all I could hear was Bosa Khuni's snoring from our side of the cabin, and Datla Nuri's from the other. When I had just about got used to their snoring, Ducktor Malek let out a strange noise. It sounded like the sudden bark of a dog. From then on he kept making that sound at regular intervals. Every time he did so, Joker woke up, and whined and squeaked until getting back to his synchronised breathing with the brothers.

I could hear everyone on either side of the curtain. Obviously, those who snored were easy to tell. With some effort I could identify the rest by their breathing, except the new woman. I kept my ear cocked to the curtain for a long time without picking up even the faintest sign of a living body beside Datla Nuri. She seemed to be hiding even when she slept. I thought I was the silent one, but compared to her I was full of noise.

CHAPTER 13

When I opened my eyes, everyone, except Ducktor Malek, was already up and had left the cabin. He was still sitting cross-legged, his eyes closed. Joker must have sprayed a lot of musk during the night as its sweetness was quite penetrating and unpleasant. I bent in front of Ducktor, thinking that he was sleeping.

"What is it, Kamal?" he said, opening his eyes.

"Haven't you slept at all?" I wrote.

"Now and then I must have dozed off for a minute or so. Every time, though, I was able to wake up before things became real."

"Aren't you tired?" I wrote.

"Perhaps not fully rested, but I had my calm periods. It's enough to keep me going."

We went to the foredeck together. It was a bright and clear morning. Ducktor Malek took the spouted pot and lumbered down the gangplank onto the island. I was getting desperate to relieve myself, because Ducktor was taking his time as he had done the previous night. I decided to go to the women's area to borrow their spouted pot. I parted the curtain and saw Datla Nuri, whose back was to me, hunched over the clay stove, frying puffed rice. The new woman, also turned away from me, was cutting onion with the chopper. Her head wasn't covered with the corner of her sari. Both she and Datla Nuri turned.

"Didn't I tell you that this is women's area?" screamed Datla.

I took the spouted pot and made her understand that I came to borrow it.

"You mustn't come in here," she said harshly. "Take it and get out."

I felt unnerved, not because of Datla Nuri's harsh words, but because of the way the new woman had stared at me. Hers wasn't a look of disgust – which I've had a lot of in my life – nor was it of pity. Her eyes just looked at me without connecting or saying anything. She was like an empty shell, someone whose memories had abandoned her. How was I to feel towards her?

It wasn't difficult to locate the spot where Datla Nuri had buried the bundle the night before. All I had to do was dig it up and reveal her secrets. But even if she proved to be a Bihari, what was I to do? As I stood over it I felt a shiver run through me as the wind rustled the canopy above, making me remember the buzzing of the voices from the school yard. I was getting drunk with thoughts of revenge. I imagined running to the foredeck with her dirty secrets, exposing her as one of those devious, bloodthirsty Biharis. No, I wouldn't hesitate at all. I imagined holding her head and pressing it tightly against the gunwale while Bosa Khuni severed it with his machete, blood spurting into the hole of my face. I looked again at the spot where the bundle was buried. Now all I could see were the empty eyes. How could you dig for empty eyes? My hands trembled as I tried to dig up the soil. Yes, there was nothing but the empty eyes, so I walked away.

Back on the foredeck, the teacher was getting anxious that we hadn't yet started moving. Datla Nuri and the new woman, her sari drawn over her face, brought in the fried puffed rice.

"Let's see your face. What are you hiding there?" asked Bosa Khuni.

"Leave her alone, you ugly face," said Datla Nuri.

"Be careful, Sister Nuri, there's a war on. If you protect enemies, you become one too," he said.

"Are you threatening me, you cowardly cutthroat? I'm not scared of you."

We waited for a long while for Ducktor Malek to return from the island to begin our breakfast. I was now desperately hungry and wanted to stuff myself as soon as the teacher served me the bowl of puffed rice, but the idea of eating in front of people was still difficult for me. I was playing with the grains with my fingers; as usual, the teacher noticed.

"Nobody will mind you here, Kamal. You're among friends," he said, and looked at everyone present. All of them nodded their heads, except Asad Khan, who pressed his chin against his throat.

"Go ahead, Kamal. Don't mind us," said Ducktor Malek.

I pulled my neck backwards, brought my face parallel to the sky, and dropped a few grains of puffed rice inside my mouth. I don't know if anyone was looking at me. There was silence, except for the noise of jaws moving, and waves lapping against the hull. I was munching with my back teeth and looking at a cloud, high above in the sky. It was Ducktor Malek who broke the silence.

"Good news, everyone. You'll be pleased to know that I've finalised the casting. I must say the divine muse has been very kind. Very kind, indeed, to me."

"I hope you haven't given the role of Sita to that ugly witch," said Bosa Khuni.

"I'm not giving it to her. Mind you, on purely artistic grounds. I thought the new woman would be more suitable for the role."

"You can't do that, Ducktor. She could be our Bihari enemy. You can't make her the heroine of our jatra," said Bosa Khuni.

"Don't question my artistic judgement, Bosa. If you cared for such things, I'd tell you that my judgement has been an inspired one. Consider the matter carefully. Like Sita the new woman is young. Although we haven't seen her face properly yet, I suspect that she is pretty too. If you dismiss both the women on board for Sita's role, then what do we do, Bosa? You must agree that we can't have Ramayana without Sita." Ducktor paused for a while, then continued, "We can have a solution to our dilemma if you volunteer to dress up as a woman and play Sita yourself."

Everyone broke into laughter at that.

"Yes, yes, you've thought of something right for a change, Ducktor. It's appropriate that an ugly brute like him plays a Hindu princess. He'll do justice to her heathenness," said Asad Khan.

Bosa Khuni popped out his already bulging red eyes, but before he could open his mouth the teacher said, "Ducktor is the director. If he thinks that the new woman is the most suitable here for Sita's role, then we should go along with this. We must obey his artistic judgement."

I was still eating my puffed rice and looking at the sky. An osprey was circling below the clouds, swooping down and disappearing only to appear again, maybe looking for fish, or just playing around.

"If the new woman is dumb, chances are that she's deaf too. In that case, how will you explain the role to her?" asked Ala Mullah.

Ducktor Malek munched his puffed rice and played with his drooping moustache.

"Thank you, Mullah, for drawing this to my attention. This is indeed a problem. We must find a way of communicating with her."

"Perhaps Kamal can assist you in this regard, Ducktor," said the teacher. "He has grown up managing his affairs in silence."

"That's excellent," said Ducktor. "His knowledge of the *Ramayana* and his expertise in silent communication makes him an ideal candidate for our task."

He turned to me and said, "I appoint you as my assistant director, Kamal. In fact, I am giving you complete freedom with the interpretation of Sita's role. You convey to her the meaning of the role and instruct her how she must play it."

Ducktor Malek had finished his food and was greedily looking at the teacher's plates and mine, as the two of us hadn't finished yet. The teacher offered him some of his portion, but I wasn't going to give him any as I was very hungry myself.

"You haven't yet told us the roles we're playing, Ducktor," said the teacher.

"Oh, yes. The discussion on Sita has somewhat distracted me. Sorry, Abbas Mia," said Ducktor. "I have already asked Kamal to play Hanuman, haven't I, Kamal?"

Bosa Khuni tensed his face hard, as if to prevent laughter pouring out.

"Anything the matter, Bosa?" asked Ducktor.

"Nothing, Ducktor," said Bosa Khuni, and burst out laughing. Asad Khan followed with a short chuckle.

"What's the matter with you two? What's so funny?"

"What do you expect, Ducktor?" said Asad Khan, pushing his chin hard against his throat to contain his laughter. "How could one entertain deep thoughts at the sight of a Kamal monkey twirling his tail?"

"Don't underestimate laughter. It may contain serious thoughts, you know," said Ducktor.

"Don't confuse us with your gibberish, Ducktor. I don't want to laugh at Kamal, but a funny monkey is a funny monkey. Right?" said Bosa Khuni.

"You wait and see. Kamal will make a memorable characterisation of Hanuman." He looked at me. "Won't you, Kamal?"

I didn't look up, but kept drawing little stars on the slate.

"How about the other roles, Ducktor? Shall we get on with them?" asked the teacher.

Taking a look at the sun, by now a quarter of the way up in the eastern sky, the teacher asked the Majee brothers to prepare the boat for the next leg of our journey. Seeing them get up, Ducktor Malek halted them and said, "I better give you two your roles." He told Harihar he would be playing the role of Prince Lakshmana, Rama's loyal brother, who accompanied Rama and Sita into exile. To Bidudhar he gave the role of Prince Bharata, Rama's youngest brother, who ruled the Kingdom in Rama's absence.

"Solid princely roles for you two. What do you think, eh?"

"We're ignorant boatmen, you respectable Ducktor, we don't know much about scripture. But aren't these princes high-caste Hindus? Would it be appropriate for us untouchables to play them?" said Harihar. "Would we not be polluting their sanctity?"

"Nonsense," said Ducktor Malek. "Don't you know what this war is all about? Why we want Bangladesh?"

"We don't know much about politics, you respectable Ducktor. All we feel is that Bangladesh will be safer for us Hindus," said Harihar Majee.

"We don't feel very safe now," added Bidudhar Majee.

"Nobody feels safe now," said Ducktor. "But Bangladesh should be more than that. Isn't that so, Abbas Mia?"

"I hope so, Ducktor," said the teacher. He paused for a while as though trying to remember what Zomir Ali would have said at this moment. "I would love to see reason and a sense of justice guiding us in our new nation."

"What are those?" asked Bidudhar Majee.

The teacher puffed on his hookah, seemingly sunk in deep thought.

"If you don't mind, Abbas Mia, I'd like to clarify things a bit for the Majee brothers," said Ducktor. "You see, in Bangladesh you can be anything you want. If you want to worship a cow or eat it,

177

it wouldn't matter at all. In the same way, if you want to marry a Brahmin's daughter, and if she is agreeable, you can do that too. Same rights for everyone, understand? That's what this war is all about."

"Oh no, I don't want to marry a Brahmin's daughter," said Bidudhar Majee.

Ducktor Malek laughed.

"You're not telling the truth about Bangladesh, Ducktor," said Asad Khan. "It's a Hindu conspiracy against Islam. If Bangladesh comes, none of us Muslims would be able to eat cows. They'd turn us into bloody vegetarians. I bet they're even planning to put their idols in our mosques."

Bosa Khuni got up and took his machete out from his gunny sack. His bloodshot eyes protruded from their sockets so much that they seemed to be floating in the air.

"Just say the word, Ducktor," he said. "I'll give you this collaborator's head."

"Stop it," said the teacher. "We want to end precisely this kind of thing in Bangladesh." He turned to Ducktor. "Would you get on with your casting?"

"That's settled then," the Ducktor said to the Majee brothers. "You two will be Prince Lakshmana and Prince Bharata. We'll talk more about it later. For the time being, try to feel princely in everything you do. You know, walk and talk in a princely manner. Understand?"

The Majee brothers nodded and moved to the rear deck to start punting the boat.

"You Asad Khan, as we have discussed before, will play the demon king Ravana. And you Bosa, you will be his mighty brother Kimbukurna. You know, the one who wakes up only for a day in every six months, and devours everything in sight. This part will suit you very well, Bosa. You will sleep through most of the play, and when you get up, you will see some rousing action – and some gratuitous violence into the bargain."

"That sounds good to me, Ducktor. But can I have the same licence with my part as you are offering the others. Can I cut some collaborators' and Pakistanis' throats?"

"Yes, everyone is allowed some licence. But there is a problem with your request, Bosa. Whatever poetic licence we take with this play, we need to maintain its basic structure. You know, the struggle between good and evil. I'm afraid, Bosa, your role is on the side of evil. So, the characters you'll be slaying in the play belong to the side of good. Now, think carefully. If you do the things that you wish to do, you'll be butchering good guys. Do you want that?"

"No, no I don't want that, Ducktor. Can't you give me a role where I can cut plenty of throats, and still be one of the good fellas?"

It was the teacher who replied. "Ducktor has years of experience in jatras and plays. He has thought very deeply before offering you the role of Kimbukurna. If I were you, I would accept it."

Bosa Khuni shook his head, but didn't contest the teacher.

"If you want, you can add one or two comic touches of your own, Bosa. Besides, I leave it to you to devise your own methods of committing atrocities on the stage. All right?" said Ducktor.

"Shall we move to the next role, Ducktor?" said the teacher.

"Before you move on, I've a few things to say, Ducktor," said Asad Khan. "First of all, I'm not very happy to be Bosa Khuni's brother. Can I also use my poetic licence to change the name of my character? To me, Ravana sounds too Hindu. Instead, can I call myself Rahman? Obviously, Rahman can't represent the forces of evil. It will be a force for goodness. If I use the earlier poetic licence that you, Ducktor, granted me, my character will be victorious. Rahman, the forces of good, will beat his opposite number. That's all, Ducktor," said Asad Khan.

Bosa Khuni, who was squeezing his brows and flaring his nostrils while Asad Khan spoke, sneezed violently.

"What gibberish the bloody collaborator is saying? I don't get it. Shall I shove my machete down his throat, Ducktor?"

Ducktor Malek ignored Bosa Khuni; he seemed to be considering deeply the implications of what Asad Khan had said.

"You can speak your mind, but no violence in this boat. Please," said the teacher. Then he turned to Ducktor Malek.

"I don't know what you think, Ducktor, but there are limits to poetic licence. What Asad Khan is suggesting amounts to a communal war. I can't permit that in my boat."

"So, you want the Hindus to win?" said Asad Khan.

Ducktor Malek flicked his long curly hair and emerged from his deep thoughts.

"I agree with you, Abbas Mia. We can't encourage communal conflict here." Then he turned to Asad Khan. "You can have your poetic licence, as long as you don't make it communalistic. Beside being contrary to the spirit of Bangladesh, it wouldn't be very artistic."

Asad Khan wanted to speak again, but Bosa Khuni said, "We've had enough of your gibberish. Shut your mouth now."

The Majee brothers were waiting for Joker to come back on board before they began punting the boat. He must have gone far for his morning fishing. While Harihar Majee beat the water with his paddle, Bidudhar whistled, but there was no sign of him. Impatient with the delay, the teacher – with his hands behind his back – walked up and down the foredeck. From time to time he stopped, roofed his hand over his eyes, and looked out over the hyacinths and lilies. It was Ala Mullah who spotted Joker first and drew our attention to him.

Joker came on board with yet another catfish. He dropped it near Bidudhar Majee on the rear deck and shook himself, spraying water. He then looked up to Bidudhar Majee with his large, dark eyes and chattered. Bidudhar Majee bent down to stroke his small, round head. That seemed to please Joker; he arched his back and went around Bidudhar Majee in short leaps. The fish was alive, still wriggling on the deck. All the men now gathered on the rear deck to take a look at it. Datla Nuri, followed by the new woman, also came out of the cabin to see what was happening.

The Majee brothers dug in their punt-poles and we were on the move again. It was hard work to cut through the densely packed weeds. From time to time Bosa Khuni, Ala Mullah and I took turns to relieve them. We punted for hours but weren't making much progress. We were caught in a vast stretch of clogged-up vegetation. No matter where we looked, the flat, green expanse, with speckles of purple and white, went on and on.

After midday we reached a stretch where the vegetation floated in small clumps, leaving enough clear water for the oars. I took the rudder at the helm and the Majee brothers were on the oars. Asad Khan came over and sat by me, but facing away.

"I don't know what the other people tell you, but I think Abbas Mia has made a grave mistake. He shouldn't have taught you how to read and write. It's most unnatural," he said.

I just shrugged my shoulders.

"I bet book-reading has further messed up your already defective mind."

"I'm happy with my life, Mr Khan. I also feel very fortunate," I wrote on my slate.

"I find that hard to believe. I am sure you don't understand the meaning of half the things that you so childishly scribble on that silly slate of yours. You see, one can only be happy by staying true to one's own station in life. Allah has assigned us to a particular place in his scheme of things, and we mustn't tamper with it."

"What's my station, Mr Khan?" I wrote.

"Well, I don't want to upset you, Kamal. You might have acquired some sensitive feelings by reading books. I also think that you must be confused about your station in life. Especially by the way Abbas Mia has indulged you. But to be honest with you," Asad Khan paused and coughed to clear his throat, "your hideous looks indicate to me the utter emptiness of your life. It goes without saying that you're the lowest of the low."

"So, can I be happy, Mr Khan, if I stay true to my lowest of the low station?" I wrote.

"Well, what I said before is only a general rule. I doubt if that applies to a wretched creature like you. Besides, for all I know, you could be an untouchable Hindu. Anyway, you can never be happy or worth anything."

"Thank you, Mr Khan for talking to me," I wrote.

"It's my misfortune that I ended up in this stupid boat and having to talk to moronic brutes like you. I bet your lot will rule the country when Bangladesh comes," he said.

"So, you're not very happy, Mr Khan?" I wrote.

"How can I be? You –" Asad Khan stopped abruptly when he saw Bosa Khuni clambering over the cabin roof.

"I hope this collaborator is not messing you up with his gibberish, Kamal."

Asad Khan lowered his head and pushed his chin hard against his throat.

"On the contrary, Brother Bosa," I wrote. "Mr Khan has been very kind to me. He thinks I'm very happy and fortunate."

Bosa Khuni looked at the slate and shook his head.

"What has he written? Read it to me," he demanded.

Asad Khan paused and hesitated for a while.

"He writes that I'm kind to him," he said quietly, almost inaudibly.

"What did you say? I didn't hear it," said Bosa Khuni.

"Kamal has written that I'm kind to him," he said much more clearly.

"Is that all? To me, the writing looks much bigger than what I've heard from you. Don't keep things from me."

"Well. He has also written my view that he is happy and fortunate," mumbled Asad Khan and got up.

"You're lucky you didn't say anything bad to Kamal. Otherwise, I would have severed your stupid head."

Asad Khan hurried over the cabin roof to the foredeck. Bosa Khuni took charge of the rudder from me. I asked the Majee brothers with gestures about Joker's whereabouts. They hadn't seen him for a while and asked me to look for him. I went inside the cabin. Joker wasn't in his den, but I heard him chattering from behind the curtain. I also heard Datla Nuri's voice sounding unusually soft, as if she was talking to a baby. As ever, the new woman was silent. I stood by the curtain and grunted from the back of my throat.

"Nephew, is that you? Come and see Joker. He's so funny, like a naughty boy."

I remembered Datla Nuri's earlier prohibition, so I was hesitant about going in.

"Come, Kamal. Only you're allowed to come into our area. If that Asad Khan or Bosa Khuni try it, I'll break their legs."

I went in. The new woman tensed up and drew the corner of her sari over her head.

"Don't mind him," Datla Nuri said. "He's my nephew. He's one of us. I look out for him."

The new woman eased a bit, but kept her head covered. Joker was looking up to the women with his mischievous eyes and chattering. He looked at me, growled, and then ran to Datla Nuri, stood on his hind legs and rested his forepaws on her thigh. She stroked him and he whimpered like a baby. I tried to touch him, but he snorted at me and ran to the new woman.

"Don't be afraid of our Kamal," Datla Nuri said, as if talking to a human child. "He will never hurt you."

Joker had climbed into the new woman's lap and curled up. When she stroked his throat, he began to whistle so gently that for a moment I thought I was hearing a cat purring. She cocked her head slightly as if Joker was whispering some secret to her. When she looked at me earlier, her eyes were empty, but now there was a hint of something. I couldn't tell what it was: perhaps Joker evoked a feeling in her or she remembered something, but she no longer appeared like a pair of dead eyes. I don't know what made me want to try to stroke Joker again, but as soon as I touched his velvety coat he growled, and gave out a shrill whistle. He arched his back and wobbled out of the cabin.

Datla Nuri was hunched over the catfish curry, tasting the gravy. She called to the new woman, without turning to face her, "Hey Kulsum, pass me the salt."

So, her name was Kulsum and she was not deaf and dumb. It took Datla Nuri a while to realise what she had done. She turned towards me.

"You heard it, Nephew. It must stay between us. Poor Kulsum has no one in the world. We must look out for her," she whispered, her voice hissing through her buckteeth.

I wasn't really listening because so many questions were racing through my mind: Who was Kulsum? Was she really our enemy – a Bihari? Where had she come from? How had she ended up in the middle of the floodplain?

I tried to ask some of my questions in gestures, but Datla Nuri wasn't very keen to engage with me.

"Leave it for later, Nephew," she said. She sucked her buckteeth and continued, "I have an idea. Why don't you take us for a trip in your dinghy after lunch? If you bring your slate, Kulsum will be able to tell you more. She is a book-reader like you."

Kulsum was still squatting on her heels with her head down, but she cast a glance at me. She hadn't gone back to her blank looks. Nor had she recoiled in disgust as people usually do before they get used to my face. She looked as though she was totally destitute and in need of my protection.

I got up to leave the cabin. Datla Nuri asked me to tell the Majee brothers to stop the boat in a short while for lunch. It was already past midday. The heat from the water had climbed onto the foredeck. Ducktor Malek and the teacher were sitting on the rattan mat with their straw and bamboo hats on. Ala Mullah and Bosa Khuni were on the rear deck, helping the Majee brothers with the rowing of the boat. When I looked at Asad Khan, who was sitting on the cabin roof, he turned his face away. I could tell that he was feeling awkward about what had happened earlier.

We were still in relatively clear waters, but no longer alone. There were quite a few sampans ferrying people, and fishermen were out in their small dinghies, spreading or drawing their nets. There was a cargo boat, carrying earthen pots. I could see island villages dotted on this expanse of green, muddy water where people were going about their normal business. It was as if the people here weren't aware that only a few floodplains away there was a war on.

We stopped by a huddle of fishing dinghies; they asked us from which village we had come. Ducktor Malek told them our story. They gave us a basketful of small fish and offered to put us up in their village. Ducktor Malek was keen to stay around here, but the teacher wanted to move on still further to the north-east. Without much wind behind us, the boat was moving slowly with the laborious strokes of the oars. I wished I had a solitary place to hide for a while, because the way Kulsum had looked at me was still playing on my mind. Despite ours being a large cargo boat, there was no hiding place in it. I sat leaning over the gunwale, and looked at the gentle waves lapping against the hull.

Although I'd never regarded myself as being the lowest of the low, people often looked at me that way. Of course, there were many people who were kind to me; I had my share of affection too, but no one had ever appeared as though they were the destitute ones when they looked at me. In our childhood, Moni Banu sought my protection, but as we grew up it was she who protected me. Now this appeal in Kulsum's eyes was a real surprise. I didn't know what to make of it, but I wondered what had made her feel I could protect her.

We stopped in a stretch of shallows. Close by there was a fishing village with nets spread out along its banks. We could smell fish drying under the sun. All of us went inside the cabin for our lunch, except Joker who dived into the water for his.

"Has she spoken yet?" asked Ducktor Malek.

"We already have you splitting our ears with your bombastics, Ducktor. We don't need any more voices," said Datla Nuri.

Ducktor turned to Kulsum. "I want you to play Sita in our jatra. Do you know about her? She was the most beautiful and right-eous of women. You don't have to talk or sing. Kamal will communicate to you the motivation of your role and how you ought to play it. I can tell that you'll be a natural in Sita's role."

Kulsum listened with her head down and walked back inside the cabin.

"At least she didn't seem to be deaf," said Ducktor.

"If she hears your voice for too long, she will go deaf," said Datla Nuri. "I thought I was playing Sita, Ducktor."

"Yes, but I had to rethink the casting a bit. I thought the role of Jatayu would suit you better. You see, Jatayu is the protector of Sita. I can see that you're looking out for the new woman, so the part is appropriate. Isn't it?"

"All right then, as long as you don't expect me to wriggle my bottom on stage."

"Jatayu is a very respectable character, you know. She gives her life trying to protect the honour of Sita. She is a noble vulture."

Bosa Khuni laughed out loud. "Ha, ha. You've chosen well, Ducktor. It's appropriate that an ugly hag like her should play a dead-eating vulture."

"You no good, big-bellied Ducktor," Datla Nuri fumed. "How dare you trick me into playing a vulture? I don't want anything to do with your stinking jatra." And she hurtled back into the cabin.

No one talked for a while as we concentrated on our eating. As I prepared my next mouthful it suddenly dawned on me how quickly I had got used to eating in front of people.

"How about the rest of the casting, Ducktor?" asked the teacher.

"Ala Mullah, as I have said before, will play Rajarishi

Vishvamitra. You know, Rama's teacher and spiritual guide. But he will do so in the guise of a suitable Muslim saint."

Ala Mullah interrupted Ducktor Malek.

"But will a Hindu prince take guidance from a Muslim saint?"

"Hasn't Emperor Akbar taken guidance from all sorts of religious figures, including Hindu pundits?"

"I see another problem, Ducktor," said Ala Mullah. "Rama's time was long before the coming of Islam. So, it wouldn't be accurate that he takes guidance from a Muslim saint."

"Give me a break, will you? We are not into bloody historical business here. We're trying to use our imaginations to amuse ourselves. Have you got it, Mullah?"

Ala Mullah stayed quiet for a while, playing with his long, thin goatee.

"I'm in favour of religious tolerance. Respecting each other and all that. Still I find it difficult to tamper with a holy book. If we take liberties with Rama, wouldn't we be showing disrespect to the Hindus?"

I could see that Ducktor Malek was getting very impatient.

"We are doing a fiction here, Mullah. You know, play-acting and all that. Haven't they taught you anything in your stupid Madrasah?"

Ala Mullah looked like he was falling into a sulk.

"Let us not trade insults," said the teacher. "Would you get on with the rest of the casting, Ducktor."

"Well, only you and I are left, Abbas Mia," said Ducktor. "I was thinking King Dasaratha for you. You know, Rama's father. His is a very dignified role."

The teacher nodded his head as though he agreed with Ducktor, but Asad Khan coughed prissily.

"I don't know much about these Hindu things, Ducktor. But doesn't Dasaratha have three hundred wives? He sounds more randy to me than dignified."

"How can I stage a jatra with all these idiots who don't understand the first thing about myths and legends? I give up, Abbas Mia. I shouldn't have entertained the idea in the first place."

"Don't give up, Ducktor. I'll make sure that everyone takes

their part seriously and obeys your instructions. Now, how about you, Ducktor? What role are you playing?" asked the teacher.

"Obviously, you can't have the *Ramayana* without Rama. So, I volunteer for that role."

After lunch, it was too hot for the Majee brothers to keep rowing. Besides, there was hardly any wind. No one objected when they suggested that we all took a rest until late afternoon. All the men went inside the cabin to take naps or at least to lie down for a while. I didn't join them.

I went for the trip in the dinghy with Datla Nuri and Kulsum. All over the floodplains silvery flakes of light were dancing, looking like the little stars that Moni Banu and I used to buy from the fair in our childhood, except where lotuses spread their leaves or clumps of hyacinths floated. Now the fishermen and their dinghies had gone. Only a sampan was ferrying people to their island villages. I paddled towards a flooded brickfield some distance away, its tower-like chimney soaring high above the water. Surrounding it were a large number of umbrella trees with spreading branches. On the way Datla Nuri picked up lotus fruits and offered them to Kulsum, who refused them.

"If you're to live among us, you have to get used to our food. You don't want to die of starvation, do you?" she said. I liked lotus fruits, but I wasn't able to eat them as I was paddling.

"You don't know what you're missing, girl," said Datla Nuri. She broke the lotus fruits open with her buckteeth and ate a pile of them before we reached the brickfield. As the women wanted to bathe, I dropped them on a bamboo platform under an umbrella tree, and waited behind the chimney. Datla Nuri called me when they had finished and had changed into dry clothes.

I tied the dinghy to the bamboo platform. It was cool under the shade of the umbrella tree. They got into the dinghy and sat together on a plank, just in front of me. Kulsum lowered her head and pulled her sari over it.

"Don't cover your head, girl. Let your hair dry," said Datla Nuri. "You don't have to be shy before my nephew. He's a pretty fella inside, you know."

Datla Nuri pulled down the edge of Kulsum's sari, baring her head, though she still had her head down. Datla Nuri said, "She's a foreign girl, you know. Not used to our ways. Would you believe that she doesn't even know how to eat rice and fish curry properly? Very strange. She also talks our language in a funny, funny way. What can I say, Nephew, she is a poor fatherless-motherless girl. Oh poor thing, she has no one to look out for her. She is also an owning-nothing like us."

I pointed to myself and gave Datla Nuri a questioning look.

"I want you to look out for her, Nephew. You know how some people can be so hateful, so we mustn't tell anyone who she is. It's also safer if we pretend that she is dumb. You know, like you, without the gift of speech."

I nodded. Kulsum looked at me without lifting her head. I could tell that it wasn't to express gratitude, but to see the face that had promised to protect her. I could also tell that this time she was a bit unnerved by my face.

"Don't be shy, girl. Talk to my nephew. He's a book-reading fella, you know."

Kulsum still didn't say anything. Datla Nuri then suggested that I should write something on my slate as a way of starting a conversation.

"Do people call you a Bihari?" I wrote.

She looked at my writing, but only spoke when Datla Nuri nudged her.

"I suppose so," she said very faintly in Bengali.

There was the characteristic accent of our enemies. I wanted to feel what Datla Nuri asked me to feel towards this poor destitute woman, but the confirmation that she was of the enemy confused me. So many questions were buzzing in my head that I felt as though a wasp had flown in through my nose. If I protected her, would I be betraying those of my people who were butchered in our school yard for no other reason than that they were Bengalis? Shouldn't I avenge them? How else could I show them that they were my people, and that I would remember them?

"I hope you haven't written anything dirty, Nephew," said Datla Nuri.

Kulsum giggled at that, but I kept rubbing my slate clean.

"What's wrong, Nephew?" asked Datla Nuri. "You're getting confused, aren't you?"

I didn't respond.

"Listen, I'm not a book-reading fella like you, Nephew. You know that I have been an owning-nothing labourer all of my life. I am not even ashamed to admit that I used my begging bowl to eat during bad times. I'm sure you heard many wicked things about me in the village. Perhaps I don't know what's right and wrong. All I know is that if someone knocks on your door, you don't ask who it is. You don't even look at their face. You just do everything you can for them. Do you follow me, Nephew?"

We went back to the boat. The men were already up and were on the foredeck. Joker gave a whistle as soon as the women came on board and whimpered around them. I went inside the cabin to lie down, Datla Nuri's harsh, rasping voice ringing in my head: If someone knocks on your door, you don't ask who it is. You don't even look at their face. You just do everything you can for them.

In the late afternoon we began moving again, heading north. I got up to help the Majee brothers with the oars. It was still windless and progress was slow. The teacher had decided that we should row until night fell. Increasingly the water was becoming free of vegetation, only occasionally a clump of hyacinths floated by. Apart from us, there wasn't a soul around. Water sang with the slight wind; the rest was silence.

Just before the sun went down on the floodplains, a flock of storks flew over us. Perhaps it was because we tried to listen to their flapping wings that we didn't hear the sampans approaching until we saw their hazy shapes in the mauve of the evening. There were four of them. Oared by many hands, they moved swiftly through the water and surrounded us before we could decide what to do. No one on the sampans gave orders but they lit their lamps all at the same time, as though following a well-practised drill. Sensing their presence, Joker scuttled about frenetically on the foredeck, and whistled piercingly.

CHAPTER 14

Some of them were already on board.

From the dark they came with their lamps and torches and dazzled us with light. Big Suban was the one who spotted me first from one of the sampans that had closed in on us from the rear.

"Kamal," he screamed.

I sensed that someone had jumped from the sampan's cabin roof to reach us, but with Big Suban's torchlight on my face I couldn't see who it was. Only when Big Suban turned the torch away from me was I able to see the face.

"Look Big Sister, it's our Kamal," said Big Suban.

As I turned around I saw Moni Banu looking at me. She had a gun, like Big Suban, hanging across her shoulder.

"Kamal," she said. "So you have taken to carrying the slate at last?"

She didn't know what had happened to Ata Banu or at the school yard. When she bent down to touch the teacher's feet to greet him, he placed his hand on her head and broke down.

"What is it Baba?" she asked. "Why are you crying?"

She didn't cry when she heard what had happened. Instead, she tightened her face and bit her lips. What had happened to Moni Banu? Why didn't she cry for her mother? I don't know, but Zafar Alam, her husband, and now the leader of this unit of liberation forces, held his Sten gun up with both of his hands. He shook it as though trying to make it speak.

"We will make them pay for it, Moni," he said. "Joi Bangla."

All the liberation fighters raised their weapons into the air, too, and shouted Joi Bangla. I was amazed to hear so much passion in Big Suban's voice and to see such rage in his eyes.

"Yes, Baba, not a single drop of our blood will go unavenged," said Moni Banu.

"I can't believe that you're saying this, Moni," said the teacher. "If you do to them what they have done to us, then what's the difference? What's the point of this struggle if we become brutes in order to defeat brutes?"

"That's what you think of me now? A brute? What crime did Ma commit to be burnt alive? Should we just grovel at their feet when they rape us and then slit open our stomachs? That's what you want, Baba?" Moni Banu spoke with such rage and grief that the teacher was taken aback. He looked baffled, as though he didn't recognise his little girl whom he'd treasured more than anything else in the world.

"I didn't mean –," he could not finish the sentence before Moni Banu stormed off and climbed down into her sampan.

Zafar Alam began to follow her, but turned back and came to stand in front of the teacher.

"Don't mind Moni, Baba, she is very tired. Fighting day and night. Risking everything. She feels the pain of our people deeply. She wants justice for them and for her mother, of course."

The teacher squeezed his face, rubbed his chin as though he wasn't really listening to Zafar Alam, as though he was lost in painful thoughts of his own.

"Are you all right, Baba?"

"Yes, yes. Do you think I don't feel pain? That I don't want justice for Moni's mother? For all those killed in the school yard?"

"Moni tells me you taught her everything she knows. She is a fighter because of you, Baba."

"I taught her the ways of reason, but not of war. I'd rather have her travelling with me in this boat, and away from the war. It seems I've no say in this matter any more. You young people do what your reason and conscience dictate, but you mustn't lower yourselves to their level."

"So, Baba, should we just let them butcher us and not resist?"

The teacher looked really troubled; I could see that he didn't know what to say to Zafar Alam. Instead he called me.

"Kamal, where is my hookah?"

I was about to go inside the cabin to fetch it, but he rushed ahead of me. It took him quite a while to come out of the cabin again.

It was decided that the liberation fighters would stay the night with us. We tied our boat to a nearby fishing platform and their sampans congregated around us. Once this was done, Zafar Alam and Big Suban came onto our boat; Moni Banu and the rest of the freedom fighters stayed in their sampans. While Big Suban went to talk to Ala Mullah, I sat with Zafar Alam.

"How is the war going?" I wrote.

"We have already eliminated a number of collaborators from the villages around here. Also, we have successfully ambushed one Pakistani gunboat. We killed about thirty soldiers there, and acquired some sophisticated weapons from them."

"So the war is going well," I wrote.

"It's just the beginning, Brother Kamal. I suspect that the Pakistanis will send reinforcements soon. You know, more gunboats and soldiers. So, there are tough battles ahead of us, but we are well prepared. You'll be glad to know that Moni is proving to be such a strategic brain and organiser. It was due to her foresight that we only lost two fighters when we ambushed the gunboat. I am so lucky, Brother Kamal."

"In what way?" I wrote.

"Moni and I are working together to liberate our country. Isn't that something, Brother Kamal? I love Moni and she is my best comrade too," he said with passion.

I'd had my misgivings about his impulse to join the war, his willingness to risk his life, and to drag Moni Banu into it as well. Now that death was all around me, it didn't seem to matter any more. Besides, what I'd already seen made me realise that we were just as much at risk as they were, even though we were trying to flee the warfront. I was also beginning to believe in Zafar Alam's commitment to see our people free. His love for our country was unmistakable. Yet, I still felt uncomfortable about the way he declared his love for Moni Banu. I wondered whether he expressed himself in these terms to impress me. Perhaps he knew that he could never share with Moni Banu what she and I once had between us.

Big Suban came and stood behind us. Zafar Alam turned to him. "Brother Suban has been our best fighter so far. He killed five Pakistani soldiers in that ambush."

Big Suban didn't say anything; he looked like someone else, someone I didn't know. Later I found him on top of the cabin roof, cleaning his gun. I tried to tell him that his axe was in my shed when they burnt it down. I touched his hand to say sorry.

"It doesn't matter, Kamal," he said, polishing the muzzle of his gun. "I don't care for the axe any more."

I stayed silent, looking at the sun going down, amidst splashes of orange on the floodplains.

"I suppose you're thinking: how does it feel to fell men, aren't you, Kamal?"

I grunted from the back of my throat.

"It doesn't feel anything. You see, the axe was a part of my hand, but the gun is not. I don't feel that the gun has anything to do with me. It just goes on its own way and kills our enemy. They just fall dead. They don't talk to me like the trees, Kamal."

I was waiting for Big Suban to talk to me about getting back to cutting trees after the war, finding himself a wife, and reminding me that I was to be his chief witness and best man, but it seemed that something else was on his mind.

"You want to know what I'm fighting for, Kamal?" he said. "It's a big question. It's for the book-reading people like you to think about. What I know is that there are times when you just have to fight. No? For me this is a time to fight. So, I will just let my gun find as many enemies as possible and kill them. I won't be happy until they are all dead, Kamal."

He paused and looked at me. I wasn't sure how he wanted me to respond. I was beginning to feel sad that the memories that tied us, made us into friends, were perhaps lost to him. He began again.

"Big Sister Moni Banu tells me: Suban, you're the liberator of your people. I don't know what people she means. Is it our village people? Or the people of our district? I'm not sure, but I like it when she says that. We all look up to her, Kamal."

I was getting so desperate to hear Big Suban talk to me in his old ways that I began to play-act a bride for him.

"I don't know, Kamal. I can't think of taking a wife any more," he said. "My mind only wants to hear the sound of the gun as it goes out felling our enemies. You see, as long as they stay up I can't liberate my people, can I?"

I wasn't going to give up on him that easily, so I mimicked the sound of an axe. I hoped that it would remind him of the times before he left the village, when for days, staying unseen, he thwacked his axe for me.

"I was a woodcutter then. Now I'm a liberation fighter. The axe doesn't sing for me any more." He then looked at me as if to console me. "Don't worry, Kamal. If I ever take a wife, you'll be my best man and chief witness. All right?"

Bosa Khuni came and sat by us. He was admiring Big Suban's gun and asking him how he could join the liberation forces. I left them talking and went to the foredeck.

Zafar Alam, accompanied by some of the freedom fighters, had gone out in one of the sampans to catch fish. Moni Banu, in the meantime, had climbed back into our boat. She was sitting by the prow with the teacher. Ala Mullah and Ducktor Malek had gone into one of the sampans to talk to the freedom fighters. I could hear Ducktor Malek's booming voice as he told them stories and their laughter. Out of the view of the liberation fighters, Asad Khan, Datla Nuri and Kulsum stayed inside the cabin. I tiptoed my way towards Moni Banu and the teacher and squatted by them. It seemed that they had put aside their differences and looked quite at ease with each other. When she noticed me, she turned to look at me. She seemed much thinner and darker, but more grown up and confident. Her voice was clear and authoritative.

"Now that you're carrying your slate, how do people treat you?" she asked.

"So far I haven't had much problem," I wrote.

"How does it feel to be seen as a learned person?"

"I feel the same as before," I wrote.

She looked at me as though trying to look inside my mouth.

"Everyone changes when a war is on, Kamal. None of us will remain the same."

"I haven't changed, Moni. I think I feel the same as before," said the teacher.

Moni Banu looked quizzically at her father, as though she couldn't quite believe him. She seemed to have changed, at least in her relationship with him, because in the past she had always dutifully accepted whatever he said.

"You are now commanding a boat, aren't you Baba? Something you haven't done before. Doesn't that change something in you?"

"Perhaps, but I am talking about one's character. I still believe in the same sense of justice and reason as before," he said.

I was feeling rather uncomfortable about Moni Banu's new sense of herself. I wanted things to remain the same, especially her. Why couldn't she stay the way she was in our childhood?

"We must let go of the past, Baba. What Zafar and I are fighting for is a new beginning. A new society, if you like, where we will have new kinds of people too."

The teacher rubbed his chin as if he were weighing carefully what Moni Banu had said, but I felt angry towards her. It wasn't so much the content of her speech that irritated me, but the way she said Zafar and I. It really got to me. I was jealous.

"You're talking gibberish, Moni," I wrote, using one of Bosa Khuni's expressions. I walked away, and climbed the cabin roof. Over the floodplains a nearly full moon was casting a bluish glow. Moni Banu followed me.

"What's the matter with you? Why are you angry with me, Kamal?" she said, sitting next to me.

I didn't make any gesture or sound to her. Nor did I use my slate, but I was aware that she didn't address me as *Beautiful One* as she had always done when we were alone.

"Let us go for a trip in your dinghy, Kamal."

We climbed down the roof and were on our way to the dinghy when Datla Nuri appeared on the foredeck.

"I hear you're a fighter lady now. How come you're still wearing a sari?" she said. "I thought you'd be wearing one of those man things. You know, trousers."

Moni Banu laughed. "How are you doing, Sister Nuri?"

Datla Nuri broke out into loud wailing. "How can I be fine, our little Moni? Those devils burnt your mother to ashes. Oh Allah, only her bones were left. She was a sour one, your mother, but she gave me food. Allah bless her soul."

She came and embraced Moni Banu and kept on wailing. "Are you going to kill those devils with your gun, our little Moni? Are you?"

I could see that Moni Banu's eyes were welling up, her lips trembling, but she didn't break into crying.

"We will, Sister Nuri. We will."

I got down into the dinghy with a lamp and the slate hanging from my neck. As soon as Moni Banu had settled herself on the prow I started to paddle. I took to the open waters to the left of the boat. It was a bit windy, but the sky was clear with an almost full moon. Moni Banu leaned over the hull and dipped her hand into the water. I could see her shadow on the dark, purple ripples lapping the hull.

"Zafar is a good man, you know. He feels for you like a real brother," she said.

As I was paddling I couldn't communicate with her either in gestures or using my slate. She sounded less authoritative than before and I could sense a pleading in her voice.

"Nothing except the war matters now. We are facing genocide at the hands of the Pakistanis. Do you understand that, Kamal?"

I kept on paddling. The wind lapped against the roof of my mouth.

"If we don't win this war we will face extinction, Kamal. So, Zafar and I are committed to it until our last breath."

Now she had a lover's pact with him and they wanted to die together. How could she be so stupid? I wondered what she called him when they were alone.

"Now is not the time to stand on the sidelines, Kamal. And no time for bookish ideas either. Sometimes I don't understand Baba at all."

I didn't like the way she talked about the teacher.

I laid aside my paddles and let the dinghy drift on the waves. She didn't say anything for a while and we stayed where we were with the dinghy continuing to drift. Then I carried the lamp and sat on a plank in front of her. She lifted her hand from the water and put it on my forehead. Drops of sweet, muddy water dripped into the hole of my mouth.

"I'm a married woman now, Kamal. So, we have to let each other go. You understand that?"

I grunted from the back of my throat. The dinghy drifted until it became tangled up among a patch of lotuses.

"Do you expect me to forget you?" I wrote.

"Don't be silly, Kamal. I don't mean that. Wherever I might be not a single day passes without me remembering you. I will always do so. You are my brother, aren't you?"

I don't know whether she heard my little grunts as the wind drove the waves over the lotuses. I don't know what got into me at that moment, but I ended up writing, "Take me with you, then. I can fight alongside you."

The wind tore the dinghy from the tangle of lotuses. We were drifting once more.

"I want you to stay out of this war, Kamal."

"You said we mustn't stand on the sidelines. Am I not worthy of even fighting for my own country?" I wrote.

"Don't be silly, Kamal. You know I don't mean that. You and Baba, you two need to look after each other now. Then, if I survive the war, I will take care of the two of you."

"I can look after myself, Moni," I wrote and then took to the paddle.

"Don't argue with me now, Kamal. Just stay out of this war and survive."

Both of us were still for a while. I don't know what she was thinking, but I was head-down and sulking. But as always I couldn't stay angry with her for long. When I looked up at her again, I almost convinced myself that it was the Moni Banu of old that I was seeing.

"Do you remember the old tiger at the circus?" I wrote on the slate and held it up before her.

"Of course, I remember the old tiger, but I don't dwell on those things much."

"I dwell on them all the time, Moni. Without those memories I have nothing," I wrote.

"Don't be silly, Kamal. I know we can't deny the past, but we must try to create new memories now. That's why Zafar and I are fighting."

"What are these new memories?" I wrote.

"We will only be able to recount them after the war, Kamal. Now we just act on our conviction. We want to free our people."

"Have you killed anyone, Moni?" I wrote.

"What do you think? What do I do with my gun? Do you think I keep it as a fashion item? I suppose if you dwell so much in the past, it's difficult for you to understand. I'm not a little girl any more, Kamal. I'm a freedom fighter. Every day I go out into the killing fields."

I was looking at a lily throbbing under the moonlight and thinking about what Moni Banu had said, but she changed the subject.

"Did you see Ma's body?"

"No. Only the bones."

"Bones," she said, her voice almost breaking. "These are new memories too."

Soon after we got back to the boat Zafar Alam returned with a basketful of fish. Bosa Khuni took them to Datla Nuri, inside the cabin. He came back to the foredeck, dragging Asad Khan with him. He pushed him in front of Zafar Alam and Moni Banu.

"You know him, don't you, Big Sister Moni? He's a collaborator, isn't he?" Bosa Khuni yelled. Some of the liberation fighters clambered on the boat from their sampans. They cocked their guns and surrounded Asad Khan.

"Yes, I know him. He's a Muslim-Leaguer. He's bound to be a collaborator," said Moni Banu, calmly and clearly.

I could see Asad Khan's panic-stricken eyes looking for someone to save him. He stooped before Zafar Alam like the most abject domestic dog and began to whine.

"You commander sir, you must believe that my family and I never harmed anyone. We are good people, ask that mouthless one," he said.

I went forward, stood before Zafar Alam, and nodded to affirm what he had said.

"You don't know the collaborators as we do, Brother Kamal. They are sly and sinister. We must interrogate him to establish the truth," said Zafar Alam.

On Zafar Alam's signal, a number of liberation fighters grabbed hold of Asad Khan, and pulled him towards the edge of the boat. Asad Khan started to scream, "They're going to kill me. They are going to kill me. Please save me, Abbas Mia. Please."

The teacher, who was on the rear deck, came over the cabin roof.

"What do you plan to do with him?" he asked Zafar Alam.

"We will take him away in one of our sampans for questioning."

"I can't permit that, my son. He's in my care."

Zafar Alam didn't know what to say; he stood there with his head bowed. Moni, looking annoyed, turned to face her father.

"Don't do that, Baba," she said. "We're on a mission to clear this area of collaborators. Without their help the Pakistanis wouldn't be so effective against us."

The teacher remained calm and absolutely still.

"You can't take him out of this boat. He is in my care."

"Don't be so stubborn, Baba. Thousands of our people are getting massacred by Islamic fascists and communalist bigots like him."

The teacher remained as impassive as before.

"You can't take him off this boat. He's in my care."

"This is not some kind of bookish idea, Baba. This is the reality of war. He is an enemy and we must take him for questioning."

The teacher looked at Moni Banu as though looking at a stranger. His lips trembled when he spoke again.

"If you want to take him you have to kill me first," he said, and turned his back on her.

Moni Banu stood, biting her lips.

"You shouldn't have done that, Baba. You're protecting our enemy."

Without a word the teacher moved into the group of the liberation fighters holding Asad Khan. When he took him by the arm, the liberation fighters looked at Zafar Alam. He nodded and they let Asad Khan go and the teacher walked with him over the cabin to the rear deck. Zafar Alam, followed by the liberation fighters, climbed down into their sampans. Moni Banu remained where she was on the foredeck.

"Let us go, Moni," said Zafar Alam. "We have a war to fight. We can't waste our time here."

When Moni Banu was about to take Zafar Alam's hand to climb down into her sampan, Bosa Khuni stopped her.

"You must know something before you go, Big Sister Moni," he said. "We might have a Bihari snake on board as well."

He led Moni Banu inside the cabin. I followed them. Bosa

Khuni lifted the jute curtain. Squatting on the deck by the clay cooker, Kulsum was grinding spices; Datla Nuri was cutting fish.

"Who are you? Where have you come from?" Moni asked.

Kulsum looked at her blankly.

"She's just a poor girl. Like our Kamal, she doesn't talk," said Datla Nuri.

"She's a clever one. She's just pretending. She has a perfect mouth and tongue," said Bosa Khuni. "Look at her, Big Sister Moni. Doesn't she look like a Bihari to you?"

Moni Banu looked at her quizzically.

"I can see that you can hear me perfectly. So, you can't be deaf and dumb. You better start talking now. Otherwise, I will be forced to open your mouth."

Kulsum began to cry.

"Leave this poor girl alone. She's just an owning-nothing girl like us," said Datla Nuri.

"How do you know that she's an owning-nothing girl? She must have talked to you – no?" said Moni Banu.

Datla Nuri looked at Moni Banu with panic in her eyes and ran to the foredeck to fetch the teacher. In her absence, Bosa Khuni stooped over Kulsum, squeezed her lower jaw with his powerful hand, and tried to open her mouth. I don't know what came over me: I pushed Bosa Khuni with all of my force. He went flying, toppling the clay cooker. Luckily it wasn't lit. I then stood between Moni Banu and Kulsum.

"She's a speechless one like me, Moni. Just leave her alone," I wrote.

"I'm not so sure about that, Kamal. Anyway, we should establish whether she's a Bihari."

"She's not a Bihari," I wrote.

Moni Banu looked at me suspiciously.

"Have I ever lied to you, Moni? I'm telling you, she's not a Bihari," I wrote.

Moni Banu stood there looking at me as if trying to remember if I'd ever lied to her. Then she walked out of the cabin.

It seemed they had decided not to stay the night with us after all. The sampans were ready to move.

"With a collaborator and a possible Bihari on board you're in grave danger, Baba," Moni said. "Your foolish ideas do not help either. We will be operating around here, so don't stray too far. We can keep an eye on your boat."

Like a dead tree trunk the teacher stood impassively as Zafar Alam touched his feet to take his leave. When Moni Banu did so, the teacher just said, "Moni."

I was sitting alone in near darkness on the stem post, hoping that Moni Banu wouldn't notice me before leaving. But she came over with a lantern and looked at me, her face tight and rigid. She whispered, "I know you haven't lied to me before, but I wonder what got into you. Why did you lie to me now? You're as foolish as Baba."

Bosa Khuni got into one of the sampans; he was going away to be a liberation fighter.

"You can't desert the jatra," Ducktor Malek shouted to Bosa Khuni. "How can I stage the jatra if I lose one of my vital cast members?"

"Isn't my role mostly a sleeping one, Ducktor? So, you won't miss me much. Besides, you can imagine that I'm sleeping on the stage."

I got up and climbed the cabin roof. I couldn't see Big Suban anywhere; he seemed to be hiding from me in one of the sampans' cabins. I was pleased by this because it showed that some part of Big Suban hadn't changed. He still found it difficult to say goodbye. On Zafar Alam's signal, the liberation fighters who were on the oars began to pull with the same disciplined rhythm as when they came. I looked after them through the bluish air of the night until they disappeared, and then I continued to listen to the faint splashing of their oars. After a while it was silent in the floodplains and we were alone again.

CHAPTER 15

That night I was so upset that I could hardly sleep. Had some of the threads that tied Moni Banu and I together been broken? Why had I lied to her? Why was I protecting Kulsum? She really meant nothing to me. I felt like getting up and going after the sampans in my dinghy, and telling her everything: sorry Moni, please forgive me for lying to you, yes she's a Bihari, she's all yours now; can we go back to the way we were?

I could often pretend that I'd taken a dip in a pond that muffled all sounds, but now the noises inside the cabin were rending my ears. Although I was spared Bosa Khuni's snoring, Datla Nuri was making up for it from the other side of the curtain. I had to contend with Ducktor Malek every so often letting out his doglike barks, and then Joker whining and chattering before going back to his synchronised breathing with the Majee brothers.

When I saw Asad Khan getting up and tiptoeing his way to the door to the foredeck I didn't think anything of it. Seeing him pass, Ducktor Malek gave one of his barks, making him freeze like a scarecrow in the dark. Ducktor asked him where he was going. He said he was going to the deck for fresh air. Since I couldn't sleep I got up with a hurricane lamp and followed him. Ducktor Malek barked again and Joker whined and chattered.

"Are you going out to practise your role, Kamal?" he asked. "Go through some of your monkey moves with Asad Khan. You know, most of your fighting scenes involve his character."

The half-moon that had gleamed earlier was barely visible, and most of the stars had disappeared too. Asad Khan appeared nervous as he walked the foredeck without looking at me. Suddenly he stopped and whispered.

"I'm taking the dinghy," he said. "I've got to get away. So, don't make any noise. Do you understand me?"

I tried to tell him with gestures that it was essential that we kept the dinghy with the boat. He pretended not to understand me.

"If I don't get away, they'll soon kill me. You don't want me dead, do you?"

He took the hurricane lamp from my hand and got into the dinghy. I thought of stopping him and waking the others, but I just stood there watching him disappear into the night.

As it was raining heavily the next day, no one left the cabin until late morning. I was waiting for someone to raise the alarm about the missing dinghy and Asad Khan's disappearance, but no one did until Datla Nuri came back into the cabin, soaked and agitated.

"That Asad Khan has stolen the dinghy," she screamed. "He's a thief from a family of thieves. I've always known that he's an evil one."

"If he wanted to go, that's up to him," said the teacher.

"Nothing will please me more than him getting caught and butchered like a fat goat," said Datla Nuri. Then she paused as though thinking seriously. "Thank Allah, at least his lecherous eyes won't be ogling my bottom any more."

Ducktor Malek gave a mocking laugh, which in turn made her hiss at him though her buckteeth.

"You can't fool me, you know. I know all about you jatra-men," she said. "You lot are always lusting after them young boys, aren't you?"

"Don't be angry, Sister Nuri," said Ducktor. "You have a star role in my jatra."

"I'm not playing a bloody vulture. You can shove your stinking play up your you-know-where," she said.

"Don't do it to me," said Ducktor as though about to break into crying. "My jatra is doomed if I lose a third cast member."

We waited for the rain to settle into a steady drizzle before moving again, but we stopped when we spotted a banana grove floating above a shallow floodplain. With Ala Mullah's help I made a raft and we set off again in the afternoon.

Now it had stopped raining, but the wind was blowing hard from the west. It must have been after about an hour or so of steady rowing that we reached a vast flow of clear water with high waves. Immediately I knew we were on a large river course. While Ala

Mullah guided the rudder at the helm, the Majee brothers hoisted the sail. The wind billowed the rainbow colours of the sail, and the boat cut through the water like the river dolphins that suddenly appeared ahead of us. Inside the cabin, Ducktor Malek stayed cross-legged and the teacher lay on the rush mat for his afternoon sleep. Datla Nuri and Kulsum were looking at the river dolphins from the foredeck.

"Come and look at these funny fish, Nephew," Datla Nuri called. "They look like bald little babies. I wonder where they come from."

Kulsum looked more relaxed. Seeing me, she lowered her head but didn't pull the sari to cover her face. Lately I had the distinct feeling that Datla Nuri wanted me to get closer to Kulsum. She made an excuse and went inside the cabin, leaving us alone. Kulsum looked ahead, perhaps searching for the dolphins among the waves. For some reason they weren't surfacing any more.

"So much water," she said faintly and with a distinctive Bihari accent, but without turning to look at me. I was surprised that she spoke to me without my prompting. She kept looking ahead, a loose strand of her hair blowing in the wind.

"Yes, we're water people. Who are your people?" I wrote and tapped on the slate to draw her attention. She looked at the slate, and then she glanced at me before gazing straight ahead again. She didn't answer my question, but I wasn't bothered because I didn't see any unease in her eyes. It was as if she'd got used to my face, or didn't see any disfigurement in it.

"Do I have to tell you? You know who I am," she said and looked at the slate. I didn't write anything else on it, but hurriedly wiped it clean as I saw Ala Mullah coming over the cabin roof. Sensing his presence, Kulsum drew the sari over her head and covered her face.

We sailed until early evening and turned left into another floodplain. The Majee brothers took the sail down and left it folded and dangling from the mast. After that they took to their punt-poles and propelled us east for an hour or so. They stopped when the sun had almost dipped. I saw the teacher climbing on the cabin roof and looking in every direction. I thought he was surveying the area to establish its suitability as a shelter for the night, but he began to hit a piece of bamboo against the mast post. We all, except Kulsum, gathered on the foredeck.

"This is the place," he announced. "We will stay here and wander around for the rest of the war."

I was surprised because this floodplain didn't look as vast as the ones we had crossed before. Later, however, as we travelled through it, it became clear why the teacher had chosen it. First, there were the long stretches of clear water that turned unexpectedly and meandered between densely packed trees and shrubs. Sometimes, we ended up in oval pools with deep, green water. They were nearly always surrounded by tall trees with inclined canopies. If we needed to disappear without a trace, we just had to slide into one of the many flooded forests. Often, at a bend of clear waters, patches of tall kash grass greeted us. Strange how their white flowers never stopped swaying in the wind. Along the edges of the shallows, dense lines of reeds offered us emergency shelter. If we were to be safe anywhere, this was the place.

Soon we were well set on a routine. We never stayed in a place for more than a day or two, but we didn't stray too far either. It was more as if we were circling the courses of a giant watery maze. Nothing seemed to be near us, but we remained vigilant. Ducktor Malek still insisted on staging his *Ramayana* with the depleted cast. Every time he saw one of the Majee brothers, he prompted them to conduct themselves as befitted their princely roles. Reluctantly they would put on stiff walks and gruff voices, which made even the teacher laugh.

"You're not playing comedy roles, you idiots. You are supposed to express dignity," Ducktor would say.

Very soon, though, the Majee brothers began to ignore him. They went about their business as though they didn't have time for his silly pranks. Undaunted, Ducktor followed them, at times almost begging them to play along with him until one afternoon Harihar Majee snapped. I can assure you that Harihar was not a man who lost his temper easily. That afternoon, after having rowed and punted for hours, he'd just sat down on the foredeck to smoke his hookah when Ducktor began to pester him. At first he ignored him, lit his hookah and puffed at it, looking far into the distance over the floodplain. When Ducktor wouldn't give up, Harihar got up and went over the cabin roof to the rear deck, but Ducktor followed him. When he came back to his old position on the foredeck, Ducktor came too. Suddenly Harihar turned around and squared up to him.

"You're oppressing us, Ducktor," he screamed. "We now feel like running from your jatra faster than we are running from this terrible war. So, please leave us alone."

After that Ducktor Malek didn't bother the Majee brothers, but he wasn't giving up on his jatra yet. One day, at midday, he was sitting under the shade of the sail with his eyes closed and his head down. By late afternoon when he still hadn't changed his posture, I thought he had finally fallen asleep. However, as soon as he saw Ala Mullah passing in front of him, he lifted his head. For the next few days he pestered Ala Mullah to come up with a suitable Muslim saint to play Rama's spiritual guide, but Ala Mullah, without showing annoyance, kept repeating: 'I'm giving it a serious thought, Ducktor.' To this, Ducktor Malek would ask: 'How deep is your thought, Mullah? You're not trying to reach the bottom of the ocean, are you?' Smiling serenely, but without answering Ducktor's questions, Ala Mullah would recite a Koranic verse, or do his ablution, or lay out his prayer mat.

Ducktor's jatra looked doomed, but I was grateful to it as it allowed me a few moments alone with Kulsum. Even after the Majee brothers and Ala Mullah had withdrawn themselves from the jatra, Ducktor pinned his hopes, apart from the teacher and himself, on Kulsum and me. As well as insisting that I practised my monkey moves, he also kept reminding me that I was to work with Kulsum in my role as his assistant director.

Late in the afternoons, hanging the slate from my neck, I would go out with Kulsum on the raft, but we never got around to discussing the jatra. I would punt, and sometimes – if the water was deep – I would take to the paddle. Somehow we would always end up in one of those flooded forests, or enclosed pools. At first, Kulsum – head down and stiffly reserved – remained squatting on the raft, not even casting a sideways glance at me. However, as time went on, I could see that she was becoming more at ease in my company. Yet her eyes never betrayed any curiosity – the way opposite sexes are curious about each other. I wasn't curious about her that way either.

When I looked at her, I mean really looked at her, I could see that she was pretty. She had thick, black hair, but it was cut short to the nape of her neck. In her perfectly proportioned face, with a strong and determined mouth, shone two bright green eyes, but like the pool of water beneath the raft they expressed nothing. She had smooth, dark yellowish skin, which was regarded as very becoming in women. Apparently such women drove many men wild with desire, but I never felt any temptation to run my fingers over her skin. She was endowed with the shapely figure of a young woman in good health, but I didn't feel uncomfortable in her proximity, as happens when the senses are provoked.

One afternoon, under the canopy of a flooded forest, I tethered the raft and squatted in front of her. She lifted her head; her eyes looked into mine, boldly.

"Why did you lie for me?" she asked.

"We are in the middle of a war. You know how dangerous it would be if your origins were known," I wrote. She looked at the shadows of the canopy, floating on the ripples of the pool.

"Do you think I am an enemy of your people?"

"I suppose so, but I promised that I'd look out for you. Nothing will change that," I wrote. She widened her green eyes, but I wasn't sure what sentiment they wanted to express.

"Who was the lady who came in with the gun? What is she to you?"

"She's the teacher's daughter. We grew up together. We're almost like brother and sister to each other," I wrote.

"I thought she meant something else to you. I saw it in her eyes as she looked at you when you lied for me."

I tapped on my slate, but wrote nothing.

"I could tell that she doesn't like me. Do you think she'll come back to kill me?"

"It's natural that our people don't like yours. It's a war between us, but I wouldn't let anyone harm you," I wrote.

She splashed water, then cupped some in her right hand, and drank it.

"Why?"

"I'm not sure, but I know that you came to us, and you looked at me. Somehow that made me feel that I ought to protect you."

"But I don't feel protected. Fear stalks me all the time."

"It stalks me too. Anyway, what can I do to make you feel protected?" I wrote. She lowered her eyes, then picked a dry leaf that had fallen on her lap from the canopy above, and crumpled it between her palms.

"If I have to stay among your people, I cannot remain a single, unmarried woman. It's just not safe. Sooner or later I'll be found out. So, I need a connection," she said.

"How?"

She let drop the broken leaf pieces into the water and they drifted away with the current. Leaning over the side, head down, she kept following them long after they had disappeared. Only when a red kite swooped down in her line of vision to catch a fish did she straighten up.

"If you marry me, I'll have connection," she said faintly, but I heard her clearly.

I didn't know how to respond to this strange request. I wondered what madness had possessed her. It took me some time to regain my bearings.

"It's not appropriate for us to discuss such matters. I don't know much about your customs, but among us only the parents should raise such matters," I wrote.

"I have no parents. They're dead," she said.

I didn't say sorry. Nor did I inquire how they died, because I wasn't prepared to face up to her emotions. Anyway, it was easy to guess that they must have met terrible deaths.

"You're a pretty-looking girl," I wrote. "You can get a much better husband than a mouthless one like me."

"Perhaps, but in the situation I'm in right now, my looks won't save my skin. It's more likely to give me away as an enemy of your people. But I feel safe with you, and I trust that you'll protect me."

"How about my looks? Doesn't it bother you to be married to a face like mine?" I wrote.

"You can't blame a girl if she finds you hideous. What girl

208

doesn't grow up imagining marrying someone with a perfectly formed face? At least someone whose lips will touch her lips?"

I knew how I looked, but I was shocked that Kulsum should be so rude and immodest as to express herself in those terms. I was upset by it, but I could see something of Moni Banu in her. Not only was she an educated girl, she was high spirited too.

"Wouldn't you find it difficult and upsetting to be my wife? Could you bear to look at my face day-in and day-out?" I wrote.

"I'm already looking at your face, but seeing nothing but your eyes. I'll only look at your eyes. If they tell me lies, I'll know. But they tell me that you'll protect me."

After that conversation I felt very uncomfortable and began to avoid Kulsum. One morning, finding me alone inside the cabin, Datla Nuri broached the subject.

"Marry the girl, Nephew," she said. "It'll please me if you do."

I looked at her quizzically; she understood that I wanted to know why it would please her.

"You know that I'm looking out for the girl. Haven't I also promised both your mother and Ata Banu that I'll look out for you? Are you following my meaning, Nephew?"

I cast my eyes down.

"If you two are married, it will be a load off my mind. I'll feel that my duties are done."

I stayed as still as the mast-post.

"Listen, Nephew, you don't know how lucky you are. Who would give their daughter in marriage to you? It's fortunate that the war is on and someone like Kulsum came along. She's pretty, and a book-reading girl and all."

I shrugged my shoulders.

"It's not safe for her. The girl needs a husband – understand? I'm telling you, nephew, you're going to marry her."

I still wasn't sure whether it was the right thing to do, but Datla Nuri had talked to the teacher about it and convinced him of the idea. Seeing me alone on the cabin roof the teacher came over and sat by me.

"I want to talk to you about a delicate matter. You see, Moni's mother has gone and I won't be here for too long. You need someone in your life, Kamal," he said. Both of us looked at the tall kash grasses some distance in front of us – wind lashing their white flowers. Rain would be coming soon.

"It's my duty to arrange a marriage for you. To be honest with you, Kamal, I'm not sure whether I can find a wife for you. People won't see your learning, but only your face. We're lucky that this girl has come along. Besides, I have the feeling that you two will get along fine. You know, you being good at silent communication," he said.

For a moment I felt like coming clean with the teacher, and telling him that Kulsum wasn't speechless, and that she was of the enemy, but I said nothing. Nor did he ask me anything about her.

"I'll get down to arranging it then, Kamal," he said, without quite realising the difficulties of his task. Since the majority of our villagers were Sunni Muslims, and the rest Hindus, they followed in marriages, as well as in everything else, the different rituals of their traditions. Although they were also supposed to have their marriages officially registered, most people didn't bother with that. How was the teacher to arrange my marriage since he knew nothing of my origins? To compound the problem he had no idea who Kulsum was either. He didn't discuss any of it with me, but I overheard him and Ala Mullah whispering to each other.

"If you'd had him circumcised and converted to Islam, things would have been so much easier," said Ala Mullah.

"You know my views, Mullah. I don't care much for religion. Besides, how could I convert him without knowing the religion into which he was born?" the teacher said.

"Even if you're not a practitioner or a believer, you still have Islam to carry you through life. Your marriage, the marriage of your daughter. And there will be deaths too. How is Kamal to go through these things?"

"I don't know. That's why I am talking to you."

"Nothing is too late. If you want I can convert him, but circumcision will be a problem."

"Let's not talk about such nonsense. Can you think of something more realistic?"

Ala Mullah suggested civil marriage, but pointed out that at present there was no authority for conducting such a ceremony. "Besides," he said, "you still need to put down the names of his father and mother…" He paused for a long time. "Though I believe that the names of adopted parents will do just as well."

How desperately I waited for the teacher to say that he would put his name forward for me, but all he said was, "You are useless. Absolutely useless, Mullah," and walked away. For the following few days the teacher made sure that he wasn't alone with me, but I knew he was mulling over the issue of my marriage. He wasn't to find a solution until one afternoon Ducktor Malek became very lucid and animated on the foredeck. We were having lunch. The food was plentiful and the cooking particularly good. Datla Nuri was in a good mood and she even indulged Ducktor.

"Oh, how thin you're getting, Ducktor. We can't have an actor who isn't as handsome as a bull elephant. I am here to feed you until you pop like a balloon," she said, and served him several large portions. On finishing his meal Ducktor belched and became very jovial.

"Wah, wah, what a beauty you are, Sister Nuri. No one is more deserving of playing Sita's role than you are. I can already see you becoming a legend throughout the swampland."

Datla Nuri laughed, baring her buckteeth. "You want to have your way with me, don't you? You randy Ducktor."

Now everyone laughed. After lunch I prepared a hookah for the teacher and went inside the cabin for a nap. Ducktor, Ala Mullah and Datla Nuri stayed with the teacher on the foredeck. I'm sure they didn't realise that I was listening to them.

"The old authority of Pakistan is dead now, Abbas Mia. Now we set the rules. So, as the captain of this boat you just assume the authority in the name of Bangladesh and conduct the marriage. Nothing can be simpler," said Ducktor Malek.

"I suppose I could do that. But I know nothing about Kamal's past before he came to us. How do we identify him? Besides, we even don't know the name of the girl," said the teacher.

"Don't forget that this boat is a sovereign territory now, Abbas Mia. You make the rules here. If you choose that a person's parentage, religion, caste and other such garbage need not enter a marriage contract, they will not enter. Anyway, the mention of such things should be outlawed in our Bangladesh."

Ducktor paused, then added. "But I suppose we will need the girl's name."

He then addressed Datla Nuri.

"Has the girl opened her mouth yet? Have you found out her name?"

"Don't be so clever with me, Ducktor. How many times do I have to say that the girl is a dumb one. So, how could I know her name?"

"No problem. In this case you just have to name her, Sister Nuri. Since you are like a mother to her, it is your privilege and duty," said Ducktor.

"Yes, yes I know, but I know nothing about naming business, Ducktor. But if I had given birth to a daughter I would have called her Kulsum."

"That's settled then. We will call her Kulsum."

So it was decided that the teacher would conduct a civil ceremony and have us married, but he still needed two witnesses. Ducktor Malek would be one of them, but he had trouble finding the second person.

"I wish I could do that," said Ala Mullah. "I know Kamal is a man of deep learning. He knows more about our holy book than I do. He is also a man of pure heart. I regard him like my own brother, but I am a Mullah. So, how can I be a witness to someone's marriage who might not be a Muslim? Please forgive me."

The Majee brothers were unwilling to be witnesses either.

"We are untouchable Hindus. If Kamal was born into a Brahmin family we would pollute him. So, you have to excuse us," they said.

Although Datla Nuri was hesitant to be a witness on the grounds that no one had ever heard of a female taking such a role in our village, the teacher persuaded her to do it.

"I know I will burn in hell for it. But I will do anything for my nephew."

Everything was ready, but the teacher still waited, hoping that somehow Moni Banu would get in touch.

"Moni would be so upset if she knew we didn't wait for her. Even with the war on, she wouldn't want to miss your marriage," he told me many times.

Soon the rain came again and with it the war was with us once more. Day after day, gunboats patrolled the waterways, and each time we dodged them by taking one of the numerous tree-lined bends. Sometimes we took shelter under the canopy of a flooded forest, at other times we held our breath in a pool of green water. Kash grasses and reeds in the shallows hid us too.

At first we could hear the fighting mostly in the distance, in another floodplain, but soon it was breaking out just behind a bend, or across a flooded forest. It wasn't uncommon for the bullets to whistle through the air above us, or a shell to land so close that splashes of water landed on the boat. These exchanges between the Pakistani army and the liberation forces could go on for the whole day, only to stop suddenly at dusk. But then, as the freedom fighters took the war to the enemy, we started to hear them at night more and more. Joker was very upset by it, and he disappeared from the boat. During the lulls, Bidudhar Majee went around the surrounding channels and pools on the raft, whistling for him, but he didn't respond to his calls.

Among us, Ducktor Malek was the most affected. He still sat cross-legged and barked through the nights. During the day he mostly lay slumped on the foredeck, only stirring his massive bulk and looking up with bloodshot eyes when he smelt food. He seemed to have forgotten all about the *Ramayana*, despite both Ala Mullah's and the teacher's efforts to animate him by reminding him of it. From time to time, Ala Mullah would bend down to his ear and speak very loudly.

"Do you hear me, Ducktor? I've got my suitable Muslim saint now. You know, to play Rama's teacher," he would say.

Ducktor Malek would grunt, and if Ala Mullah persisted, he would mumble: "Rama, oh him. Oh Allah, he's so hungry. Can't you see that he's cooking his rice? So, bugger off."

When bullets flew and bombs fell he would go into a frenzy, shaking his long curly hair, and acting out one of his roles from a jatra. His favourite, as ever, was Mir-Zafar the traitor, but there was no silly walk, high-pitched voice, or rolling of the eyes. It wasn't funny, and no one laughed.

The teacher came up to me and said, "What are we going to do, Kamal? Ducktor has lost his mind."

After a particularly fierce spell of fighting that lasted for two days, during which Ducktor finally fell asleep, we had a period of relative calm that also went on for days. We didn't have silence, though, because Ducktor snored so vigorously that it felt as though machine guns were being fired inside the boat.

Despite the fact that Moni Banu hadn't been in touch with us, the teacher decided that it was time for me to get married. The Majee brothers went around looking for a duck to trap, but the clamour of the war had driven all the ducks away. They did, however, collected enough lotus flowers for two garlands. After a prolonged absence, Joker – with yet another catfish between his paws – made his appearance. For Kulsum there was no red sari to wear, nor henna paste to paint her hands with, but Datla Nuri sang marriage songs in her harsh, rasping voice.

It was raining heavily again and we gathered inside the cabin for the ceremony. The teacher sat against the mast pole in the middle. To his left sat Datla Nuri with Kulsum next to her. I sat to his right with Ala Mullah next to me. The Majee brothers squatted behind us, but Ducktor Malek was still snoring. The teacher called him many times, but he didn't respond. Bidudhar Majee went for Joker and made him whistle into Ducktor's ears. Ducktor gurgled like a slaughtered bull, flailed his arms and legs, and opened his eyes. He stared at us blankly. When the teacher asked him, "Are you ready to be a witness now, Ducktor?" there was no response. He didn't seem to hear the question, let alone comprehend its meaning. I knew that he'd been scared of falling asleep and dreaming, because he didn't want things to become real for him, especially the things that had happened in the school yard. I realised that I shouldn't have let him fall asleep.

"I know how to fix his type," said Datla Nuri. She went behind the curtain and came back with a large plate of rice and catfish curry.

As soon as she placed it before Ducktor, he hunched over it and gobbled it like a duck.

"He might have gone foolish in his head, but he's as greedy as before," said Datla Nuri.

As Ducktor still stared at us blankly and didn't respond to Ala Mullah's questions, the teacher declared that Ducktor – having lost his mind – was not fit to be a witness. He was about to postpone the wedding when we felt a thud against our boat. I held my breath, fearing the worst, until Big Suban's voice reached me over the sound of the rain. He'd come alone in a dinghy. He looked very glum and serious.

I don't know whether it was a wild coincidence or a miracle that Big Suban arrived just in time to be one of the witnesses to my marriage. Once the ceremony was over, Bidudhar Majee played his little flute and his brother Harihar sang. Then they sprinkled a handful of lotus petals on Kulsum and I. Datla Nuri didn't sing again; she got busy serving us rice and catfish curry. When she served Ducktor Malek another large plate, he finished it in the same manner as he had done the previous one. I thought Big Suban had something to say to me, but he still looked glum faced and remained silent.

It was only after the meal that Big Suban gave us the message he had come to deliver: Zafar Alam had been killed in action. My immediate thoughts were: now that Moni Banu was a widow, what would become of her? I wished I were with her, that I could hold her, and make her feel that I would always be there for her. I left Kulsum alone, wearing the lotus garland that I had put on her only a short while ago, and got onto the raft. I began to punt away with Datla Nuri shouting after me: "Come back, Nephew. You're a married man now. Stop acting so foolish."

I turned back.

CHAPTER 16

Big Suban took Kulsum and I for a trip in his dinghy.

It was the only thing he could do, he said, to treat us on our marriage. It was afternoon, and despite the sky being clear and the wind blowing gently over the reeds, it was far from tranquil. From beyond the bends of the watercourse, echoing sounds of bullets and bombardments had driven all the birds away. Not even a single kingfisher could be seen wagging its tail from the branches hanging over the water. Big Suban told us not to be alarmed, because the sounds were coming from several miles away. He ought to know it, he confided, as it was his unit we were hearing. Apparently it was engaging the Pakistani army in one of its routine exchanges of fire. He told us that it was Moni Banu who was in command now.

"When Zafar Alam died she didn't cry. Not even a tiny drop, Kamal," he said.

Kulsum kept her head down, her sari over her face. We edged past a bed of reeds, and through the hyacinths, headed towards the flooded forest. I wasn't surprised to hear that she hadn't cried for Zafar Alam. If she didn't cry for her mother, surely she wouldn't cry for anyone else. I supposed the war had changed her and made her hard inside. Or, perhaps she needed to express her grief in a different way in her new position as commander.

"She just opened her eyes like a pair of polished stones as the waves carried his body away," said Big Suban. "Within minutes we were on a raid with Madam in charge. She fought like a trapped tigress that day. We slaughtered about fifty collaborators. All belonging to the hateful Jamat-e-Islami."

Hearing Moni Banu being called Madam sounded so strange in Big Suban's mouth that I gave him a look of surprise.

"When she took charge, we didn't know how to address her.

But when a man in our group, a book-reader like yourself, began to call her Madam, the rest of us followed him. I don't know what Madam means, but it sounds very important. You see, Moni Banu is our leader. She is very brave and cunning in her dealings with the enemy. So it's right that we should call her Madam."

We entered the flooded forest; it was cool under the shade of the canopy. Deftly, Big Suban guided us between the trees. He halted the dinghy under a fig tree and addressed Kulsum.

"Oh my brother's wife," he said. "Where are your people? Where have you come from?"

Kulsum stayed head-down and silent. He then addressed me.

"War is a funny thing, Kamal. It plays tricks with your destiny. Look, how it has brought you a matching bride. Just as speechless as you are. I bet the two of you can make perfect sense of each other without using a word."

I looked up and smiled with my eyes; he continued.

"At least one of us is married, Kamal. Isn't it funny that it's you who should be the one to get married? But thank Allah that I was on time to perform my duties for you."

Later that day Big Suban, as ever, slipped away, disappearing into the darkness of the evening without saying goodbye.

Now that we were married, the other side of the curtain became Kulsum's and mine. Datla Nuri moved over to my spot in the front part of the cabin. Kulsum and I slept side by side, but without touching each other. She lay with her back to me, curled up; she didn't move. Nor did she make any sound, except her breathing fluttering like a soft plume in the wind. It suited me because I was trying to imagine Moni Banu in her new role as Madam and commander, but failing to make any headway. My mind was going back over the moments when she became a woman: her head in my lap, I stroking her hair, and she asking me what I was to her. Neither of us knew how to answer that clearly, so we hid from our feelings, but sometimes a ripple on the surface caught us unawares. In those moments we looked at each other without shame in our eyes. Afterwards I never regretted those feelings, but tried my best to drown them. Recently I'd started to accept her as a sister and nothing more. Now that she was a widow, what was I to feel?

In the morning we woke up to light rain. Datla Nuri looked at me mischievously.

"Nephew, have you become a real married man now? I hope you've sowed the seed of a little grandchild for us." She giggled, rolled her eyes, nudged Kulsum with her shoulder, and giggled again. The teacher and Ala Mullah, though sitting nearby, pretended that they hadn't heard. Harihar Majee smiled quietly and walked over the cabin roof to be on the rear deck. Bidudhar Majee was trying to make Joker go fishing, but he didn't seem very keen and kept whining. Ducktor Malek was still in bed. Since he'd fallen asleep, he snored day and night, except from time to time sitting up briefly and screaming. He only woke up when Datla Nuri served us meals. He didn't speak to anyone; he just gobbled up his food and fell back to snoring again.

By the late morning, the rain had stopped. Realising that it was impossible for us to be alone in the boat, Datla Nuri insisted that I take Kulsum out on a trip on the raft.

"You have to get to know the secret ways of your wife, Nephew. Otherwise you two will remain dead fish to each other and stink like hell."

I had no intention of knowing her secret ways, but it was impossible to ignore Datla Nuri. So I went out with Kulsum. I punted for a while, then took the paddle in clear water, and after turning several bends came to an enclosed pool with lotuses. Kulsum looked at me with a steady gaze as if trying to fathom the secrets of my eyes.

"What am I to you?" she asked.

"Didn't you want me to protect you? I'll protect you," I wrote on the slate.

"I didn't mean that. I wanted to know how you feel about me."

"The fact that I have taken you as my wife doesn't mean that there is anything between us. I hope you are clear on this."

"Yes – it wasn't supposed to mean anything. I'm grateful that you have done this to protect me. I wish I could do something to pay back some of my debts to you, but I have nothing." She lowered her eyes, and said, "If you want to exercise your rights as a husband on me, I wouldn't mind." She spoke quietly, but I heard her.

She kept her head down, but arched her eyes to see if I had written anything. Instead of writing an answer I wiped the slate clean. She stayed quiet. The water lapped against the smooth, round trunks of the banana trees that formed the raft, wobbling it slightly.

"Am I that ugly to you?"

"No. You're too beautiful, Kulsum. I don't deserve you. If it weren't for the war, and if you hadn't found yourself among us – your enemy – you never would have come anywhere near me."

"I don't deny that. Since circumstances have brought us together, what are we to do?"

"We can pretend that we're married until the end of the war, then you can go back to your people."

"Even if I survive the war, I wouldn't know where to go. My parents and my brothers and sisters were my only people. And they are dead."

"You can go back to Pakistan, can't you?"

"I know nothing about Pakistan. I have no one there."

Humidity was rising again after the rain had stopped, and despite our raft being in shade, it felt hot. On Kulsum's face tiny globules of sweat were gathering and hanging like morning dew on a blade of grass. I was thinking of returning to the boat, but suddenly she straightened her head up and said, "I want to wet my hair. Do you mind?"

I had no reason to mind, but I wondered how she meant to do it as we carried nothing suitable to draw water with. For a moment I thought she might jump into the water, but she didn't do that. Instead, she looked at me in a way that really unnerved me, because she seemed so much like Moni Banu when she wanted me to do her a favour. Then she loosed her hair and sat hunched over the raft's edge and waited. How could I refuse her?

From the pool I scooped water into the palms of my hands and poured it over her head. Water slid down her thick, oily black hair and returned to the pool. Then I scooped water with one of my hands and rubbed her hair with the other. It was the first time that I had touched her. It felt strange, as though I was brushing against the dense feathers of a black bird.

"I've no country, no people. You are my only home now."

I was so taken aback by what she said that I was no longer mindful of the hand that lay on her head. It slackened. As she bent further down, it slid down her nape, over the smooth yellowish brown of her skin. How was I meant to be a home to her? Was she wishing to enter into my inside and build her little nest there? Then without quite realising what I was doing, I began to caress her nape and she lay so quiet, as though she was holding her breath.

Before I had a chance to react she rolled over the raft and sank into the pool. I waited for her to surface, but there was no sign of her. Only bubbles came up from the depths. What was she playing at? I dived in and frantically searched for her among the tendrils of lotuses. Where was she? At last I found her curled up like a foetus on the muddy bottom. I dragged her up to the raft.

I was gasping for air, but she seemed calm. I was about to show her my annoyance when she looked straight into my eyes. How could I be angry with her? She seemed to know all the tricks that Moni Banu used to play on me. She took one of my hands and pressed it against her cheek. I expected it to be cold, but it was burning.

"You saved me. You're my home," she said.

How could I be your home, Kulsum, without being able to touch you with love? I have nothing left; I have given all my love away to Moni Banu.

Kulsum kept my hand pressed against her cheek and I felt her tears wetting my skin.

Suddenly we heard a noise coming from just beyond the trees enclosing the pool. I immediately sensed danger and dragged the raft to the pool's edge, and then swam between the tree trunks and waded through the water to get to the other end. I stopped behind a rattan bush from where I could just about hear the people who came by in a boat. I didn't have to listen for long to realise that they were a gang of collaborators. Then I heard a gunboat approaching. It dawned on me that it was a joint raid by the Pakistani army and the collaborators, but who were they hunting? Who else but us?

I swam back to the raft, punted, and then paddled as fast as I could to reach our boat. They had also heard the gunboat and knew that it was a raid. No one had panicked and the teacher looked in command. Standing by the mast post on the cabin roof he gave us orders in a loud and clear voice. If Moni Banu had been there she would have been proud of him. I was proud of him. He directed us to row with all of our strength and in unison. We did just that and the boat raced through the twists and turns of the watercourse. After several bends he directed us into a flooded forest. The teacher came down to the foredeck and walked its length with such a look of purpose and confidence that we felt nothing could touch us.

We heard the gunboat again. It was still some distance away, but the teacher wanted us to keep moving. While Ala Mullah guided the rudder at the helm, the Majee brothers and I punted, then, reaching clear waters, we rowed. Climbing onto the cabin roof again, the teacher directed us through several bends, then he led us into a dense patch of tall kash grass. There we remained hidden under their arching stems, their white flowers swaying above us. It was late afternoon by now, and the rain clouds were gathering again, low in the sky. Despite the fact that the Majee brothers, Ala Mullah and I stayed on the rear deck, ready to propel the boat at a moment's notice, we were relaxed. For some time now there had been no sign of the gunboat. Joker was relaxed too; he went around us, sniffing and chattering, but when I tried to touch him, he looked at me with his bright, dark eyes and snorted. He gave out a shrill whistle, stood on his hind legs, placed his forepaws on Bidudhar Majee's lap, and began to nibble his fingers. I looked at Bidudhar and tried to ask him with gestures why Joker didn't like me, but he didn't understand my question. So I wrote it down on my slate and showed it to Ala Mullah, who read it out.

"He hasn't seen a face like yours, Kamal. He can't quite decide what kind of creature you are," said Bidudhar.

"If you're kind to him, he'll get used to your face," added Harihar.

Pushing Joker aside, Bidudhar lit his chillum. Joker ran to Harihar, whimpering, but as soon as Bidudhar gave a whistle he jumped off the boat.

"Where's your family?" Ala Mullah asked the brothers.

"We don't know. We were on a job, many miles away from home. When we came back we found our village burnt down and everyone gone," said Harihar Majee.

"Perhaps they've gone to the refugee camps in India. Have you been there?" asked Ala Mullah.

"No, we haven't," said Harihar. "We're poor boatmen. We only know the rivers and floodplains around our swampland. When the teacher offered us the job, we said to ourselves: even with the war on we must do what we were born to do."

"How is the teacher going to pay you? Surely, with the war on he has nothing to pay you with," said Ala Mullah.

"We know that. We're not asking for any money. Anyway, it's useless now. But he promised to give us a new boat after the war."

"How can the promise of a boat be more important than looking for your family?"

"We don't know the answer to that. All we know is how to sail boats. If our family has gone to India, we'll find them after the war."

"As Hindus you're in more danger than we are. I believe a refugee camp would have given you a better shelter. Don't you have to survive the war first to enjoy your new boat?"

"What you said is true, but we don't think like this. We feel that the boat is our world. When we row it, we feel at home and safe."

"I don't follow you, Harihar Majee. If the boat is your home, then where is your country?"

"We don't understand the meaning of country, Ala Mullah. We only know boats, water and the sky above our swampland. We live in it like a fish does, that's all."

When we heard the gunboat again from some distance away, the teacher came running over the cabin roof. Seeing him, Bidudhar Majee whistled for Joker and we lowered our punt-poles. We were almost clear of the patch of kash grass when Joker clambered on board. Reaching the clear water, we took the oars, and rowed swiftly through the channels between dense lines of trees. Yet, several bends later we could still hear the gunboat. It seemed to be taking the same course as we had.

Suddenly the gunboat stopped. We had no idea if they had given up or had just changed their tactics to surprise us, but the teacher didn't want to take any chances. He made us row and punt as hard as before. We kept on going through the tree-lined channels, flooded forests and pools. We were happy believing that we were reaching the heart of our swampland where they would never find

222

us. Finally the teacher ordered us to stop in an enclosed pool. It was almost evening and the sky, dense with rain clouds, was dark. It was about to rain at any moment.

Overhead, wind blew hard among the arching branches. We took shelter in the cabin as the rain came. We felt so safe that Datla Nuri lit the clay cooker to make us tea. Ducktor Malek woke up unexpectedly and remembered the jatra. From his lying position he pestered the Majee brothers to conduct themselves like princes, then he hauled his enormous bulk up. He went around the cabin pretending to be Lord Rama with his bow and arrow, hunting demons. When he noticed Kulsum sitting head down, he put on a soft, tender voice to address her. "Forgive me my queen for mistrusting your virtue," he said. "My sorrow is as deep as the ocean for making you walk through the fire. Forgive your foolish lord, forgive me my beloved."

Kulsum lowered her head further as if she wanted to burrow beneath the deck's planks. Datla Nuri noticed her discomfort and came to her aid.

"You mindless glutton, leave her alone. Go and sit in your place and be quiet. I'll give you something to eat soon," she said.

Ducktor Malek sat cross-legged and began to snore again. Unlike the rest of us, the teacher still looked worried. He put his bamboo-and-straw hat on and went out to the foredeck. I put on mine and followed him. We looked at the drops of rain splattering on the brown water of the pool. Cocking his head, he tried to listen as if to hear beyond the sound of the rain and the wind.

"I've the feeling that they're still here, looking for us. Perhaps we should move on."

I thought he would go inside the cabin and ask the Majee brothers to start rowing. Instead, he stayed on the deck, looking at the rain.

"After the war I want you to take Moni back to our homestead. Now that she's a childless widow, it wouldn't be nice for her to stay with her husband's family. You have to look after your sister, Kamal."

I was startled because it was the first time that I'd heard the teacher mention Moni Banu as my sister. I couldn't quite fathom the consequence of it then, but remember being very pleased, because it meant that the teacher considered me his son. The rain came to us slanting and heavy, and despite our hats, our lungis became totally soaked, but we stood looking at the rain, our eyes wide open, the way we had done so many times in the past, when we used to watch the rain fall on our pond. He put his hand on my back and caressed me.

"I'm proud of you, Kamal. I know you'll look after your sister," he said again, his voice almost breaking with emotion.

We heard a sound, but it wasn't thunder. While the teacher went inside the cabin to alert the others, I ran to the rear deck to take a punt-pole. Soon the Majee brothers joined me and Ala Mullah took up his position at the helm, but it was too late. All we could do was turn the boat around. At the far end of the pool were the sampans, barely visible in the rain, but they were heading towards us. Suddenly we heard the engine of the gunboat starting again. From the cabin roof the teacher shouted at us not to give up. "Forge ahead. Show them what you're made of. No one can catch us on water. Go with the power of the wind."

We dug in the punt-poles with all of our strength and managed to push the boat through a patch of reeds to our right that took us into a narrow watercourse. Then we took the oars with the teacher joining us. The four of us rowed and rowed, zig-zagging through several bends, but suddenly we found ourselves on a long watercourse with the gunboat behind us. We didn't panic as we slid into a flooded forest, just to our left. We were relieved to hear the gunboat passing us by and moving on. By then it was night and the rain had stopped falling; it was very dark without the moon. From all over the forest crickets began their chirping. I didn't expect to see glow worms, but there they were: looping lines of flickering light between darkened trees. After waiting for an hour or so, and hearing nothing untoward, even the teacher was beginning to relax. Surely they had returned to their base by now. We heard that they didn't like staying away from their base at night. Perhaps that's why they had given up.

As we punted our way out of the forest, Harihar Majee began singing a boatman's song. As always, I began to drift with the boatman, our nomad of the waves, his voice sliding up the waters into the endless blue above. So much loneliness and so much passion for the journey that never ends. Ah, the soul of our swampland. Suddenly Harihar Majee stopped as we heard the sampans cutting through the water.

This time we could do nothing. Four sampans rushed towards us with lightning speed and surrounded our boat from all sides. With their torchlight and lanterns the collaborators came on board. I was a bit dazed but I had no problem recognising Asad Khan as he passed me by with a rifle in his hand. He didn't look at me. He went straight for the teacher and knocked him down with the rifle butt and then started kicking him.

"Let's see who's the big-shot Noah now. No one escapes the wrath of Allah," he said and fired a shot in the air. Within minutes the gunboat with Pakistani soldiers arrived. On their orders we all gathered on the foredeck, except for Ducktor Malek, who was still sitting cross-legged and snoring. Asad Khan, accompanied by a number of collaborators, went inside the cabin and dragged him out. Half awake, he kept on asking if dinner was served.

"You'll get your dinner in a minute, you dirty glutton," said Asad Khan.

"Who is this man?" asked the captain in charge of the Pakistani forces.

"This son-of-a-bitch is a big polluter, sir. He dabbles into Hindu things in a big way. Only Allah knows how much stain he's put on our Islam. He even made us take part in a heathen Hindu play. Shall I feed him his dinner, sir?"

The captain nodded and Asad Khan put the muzzle of his gun into Ducktor Malek's mouth.

"Do you want your dinner now? Roast, kebab and pillau rice are coming," said Asad Khan and pulled the trigger. Ducktor Malek's brain scattered on us; his body shook for a while before becoming still. Joker whistled as though he was crying for all of us. The soldiers and the collaborators shot at him, but he managed to jump off the boat safely.

"You're an honest soldier of Islam. With men like you, Allah willing, we'll save Islam in East Pakistan," said the captain.

"He's a wicked lecher and a thief," shouted Datla Nuri, pointing her finger at Asad Khan.

"Who's that woman?" asked the captain.

"She's a foul-mouthed old hag, sir. When she had flesh on her body, she was a dirty whore. Another big polluter, sir."

The captain nodded and two soldiers leapt forward and bayoneted Datla Nuri to death. Kulsum, who was sitting next to her, screamed and slumped to the deck floor.

"Who is this woman?" asked the captain.

"She's a good Muslim, sir. One of your people – a Bihari."

"What is she doing here?"

"She has been kidnapped and dishonoured by this heathen lot, sir," said Asad Khan. On the captain's order, two of the soldiers carried her into the gunboat. Once Kulsum had gone, Asad Khan ran to the Majee brothers, and asked them to stand up.

"Do you want to see genuine Hinduness, sir?" he asked the captain, smiling.

"What is that?" asked the captain.

Asad Khan then pulled the Majee brothers' lungis down. They stood head down, naked. Asad Khan poked their private parts with the muzzle of his gun.

"Look, sir," he said. "Look at their heathenness."

The captain then ordered two soldiers to put ropes around the Majee brothers' necks and make them dance like bears. The soldiers pulled them hard, but the Majee brothers stood their ground. Bidudhar Majee began to whistle, a tune I hadn't heard before, but it went through me as though something was whispering from the depths of the floodplains. The captain pulled his handgun out and shot them both through the temples.

When the captain faced him, Ala Mullah started to recite long Koranic verses.

"What are you doing in this heathen boat? You should be fighting with us for the integrity of Pakistan and the glory of Islam."

"Every moment of my life I serve Allah and Islam. I am a mullah, sir."

"He's a double-faced mullah, sir," said Asad Khan. "He's too friendly with the enemies of Pakistan and Islam. He never spoke up against the enemies who are fighting to destroy us."

"Take him with you. Do as you please with him," said the captain. Two of the collaborators dragged Ala Mullah into one of the sampans.

I didn't know whether the teacher was unconscious after Asad Khan knocked him down with his rifle butt. He was still on the deck floor, his body crumpled into a ball. One of the soldiers threw a bucket of water on him and made him sit up. He sat with his head slumped between his knees.

"He's the ringleader, sir. Full of un-Islamic views," said Asad Khan.

"So, let's hear your views," said the captain. Blood was still dripping from the back of the teacher's head, his clothes drenched red. One of the soldiers pulled his blood-soaked hair to lift his head up, his eyes barely open.

"What are your views then?" asked the captain again.

"Reason and justice," said the teacher faintly. The soldier let go of his hair, his head slumped again between his knees. Asad Khan came forward and kicked the teacher again.

"He talks rubbish like this all the time, sir, but he pretends that he's a righteous one and know-it-all."

Asad Khan put the muzzle of his gun into the teacher's mouth but the captain stopped him, saying that he wanted to take him alive as he could be a good source of information.

Finally it was my turn.

"Who's this ugly brute?"

"He's just an ugly brute, sir. He doesn't understand the meaning of anything. Absolutely dull-witted, sir."

"What should we do with him?" asked the captain.

"Let him go, sir. He's so stupid that even if he doesn't like us, he can't do us any harm."

The captain thought about it for a while, and then said, "Sometimes stupid ones are good sources of information. We will take him back to the camp. But we need to establish who he is."

"He's our village idiot, sir. We call him Kamal, but he's just an ugly lump of flesh. We consider a goat or a chicken worthier than him. So, there is nothing to establish about him, sir."

The captain narrowed his eyes, creased his forehead and regarded me. "So, you are the beautiful, the perfect one. Now tell me who you are. I don't expect you to speak, but give me a sign. I'm good at reading signs."

I looked at him blankly and widened the hole of my mouth.

"Look at his ugliness, sir. Surely the most hideous thing you have ever seen. Doesn't he seem a pure vegetable to you? In fact, I'd bother more for an aubergine than him."

"Perhaps, but we must at least establish that he's not a Hindu."

"How can we do that, sir? He has no notion of such things. He's nothing," said Asad Khan.

"He can be a Hindu without knowing it like a goat can be a goat without knowing it. It's very easy to establish. All we have to do is examine his private parts."

I thought I'd really had it: I wasn't circumcised and when they found it out they would slaughter me the way they had slaughtered the Majee brothers. I was thinking of Moni Banu on that day in the mango grove during the early summer storm. She was whirling in the rain and the wind and asking me to become a sorcerer. Yes, I was her sorcerer then.

"Let's see what you are hiding there," said the captain and came forward. He was about to pull my lungi down when the teacher rose from the floor, flew at the captain and knocked him down.

"He's my son. Yes, my son. You want to see my private parts, do you?" the teacher screamed like a mad man and took his lungi off. He stood naked over the captain, still screaming, "Are you satisfied now? Do I look Muslim enough for you?"

The captain took his handgun out and shot the teacher several times. His body slumped at my feet, but before I could bend down to touch him two soldiers grabbed me. They tied my hands behind my back and put a rope around my neck.

"We will take him to the major. He will know how to get the truth out of him," said the captain.

They dragged me to the gunboat and pushed me into a dark room without windows. As soon as they had left, Asad Khan came in with a torch.

"Don't cry over that stupid teacher. He got what he deserved. Luckily they don't know that he fathered that bitch Moni Banu. So, they have no idea that you have anything to do with her either. I told them nothing. If they find out, you'll be as good as dead. If I were you I would stay quiet about that reading and writing business too. Always act as stupid as you look. Do you understand me?"

I didn't want his help. I would rather be dead than be protected by that vile creep. If my hands had been free, I wouldn't have hesitated to grab his throat and squeeze the life out of him. I have never bemoaned my deformities, but at that time how I longed to have a tongue so that I could spit in his face. All I could do was grunt like an angry dog from the back of my throat and open my eyes wide with venom.

"Show some gratitude for saving your skin. I don't know why I bother with an ugly brute like you," he said and hurried away.

They took me to the regional military headquarters for questioning. Although I discovered that Kulsum travelled in the same gunboat as I did, I didn't see her during the journey.

CHAPTER 17

About midnight the gunboat reached the ghat by the river. I heard the soldiers getting off and on, their boots stomping the gang-plank, but they didn't come for me until an hour or so had passed. Two soldiers dragged me by the leash, my hands tied behind my back. Despite the rope cutting into my neck I tried to look around, but I didn't see Kulsum.

I recognised the compound immediately because it was illuminated with bright lights. During the colonial period it had been the regional administrative centre and it continued to be so after partition. It housed the court building, the district magistrate's office and his bungalow, the police headquarters and the superintendent's bungalow, and the government rest house. All of them were brick-built and red.

At the landing, the soldiers dragging me asked the captain what they should do with me.

"Take him to the major."

Through intense bright lights and patches of darkness they dragged me to the major's office. The captain came in behind us.

"What you got there?" asked the major.

"As you can see, sir, a horrid cripple. Perhaps also mentally deficient."

The major played with his lush, heavy moustache and regarded me in silence for a while.

"What can I do with him?" he asked.

"He might know about the terrorists, sir. Perhaps he can lead us to their hideout."

"Even if he knows something, how am I to get it out of him? Obviously no speech can come out of that mouth. If he is mentally deficient I don't expect him to write either," said the major.

"We brought him to you because you are the best, sir. If anyone can bring the truth out of him it would be you, sir."

The major asked the soldiers to bring me near to him. When they dragged me next to his chair he turned around and looked into me as though he was an eye doctor.

"Interesting eyes," said the major. "Keep him. I'll deal with him later."

The soldiers took me out, tethered me to a tree and left. It was in a dark patch somewhere in the middle of the compound. All I wanted to do was curl up and fall asleep, but with the rope pulling on my neck I couldn't lie on the ground. I sat on the soggy mud and leaned against the tree.

I heard gunboats leaving and arriving, and columns of soldiers marching, and then a strange silence descended on the compound. I could even hear the crickets chirping. From time to time thunder rumbled in the distance, but there was no rain. I was so exhausted that I could have fallen asleep sitting up, but the teacher's face kept coming back to me. Why had he been so stupid as to call me his son and give his life to save me? What was my life worth? Sometimes he was so hard to understand, but he was my father. When the captain shot him he opened his eyes wide, the way he used to open them to see through the rain. He kept on searching for my eyes to the last moment and telling me that I was his son. I was crying and sobbing so much that a soldier on sentry duty came and pointed his torchlight on me.

"Quiet, you ugly son of a bitch," he said, but I couldn't stop. So he hit me with his rifle butt, and the rest I don't remember.

I don't know for how long I was unconscious, but when I came around it was still night. I heard thunder, then light rain began. The canopy above wasn't thick enough to protect me: I was getting wet and cold and began to shiver. For a while I thought I had fallen asleep and was dreaming, then I realised that the noise was coming from the police headquarters building, which wasn't too far to my left.

Allah, the screaming and shouting was so terrible, as though they were skinning them alive. Who were they torturing? At least the teacher didn't have to go through that. Oh how soft he was, reading books; he was better off dead. Why are you keeping me alive, Allah? I don't want to remember anything. Sorry Sona Mia, sorry, but you'll have to find someone else to remember you all. Then the buzzing of the prayers began, the same as I heard in the school yard.

I didn't want to hear it, but I couldn't close my ears as my hands were tied behind my back. I began to grunt as loudly as possible, praying, really praying for the sentry to come and finish me off. He came in after a while and put his torch on my face.

"What's the matter with you? You motherfucking heathen. Why are you making that ugly noise? If the major didn't have business with you I'd have thrown a grenade down your ugly hole."

The rain became heavier and I didn't hear the buzzing any more. I was totally drenched and shivering. I don't know whether I had fallen asleep briefly or not, but I heard the morning azan. It wasn't like Sona Mia's voice floating in to drape me with the warmth of Allah's love. As soon as the azan ended there were several volleys of gunfire. Were they executing the prisoners who survived the torture during the night? If so, at least they would be at peace now.

Late in the morning the major stopped by to see me.

"How are you? Did you have a good night's sleep?"

I heard him clearly, but I remained still with my head slumped on my chest. He came forward, lifted my head with one hand, and opened one of my eyes with the other.

"I see you didn't sleep during the night. Only intelligent people have trouble sleeping. If you were a real vegetable you would have slept like a log. So, don't play-act with me. You understand what I am saying, don't you?"

I stared at him blankly and dropped my head on my chest when he withdrew his hand.

"Perhaps you will be in a better mood to talk if you have a dry place to sleep. I suppose you also need a good breakfast. Yes?"

On his orders two soldiers dragged me to the police headquarters building and put me in a huge room with electric light. In the middle of it there was a large and deep earthen tub full of foul-smelling water. Around it, several ropes hung from iron rings fixed to the ceiling. There were several stools scattered in the room; and a very high and bulky chair with leather straps. My hands were still tied behind my back; and the soldiers who dragged me in tethered the rope around my neck to a window grille. They put the light off and left. I curled up on the floor and fell asleep.

The major woke me up in the afternoon.

"We did not want to wake you up. Unfortunately you missed breakfast and lunch. Don't worry, we'll make up for it with a good dinner. How does that sound to you?"

I again looked at him blankly, as though I had no capacity to catch his meaning.

"I suppose most people judge you by your appearance only. Please be assured that I'm not one of them. I like to think that I judge a man by his inner wisdom and beauty. A real man always lies under his skin. Am I right?" He spoke Bengali correctly, but with a strong accent typical of the Pakistanis.

I looked down, hiding my eyes from him.

"Forgive my oversight. I should have brought you pen and paper. I bet you can write more intelligently and faster than I can speak." He went out and came back with a blue writing pad and a fountain pen. He sat on his chair and placed them on my lap. I slid my fingers over the pen as if it was a mysterious object about whose nature I hadn't the faintest idea.

"No problem. You don't need writing to communicate, do you? Besides, I am of the view that writing is not the only mark of intelligence. As far as I am aware, our prophet never wrote anything in his life. Perhaps, you could respond to me in gestures. We can have a meaningful conversation that way too. No?"

I still pretended that I understood nothing of what he was on about.

"You see, I served as an intelligence officer for years before my present command. So, I can tell who's avoiding me. You might try to hide your eyes, but I've already seen them. And they tell me that you heard and understood everything I said. Yet, I wonder why you pretend not to," said the major. "You will be a tough case, but then I'm a specialist at tough cases."

He freed my neck from the rope and untied my hands before he left. I got up and walked the room. The floor was littered with little pebbles of goat's droppings. So, they kept their goats there. Considering the amount of rain we were having, it was a sensible idea. I knew how much my cows suffered during the rainy season. I touched the dangling ropes and wondered what they were for. Perhaps they use them to tether their goats. I didn't see any need for that in a room with doors that could be locked. Dead, bloated rats and faeces floated in the tub's water. Surely, this water wasn't fit even for the goats. I had always thought that animals needed clean water as much as we humans do.

I moved to the open window with the iron grille. A large number of Pakistani soldiers in uniform were moving about between the buildings. The whole compound was dotted with bunkers from which barrels of machine guns protruded. There were sentry posts and high watchtowers too. I spotted a group of armed collaborators sitting under a tamarind tree. Not far in the distance the roofs of several gunboats could be seen just above the high riverbank.

I turned around when I heard the door open. It was a strange sight. Two soldiers came in with two goats, two earthen pots and a gunny sack.

"On the major's orders we're bringing you dinner," they said in unison in Urdu, but I had no problem in understanding them. The goats bleated and rushed towards me. For a moment I thought they were charging me with their horns, but they stopped just in front of me and bleated again.

"They want their dinner too," said the thin, small soldier with large eyes. His companion was tall and fat with a huge face, but small and beady eyes. Both of them had innocent smiles like many of the sharecroppers in our village. I wondered if they had come from peasant families. I would have loved to know if they grew rice on their land.

"Are you a traitor to Pakistan and Islam? If you are, our goats won't like you. You see, they are devout Muslims. Can't stand the sight of polluters and heathens. But they seem to be taking a shine to you. I can see that they are very keen to make you laugh," said the small, thin soldier and broke into a giggle. He was called Sergeant A Khan, and his friend – the tall and fat one – Sergeant T Khan.

"We're a double act. We're the jokers in the camp. Some call us Laurel and Hardy, but we prefer to be called Sergeant Goatmen," said Sergeant T Khan and smiled shyly, closing his beady eyes. "Nothing pleases us more than making people laugh."

I didn't know how to take them. They were funny, but I knew that the major had sent them to work on me. So, I gave them the same blank looks I had given to the major. Sergeant A Khan looked at me with his large eyes and shook his head.

"I have never seen a mouth as large as yours. I bet you're a mighty big eater. Nothing to worry. The major has sent you plenty of food, but he was very insistent that we make you laugh. You see, we're goatmen, we're funnymen," he said.

The smell of richly spiced curry cooked in ghee and parata made me realise how hungry I was. I hadn't eaten anything since yesterday morning, before I had gone out with Kulsum on the raft. By now, after living on the boat for so many weeks, I was used to the idea of eating in front of strangers. So, without thinking twice about the presence of Sergeant Goatmen, I reached for the lid.

"Not so quick," said Sergeant A Khan, lifting my hand off the lid. "We haven't had a laugh yet. I'll tell you a secret. Laughing heightens the appetite, and makes food all the more enjoyable."

"Perhaps you want to have the laugh a bit later. Now it will please us if you give us a little sign. You see, it's not funny if we don't see the audience is in tune with us. All you have to do is to raise your hand to a question we will ask you. Just to show that you're with us. You know, us funnymen feel very sad when we don't see our audience with us. Just raise a quick hand, and then you can get on with your dinner," said Sergeant T Khan, rubbing his chin.

I had a bad feeling about it, so I kept my eyes lowered.

"It's a simple question. Raise your hand to it, so that we know we're getting through to you. No funnyman can make anyone laugh without that. I'm sure you'll appreciate that. Here it comes," said Sergeant A Khan.

"Are you a Hindu?" asked Sergeant A Khan in a baby voice.

I didn't even move my eyelids to his question.

"You are a Muslim then?" asked Sergeant T Khan, biting his lips like a fat little boy.

I kept my eyes down and my body as rigid as possible.

"Are you a man?" asked Sergeant A Khan, his baby voice cracking slightly.

I stayed like a stone.

"Are you a baby dog – bow wow?" asked Sergeant T Khan as if the little fat boy was angry.

I continued to pretend I had no comprehension of human speech. For some reason I imagined myself as water.

"Perhaps we should have a laughing session to break the ice. That will allow us to feel comfortable with each other. No?" said Sergeant T Khan, and broke into a chuckle.

Suddenly both of them jumped on me. They lifted me up, put me into the tall, bulky chair, and fastened me tightly with the leather straps.

"You look like a king on a throne," they said bowing to me. "Give us permission, your majesty, to entertain you. Shall we begin by washing your feet?"

They nudged each other with their shoulders and giggled like silly, innocent boys. Then they took out an aluminium bowl from inside the gunny sack, filled it with water from the tub, and wetted the soles of my feet.

"Are you ready, your majesty?" said Sergeant A Khan and plunged his hand into the sack. Sergeant T Khan did the same. Each brought out a handful of salt and smeared the soles of my feet. No sooner had they done this, the goats began licking my soles with their harsh and almost sandy tongues. It felt ticklish, but I was determined not to laugh. I fixed my gaze on the portrait of General Yahiya Khan on the wall in front of me. I was particularly drawn to his heavy brows, which hung like palm fronds over his eyes, but that was a mistake. For some reason I found them so funny that I couldn't contain my laughter. Sitting leisurely on the floor, on either side of me, Sergeant Goatmen smeared salt on my soles again and the goats slurped as they licked them clean. Once I started to laugh I couldn't stop.

"Laugh your majesty, laugh. It will please the goats. We've learnt this trick from our Chinese friends. You see, China is a big friend of the pure land of Islam. They'll also be happy to learn that the trick is working," said Sergeant A Khan. Sergeant T Khan looked at me with his beady eyes and smiled like a naughty boy.

"Are you a snake – hiss, hiss? Just roll your head to your right to say yes and to the left to say no."

I was laughing so much that my stomach was hurting, but I couldn't stop.

"You see, our goats love making people happy. Unless you roll your head to say yes or no, they will keep on making you happy," said Sergeant A Khan.

I didn't pay him any attention. I don't know how much time had passed as Sergeant Goatmen kept on smearing the soles of my feet with salt, the goats kept on licking, and I kept on laughing. Until the goats licked my soles off and got into my flesh. Sergeant Goatmen looked at each other, rolled their eyes, and giggled together. Then they said that the real funny part was about to begin, before putting salt on my raw flesh.

"We don't want to brag about it, but people say it's a comic masterstroke. It's so funny it can even kill a man," they said in unison and continued to giggle. The goats licked me like some man-eating demons. It was so painful that I thought it would be a relief if I died. I gurgled from the back of my throat, foam spilling from my mouth, but no matter how hard I tried I couldn't move. Nor could I scream.

"How about a drink, your majesty?" asked Sergeant A Khan. He scooped some dirty water from the tub with the aluminium bowl, poured a huge quantity of salt into it, and mixed it with the toecap of his boot. While Sergeant T Khan held my head, Sergeant A Khan poured the water down my hole. Strangely I didn't feel sick. Still slurping, the goats were licking my open wounds. Sergeant Goatmen smeared another round of salt on my soles. I couldn't take the pain any more. I was on the verge of passing out, but I could still hear Sergeant A Khan. He whispered into my ear.

"You are a goat, aren't you? No wonder our goats have taken such a shine to you. Yes, you are a goat? Just roll your head to your right to say yes or to your left to say no. Hurry up. Your dinner is getting cold, you know," he said.

I don't remember much, but I must have looked at him blankly before passing out. When I woke up I found my feet were bandaged and the major was sitting by me. He had a glass of water in his hands and some bananas. He looked at me with concern and offered me the water, which was clean and cool. Then he peeled a banana for me. Every time I moved I felt an intense pain searing through my feet.

"Sorry about the clowns. They get a bit carried away with their comedy routine, but they are kind souls. So anxious to entertain people."

I kept my vigilance up and didn't give him any indication that I understood him. The major narrowed his eyes and looked at me suspiciously.

"The clowns tell me that you're just a vegetable. You have no comprehension of things happening to you. Apparently, you're as stupid inside as you look. But I don't believe that. They might be good at making people laugh, but are very poor judges of character. I know you're very intelligent and understand everything we say to you. So, I'm puzzled why you won't talk to us."

I lay curled up on the floor.

"I'm afraid the clowns want to entertain you again. Apparently they have a new routine they want to show you. Perhaps you've had enough of their silly clowning. Shall I ask them not to come?"

I would have done anything to stop the clowns from visiting me again, but I wasn't going to fall for the major's tricks by answering him. So, I lay curled up, feigning my incomprehension as before. The major got up, exasperated.

"So, you want to be entertained by the clowns. Well, it's your choice. But I must warn you about their new routine. It's funny. I mean, really funny," he said and left.

While I waited for Sergeant Goatmen, it occurred to me that despite my best efforts my secrets could still be out. So many ways it could happen, but most of all I feared that Asad Khan might change his mind. I don't know why he had decided to protect me in the first place, but if he could butcher Ducktor Malek in such a cold and calculated way, and beat up and humiliate the teacher – who had risked his relationship with his only daughter to protect him – he would be capable of anything. Besides, irrespective of what had happened between us, Kulsum still belonged to the enemy, and it wouldn't take her much to betray me. Perhaps she was entertaining the idea of avenging her family, but I also knew that when she said I was her home, she meant it. Would she be my home too?

Sergeant Goatmen had just entered the room. Oh Allah, they had brought the goats along. Please, please, not the goats again. I would do anything, tell you everything you want to know, but please don't use the goats on me any more.

Sergeant Goatmen brought their faces close to mine and smiled. I was relieved that they didn't address me as *your majesty* and lift me into the high chair with straps.

"How about a bath? We can't keep our guest dirty. Oh, no," said Sergeant A Khan. Sergeant T Khan closed his eyes, and covered his mouth with his hand to hide his giggles.

"Goats are not in a funny mood today, but tell us if you fancy a laugh. We might be able to persuade them. But we are here to give you a bath. We will be your nurses today. You'd like that, wouldn't you?" said Sergeant A Khan. I was somewhat relieved to hear that the goats weren't in a funny mood, but was beginning to suspect what kind of bath they meant to give me. They dragged me near the tub.

"Baths do wonders for your health, but it's funny how some people don't like too much bath. In case you're one of those people, we thought we should establish a procedure. We will ask you a question before we put you into the bath. Nice and easy question. If you want to answer it, just raise your hand, we'll stop. Is that clear?" said Sergeant A Khan.

Sergeant T Khan picked me up with his enormous hands and sat me on the edge of the tub. He looked inside my mouth with his beady eyes and twitched the corner of his mouth.

"What do you see?" asked Sergeant A Khan.

"Nothing except a little pink thing at the back of his throat. It's horrible," said Sergeant T Khan.

"I told you, he's totally empty, didn't I? Just a lump of godforsaken flesh. I don't think he understands anything," said Sergeant A Khan.

"Let's give him a bath. If there is anything human in him, we will find out," said Sergeant T Khan.

"Sure, we will," said Sergeant A Khan. Then he addressed me. "Are you human? If you are, just raise your hand, and we will stop. Yes?"

The Sergeant Khans lifted me up over the tub. While A Khan held me by the legs, T Khan wrapped an arm around my neck. My nose was almost touching the thick, dark water with bloated rats and floating turds. Suddenly T Khan tightened the grip around my neck and pushed my head under the water. Foul water rushed in through the hole in my mouth. For few seconds I struggled to free myself, but the more I tried, the more T Khan tightened his grip. I thought he would strangle me before I had time to die of drowning.

I don't know how I managed it, but I didn't raise my hand to say: yes, yes, I'm human. Before I lost consciousness, Moni Banu came to me and told me, Beautiful One, I'll look after you, but she didn't make me wear the red scarf around my mouth and walk around her any more, nor did she lead me through the summer storm to the mango grove, bite my finger until it bled and tell me, Beautiful One, you're not my brother. But I am your brother, Moni, yes I am; even the teacher told me to look out for you because you're my sister; I'll never again look at you with fire in my eyes, but I will always look out for you because you're my sister.

I don't know when they pulled me out of the water because I don't remember anything. Nor do I know how they revived me. The next thing I remember was the major sitting in front of me and Sergeant Goatmen on either side.

"This one is pure vegetable, all right, sir. His inside is totally vacant. You can't even call him human. Not only did he not raise his hand, he didn't even move. I don't think he has any comprehension that he was dying. In this sense, he is not even an animal. When we slaughter our cows they struggle to live, but not him," said Sergeant A Khan.

"What are we to do with him now?" asked the major.

"We can't do anything more with him, sir. Our job is to get information out of people, not to execute them. We're finished with him, sir. He has nothing, so there's nothing we can extract from him," said Sergeant A Khan and stood up. Then Sergeant Goatmen saluted the major and walked out with their bleating goats. I opened my eyes with the major looking on at me.

"You might have fooled the clowns, but I'm not so sure. Your eyes tell that you're more intelligent than both the clowns put together. And you know what you're doing – don't you?"

The following morning they again tied my hands behind my

back, put a rope around my neck, dragged me out of the building, and tethered me to the same tree as before. It was only then that I realised that it was a calabash tree. This time they tied me to one of the lower branches, which allowed me to curl up on the wet muddy ground and fall asleep. About midday Sergeant Goatmen, who were on their way to the police headquarters building, woke me up. They brought a bowl of gruel and a tumbler of clean water.

"Our goats don't find you funny any more. It's never happened before. You must be the most wretched abomination in Allah's creation," said Sergeant A Khan, this time without giggling.

"Our goats are most offended because we called you a goat. You see, they have more brains than you have," said Sergeant T Khan. He didn't giggle either.

Even though it was painful, I pulled myself up and sat leaning against the calabash tree. All around me there were hundreds of Pakistani soldiers, fully armed and in combat fatigues. They were either marching towards the gunboats by the riverbank or returning from action. I was desperately hungry, but as my hands were tied behind my back, I couldn't eat. I went down on my knees and bend my head over the pot of gruel, but without a tongue I couldn't lap it up.

In the afternoon the major stopped by.

"You are either the cleverest or the stupidest man on earth. I intend to find out. You will be tied to this tree until you give us a sign. If you do that we will free your hands and you can eat your food. Otherwise, you die here," said the major.

He stood before me playing with his moustache and observing me as though trying to decipher my involuntary movements and twitches. I thought he would go on watching me for hours, but luckily the sky broke into a torrential downpour. He ran to his bungalow, the previous colonial magistrate's residence, which lay about thirty yards to my right.

The foliage of the calabash tree wasn't dense enough to protect me from the rain. I was drenched within minutes, but I was able to drink. I lay face up and widened the hole of my mouth. I stayed in this position until I'd had my fill of water, and then curled up, shivering in the rain. Hours must have passed as I lay there. From time to time thunder struck and the wind whistled between the bungalows. I pulled myself up as I heard the goats bleating and saw a group emerge from the rest house with torches and flambeaux. They passed just in front of me and headed towards the riverbank. Sergeant Goatmen, at the head of the group, walked briskly with their goats. Behind them were the prisoners, heads down and lumbering, dragged along by soldiers in raincoats. A few minutes later, I heard the gunshots from the riverbank. I knew they had shot the prisoners, and wondered why, so far, I had been spared.

It was my third day in the camp. Apart from the few bananas the major had given me on my second day, and drinking rainwater, I'd had nothing to eat. In the morning Sergeant Goatmen brought me a fine breakfast composed of scrambled eggs and chapattis and a glass of sweet milk. As before, with my hands tied behind my back, I wasn't able to eat any of it. As intended, the sight and smell of the food made my hunger more difficult to bear. An hour or so later, the major came to see me.

"I hate to see this fine breakfast wasted. All you have to do is give us a sign. You must be very hungry, yes?"

I wasn't going to fall for his tricks. I stayed curled up on the mud as if I was a dead lizard. When he was gone I sat up against the calabash tree and swivelled my head around to take in the view, but froze as I turned to my right. There on the major's bungalow was Kulsum, wearing salwar and kameez, and sweeping the veranda. She stopped for no apparent reason and looked in my direction. She stood up looking at me, but I could see neither her eyes nor the expression on her face. I wondered what she was thinking, especially now that she was safe and secure among her own people. She didn't need to pretend to be married to me any more. She was free to imagine a life with a man with the kind of face she, perhaps, had dreamt of when she became a woman. Surely not a man who had a hole for a mouth, who couldn't even touch her lips with his in the most intimate of moments or whisper sweet words of love in her ears. How did she feel about me? I had no way of knowing, but I liked her standing there on the veranda, looking at me.

Suddenly the major came onto the veranda and Kulsum hurriedly resumed her sweeping. I wished he would leave, but he sat on the recliner. Kulsum brought him a drink. Perhaps tea. I had no way of knowing, but I felt that the major – despite the appearance – wasn't using her as a maidservant, but treating her like a daughter. I was sure that he would have been moved by the story of a young orphan Bihari girl, who was bright, beautiful and well educated. He would be protective towards her, the way he would be towards his own daughter. I realised I should have thought about this before; suddenly fear crawled up my spine as it occurred to me that he would no doubt ask her questions about me. Even if she didn't mean any harm, perhaps as a way of throwing some good light on me, she might tell him how I was a book-reader and perfectly capable of communicating in writing. That would be enough to undo my ploy and bring me before a firing squad, but I feared something else even more. If she had told him that I was married to her, this was bound to outrage him. Oh the horror of it! Doesn't even bear thinking! Can you really imagine that ugly cripple with such a charming, well-bred young woman? It would be natural for him to think that I had taken advantage of a defenceless Bihari girl and taken her as my wife by force. Death by firing squad might well be a desirable end.

While the major was still sitting on the veranda, sipping his drink, Kulsum disappeared inside the bungalow. When I thought about it again I realised that she, for whatever reason, hadn't told him anything about me. Otherwise, I would have been dead already. But would she keep her mouth shut in the future? The major got up and headed towards the riverbank. Perhaps he was going out with his troops on an operation. I could hear the gunboat engines starting up. I didn't care where he went as long as he wasn't on the veranda. As I lay there thinking about Kulsum, she – as if responding to my secret summons – came out and stood once more beside the pillar, looking at me.

She was wearing a white salwar and a blue kameez. From the distance, and with the morning sun falling on her face, she looked almost cheerful. When someone passed between the bungalow and the calabash tree, she hurried inside, but soon appeared on the veranda again. She walked a little, stretched her arms, looked at me, but never left the veranda. How I wished for her to come over and sit by me, but she couldn't have done that without being seen. From a sentry box to my left a soldier was keeping an eye on me. Besides, there was the high watchtower that afforded a clear view of the passage between the bungalow and the calabash tree. Luckily, the veranda itself could be seen neither from the sentry box nor from the watchtower.

The sun had moved right over the bungalow, putting Kulsum in the shade. She looked more sombre now, as though burdened by distressing thoughts. I wondered what she felt, seeing me with my hands tied behind my back and tethered to the calabash tree like a goat. Was she feeling sad for me? I hoped she wasn't.

Just after midday Sergeant Goatmen appeared again. Kulsum ran inside the bungalow. They brought in the lunch: chicken in thick spicy sauce and paratas.

"It's hot," said Sergeant A Khan, as though making casual conversation with me.

I didn't even twitch a muscle in response.

"It's cold, yes?" said Sergeant T Khan.

I was beyond language, the way the mud on which I sat was beyond language. They shook their heads, picked up the untouched breakfast and left.

The sun had moved towards the western sky. It was still bright and hot. I waited for Kulsum to appear again, but hours passed and there was no sign of her. What was she doing, and why wasn't she coming to the veranda? I had no claim on her; she owed me nothing, but I wanted to see her looking at me. I felt that if she didn't keep looking at me I would cease to exist and disappear in the mud, without leaving a trace.

It was evening and the sky was red with orange patches; then the purple descended before the darkness of the night. I saw the major climbing the steps to the veranda. With his return my chances of seeing Kulsum were gone, at least until the next day.

The eyes from the sentry post and the watchtower were as vigilant as ever, but nothing much was happening in the compound. In the distance, hollow, echoing sounds drifted in, signalling the gathering of rain clouds. I wished it wouldn't rain, because I would be drenched, forced to wallow in the mud, and unable to sleep. But then if it didn't rain, I wouldn't be able to drink.

The rain was holding off and I tried to sleep, but the smell of spices awakened my hunger. I sat up thinking that somehow I would find a way of eating the chicken curry that Sergeant Goatmen had left for me. As I crawled towards it I realised that my leash wasn't long enough. The rope cut into my neck, strangling me, but still I couldn't reach. I gave up and lay curled on the wet ground. I could hear the wind among the calabash leaves, whistling like a giant kite, and already a few drops of rain were falling. I remembered the teacher and couldn't stop crying again. Sergeant Goatmen, returning from the police headquarters building with the goats, stopped by.

"Are you laughing all by yourself? If you laugh like this, what's going to happen to our goats? They'll lose more than their jobs, you know. Most likely they'll end up in the cooking pot," said Sergeant T Khan and laughed like a little boy.

Sergeant A Khan picked up the curry and the paratas.

"I hate to see food go to waste. We will make it easy on you. We will ask you a question and all you have to do is make a noise. You can grunt, you can cry, you can laugh. If you like, you can even fart. We don't mind. We funnymen are used to that kind of thing, you know."

Both the sergeants laughed as through they were sharing some private joke.

"You are a real potato head, yes?" said Sergeant T Khan. He kept asking me this question while Sergeant A Khan put the food down and pressed his ear just before the hole of my mouth. I held my breath until he moved around to listen to my backside.

"Just a tiny fart. Please don't deny your poor, funny friends. Give us a little fart. We don't mind if it stinks like hell," said Sergeant A Khan.

I closed and hardened my body as though I had become a fossil.

"You are very clever, aren't you?" said Sergeant T Khan. He kept repeating this, and his companion, as he had done before, tried to listen to my body. My response was the same.

When they'd been gone for a while, I sat up and looked in the direction of the bungalow. From the veranda, a dim light, perhaps a torch, was going on and off. It was too dark to see her face, but I knew it was Kulsum saying goodnight to me. The light went on and off few more times, then it disappeared inside the bungalow.

She didn't need me, so why was she doing this? I knew she had been cool and calculating, not to say rather shameless and forward, when she asked me to marry her. In our part of the world who'd ever heard of a young woman proposing marriage to a man? I know people do desperate and unexpected things to survive, but why was she appearing on the veranda and looking at me? Was it to gloat at my misfortune? No, it couldn't be that, because I knew that when she said I was her home, she really meant it, but then there was no past between us, the way there was between Moni Banu and I. We hardly knew each other, and I had never given her any sign that I might care for her in any other way than just protecting a poor war refugee. Kulsum, I didn't know what your intentions were, but every time I saw you I felt that you were offering me a home too.

For the following few days I saw neither Sergeant Goatmen nor the major. I had no idea where they had gone. I had seen the goats wandering on their own in the compound. An eerie silence had descended on the camp. I was still tethered to the calabash tree. No one had brought me any food or asked questions. It seemed they had forgotten about me. From time to time it rained to provide me with drinking water.

Now, when a soldier or a collaborator passed me by they didn't even turn to look at me, but Kulsum was there on the veranda. It didn't escape my notice that she wasn't wearing salwar and kameez any more. During the day, wearing the sari she wore in the boat, she would stand for hours looking in my direction, and only hurried inside when a soldier came down the path between the bungalow and the calabash tree, which was happening less and less. At night she would come out with a hurricane lamp and swing it from time to time. I began to feel she was staying awake the whole night, and that if she'd had the slightest chance of running towards me unnoticed she would have done it, but the eyes from the sentry box and the tower were still watching.

But whatever her reasons for keeping vigil over me, I was glad that she did because she kept me alive. Every time I felt a drowsiness that almost made me give in to that silence where even a conch shell doesn't echo the whisper of the wind, the only thing that made me open my eyes was to see Kulsum looking at me.

I wasn't sure how long had passed since they'd brought me into the camp, perhaps a week. Between periods of sun there was rain, and days merged into nights. Then one morning bullets began to fly all over the compound and mortar shells landed close by. The watchtower was hit and I saw the soldier on duty falling to the ground like a dead branch. At first I thought the liberation fighters were only coming over the ground, from behind and from the right side of the camp, but then I realised that heavy fighting was also taking place by the riverbank. It seemed like a well co-ordinated attack from both land and water. I wondered if Moni Banu was there, directing the operation from a sampan. If she was, she was doing a good job, because panic had set in among the soldiers. From the sentry box the soldier on duty came running towards me, climbed the calabash tree and fired a round of bullets from his automatic rifle. He then climbed down, changed the magazine of his rifle, and pointed it at me. I thought he was going to shoot me and closed my eyes, surrendering to the inevitable, but he didn't pull the trigger.

"If it weren't for the major's order to keep you alive, I'd pour the whole round into your ugly hole," he said and ran towards the riverbank. He hadn't gone far when he fell, riddled with bullets. I lay curled up on the ground with the battle raging around me. It went on and on, and I didn't open my eyes to see what was happening until I felt a hand on my forehead. It was so gentle and loving that I thought it was Moni Banu coming to rescue me, but I was wrong. I opened my eyes and saw Kulsum peering at me.

"This is our chance. We have to get away," she said and cut the rope which tethered me to the calabash tree and untied my hands. I didn't have the strength to stand up, so she tried to lift me. It was painful as the soles of my feet were still sore.

"It's safer to crawl," she said. I was so weak that I had to push myself even to crawl, but she got down on all-fours and crawled beside me, encouraging me to carry on. We reached the bungalow safely. She brought me a tumbler of clean water with a large amount of sugar and a bundle of food. I got some strength from the drink and a piece of bread from the bundle.

There was no time to waste, so we crawled to the right of the bungalow, avoiding the soldiers in their trenches, bullets flying over our heads, and pushed through undergrowth to reach the betel-nut grove next to the camp. The freedom fighters seemed to be shooting from above us, from the fronds of the trees. I was praying that they wouldn't mistake us for the enemy. When we passed a dense creeper bush a group of freedom fighters jumped from nowhere and surrounded us. They questioned us as to who we were and what we were doing there. Kulsum couldn't open her mouth without betraying her origins. I tried to explain with gestures that my wife and I were prisoners and were trying to escape, but they didn't understand me.

"He must be an enemy spy. Let's shoot him," said one of the freedom fighters.

"The woman looks like a Bihari. That's why she doesn't open her mouth," said another.

Big Suban must have seen us just in time. He slid off a betel-nut tree and came running towards us, shouting.

"What are you doing? This is our Kamal, my bosom friend. She's his wife. Can't you see that both of them are speechless?"

Big Suban wanted to know how I ended up in the camp. I told him that we'd been caught while we were on a trip on the raft, because I didn't want to tell him what had happened on the boat, I especially didn't want Moni Banu to know about the teacher. At least not like this, from someone else. I would tell her myself. Big Suban told us that she was indeed there, leading this operation, so it was impossible to see her just then. He took me on his back and carried me through the betel-nut grove, to the riverbank a few hundred yards away from the ghat in front of camp. There were several sampans belonging to the liberation fighters waiting there with supplies.

"You stay here, Kamal. After the operation we'll take you back to our camp. You will be safe among us. And Madam will be very happy to see you," said Big Suban.

When I expressed my desire to get back to the boat, he was surprised. I persisted, and in the end he agreed to let me go. He asked one of the sampans to take us to the other bank of the river, where we could get a dinghy to make our way to the boat. I don't know why I wanted to go back. No one was there. Besides, I didn't know where to find it. It could have drifted anywhere in this vast floodplain. Yet, I felt an inexplicable urge to get back there. Now thinking back on it I realised that the boat, despite what had happened in it, was a kind of refuge. Moreover, where else could I take Kulsum? I couldn't take her among the liberation fighters because sooner or later they were bound to find her out. A Bihari, an enemy.

"Stay alive, Kamal. Now you have a wife to look after," said Big Suban. "We will liberate the country soon. I'm thinking about my axe again and cutting trees. After the war who will come to interrupt me in the forest if not you?"

It was the first time that we parted company by saying goodbye to each other. We were taken to the other bank, then put in a dinghy. Although by then I had eaten some more of the food that Kulsum had carried in the bundle, I didn't have the strength to paddle. Kulsum insisted that I rested. While I lay in the dinghy with my head on the stem post and fell asleep, Kulsum paddled. I have no idea from where she got the know-how or the strength, but she paddled and paddled across the river, then through the floodplains until the evening. Kulsum only called me up when we reached the boat. It was tangled up among hyacinths in the middle of a vast floodplain. There was no wind, and not a soul was around; only the silence under a red and purple sky. It seemed we were alone in this waterworld. I pointed to the boat and held up my hands as if surprised. She smiled and said, "I have always been good at remembering. I hardly ever forget things. I came back to where we were, then I followed my hunches to reach here."

I didn't know how to feel when we got into the boat. It looked almost the same, except for the bloodstains on the foredeck. I didn't see Joker anywhere but the strong, sweet smell of his musk was reassuring. I knew he must be around. Kulsum got busy tidying up; she found my slate in the fold of a rush mat. She hung it around my neck and said, "Now that we're only the two of us, we can talk and talk. We won't be alone any more."

I took the slate and cleaned it with the steam of my breath.

"You should have stayed among your people, Kulsum," I wrote. "It's not safe for you here."

"I only feel safe with you. You're my home, aren't you?" she said.

CHAPTER 18

For the next few days, I lay in bed. If I wasn't sleeping, I kept my eyes closed as though I was afraid, like Ducktor Malek, of what I might see. My wounds were still raw and I had a high fever. Moving quietly like a cat, Kulsum nursed me through the days and nights. She cleaned my wounds and changed my bandages with pieces of cloth she cut from Datla Nuri's old sari. Most of the time she sat by me, put a wet rag on my forehead, wiped my brows, and ran her fingers through my hair. From time to time, she mumbled to herself something that I didn't follow. She left me alone only to cook rice and lentil soup, but came back as soon as they were ready. She mixed them with her fingers and placed them gently deep into the hole of my mouth. No one had nursed me like this before. In fact, I had never been nursed.

Since we'd returned to the boat, there was hardly any wind, and the boat remained trapped where we had found it. We didn't hear any bombardment or gunboats. Perhaps the liberation fighters had overrun the camp and driven the Pakistani army out from this stretch of the floodplain. Silence had brought some of the birds back. I could hear ducks flying over us and the cry of the ospreys. Joker was back on board too. I don't know where he went while we were in the camp, but I was pleased to hear him chattering and whimpering again.

I was feeling much better after a week or so. I no longer had fever, but my feet were still sore. Seeing me restless in the cabin's shadows, Kulsum lifted me up. I leaned on her shoulders and hobbled to the foredeck. It was late afternoon; she settled me against the gunwale and went back inside the cabin. I scanned the horizon, but saw no movement, except for the gentle fluttering of odd patches of hyacinths or lilies. The rest was just water as far as I could see. I looked up in the sky and saw a group of vultures circling up and up until they almost disappeared, then they began their descent. I realised that this was only a lull and that the war was not over yet. I could tell that the vultures had spotted a meal somewhere in the floodplain. I was wondering who these dead were when Kulsum came back with a bowl of rice pudding. As she fed me with her fingers, she asked me how she should address me.

"Should I call you husband? Or, should I not address you by any name whatsoever, as is customary here?"

Although Kulsum had hung the slate round my neck before bringing me out to the foredeck, I wasn't keen on using it. So I shrugged my shoulders and kept looking at the changing colours of the water as the afternoon drifted into the evening.

"Calling you husband or calling you nothing belongs to old customs. It wouldn't suit an educated couple like us. What do you think?"

I agreed with her views, but I was surprised to hear myself referred to as a part of a couple. Besides, I wasn't sure I was an educated one. Yes, I had read some books, and I suppose – as the teacher was in the habit of reminding me – they had given me a particular window to the world, but I had never attended any school, or left my village to be acquainted with the ways of the world. What bounded my horizon was no more than the wind dancing over the yellowish stalks of rice fields, or water ebbing and flowing until the light in my eyes dimmed into throbbing grey far into the distance, or village folks ploughing their land and tending their animals, and always being at the mercy of flood and praying to Allah for deliverance. This was the stuff of my reality, not the books.

I stayed quiet and closed my eyes.

"I don't want to call you Kamal either. Sister Nuri told me that the teacher imposed that name on you," she said.

I didn't like her for talking badly of the teacher, so I waved my hand to show my annoyance.

"What did your birth parents call you? Perhaps I should call you by that name."

"As far as I know, they never gave me a name," I wrote on my slate.

"What should I call you then?"

I dropped my writing stick and looked out at the floodplain again. She stayed silent for a while as though deep in thought.

"I know what I will call you. You are Allah's gift to me. So, how about Ata Allah?"

I like being called Kamal, but if it pleased her to call me Allah's gift I wouldn't make a fuss about it.

"Now that I can call you by a name, I can tell you stories."

I shook my head but with a half-smile. She didn't need to call me by a name to tell me stories.

"If I tell my stories to someone without a name, I might feel that I'm telling them to nobody. I can't do that."

I raised my brows and fluttered my lids in a way to suggest that if she wanted to tell me stories she should get on with them. I returned to my half-slumber.

"I was born here, you know. In East Pakistan, or what your people now prefer to call Bangladesh."

I opened my eyes at that and grabbed hold of my writing stick. I couldn't let her presume that I didn't mind whatever this land was called.

"I myself prefer to call it Bangladesh. Pakistan died on us a long time ago," I wrote.

She looked at me as though surprised by my response. She stayed silent for a long while and bit her nails.

"I know nothing about Sind, Punjab, Baluchistan, or the Frontier Provinces. Nor do I have anyone there, but the idea of Pakistan, you know, will never die on me."

I felt such fury at hearing these words that I grabbed the bowl of pudding from her hand and threw it in her face. I was gurgling loudly and saliva was dripping from the hole of my mouth. I didn't look at her, but head-down I scribbled on the slate.

"You rabid Pakistani dog. You're evil, I hate your face," I wrote. It was only when I thrust the slate in front of her face that I saw the cut. She sat with her eyes wide open with fear and blood dripping from one of her cheeks. I didn't feel sorry for her, but on the contrary, the sight of blood enraged me further. I was gulping so much air that I almost passed out.

I hardly noticed when Kulsum got up and went back inside the cabin. I remained on the foredeck; Joker chattered and scuttled about but never came near me. Suddenly darkness fell on the floodplain. Hours went by and I was still sitting alone and in the dark on the deck. I didn't know what Kulsum was doing inside the cabin. Perhaps sulking, but I was still furious with her for her attachment to Pakistan. Didn't she know what Pakistan had done to me and my people? How could she still be loyal to the genociders and the rapists? Had she already forgotten Datla Nuri?

She came out with a hurricane lamp and said, "Ata Allah, let's go inside. I've cooked you something nice."

I leaned on her shoulder and hobbled inside. It was hot and humid. She'd made a khichuri with rice and lentils and fried some eggs. She served me a plate, and while I ate, she fanned me.

"Perhaps we should never mention the names of our countries again. They are like ghosts, aren't they? They haunt you, but remain unreal. Can we begin with something real, like home? You are my home, that's what really matters, isn't it, Ata Allah?"

I looked at her and felt relieved that the cut in her face wasn't deep. I was beginning to regret having thrown the bowl at her. I stopped eating and slid the back of my hand over the cut. She lowered her head and sobbed. That night when we lay next to each other, with the lamp off, I felt an uncontrollable urge to hold her and bury myself inside her. I had the feeling that she was reading my thoughts, because when I touched her skin she opened her pores as though I had melted into tiny particles of water that could easily slide into her. Yes, I travelled through her pores and came face to face with her strangeness. Yes, it was strangeness, but I didn't feel like turning my face and running away from it, rather I wanted to give myself to it as though I were its captive.

"If you come inside me, I'll never get lost," she whispered, "because, I will know where to find my home."

Next morning when I woke up I heard Kulsum playing with Joker as though with a baby. I leaned on one of the oars and hobbled to the foredeck. She smiled at me as though we'd been intimate companions of many years and had no secrets between us. But I knew very little about her, apart from the fact that she belonged to our enemies.

"You must be missing your fish curry," she said. "We should ask Joker to fish for us."

"You need to give him a signal by whistling. That's what Bidudhar Majee used to do," I wrote. "You'll have to do it, you know."

Kulsum said that she knew how to whistle and puckered her lips to demonstrate. Joker looked baffled; he widened his large, dark eyes and shrieked; then he jumped into the water. Kulsum kept whistling but there was no sign of him.

"He's a naughty boy. He doesn't want to listen to a woman," she said and went inside the cabin.

She came back with a pot of gruel and molasses for us both.

"I'm not used to this kind of food. You Bengalis are rice people, we're bread people. Perhaps that's why we can't live together."

I mixed my gruel into a ball with molasses, dropped my head backward, my face pointing to the sky, which was darkening with rain clouds. Then I dropped the ball inside my mouth. She didn't speak again until we'd finished our gruel, which I enjoyed as ever.

"Ata Allah, can I continue with my story?" she said. "I don't want to remain a stranger to you."

I washed my hand and picked up the writing stick.

"I may become more of a stranger to you if I know more about you?" I wrote.

She thought about it for a while, biting her lips, then she said, "Yes, there is that danger, but I want you to know my story."

I shrugged my shoulders.

"I have already told you that I was born in this land. I grew up in a railway town in the north. You see, my father and my grandfather were railway men. They were also born in Bengal, but in the western half. In Calcutta, to be precise. They didn't consider themselves as Bengalis, nor did they speak the language. We spoke Urdu at home. I am not sure from which part of India my great grandparents originally came. Perhaps, not from Bihar at all, but like the other non-Bengali Muslims living in Calcutta, they were known as Biharis. It didn't bother my parents or grandparents, because the only thing they cared about was being Muslims. So, they wanted Pakistan with all of their hearts. And after the partition they moved over the border and came here. We lived in an enclave within the railway town, surrounded by Bengalis. We kept ourselves to ourselves, content to be Muslims and Pakistanis. Then the problems started. You Bengalis wanted to speak your own language, wanted to maintain your customs, which, you must admit, are against the spirit of Islam and Pakistan."

I felt myself getting angry again. I couldn't bear to listen to such rubbish. I got up and hobbled inside the cabin. The sky was rumbling and I lay in my bed. Kulsum stayed out on the foredeck until the rain came.

"You knew who I was when you married me," she said, sounding cross. "No matter how much you wish, the difference between us will remain. So, what do we do?"

She sat far from me, opened the shutter to the cabin window and looked at the rain outside. I had known that I was marrying an enemy, known the differences between us, but I didn't know that it was going to be so difficult. The rain went on and on. I got up and approached her.

"Tell me your story Kulsum, I like to hear it," I wrote.

She looked at me, puckering her lips.

"I told you that if your eyes lie, I would know it. You are lying now – aren't you?" She turned her eyes to look at the rain again. I didn't know what to say to her, so I opened the other shutter and looked at the rain too. After a while Kulsum got up to cook; we ate our lunch in silence, then we lay down to rest, keeping distance between us.

In the afternoon the rain stopped. Kulsum went out to the foredeck and I followed her. She whistled for Joker, who suddenly surfaced with a fish between his paws, and came on board. She stroked his head and said "Good boy," then she looked at me and smiled.

"We will have fish now. I'll cook it the way Sister Nuri taught me." When she was taking the fish inside the cabin I tapped on the slate to draw her attention.

"Tell me about you. How you came to be here, in the middle of this floodplain?" I wrote. She looked into my eyes and smiled again.

We sat on the cabin roof. In the soft sun of the afternoon the floodplain felt so vast, so silent, and so solitary, as if we were the last two humans alive on earth. Joker came to lie beside Kulsum, curled up like a cat, and she stroked his fur.

"When the Pakistani garrison in our town cracked down on your people, we were happy. My mother made sweets and all of us did special prayers. My father even volunteered to work with the army."

I was feeling the anger welling up inside me again, but I was determined not to show it. Luckily Kulsum didn't look into my eyes.

"You see, the Pakistani garrison was very small, and it was further weakened by the desertion of its Bengali members. The deserters and the mob soon overran it; then they came after us." I could see her lips trembling as though she was trying to suppress a sob. I looked away because I couldn't give my eyes to her in sympathy. Whose fault is it if you get a taste of your own medicine?

"I've already told you that my family died. I don't want to go into details. I'm sure you have already heard too many horror stories. Besides, it is not easy for me to tell," she said, her eyes watery, but her face rigid as if sculptured in stone.

"How have I ended up here? Well, it's a long story. Let us say that somehow I escaped. One of the mechanics, who worked under my father, found me. I was hiding in the depot, under an old steam engine. He is from this region. He took pity on me, made me wear a veil, and brought me along with him. I pretended to be his wife." She said all this almost mechanically, as though recounting some news items in which she didn't have any personal stake. Yet, I felt uneasy – perhaps a bit jealous of the man who pretended to be her husband. I wondered if she felt anything for him.

"You see, that's how I got the idea that I needed to marry one of your people to be safe. Thank Allah that he sent you for me. Anyway, I was planning to stay with his mother. When we got to their homestead, it had already been burnt down. And his family was gone. I travelled with him for a while in the boat, but increasingly we were meeting patrols belonging to your libera-tion forces. He was scared that I would be found out. You see, he didn't want to be seen as a traitor. So, he left me on the island where you found me. He said before leaving, 'If you put such faith in Allah, he will look after you.' Yes, Allah is looking after me. Otherwise, he would never have sent you to me."

I wondered whether Kulsum had reckoned that I would be a traitor to my people for her sake. I hoped not. Yes, I would take care of her, protect her, even let her build her little nest inside me, but I would never be a traitor. How could I betray Ata Banu, Zomir Ali, Datla Nuri, Ducktor Malek, the teacher, and all those who were butchered in the school yard? Even though their faces did not express anything, like pieces of pristine white muslin, and their eyes had stopped being hungry for light, they called out to me to give them shelter in my memory. How could I deny them?

I couldn't look at Kulsum. Instead, I cast my eyes at the sun, low at the very edge of the floodplain; it was so large and red that the water shimmered as though thousands of kapok flowers floated on it. Kulsum asked me what I was thinking. I shrugged my shoulders and evaded her eyes.

"Now that I've told you my story, you know who you are married to," she said and went back inside the cabin.

Suddenly the sun dropped behind the edge of the floodplain and everything went pitch black. Not even the fireflies were out to relieve the dark monotony. Nor could I hear the crickets, only the lapping of the water against the hull, and the slight wind whistling past the mast. I don't know what happened to me, but I was swaying my body, my head arching over my knees and then straightening up, on and on, and the humid air was hitting my palate and the back of my throat. Still, I couldn't shake off the questions: Am I a traitor? What do I do with my rage at the enemy? Shouldn't I rip them up limb from limb, or cut their throats? How else can I avenge my brothers and sisters? Besides, how was I to answer Moni Banu if she looked at me with accusing eyes: Yes, yes Beautiful One, you have not only betrayed our love, but our motherland too in her desperate hour of need, and all that for a Bihari whore – how could you sink so low? I rocked my head to and fro and kept on rocking until the night had filled my inside so much that I couldn't think any more, but only vaguely felt the whistle of the wind across the mast post and the water lapping against the hull.

When I made my way inside the cabin, Kulsum was lighting the lamps. Joker was whimpering and following her. I stepped in front of her as she was hanging one of the lamps from the mast pole. She opened her eyes to me with the lamplight flickering in them. She looked as though she was scared of me. I wondered if she was feeling that way because she had realised that by telling me her story she had revealed her secret soul to me, which belonged to our enemy.

I don't know what came over me as I looked into her eyes. I was trembling, because all I could see was the destitute one seeking a home inside me. Yes, Kulsum you belong to our enemy, but I will wrap you up with my skin. I touched her on her face, she tilted her head to press her lips, dry as baked earth, against the back of my hand. Somehow, though, it felt so tender that my eyes became blurred. The more I looked into her eyes the more I felt that it was not I but she who was offering a home.

For the following few days nothing could separate us. If our liquid bodies stopped pouring into each other for a moment, we wrapped each other with our skin. We entered each other through the eyes as though we were being taken to cradles to be rocked to sleep. I realised I was wrong to think that I had no love left in me because I had given it all to Moni Banu. Yes, I had opened my inside to Kulsum with love. She was mine and I was hers.

One morning I was awakened by a thud that rocked the boat. Kulsum woke up too. We looked at each other, wondering who or what it could be intruding into the home that we had built.

"Brother Kamal, are you in there?" Bosa Khuni shouted out.

I went out to the foredeck and saw Bosa Khuni looking up from his dinghy, next to the boat. Clouds were gathering low in the sky. Despite the friendly smile with which he greeted me, he looked as fierce as ever with his pockmarked face and his red bulging eyes. He had a gun slung across his shoulder, but he was still carrying the familiar gunnysack in which he kept his machete.

"So pleased to see you alive, Brother Kamal. We were so worried for you," said Bosa Khuni and extended his hand to me. I helped him climb on board.

"Especially, Madam. You know, Big Sister Moni Banu," he said. "She was so worried that she sent me to look for you. Are you alone, Brother Kamal?"

I didn't give him any sign. He followed me to the prow where we sat down.

"We know what had happened, Brother Kamal. We know of the massacre on board. About the teacher, Ducktor Malek, the old hag Datla Nuri, Ala Mullah, and the Majee brothers. We know what the collaborator Asad Khan did, but we got him. He grabbed my feet and whined like a domestic dog. I didn't do a clean job on him. I did it real slow. It must have been a relief to him when I finally cut his head off."

I knew Asad Khan deserved what Bosa Khuni did to him, but I was feeling sad for him. I knew that he despised me, but he protected me as well. Sometimes the things you saw in this war were so strange they didn't make any sense at all.

"We know of your marriage. You shouldn't have done it, Kamal. Madam was really upset. Why did you have to marry one of our enemies? It's treason, you know. You are lucky that Madam is in command here. Otherwise, our boys would have hunted you down as a traitor. I know, I know, she must have talked a lot of gibberish and you fell for it. We don't blame you, but I'm here to remedy the situation," he said and popped out his red, bulging eyes.

I felt as though a snake crawled up my neck. What did he mean by remedying the situation?

"We know that when they tortured you, she had it real good in the camp. Living it up in the major's bungalow. It's natural that they should be looking after their own kind. But you mustn't betray your own people for a piece of dirty flesh. Madam was really upset, you know. You should be a genuine fella-who-loves-his-country like me, Brother Kamal."

I do, I do, I tried to gesture to him, but he narrowed his eyes and looked skyward, which was almost dark now with rain clouds. What did he mean to do with Kulsum?

"It's true that Madam wanted to know if you were safe, but she sent me on a special mission. I must take the Bihari woman with me. This is still a war zone, you know. You must understand that it's not safe with the likes of her around. She can do us a lot of damage."

I was desperately searching my mind for what I could do to persuade Bosa Khuni not to take Kulsum from me. I knew in my guts that his mission involved cutting her throat. He looked at me and said, "I hope you are not trying to say some gibberish to me. I like you, I respect you, Brother Kamal, because you are not into gibberish like the others."

I don't know what I meant to say to Bosa Khuni just then, because both of us turned our heads to see Kulsum bringing two bowls of gruel with molasses and glasses of water for us.

"You must have travelled a long way. You must be tired and hungry," she said to Bosa Khuni in her distinctive Bihari accent. "We have nothing much to offer you except these bowls of gruel."

Bosa Khuni smiled, his red bulging eyes dancing; it was as though he had known from the very beginning that Kulsum was a Bihari – our cruel enemy.

"So, you're a Bihari and you can speak. I must say I'm impressed by your play-acting. You must be real good to keep it up for so long. Now that you have opened you mouth, please don't speak any gibberish," he said.

"What do you plan to do with us?" asked Kulsum.

Bosa Khuni mixed his bowl of gruel with molasses and began to eat as greedily as ever, like a duck.

"For a Bihari you make a good gruel, but that doesn't change anything. I'm here to fetch you."

"Where do you plan to take me?"

"I can't tell you that, but you are to come with me."

"But I don't want to leave my husband. What's going to happen to him?"

"Please don't confuse me with your gibberish. I'll finish my gruel, then we will set off. Yes?" Then he looked at me and said, "Madam wants you to stay in hiding for a while. The war will be over very soon, you know. She will come looking for you and she will take you home. She really means it, Brother Kamal."

I didn't touch my gruel. Wind was lashing the hyacinths and whistling like a demon past the mast. Once Bosa Khuni had finished his bowl, he said, "Have we still got the old hookah on board?"

I went inside the cabin, prepared the hookah, picked up one of the paddles, and came back. Bosa Khuni took a few puffs and, handing me back the hookah, said, "I don't like the look of the sky. It's going to be a bad storm. We must get going."

He turned, but before he could reach Kulsum, I was between them. Trembling, I gripped the paddle with both hands and rested it on my right shoulder, then I looked at him hard as if I wouldn't hesitate to split his head if he dared – yes, even moved an inch towards her. The wind was now blowing harder and the boat rocked from side to side. Bosa Khuni looked at me calmly; I had the feeling that he had expected my response.

"Brother Kamal, what are we to do with you? I understand that you are a bit upset. I suppose you never thought that you were destined to taste human flesh, did you? It must have felt real nice. Good on you, Brother Kamal. Now would you stand aside, please."

I gurgled from the back of my throat and stood my ground.

"I can see that she's a pretty one. Her smell must have made you feel like a bull on heat. It's easy to fall for the likes of her, but don't forget that she's a Bihari whore. It's war, you know, and I have my orders. I can't leave without her."

I stamped the paddle's head on the deck. Suddenly the sky broke and the downpour came amidst thunder and lightning.

"Brother Kamal, I'm glad that you are not messing my head up with gibberish, but I must move on. Please, step aside. Otherwise, I'll be forced to deal with you as one of the traitors."

My whole body was shaking but I stood my ground.

"I'm not just a cutthroat any more, Kamal. You understand that? If I were, perhaps I could have made an exception. But I'm now a genuine fella-who-loves-his-country. So, I can't let you enjoy that Bihari any more. I must take her. It's Madam's strict order."

He snatched the paddle out of my hand and threw it into the water. Then he pushed me aside so violently that I lost my balance and fell on the deck. He took his machete out and advanced on Kulsum. She gave a piercing cry – Ata Allah – then she became silent like stunned prey. Bosa Khuni put the sack over her head and tied her hands behind her back. I crawled and grabbed around his legs. He lifted his machete and said, "Let me go, you traitor. If it weren't for Madam's strict order, I wouldn't have hesitated, yes, to cut your head off."

He tried to shake me off, pulled me by my hair, and hit me with the butt of his machete, but I didn't let go of his legs.

"What do we do now, Kamal? I can't go empty handed," he said, and handed the machete to me. Then he lay flat, face up on the deck, and bared his throat.

"If you want to keep her, you have to cut my throat. I can't go empty handed."

My hands were shaking so much that I was finding it difficult to keep hold of the machete.

"Come on, it's not difficult. Think of me as a cow. Put the blade on my throat and push it. I promise I won't move."

I looked at him, his eyes closed, rain falling on him, but I couldn't do it. When the machete fell from my hand, Bosa Khuni got up and touched my head, "You can still be a genuine fella-who-loves-his-country, Brother Kamal. You don't want to go to your grave as nothing, do you?"

He picked Kulsum up like a doll with his massive hands, climbed down into his dinghy, and paddled away. I sat sobbing on the foredeck, rain falling on me. I don't know for how long; I didn't even care when the wind, which by then had turned into a fierce gale, began to toss the boat sideways, up and down as though it was about to tear it into pieces. Huge waves came galloping over the patches of hyacinths and rolled over the deck, flinging me across it. I clung to the prow as the wind howled like a demon, and snatched the boat free from the hyacinths in which it had been trapped. Once in the open waters, the boat tossed and turned and drifted at breakneck speed. I must have clung to the prow for hours as the storm raged on. It was so dark that I couldn't see where the boat had drifted. It would have been easy to let go and be free at last in the silence at the bottom of the floodplain, and I don't know why I decided to live. Perhaps, I felt that if my life had any meaning, it could only be from carrying my body across time. Besides, someone had to carry on and remember all those dead and taken away.

When the storm subsided I crawled inside the cabin. I was shivering so much that I couldn't stand up or look for the hurricane lamps. I groped on all fours and found my bed, took my wet clothes off, and lay with a quilt over me. The boat was still drifting, but smoothly, and I was so tired that I was almost asleep when I heard Joker whimpering near me. He gave a soft whistle, curled into a ball next to me, and began to breathe in his usual rhythmic way. I had no idea where he had been during the storm or when he came on board. We drifted and drifted with the current. I don't know for how long I slept, but when I woke up the boat was still drifting. It continued to drift for days until it came to a halt, trapped in yet another clump of hyacinths and lilies.

ISLAND

*It is my responsibility before a face looking at me as absolutely
foreign that constitutes the original fact
of fraternity.*

Emmanuel Levinas

CHAPTER 19

I am looking out at the island from the foredeck.

I can't see much further than the prow. I wait for the sun to burn the mist away and when it does, the island looks as lifeless as before. Nothing moves here. There is hardly a cloud in the sky, but thunder is still rumbling somewhere far in the west. I have no idea what has happened to the islanders, whom I deduce to be fishing folk from the numbers of nets I see spread out for drying, from the types of boat moored at the ghat, and from the smell of rotting fish. Perhaps they fled the island or they have been killed. Or, perhaps it has been taken over by the enemy and they are hiding and waiting to ambush the likes of me. Fear triggers a cold tremor through my body, but I know the island awaits me. I have to go there. I can't stay trapped in the boat for the rest of the war. So I climb on the cabin roof – which was badly damaged by the storm – still hesitating about what I must do next, when suddenly I see Joker surface in the clear water just beyond the patch of hyacinths and lilies in which the boat is trapped. He is swimming towards the island. Perhaps he has already checked it out and found it to be safe. I know he wants me to follow him.

From the boat I swim under the tangled weeds and emerge in the clear water. I look for Joker but I can't see him anywhere. His absence unnerves me, but there's no turning back. I carry on swimming, and after about fifty yards or so, reach the boats moored at the ghat. I climb into a fishing boat, on whose deck I see a net lying piled up into a ball, and a coconut hookah dangling from the mast post, but there's no sign of anyone having used it recently. It's no more than a step from the boat and I will be on the island, but I wait on the stern-post and survey its length and breadth. Nothing moves except for the leaves on a creeper bush by the bank. Even they seem to be struggling to breathe. What lies in wait for me here? My guts tighten and I gasp for air. I lose courage and instead of jumping from the prow onto the island, I climb down into the water, knee high, and crawl up the slope. Before the top of the bank I pause, keep my head down, then look around, and only push myself up on my belly when I am convinced that the island is truly deserted.

I crawl behind a banyan tree, its tangled roots hanging like dead snakes, and stand up to survey the island again. At some distance from the shore I see clusters of small adobe huts with bamboo walls and thatched roofs. Between the bank and the huts there's a large muddy area in which rows of nets are spread out on small bamboo poles. I feel sick at the smell of rotting fish – so many of them. The fishermen must have laid them to dry before the rainy season began, and then fled in a hurry, leaving the fish to rot under the rain. I run between two lines of nets, and on reaching the first cluster of huts, I pause only for a quick look around, and then I enter one at random. Everything tells me that its occupants left in a hurry. Someone must have been eating on the reed mat when they had to run. There is rice on a brass plate that has rotted and dried, then formed into hard brown and green ridges. Beside the plate a clay bowl and a tumbler lie on their sides, no doubt kicked by panicking feet. It's clear that no one has lit the clay oven for a long time. I move from hut to hut and each one tells a similar story. There's not a soul around.

Several paces on from the hut I find a Hindu temple. It is brick built and its door is wide open. I look inside and my eyes are drawn to the goddess Kali, her black skin, the garland of skulls around her neck, and her tongue protruding and dripping blood. No one seems to have lit the tiny lamps around her for a long time. I feel the urge to light the lamps and seek blessings from Mother Kali. Perhaps I was born a Hindu. There are no matches, but I pray to Mother Kali to protect me. I think that Sona Mia and Allah wouldn't be upset with me for praying to Mother Kali. No matter who I am and what I do they will always love me. I move behind the temple and find a large storeroom: it is stacked with rice, potatoes, lentils and spices. If I stay here, at least I will not starve.

When I leave the granary I have the feeling that someone is watching me, shadowing me with the stealth of a tiger. I hide behind a hut, wait and look, but I don't see anyone moving. Nor do I hear any unusual sounds, but I feel in my bones that something is there. What does it want of me? In a panic, I run to a hut towards the end of the village and close the door tightly behind me. Time passes and I wait and wait, gasping for air, my heart thumping as though it will break out of my ribs – until I hear Joker whistling. I open the door. He runs towards me, chattering. He sniffs me, climbs on me. He looks at my face with his bright, dark eyes, and whistles gently. It seems he has got used to my face. Or, perhaps he has realised that he has to relate to me nicely, because he has no other choice of companion. I have never been so glad to see him.

We go back to the large, tin-built hut next to the granary. In the middle there's a large bed covered with an embroidered quilt. This looks like a merchant's hut, but what is it doing in a fishing village? I can think of no reason, but don't let this bother me as I climb onto the bed and lie in it. I can smell Joker discharging his musk in a corner. I'm glad he's got busy building his den again. From now on this hut will be our home.

From the corner of my eye, to my right, I see clothes hanging from a string that crosses the length of the hut. Besides women's clothing there are long white shirts and fine cotton dhotis as worn by Hindu men of wealth. I could do with these clothes as my lungi and shirt are frayed and smelly. No doubt I will look very strange in them, but who's to look at me except Joker? For all he cares, I could go stark naked like him.

I get up to explore the hut. To the left of the bed there's a low desk with a cushion next to it. On the desk there are fountain pens with metallic caps and pots of ink. I sit on the cushion and open the desk flap. Inside there are piles of ledgers. I flap the pages, ledger after ledger, and numbers flutter before the hole of my face. Nothing but numbers in black ink. I have seen enough of them, but when I'm about to give up and move on to explore other things in the hut, I come across several more ledgers with bright blue covering. I pick one up and flick the pages with my thumb; they still smell of fresh tree pulp. I can't resist running my fingers over them. They are all empty: not a single ink mark between the lines and the columns to tarnish them.

I pick up one of the fountain pens and write: Kulsum, I'm missing you. I realise uneasily that this is the first time I've written on paper. It dawns on me that my previous writing, done on slate, had only a momentary existence. What I have just written can – if the paper is not consumed by fire or rain, or eaten by a goat – last a long time. Perhaps long after I die. I shiver at the thought and it makes me look at my writing again. I brush the tips of my fingers over the words, feeling that they will bear my anguish for the rest of my life and beyond. Kulsum, I'm missing you. Tears cloud my vision and the words become blurred. As I dry my eyes with my sleeve I hear something move behind the hut. Joker has noticed it too. He whistles and comes near me, hobbling, looking anxious. I know I should open the door and investigate, but I have lost my nerve. Instead, I push the wedge to fasten the door tighter, but it is still there. I can sense its mouse-like rustling just behind the tin panel at the back of the hut. Has it come to smell me so that it can trace me in the dark? Oh, Allah, how long do I have to endure this terrible thing? It is evil and it is strangling me. Suddenly Joker whistles piercingly and the creature scuttles away. Thank you, Joker, you have saved my life.

I stay sitting on the floor for a long time with Joker resting his head on my lap. It is after midday when I open the door. I am slightly dazed as I look at the sun baking the mud yard. A few yards in front I see the coconut fronds swaying gently with the wind, but I don't hear their music. Nor do I hear the creature. Perhaps it has moved on, looking for other victims.

The monsoon season is nearly over. It will rain for a few more days, then the sky will rumble without the rain a bit longer, and then the long dry season will come to stay with us until the monsoon comes again. I wish I could take comfort in the same old cycle of nature, but so many things have happened, and nothing will be the same for me again. Suddenly I feel the urgency of taking a bath and peeling off my torn, dirty clothes. It's about time I put on something nice and fresh. I laugh to myself: Kamal, you should become a snake, shedding your old skin for the new.

I pick up one of the merchant's long white shirts and a dhoti from the string and step out into the courtyard. Joker follows me, squeaking and chattering. Despite my need to believe that I am alone on the island, I feel that there is something here, but I don't know what. What does it want to do to me? Does it want to enter me and eat me up from the inside? I stop and look around. Joker stops too, his ears erect and his sharp inquiring eyes wide open. He sniffs the air, arches his back, and walks ahead of me with his funny little jumps. I follow him, somewhat reassured. Whatever is on the island, it cannot be nearby or moving towards us. Otherwise, Joker would have detected it and shrieked nervously.

I am almost relaxed now and look ahead to the boats by the shore, but then I notice the marks on the mud. I wish I could ignore them, but instead I hunch over to examine them closely. They puzzle me. They don't look like the footprints of a human or of any animal I know of. I look around, my heart pounding. To make matters worse, Joker has gone ahead, leaving me alone. I know I should run, but I can't help taking another look at the marks. For a moment it occurs to me that there may be human handprints, but there's no sign of any palm – only of fingers. But how can anything walk just on fingers? Then I notice the dimples, as though made by the rear end of something. What kind of animal is this? In panic I run towards the water and get into one of the fishing boats. If I see anything dangerous I will row away as fast as possible. I feel that this island is full of malice.

I untether the boat intending to put miles between this cursed place and me, but pause, seeing Joker happy in the water, diving, catching fish, rolling on his back and eating them. Perhaps he knows something I don't. I look around and wait, but there's no sign of anything. Perhaps I've been imagining things. I get into the water for a quick bathe, then put on the merchant's long white shirt and dhoti. On the way back I look at the prints again, but my eyes are drawn ahead to others. These seem freshly made and they lead to the veranda of the tin hut. Is it waiting for me inside the hut?

I hide behind the palm tree, my hands shaking, but Joker has gone inside the hut, snorting. I hear his piercing whistle and something banging against the tin panelling, and then everything goes quiet. I wait, barely able to look at the hut, then something appears on the veranda. I duck behind the palm tree. I don't want to see the evil one. I tense up to run, then I catch it with the corner of my eye.

I have to look twice to make sure that I am seeing a boy. He doesn't have any legs; his arms are as long as an orangutan's. He balances himself on his fingers, swings his body forward, and then lands on his backside to repeat the movement. So, this explains the handprints in the mud, but what is he doing here on his own? I am sure he has been observing me since I arrived on the island. Now I suppose he has decided that I mean no harm to him, or he wouldn't have revealed himself to me. Yet, he sits cowering against the steps to the veranda. Joker comes around, snorting, but this changes into a whimper as I come close to the boy. I am not sure about his age, but I'd guess about fourteen. Coming closer to him I notice his little stumps; they end before reaching the knees. Perhaps he was born legless, the way I was born mouthless.

I fetch the ledger and the pen from inside the hut and write on it. He gazes at it blankly and shakes his head. He can't read. Then he looks at me from head to toe as though trying to judge who I am. I feel very exposed in the merchant's clothes. Does he see wretched mimicry? I want to burrow under the earth and disappear. He lingers on my face; I'm sure the hole puzzles him. He lowers his eyes, surprisingly not out of aversion, but out of reverence, as though I am his superior.

"You're the new master, then?" he asks.

I give him no sign, but turn my face up, which possibly conveys to him that I am being haughty.

"I was the old master's servant boy. I'm legless but my hands are strong," he says, and shows me his hands. "I can do most jobs."

I keep looking over his head at the palm tree. I don't give him any sign to say that I am *not* the new master.

"Can I be your servant boy? I will do anything you want me to. You see, there are no other masters around."

I don't know what has come over me, because I nod my head. He smiles and moves towards me. He doesn't swing, balancing on his fingers, but crawls using his stumps and hands. He comes over to me and touches my feet.

"I have no one. Thank you for taking me in, Master," he says.

He gathers firewood and I light the clay oven in the kitchen next to the hut. I don't have to go to the storeroom for provisions; there's enough rice, lentils and cooking oil here to last for several days. I mimic chopping food and cooking it and point to myself. He looks at me with surprise, as though masters do not do such tasks.

"I will do the cooking for you, Master?" he says.

I gesture with my hand to indicate our respective heights and ages. He is only a boy and surely he can't cook.

"I live on my own since the old master left me. Months ago. I do my own cooking. Very tasty."

I don't want to engage with him on this matter. I want to tell him that I simply prefer to do my own cooking. What comes out is a dismissive wave to try to close the discussion.

He laughs knowingly. "I see. You are a Brahmin, Master. You don't want me to pollute you. I understand."

I don't respond to him. Instead, I get on with the cooking. He crawls on his stumps and hands and approaches Joker who – to my surprise – doesn't grunt at him, or whistle piercingly. He whimpers gently as he touches him. He plays with him for a while, then he asks, "Shall I fetch some water, Master." I nod. He hangs a tin can from his neck and crawls out. Joker discharges more musk in his chosen corner and curls up to sleep. It is taking so long for Legless to return that I've finished cooking and am desperately hungry, but where is he? I go out to look for him, but there is no sign of him. Then I see him crawling through the mud with the tin can dangling from his neck. I see he is struggling with the full can, so I run to help him, but he doesn't let me.

"You're very kind, Master, but this is my task. If you do this, how can I be your servant boy?" I let him drag the can into the kitchen. I tell him with my hands and eyes that we are to eat together.

"I cook my own food," he says. "It is not right that I eat with you, Master."

I look at him sternly, making him understand that it is an order that he eats with me. He lowers his head and doesn't protest any more. I put two plates on the floor, but before I can serve the rice and the lentils he swings his torso out of the door in two or three quick movements. I have no idea why and where he has gone. He comes back shortly with a clay bowl and a tumbler.

"I eat from these," he says. "If I eat with your plate, I will pollute you, Master."

I serve him his food. He takes his clay bowl and the tumbler to the door as though to maintain a respectful distance between us. During my stay on the boat I lost my inhibition over taking my food in front of strangers, but now I'm feeling self-conscious again. What will he think seeing me arch my head backwards and dropping food into my hole? I can see that Legless is a clever one: he not only gets my meaning from the hints that I give him with my eyes or hands, but he also seems to detect – without my giving him any signal – what is on my mind. He senses my discomfort and turns his back to me before he begins to eat. Now that his eyes are not on me, I can eat my food, but still the sense of unease doesn't leave me.

When we finish eating, Legless takes the plates out to wash them. On his return he asks if he should prepare the hookah for me. I don't bother to look at him, What kind of idiot is he? Can't he see that I have no lips for drawing on the pipe? When I see that he is waiting for an answer, I shake my head.

"I see, you don't smoke, Master; the old master used to smoke all the time," he says, as if this is the only difference between us. Hasn't the idiot noticed the gaping hole of my mouth? Doesn't he realise that my face, my disfigurement, has consigned me – just as his legs have done – to the lowest rung among the order of men? I go to the tin hut and stand on the veranda. He brings me a rattan stool. It is early afternoon and the sun, despite the distant rumbles in the sky, is bright, but it is not nice out here on the veranda with the smell of rotting fish. I am feeling nauseous, so I stand up. Legless seems to understand the reason for my discomfort.

"I see that the smell is bothering you, Master. I will sort it immediately. It is not right that you have to smell rotting fish," he says, and swings himself out of the veranda at lightning speed. I wait until I hear the spade thumping the ground, then I walk towards the shoreline. I see him, putting his weight on his rear end, digging a hole near the nets from where the rotten fish are giving off that nasty smell. He gives me a submissive smile, then swings his head, down and up, as though reading the Koran. He digs without looking at me again. I kick the little mound of mud that he has already made next to him. He looks up and I show him that I need a shovel too. He looks baffled, "You don't dig, Master. It's a servant boy's job." I show him forcefully that I want to dig.

He looks at me with panic in his eyes, as though he has just noticed my face. He doesn't say anything; he lowers his eyes and fiddles with the soil he has unearthed. Is he thinking that he has made a serious mistake in regarding me as a master?

I leave him to his digging and walk to the shoreline. I get into a boat, climb on its cabin roof, and look out over the floodplain. Dark clouds are gathering low in the east, but the sun, which has already travelled far down the western horizon, is casting a soft light. Apart from Legless's digging and the lapping of the waves on the shore and against the boats, there are no other sounds. I don't understand what has happened to me? Why am I letting Legless presume that I am his master? Before it goes any further, I should make him understand that I am really one of his kind. Is it pleasing me to be called Master?

Legless is still digging. Joker jumps into the water and dives under for a long time. He surfaces quite a bit away with a fish between his paws. I walk back to the tin hut. When I pass Legless he doesn't pay me any attention. He keeps digging. I sit on the rattan stool. I wish for the rain to come and drown out the sound of his shovel cutting into the ground. It's annoying me now. If he takes it upon himself to be my servant boy, then what can I do? If he's so stupid, he deserves to be a servant.

Now the wind has picked up. The fronds on the palm trees are shaking wildly. I go inside the tin hut, but before I can light the lamps the rain comes. It is pattering on the tin roof and I can't hear Legless's digging any more. Thank Allah, at last I can have some peace of mind. I light the lamps and sit on the bed with the embroidered quilt over my legs. I have locked the door but keep an ear open for Legless. Hours pass and it is already night, but no sign of Legless. Is he still digging? I go out to the veranda with the hurricane lamp. It's so dark, and without the lightning flashing on the island, I can't see a thing. I can only hear the wind screaming in tandem with the rain. I come in and close the door behind, then open it again to stand on the veranda with the hurricane lamp. After doing this several times I'm getting really worried for him.

I go out to look for him, heading in the direction of the shoreline, but a few paces on, the hurricane lamp, battered by the wind and rain, blows out. It's completely dark, but I'm not unduly concerned as I consider myself to be an excellent night tracker. I grope towards the place where I sense Legless is digging. I go round and round, finding nothing to orientate myself. I realise that my gift for finding my way in the dark can only be used in the familiar terrain of our village. Here it is useless. I rush on all fours in one direction, then another. I'm bruised and scratched as I hit trees and scrape through bushes. How I wish I could scream, but nothing comes out of my mouth except for muffled grunts. Exhausted, I lie on the mud, the rain falling on me. I am almost resigned to stay out here for the rest of the night when I hear something stirring near by.

"What are you doing here, Master?" asks Legless.

He takes me back to the tin hut. I clean my wounds, change into another of the merchant's long white shirts and dhotis, and lie on the bed. There's no sign of the rain relenting. Legless asks me what I want to eat for my supper. I show him that there are enough leftovers from the lunch for both of us. He asks me if I fancy some green beans and aubergine.

"I've grown them myself, Master," he says.

He takes my sitting up as a signal that I have said yes to him. He runs out of the door into the rain. He comes back with a handful of aubergines and green beans, then he lights the fire on the clay oven. While I cook he sits with his wet clothes on, next to the fire. I inquire if he wants to change his wet clothes. He tells me that he has no other clothes than the ones he is wearing. I get up and bring to him some of the merchant's clothes from the string. Legless looks at me with panic in his eyes.

"I can't wear your clothes, Master. It will pollute you. You must know that I'm of the untouchable caste."

I flutter the shirt and the dhoti I am wearing with my fingers. I want to show him that they belong to the merchant, and that my station in life is no higher than his. I am no master. Perhaps, like him, I also belong to an untouchable caste. He looks at me baffled and doesn't understand what I am trying to say. How can I get through to him? If only the idiot knew how to read. He gives me a silly smile.

"Those clothes are very becoming on you, Master."

I let him be with his wet clothes and sit down to continue cooking. Legless gets up to open the door when we hear Joker chattering on the veranda. He shakes himself, throwing globules of water all over the hut, and runs to his den.

"Can he catch fish for us, Master? The only thing I don't know, is how to catch fish."

I point to Joker and make a u-shape with my thumb and middle finger to mimic the action of whistling loudly.

"I'll whistle to him tomorrow. You can't live just on rice, lentils and vegetables. You need to eat fish, Master."

I serve him his food, but I don't want him to sit far away from me. I point to the spot where he should sit. He hesitates, but when I tap the spot insistently he accepts. He mixes his food nervously but after several handfuls eases himself, enjoying the flavour of my fried green beans with aubergine. When I've finished I belch in satisfaction to show that I am pleased with his company. Then I grunt from the back of my throat to draw his attention. I point to my ears, point to him and mimic a talking mouth by opening and closing my thumb and fingers. I want to know how he has survived on the island on his own. After a time he gets my drift.

"When the old master and everyone left, I was scared. I knew that the Pakistani army and the collaborators would come here to kill, especially an untouchable one like me."

He flicks a ball of rice inside his mouth, chews it silently and rhythmically like the way my calf used to masticate grass, and continues with his story once he's finished swallowing.

"There's an old ruin on the island. I'll show it you tomorrow, Master. Even before the war no one went there. It is said that very bad types of ghosts and cobras live there, but they don't bother me. I dug a tunnel there. I was ready when the first army raid came. As soon as I saw the gunboat with the Pakistani flag coming I ran into my tunnel. They looked everywhere, but they never found me. You must also know that they can't stand the smell of stinky fish, so they couldn't leave quickly enough. After that they came a few more times, but every time the same thing happened."

He takes a long break to finish his plate, licks his fingers, and then drinks a tumbler of water. I'm thinking that I shouldn't have prompted Legless to bury the rotting fish. How are we to protect ourselves if the Pakistani army decides to come here again?

"Freedom fighters also come here. They like me, Master. They say, 'Legless, you're in charge of this island. You look after it until liberation comes'. Now that you are here I am happy to be a servant boy again."

I turn my head so that he won't see the lies in my eyes.

"I grow green beans, radishes, sweet potatoes, aubergines, cabbages and chillies. I climb coconut trees, mango trees. And there's a lot of rice and spices on this island. So, I eat, sleep, hide and the time passes."

I'm so tired that I am dozing off. Legless notices it and gets up to wash the plates and pots. I show him that he should sleep in the tin hut with me.

"It is not right that I should sleep with you, Master. I sleep better in my tunnel," he says and leaves me. I close the door behind me. I pick the ledger up and write in it.

So I have become a master and it feels good.

I lie in the bed and cover myself with the embroidered quilt. Rain is still bouncing off the tin roof, but suddenly I hear other sounds in the distance. Firing and bombardment have begun again. During the last few days, the Pakistani army must have sent reinforcements to man the camp and continue with their war in the floodplains. The firing and bombardment goes on and on. It is well past midnight when it stops. The rain has stopped too, but I can't sleep. So, I get up to write in the ledger. It then occurs to me that perhaps I should write the story of my life and what I have seen during the war. Perhaps it is the best way that I can preserve the memories of the dead.

I begin: I have a hole for a mouth.

I write and write, and suddenly I remember the promise I made to Zomir Ali. Yes, Venerable Scholar, from time to time I will be your eyes, and see the world for you. I look around the room and see nothing but darkness. So I get up, light the hurricane lamp, and open the window at the back. The air is much clearer after the rain. Under a three-quarter moon the island is draped in a bluish light. Yes, Venerable Scholar, I am seeing the dark mass of the trees for you. Yes, they are dancing for you. You see, I haven't forgotten my promise.

I wonder again why Legless regards me as his master. Perhaps he needs a master. Perhaps his life appears meaningless and full of frightening holes without a master. Perhaps he knows that I am a servant like him, but wants to put me in the position of being a master for his own benefit. Am I not simply obliging him? I can almost hear Zomir Ali's sarcastic laughter: Who do you think you are kidding, Kamal? Enough. I've had enough of these thoughts; I'm really getting tired. I move from the window and lie on the bed.

I never thought it would come to this, but right now Moni Banu makes me feel angry and bitter. Why did she have to send Bosa Khuni to take Kulsum away from me? I even wonder if she instructed Bosa Khuni to cut her throat real slow. To do a messy job on her. Why Moni, why did you have to do that? I know Kulsum is our enemy, but I love her.

Where are you, Kulsum? How can I bring you back to me? Perhaps I should remember every part of you, bit by bit, and then glue you together in my imagination. You are bound to come back to me then, aren't you? First I gather the tip of your nose, then up the ridge, the sockets of your eyes, then slightly down your cheekbones high up on your face, the yellowish brown of your skin, so smooth that my fingers slide over it. I try to feel the little tremor that runs through your skin as you stretch your mouth into a smile, but you give me nothing. What can I say about your hair, yes your hair, thick black and oily, that rests on your nape? I plough my fingers through the furrows between its strands, then I gather a bunch and brush it over the hole of my face; it tickles my palate, but it doesn't smell of the coconut oil you rub on it every time you take a bath. I don't know how I have reached your lips, but I touch them and they feel harsh and dry as cracked earth, then I push my fingers between them, but they are shut tight as though they are sewn together with iron wire. Why are you sealed up, Kulsum, why don't you want to let me enter you? The same yellowish brown as the skin on your cheeks runs down your neck, then to the mounds of your breasts, hard as polished stones, from which my hand slips down your navel. With high hopes I rub between your hipbones, on the valley of your stomach, but the pores of your skin are just as closed as your mouth, offering me nothing but the outside. Further down, between your legs, my hand crawls through your tuft of hair like a lost traveller in some foreign land. I push my fingers in the furrow between the ridges, but it is as dry and as closed as your mouth. Why have you closed your inside to me? Your thighs, then your calves. There I find the same polished surface, but the soles of your feet are black with dirt. I wash your feet. I keep washing them until they are clean. I feel that you are opening slightly for me, but I can't be sure.

Not wishing to leave any part of you untouched, I turn you face down and carry on along your back, bit by bit from your heel to the crown of your head, and do it all over again, but I can't glue you together. How can I do this if you only give me your surface? Perhaps you should come into my insides, Kulsum. Remember, you wanted to build your home there, and I have opened it all for you.

It must be morning now. I hear Joker getting up, whimpering and walking around the door. I know he wants to go out, so I open the door for him. The island is still shrouded in mist.

CHAPTER 20

Legless appears from the mist.

He swings onto the veranda and tells me, "Do you want to see the island, Master? I will show it to you."

We take breakfast. Legless washes up, then he sweeps the hut. I sit on the veranda and wait for the mist to lift. When the palm tree in front comes into view, Legless swings out of the veranda into the mud yard. I follow him. He shows me the patches where he grows his vegetables. I am astonished at the abundance and variety of his cultivation. They are of excellent size and quality too. I recognise the green beans that I cooked last night, but my attention is drawn to the particularly large and succulent gourds hanging from the same trellis as the beans.

"Do you like gourd, Master?" asks Legless. Before I can reply he climbs, with his little stumps, up the ladder next to the trellis. He yanks a gourd off its stalk and offers it to me.

"They are very nice with fish, Master. I will make Joker fish for us. He likes me, Master."

I walk between his rows of aubergine plants, laden with purple fruit of the fat-bottomed variety. While I look at the cabbage patch, drooling over the pale green orbs, and thinking how nicely they would go with goat meat, Legless is busy digging the patch next to it. He brings me a handful of sweet potatoes and says: "They are very sweet and tasty roasted, Master."

I nod. He takes the gourd from my hand.

"I will take them to your hut, Master," he says and swings his way back to the tin hut. We continue when he returns. On the edge of his vegetable patches runs a long line of coconut and betel-nut trees. Legless holds a cutlass between his teeth, puts a rope around his stumps, and with little jumps – not unlike Joker – he propels himself up a coconut tree. He drops a bunch on the soft mud, then back on the ground he chooses a young green coconut for me. He cuts it with two swipes of his cutlass. Offering it to me he says, "This is very good for you, Master. I will bring you the best ones. Every morning and every afternoon."

I try to drink the fresh, sweet water, but it spills on my clothes. The front of the merchant's long white shirt gets totally soaked. I feel awkward and embarrassed. Surely Legless is having fun seeing his master making a fool of himself. I must admit, though, that Legless makes a very tactful servant. He lowers his eyes and fiddles with the coconut shell as though he hasn't noticed anything.

We come back to the cluster of huts and walk inland from the shore where I first landed on the island. Some distance away from the huts, and near to the west bank, he takes me to an isolated hut. My heart pounds with excitement as I enter a blacksmith's forge.

"He was a grumpy one, the old blacksmith. He didn't like talking much, but he went clank, clank the whole day," he says.

The forge looks in perfect working order with all the necessary tools. I sit on the low floor-stool and pull the string to the bellows. It whooshes, blows charcoal dust into the hole of my face, making me spit out a lump of saliva. Legless swings out of the forge and comes back with a container of water dangling from his neck.

"You need to wash your face, Master," he says. I don't look at him because I don't want him to fuss over me every time I make a fool of myself. I know I must be more cautious not to draw his attention to my deformities. Otherwise he will begin to doubt whether I am really a master. I can't let that happen, so I kick the container and shoo him away with my hand. He is baffled, then fear flickers in his eyes. He cowers and crawls away. At last I can have some privacy.

I am still sitting on the floor-stool with my hand on the string to the bellows, and imagining that I have become a real blacksmith. In the past our village blacksmith allowed me to pull the bellows for him, and sometimes, when in a good mood, he let me beat into shape the objects he was working on. This stood me in good stead when I had to make the nails to repair the cargo boat, but I'd never made anything of my own. Now that I have the forge at my disposal, I can make whatever I want. Perhaps a shovel or a knife, though this island is full of them. Yes, I can almost hear the old blacksmith going clank, clank the whole day, as Legless puts it.

It then occurs to me that I might as well make something useless. At first I'm horrified by this thought. How can anyone spend effort and good metal to make a useless object? I know that people have been using metal for a long time to make things that do not have any practical use, and for the sheer beauty of their shapes. I suppose that's how art objects are made, but how could I be an artist? Perhaps I should make something for Kulsum. Yes, I will do this, but what? Nothing comes to mind immediately. I take a tiny hammer and tap it on the anvil; it tinkles like an ankle bell. As I continue tapping I have the strange sensation that Kulsum's feet are walking around me. No face, no body – just the feet on their own. They are so soft on the ground they are almost inaudible. Yet, they roar inside me like the wind trapped deep down in a well.

I get up from the floor-stool knowing that I have to make one of Kulsum's feet. I wonder what people will think if they see the result of my endeavour. I can see them laughing: Look what a funny business – a mouthless artist! Oh how lucky I am that there's no one here to see me except Legless and Joker. Well, Joker is Joker; I know he's a crafty sod, but he doesn't give a damn about what I do as long as he has my company. Sometimes I wish he would go wild because he doesn't need me to provide for him, but I suppose he has lived too long in human company to do without it. Although Legless notices everything and preoccupies himself with me, he doesn't dare laugh at me as he is in awe of me as his master. Where is he now? I look for him, but I don't see him anywhere. Is he upset with me? I feel really bad that I've been cross with him. Perhaps this master role is not for me. It's already making me feel that I have the right to take advantage of him and mistreat him. Was I not in his position only a little while ago? Yes, I will come clean with him. I know he will feel angry with me for deceiving him, but if I don't stop playing this master role soon, it will turn me into someone like Asad Khan. If that happens, may Allah save my soul.

I turn a corner around the cluster of huts and see Legless sitting with his head down. I approach him, but he doesn't look up. When I touch his head he senses affection. He looks up and smiles.

"Do you want to see my home, Master?" he says. I nod, and I don't make any attempt to tell him that I am not his master. Perhaps I will come clean with him later. He swings his body southwards and I follow him. He takes me across some rice fields, then through a clump of blueberry and fig trees. We arrive before a bamboo grove surrounded by dense rattan bush and creepers. Only when I enter the grove do I see the ruin. It is a large structure and its roof has fallen. From its thick walls ancient roots have shot up with spreading branches. It smells of human waste. If evil spirits have their home anywhere it is here. He takes me though the ruin and we come to a door that leads to one of the back rooms. It is packed with mangled beds and broken chairs, piles of bricks and firewood, tattered and smelly quilts and clothes. It seems that no one has set foot in this room for many years, and it is impossible to enter it. Legless pauses a few seconds before the door and gives me a knowing smile, then he slides through the rubbish tip. I follow him, but it is not an easy task: I scratch my arms and legs in the process, but manage to land on a heap of hay piled high against the outer wall. I follow Legless as he wriggles through the hay and we come to the mouth of a tunnel. We crawl in the dark, take unexpected turns, and at last we reach an illuminated area. It is low and round like a cave. This is Legless's shelter.

"Do you like my home, Master?" I nod to say yes. "No one can find it unless I show it to them."

I sit on a quilt over a cushion of hay. He zooms out; I have no idea where he has gone. I get up to explore. It has little in it, but surprisingly I find a large mirror and many hurricane lamps. I wonder what they are for. Perhaps Legless loves to put all the lamps on and look at himself into the mirror. Does he imagine that the person he sees in the mirror is not really him, but a stranger, or perhaps a friend whom he can engage in a long conversation? Perhaps that's how Legless bears his solitude. For myself I don't like mirrors. I don't like looking at myself. I know if I see myself in one I will slide through to the other side – like the English girl in a book that Zomir Ali translated. I'm always fearful that if I go to the other side of things I will not be able to come back. So I keep a large distance between the mirror and myself.

Legless comes back with a brass pitcher. "I have brought you milk, Master. I have a cow and she gives me milk. I will be very happy if you drink it, Master," he says.

He sits with his back to me; I suppose this is to allow me privacy. I tilt a few drops of milk from the pitcher into the hole of my mouth. It is still warm and tastes sweet and creamy. It is strange, at first I don't know why, but at this moment I remember *Hayy Ibn Yaqzan*. It is ages since I read that book. My memory of it is not altogether pleasant: I remember being pestered by Zomir Ali to engage with him in a learned conversation about it. When I refused, he was cross and insulted me. Yes, I suppose I remember it now because, like Hayy, I find myself on a desert island. Two solitary souls lost on desert islands. Well, this is not wholly true as Legless was already here when I came. And as well as keeping me company, he is looking after me, too.

Ah, I know exactly what triggered my recollection of Hayy: it was the milk. When the baby Hayy found himself marooned on a desert island, he was suckled by a deer. She became a mother to him. Now Legless mothers me like the deer. Should I not treat Legless like my mother?

"Is the milk nice, Master?" he asks. It sounded sweet to my ears before, but now I can't bear being referred to as Master. What game is he playing? Doesn't he know what I might do to him if I become like Asad Khan? I crawl out of Legless's cave, rush through the ruin, and reach the bamboo grove almost breathless. Legless comes after me.

"Don't you like my home, Master? I am poor, but my home is very safe."

I head for the tin hut without looking back at him. I close the door behind me and lie on the bed. I cannot get Legless out of my mind; I must tell him without any delay that I am not his master. I get up and open the door. Legless is sitting on the veranda.

"Do you want anything, Master?"

I use my hands and eyes, my little grunts, and all the other gestures that I have perfected over the years, to communicate with him. I tell him, Legless, I am not your master. He doesn't seem to understand me at all.

"Are you feeling unwell, Master? Should I massage your head?

I am very good at it. The old master used to love it." I push him away when he comes near me.

"Have I done anything bad, Master?"

I go inside the tin hut and take off the merchant's long white shirt and the dhoti that I have been wearing since I have settled on the island. I put on my old, dirty rags and I go out to the veranda. I try to tell him, Look Legless, look at me. I am no master. I am really like you. I have been a deformed servant all of my life. He grins at me and says, "Ah, I understand it now. You want me to wash your clothes. I will do it right away, Master."

He swings inside the tin hut, gathers the merchant's clothes that I have just taken off, and heads for the shore. I can't figure him out: if he understands my slightest hints in other matters, why doesn't he follow my best efforts in this? In desperation I take the ledger out and write in big letters: Legless, I'm not your master. I know he can't read, and yet I run to the shore by the ghat and show it to him. He looks scared.

"You don't like my washing, Master? I am really good."

It is about midday. There are some clouds in the sky but they are high, scattered, and drifting. It doesn't seem like it will rain. Perhaps the monsoon season is over. I leave Legless beating the clothes on the ghat and head for the forge. I haven't gone far when I hear the firing and the bombardments. It began early today and seems as if it's coming from much nearer than yesterday. I should be used to it now, but every time I hear it I feel panic. I walk briskly to the tin hut and open the ledger. Legless is spiteful, I write. Perhaps he doesn't want to share the island with me. I am sure he understands me perfectly when I try to tell him that I am not his master. Perhaps he is playing the game of master/servant to drive me crazy. He is devious.

He comes into the hut. "I have left the clothes out to dry. They are really clean, Master," he says. I ignore him. He waits for a while, then he leaves. The firing and the bombardment are more intense now. Perhaps a large and decisive battle has started.

I make a khichuri with rice and lentils and gourds. I serve a good portion on Legless's plate, then I serve myself. I wait and wait, but he doesn't come. I go to the veranda and look in every direction, but there's no sign of him. If he's playing upset, I can play that too. I eat fast. When I'm nearly finished, Legless comes in with a broad smile.

"I have brought you mangoes, Master. They are very sweet." Then he sits down to eat as if nothing has happened.

After the meal he goes out with Joker to make him catch fish for us. I lie down for a rest, but the firing and the bombardment makes this impossible. I drift into memories of the story of Hayy Ibn Yaqzan again, especially when he becomes an eagle. When the great eagle is dead, he puts on its beak, feathers, wings, and then – brimming with its power – he swoops down on the island. He scares all the animals and they submit to his lordship. But I have done nothing to scare Legless. All I have done is put on the merchant's silly clothes – and he calls me Master. Surely, this is not right. If we are to have a master on this island, it can only be Legless. He has a rightful claim to it. He was here before me; he safeguarded the island and cultivated it.

I resolve to do everything to convince Legless that I am not his master. I move out of the merchant's large tin hut and into a small straw and mud hut near the forge. Now my old rags and the poor shelter ought to convince Legless of my lowly status.

Feeling much more at ease with myself I walk to the shore. Sitting on the ghat's top step I observe Legless; he is below me on the bottom step. He's whistling, but Joker doesn't bring him any fish. I don't know whether Joker isn't hearing him properly with all the bombardment going on, or whether he is ignoring him wilfully. After a while he seems exasperated with Joker and stops whistling. He crawls up and sits beside me.

"Joker thinks he's his own master. He won't listen to me."

I try to tell him that he is his own master too. He doesn't follow my meaning. Instead, he looks at my clothes.

"Your clothes must be dry now, Master. Shall I bring them?"

I look at him angrily; he lowers his head. I get up and head for the new hut. He follows me.

"Do you feel alone in the big hut, Master?" he asks. I say no and he understands me clearly.

"Ah, I see, you want to be a shadu, Master. You want to do ascetic practices, yes? So, you wear poor clothes and live in a poor hut."

I can't take this any more. I almost thrust the hole of my mouth against his face. I want him to see the cave of my mouth and the pink little thing at the back of it. I gurgle and exhale a foul wind from my guts. Then I go into the hut and close the door behind me.

For the next few days Legless keeps his distance. I see him swinging across the island, tending his vegetable patches, and climbing trees. He fells coconuts but doesn't bring me any. If I go bathing, and he happens to be on the ghat, he hurries away as soon as he senses my approach. He doesn't even look at me when he passes me. It is as though I do not exist for him any more and that he is alone on the island again. I don't know what he is thinking, but I can't get him out of my mind. How can I make up for the wrongs I have done him?

It hasn't rained for several weeks now. Perhaps it won't rain again until next summer. For the last few days I haven't heard any firing. Perhaps the Pakistani army and the collaborators are finally defeated. Perhaps they will not return to our swampland again. If this is the case, then I am living in a liberated zone. I say to myself, *Joi Bangla*.

I now spend most of my time at the forge. It takes me some time to start the fire, but once it is started, with plenty of good quality charcoal and wood at hand, I have no problem keeping it going. First I put a square slab of iron into the fire and pump the bellows, and keep on pumping until the iron throbs like a liquid sun, then I take it out with tongs. I beat it with a large hammer on the anvil, then I dip it into the water. I repeat the process many times over to shape its topside into a sloping ridge. Once I achieve this I will use chisels and a light hammer to transform the iron into the likeness of Kulsum's foot. My job would have been easier if I'd been able to make a wooden mould and melt the iron, but I don't have these facilities here. Besides, I don't know how to do such things. I have to make do with what I have and know.

The sun shines again and the air feels mellow but sombre. I begin working at dawn and keep on working until night falls, only taking a short midday break for lunch. I'm so absorbed in the whoosh of the bellow and the sound of the hammer on the slab that I never get tired or bored. The anticipation of seeing Kulsum's foot breaking free of the metal drives me on.

Using the chisel and the light hammer I begin to chip away at her instep, the round of her heel, the undulation of her muscles, her tendons, and the twisting but delicate elongation of her toes. I'm so absorbed that I don't notice Legless's arrival. Only when he's within touching distance do I see him. I bend to look at him. His eyes are burning, his lips trembling. He rears up on his stumps and shoves a handful of mud into the hole of my mouth.

"You are ugly. You are mean. I hate you," he says, and swings away.

I stay where I am, stunned, with the mud still in my mouth. I look out into the mud yard and the cluster of huts. Despite being bathed in clear sunlight they look desolate and dull. I want to run away from this island – as far as possible from Legless. How can I show my face to him again? I pull the bellows, pull them harder and faster. In the hearth the charcoal hisses madly as the fire spurts up like an amber fountain. I don't know what I am doing; I'm in a trance. I drag the glowing block of iron out from the fire and almost grab it with my bare hand, but something makes me pause. It occurs to me that Legless is not so blameless either: if he wasn't so desperately in need of a master he wouldn't have mistaken me for one. I'm not even sure if it *was* a mistake on his part. I don't deny that being treated as a master pleased me, but I couldn't have played that role without his servantly conduct. So why should he put all the blame on me for what has happened? For all I know, he could have planned the whole thing. I feel angry with Legless. I go to the ghat and wash my face, then I shut myself in the new hut.

For the following few days I work away with the chisel and the light hammer after softening the iron in the fire. Shut off from everything around me, including my memories, I carve and shape those details that will finally give me Kulsum's foot. Now I don't stop even when night falls. I hang the hurricane lamps from the forge's ceiling, and under their dim yellow light, I work and work until my vision goes bleary and my hands seize up on me. The closer I get to the shape of her foot, the more I tremble with so much feeling I think I will break into pieces. The curves of her heels. The ridges of her tendons. The sudden drops that create the valleys between her toes. The nails.

Since the incident with the mud, I haven't seen Legless anywhere. He doesn't tend his vegetable patches, doesn't climb the coconut trees, and doesn't even go to the ghat to bathe. He seems to have shut himself up in his shelter. I sense his passing only in the dark of the night, and even for that I have to be very alert. He is a barely noticeable swish through the air, then nothing. How long will it take him to forgive me?

It is several weeks since I began working on the foot. I feel that I could work and work on it to the very end of my life and still not finish it. At night, I hear the buzz of the insects as they circle the hurricane lamps, the chirping of crickets from the tall grasses. I make final, delicate chisel cuts to mark the edges of her little toe, then I douse the fire for the last time. What others will make of the piece I have no idea, but I look at it and I see Kulsum placing her right foot on the front steps to my door. She is hesitant, full of a stranger's nerves, but before she can knock I am opening it to welcome her.

I carry the foot to the shore and climb down the ghat. The floodwater has already receded several yards from where it was when I arrived on the island. Most of the fishing boats lie stranded in the mud. Walking on the muddy but firm ground I reach the new shoreline, then I gather water in the cup of my palms. I wash Kulsum's foot; it is not cold metal any more, it is not dead substance. I wash her foot again, clean the dirt between her toes, then wash it again. I promise you, Kulsum, there is not a single stain on your foot now. Yes, you are a stranger, but my door is open for you. All you have to do is step right in.

Weeks have gone by without seeing Legless. Time passes. Apart from cooking and a few hours of sleep, all I do is watch the floodwater recede further and further from the ghat. Water now flows only through the river channel. It looks marooned between mud plains that will dry into dust in a few weeks' time. Several times each day I look at Kulsum's foot and I examine it closely to see if any dust has fallen on it. Even if I don't find any I wipe it with my sleeve, then take it down to the river to wash it clean. I don't want any dirt staining her foot. Sometimes I take out the ledger to write the story of my homestead, then of the journey, and finally of the island.

One morning I get up early and grind rice. I make breads with it and, leaving them to steam, I walk out. The island is still shrouded in morning mist. Everything tells me that winter is almost on us: the chilly air is making me shiver. I head to Legless's vegetable patch. It's impossible to see more than a few yards in front, but I wait and listen. It would be a shame if I got caught stealing his vegetables. I hear only the birds. So much twittering and chirping, but it's the harsh guttural cry of the ospreys that pleases me most. Now that the firing has stopped they are back and have resumed their old ways.

I pick a cabbage, some green chillies, and run back to my hut. By the time I finish frying the cabbage with turmeric paste and green chillies, the rice breads are done. Going out again with the cutter I bring back a banana leaf and wrap up the food I've just cooked.

My heart races as I reach the ruin. In front of it I see a cow and a calf tethered to a pole. I presume that the milk Legless offered me comes from this cow. I'm nervous that they might moo and give me away, but they stay quiet. Making my way though the cluttered room, under the pile of hay, I reach the mouth of the tunnel that leads into Legless's cave. Perhaps he is already up and out and watching me. No time to linger. I drop the bundle in the tunnel and scamper out.

Several days pass and still I haven't seen Legless. One afternoon I am sitting by the river, watching Joker diving and surfacing in the water. From time to time he catches a fish and eats it floating on his back. I don't see Legless coming to sit beside me, but sensing his presence I feel nervous. Not daring to look at him, I keep my focus fixed on Joker. Legless whistles to Joker, but as before, he doesn't bring him any fish.

"Joker is a greedy one. He wants all the fish for himself," he says. When I turn to look at him, he keeps looking at Joker, but says, "Your fried cabbage and rice breads. They were very tasty."

I'm pleased that he hasn't rejected my offer. I expect him to say something about what has happened between us, but he doesn't say anything. We watch Joker in silence, then suddenly he says, "I look nice, but you look ugly, don't you?"

I lower my head. Joker comes up the bank with a fish, but he doesn't bring it to us. When Legless approaches him, he dives into the river.

"I haven't eaten fish for a long time. I love to eat fish."

I tell him in a mime of spearing fish, which he perfectly understands, that I can catch fish for him. He keeps a straight face, but I can tell that he is pleased.

"You're useful, then. Very good," he says.

I run back to the hut to fetch a spear. I put it in one of the dinghies stranded in the mud bed. The distance between it and the river channel is considerable. While I drag the dinghy over the mud, Legless follows me, crawling. I'm sure he knows how difficult it is to drag a dinghy over such a terrain, but he doesn't help me. I am pulling with all of my strength and soon I am exhausted. I know he hasn't got legs, but if he wanted to help me, he could have found a way. He is out to punish me. When I stop to take a breather, he says, "You're not very strong, are you?"

We make it to the river. My muscles are aching and I'm out of breath. Legless sprawls on the prow, leaving me to paddle. He directs me to go west, where we'll find a shallow lagoon. When the floodplain dries up, he tells me, fish gather there in large numbers.

"Even an idiot can fish there," he says, looking at the sky.

I paddle for some time, but there's no sign of the lagoon. The course of the river twists and turns. Legless clears his throat and I think that perhaps he will say sorry for misleading me. Perhaps he will show remorse for having shoved mud in the hole of my mouth. Or, perhaps he will even admit to tricking me into playing master.

Instead, he asks, "You are a blacksmith, then. Yes?"

I shake my head to say no.

"Why were you going clank, clank like the old blacksmith, then?"

I cannot really explain with gestures what I was doing. But I point in the direction of the huts and hold at an imaginary object in my hands. I want to tell him that when we get back I will show him what I have made. I don't know whether he understands this. I return to paddling, but there's no sign of the lagoon.

"You see, lagoons are very funny. They are in the habit of moving all the time."

I've had enough of his pranks. I stop paddling. I plunge the punt-pole into the riverbed and tether the dinghy to it. He looks at the water and nods.

"You have chosen well. You are not as stupid as you look. This is a good place for spear fishing."

I get out of the dinghy with the spear. The water here comes up to my waist, and it's so muddy that I can't see a thing beneath the surface. For spear fishing you need clean shallow water. I stoop and circle around the dinghy, then stand up to look at the sky.

"Why are you looking at the sky? Fish don't live in the sky."

I wade further away from where I tethered the boat, come closer to the shore, but the water doesn't get any shallower or clearer. I find nothing to throw my spear at. I know Legless is watching me; it makes me feel tense.

"Any idiot can catch fish here. You are not very good, are you?"

In desperation I fling my spear, hoping that by some miracle it will home in on a fish. No such luck.

"You're worse than a blind old heron," he says. "Don't waste any more time. Come on board."

I get into the dinghy and paddle. Legless is still sprawling on the prow. When I see the sun sinking on the river I stop and let the dinghy drift. I don't look at Legless. I don't want to see his smug face grinning at me. Then quite by accident, looking at something else, I catch his expression. He is not grinning at me. Instead, he is looking towards the horizon, his face glowing, as though every bit of red from the water has seeped into him. I can't take my eyes off him. Then his face slowly turns bluish in sympathy with the purple that descends from the sky, darkening the water, but I have no idea what he is thinking.

"I will bring you coconuts. And you will do the cooking. Yes?"

I have the feeling that this is Legless's way of forgiving me. Perhaps he wants to move on. I have no intention of dwelling on what happened between us since I arrived on the island. Perhaps we can now become friends.

Back in my hut, while I prepare the clay oven, Legless goes out to pick vegetables. He takes a long time, so I go to check on Joker. You see, he has refused to move in with me to my present, humble fisherman's hut. Instead, he prefers to stay in the merchant's large tin hut. I find him curled up in his den, but he gets up when he sees me. He whistles softly, climbs on me, nibbles at my fingers. When I leave he whimpers but doesn't follow me.

Apart from aubergines, beans and gourds, Legless has also brought a large, ripe jackfruit. He asks me about Joker. I tell him that he refuses to leave the merchant's hut.

"Joker thinks he is the master now. He's very naughty," he says, laughing. "Shall we go and beat him up?"

I sense that it is not Joker but I who is the target of his remarks. I get busy chopping the vegetables, but I need water to wash them. I tell Legless to fetch water.

"It's easier for you to fetch water than me," he says. "So, from now on, you fetch water."

I am not happy about this. I'm in the middle of cooking, so he could at least fetch the water. Reluctantly I get up with the pitcher and go to the well. When I return, I see him handling Kulsum's foot. He puts his hand into the foot through the hollow that descends from the shank, then through the ankle to the insole.

"What is this? Is it what you were making?"

I nod and show him my foot.

"You're funny, you know. This doesn't look like a foot."

I take it from him, place it next to my foot, and gesture him to look at it carefully. He throws a cursory glance at it and smiles.

"You're not very good at shaping metal and making a likeness, are you? But I like this metal. I like its hole."

I put the foot back where it was, turn my back on him, and get on with the cooking. He stays silent for a while, then goes out. He comes back only when I am about to serve. Before, he used to eat quietly, as if he wasn't really there, but now he eats as noisily as Ducktor Malek. I suppose now that I am not his master he can be as uncouth as he likes.

After the main meal he breaks the jackfruit open; it's very tasty and full of flavour. It lightens my mood and Legless notices this.

"This is very tasty, isn't it?"

I nod my head.

"I will bring you coconut, I will bring you jackfruit. Every day."

It is a very large jackfruit. Although my stomach is full I can't stop eating. It reminds me of Big Suban. Ah, yes, during jackfruit season he and I used to have so much fun and adventure stealing them. I wonder what he's doing now. He must have taken part in many ambushes and battles since I saw him last. Has he survived? Will we get to share a jackfruit again? I know the gun and the war will have changed him, but I hope he hasn't changed as much as Moni Banu.

"I'll do the washing up," he says. "You cook, I wash up. Yes?"

This pleases me. When he goes out to wash I take the ledger out.

I got off lightly, I write, for playing master. Legless is more just in dealing with me than I was with him.

When he comes back I want to ask him what he thinks about in his solitary moments. I make a pantomime of pointing to his temples and raising my eyebrows to suggest what I hope is a questioning face. He makes what is, I suspect, a random but successful guess.

"All I think about is how I can be safe – and that I don't want to be beaten up by a master."

I gesture with a beckoning of my hand that he should say more.

"I like you," he says. "When you were master, you didn't beat me."

How can I tell him that I'm really sorry for pretending to be his master? I give him a rueful, downcast, apologetic look. He smiles, but doesn't say anything. I want to ask him why he presumed that I *was* a master, but can only look at him as if expecting him to say something more. He lowers his face and rubs the smooth edge of one of his stumps. He stays silent for a while, then he says, "You and I are friends, yes?"

He takes out a little knife from his pouch and gives it to me.

"The old blacksmith gave it to me. Very nice," he says. "I want you to have it. Now we are friends, yes?"

I take it, but he keeps looking at me. I know I have to give him something to show that I have accepted his friendship, but I have nothing of my own, except my torn and dirty clothes. He looks at me, looks around the room, then at me again. Since I have written in the ledger I suppose I can claim some portion of it as my own. So, I offer it to him.

"What can I do with this? I can't read," he says. "Sometimes when the old master wrote in them, he used to beat me up."

He looks around the room and fixes his gaze on Kulsum's foot.

"If you want to give me something, give me the metal piece."

I'm taken by surprise. I don't want to give it to him, but feel I can't refuse him either. I ask him what is he's going to do with it. Surely it can't be of any use to him.

"I can plant the flag in it. You know, Bangladesh flag. Yes?"

I don't know what to say, and look at him blankly. He gets up and picks up the foot and shows me the hollow through which he slid his hand earlier.

"This will be very good for standing the pole. We will put a nice flag in it, yes?"

I want to say, Please, Legless, anything but this. If you wish, I will be your servant, but please don't take this from me. He gives me a broad smile.

"We are friends now. Yes?"

Legless hangs Kulsum's foot from his neck and crawls out of the hut. I stay there, fuming at him. My breathing becomes faster and louder, and I want to rush to his den, beat him up, and snatch the foot away. If the bastard resists I will kill him. My anger doesn't lessen even when I go to bed.

Now winter is coming. I can feel the chill in the air. I wrap the quilt around me, but can't sleep. The chirping of the crickets annoys me. Why can't they shut up for a change? Then I feel sad, as if I have lost Kulsum all over again. I get up and write in the ledger. I don't fall asleep until well past midnight.

I wake up when I hear banging on the door.

"Get up! Quick!" I hear Legless, his voice panic-stricken.

I open the door for him.

"Someone has come on our island. It's very dangerous," he says. "Come and hide in my place."

It's still dark outside. The morning birds have not risen yet. We go to Legless's cave, keeping our ears open. I wonder who has come? We wait and wait, but hear nothing. Then a faint voice reaches me. At first I am not sure what that voice is saying and to whom it belongs. When I listen to it more carefully I recognise it. It is Bosa Khuni and he is calling me. My first thought is that he has come to finish me off – convinced that I am a traitor. I have to stay in hiding.

"I got your Bihari with me. Don't you want her?"

Legless doesn't want me to go out, but I ignore him and make my way up the tunnel. Before I meet Bosa Khuni I want to make sure that he is not tricking me, and that Kulsum is really with him. I pause for a few seconds outside the ruin to locate the position of his voice and edge around so that I can observe him, unnoticed. It's so dark I can hardly see anything. I grope around a bush and suddenly a bright concentration of light flares into my eyes. He must be carrying a flambeaux. I creep stealthily around him. The view is not clear in the dense fog, but he seems to be standing next to a figure, much smaller than himself. I need to hear her say something before I can be sure it's Kulsum. I hear only Bosa Khuni's voice. Is Kulsum there? I know I have to risk everything, yes everything, to find out.

"Brother Kamal, what took you so long?" asks Bosa Khuni when he sees me. Kulsum looks at me as though she is looking at a ghost, then she lets out a strange noise. I am not sure whether it is of surprise, anguish, or joy.

We go back to my hut. At the door Legless is waiting for us with Joker. Seeing Kulsum, Joker whistles excitedly, and then climbs onto her, chattering. She strokes his fur.

"Give us something to eat, Brother Kamal. We haven't eaten anything for ages."

While Legless goes out to pick fruits, we go inside the hut. I get busy frying the leftover rice and the vegetable curry from the previous night. Kulsum is still with Joker. He is now nibbling her fingers and whimpering. As Bosa Khuni is sitting next to me, I don't dare look at her straight on, let alone meet her eyes.

"I know you didn't say much gibberish to me – thank you for that, Brother Kamal – but when I left the boat I saw gibberish in your eyes," he says. "It's been doing my head in. So I brought her back."

I don't look at him and continue cooking. Legless comes back with green coconuts and mangoes. Bosa Khuni asks him who he is.

"I am Legless," he says and points his finger at me. My heart sinks. I feel he is about to denounce me for playing his master. Instead he says, "He is my elder brother and I look up to him."

Bosa Khuni laughs and says, "So, you have a brother now, Kamal. You are doing very well in this war, aren't you?"

Legless cuts coconuts for each of us. Bosa Khuni drinks and says, "I will miss these things, but one day I'll be back again in our swampland."

I'm puzzled. Where is he going? I look at him inquiringly.

"You will know soon, Brother Kamal. I believe you can even help me get there."

Legless swings out. So where is Bosa Khuni going? What does he want to tell me? From outside, Legless calls us out, his voice breathless with excitement. Kulsum and Joker stay where they are, but Bosa Khuni and I go out. Legless has placed Kulsum's iron foot on a small mound of earth and has attached a red and green Bangladeshi flag to a bamboo pole.

"Elder Brother," he calls me. "Can you help me?"

Together we place the pole inside Kulsum's iron foot. The flag flutters gently in the wind. Bosa Khuni sings, his voice as harsh and rasping as Datla Nuri's:

My Bengal of gold, I love you
Forever your skies, your air set my heart in tune
as if it were a flute…

I feel choked with emotion. As ever, I become a flute playing in the sky.

We eat fried rice, then the mangoes.

"Do you have a hookah here, Brother Kamal?" Bosa asks. "It would be nice to have a last smoke."

Last smoke? What is he on about? Legless swings out and brings back the merchant's hookah. He fills it with tobacco, lights it, and offers it to Bosa Khuni.

Bosa tells Legless, "You are a genuine fella-who-loves-his-country."

Legless looks very pleased. Bosa Khuni sucks at the hookah vigorously, and swirls of smoke dance and envelop him.

"Brother Kamal, it's time to go. Would you come and see me off?"

The last thing I want to do now is to go with him. All I want is for him to be gone so that I can be alone with Kulsum. Since she arrived my heart has been racing wild for the moment when I will give myself to her smell, to her voice, to her skin, to the green orbs of her eyes. I feel that if I have to hold off any longer I will burst into flames.

"I will go with you if you like," says Legless.

"It's very kind of you, Legless, but I have something to say to Brother Kamal. It's very important that he comes with me."

Reluctantly, I get up to follow Bosa Khuni, but as I do so, Kulsum breaks into crying. What is she crying for?

"Shut up your Bihari mouth. I've had enough of you," Bosa screams, his red eyes bursting out of their sockets.

I follow him outside, and we make our way down the ghat and on to the muddy plain. I have to walk briskly to keep up with him, but the plain seems to go on and on. By the time we reach the river, the morning mist has lifted. We stop when we finally reach the dinghy. I wait for him to tell me whatever it is he wants to tell me, but he doesn't say a word. Instead he gets into the dinghy. I don't move.

"Aren't you coming, Brother Kamal?" he says. "Let's paddle a bit. You know, so that they can't see us from the shore. I promise you it will be very quick, then you won't see me again."

I am still hesitating.

"Come on, Brother Kamal. Only a few minutes of your company. Don't deny that to an old friend. Please," he says, and extends his hand. I take it and climb into the dinghy. He pushes the dinghy away from the bank and starts paddling furiously. Where is he taking me? What does he want to do to me?

I notice the gunnysack in which he carries his machete. It's lying on the inside curve of the hull, just in front of his leg. What am I to think apart from the obvious, that he plans to take me out and cut my throat? Suddenly my whole body is trembling so much that Bosa Khuni cannot but notice it.

"Don't worry, Brother Kamal. Just a talk. I promise you I will speak no gibberish."

He paddles on, turns a bend, then stops when we reach the middle of the river. He looks at me in a strange way and smiles. I become even more convinced that he means to cut my throat. My mind is racing: if I jump into the water, perhaps I'll have a chance, yes, I'll jump. But my body stays glued to the plank where I'm sitting. I open the hole of my mouth wide and scream. Only a tiny grunt comes out.

"You want to say something, Brother Kamal?"

We're in the middle of the river and the dinghy is not tethered to anything. Yet it doesn't seem to be drifting at all. The current is very sluggish and there's hardly any wind.

"Well, Brother Kamal, here we are. Will you hear me out?"

My head is buzzing so much that I don't hear clearly what he is saying.

"As I told you before, I've brought the Bihari woman back because of your bloody gibberish. I know, I know, you didn't speak it, but it was in your eyes. Right? Bloody hell, they've been bugging me. Real bad."

I don't look at him. I can't help but direct all my thoughts to his sack and the moment when he's going to bring out his machete.

"You judged me, didn't you? I saw it in your eyes. Bloody gibberish. You thought I was worse than a shit-eating hog. Right? Ha, ha, Bosa a genuine fella-who-loves-his-country! I tell you something: in my old profession I wouldn't have given a bloody damn about it. I would have butchered your ugly face before you could even grovel at my feet. But things have changed."

I stop shaking. I suppose I have accepted the inevitability of it all. I look at him as if to say: So, you have come to butcher me now. He seems to get my meaning.

"Let's face it, Kamal. You're a bloody traitor. Yes, I should have butchered you then. Real messy and slow. But as I said, things have changed. No matter what you think of me I'm no longer a professional. Yes, the cutthroat is dead. I am now a genuine fella-who-loves-his-country. I suppose that's why your gibberish gets to me."

I look at him boldly as if to say that it is he who is talking gibberish now.

"Yes, yes, I know, but what can I do? You must know that I've never opened my inside to anyone but you, Kamal. I suppose that once I did that I became infected with gibberish like everyone else."

He looks up at the sky and squints at the glaring sun.

"Soon after I left you in the boat I was getting ready. You know, to do your Bihari in. I promise you, Kamal, I meant to do it quick and clean. Then I remembered your gibberish. Bloody hell. You really love that whore, don't you? Love? I never cared for that bloody shit. What I don't get is that you read plenty of books and things, and still all you become is a bloody traitor. All for a dirty Bihari whore. I don't understand this world. It's full of gibberish. Anyway, I couldn't do your Bihari in."

The dinghy is circling gently, as if caught in a gentle whirlpool. He looks at the water as if he has lost himself.

"When you become a genuine fella-who-loves-his-country everything changes. You get bloody smashed up by gibberish. So, I take your Bihari to my sister's place. And I tell her not to open her mouth, and play a stupid dumb. My sister says, 'Bosa, is that your wife? How come you didn't invite your own sister to your marriage?' Anyway, I shut her up. So, your Bihari stays with my sister and I go back to the war."

He starts to paddle again and reaches the other bank of the river.

"When I went to report back to Madam, she asks me if I found the Bihari and you. I say, 'Floodplains are vast, Madam. It's not easy to find a boat there, but I looked and looked. Not a trace of them. You must know that the traitor and the Bihari are very crafty, Madam.' I knew Madam didn't believe me, but she didn't question me further about it. You see what you made me do. You made me lie to my commander, Kamal. Bloody bad business. Yes, I lied for your Bihari whore."

It is about midday. The sun is pouring down on us from a clear blue sky. He drags the dinghy up the muddy slope, and then we climb the bank. We see before us the mud plain stretching for miles towards hazy lines of trees in the distance. Nothing moves and everything is quiet. He runs to the dinghy and comes back with his gunnysack.

"War for us is over, Kamal. It's only a matter of days before the rest of the country is liberated. I've already told you this, haven't

I? Oh, I am becoming so forgetful. Anyway, the war allowed me to become a genuine fella-who-loves-his-country, so I have no desire left in my life. I know, I know, it's bloody gibberish, but I feel fulfilled. You're an educated man, Kamal. You must understand this."

We walk over the mud. An osprey flies in from nowhere and ruptures the silence with its harsh cry. He screws up his eyes and watches it flying low over the river.

"Let's take a walk," he says.

We walk the muddy plain. My time is up: he will cut my throat somewhere in this lonely place. I do not care for myself any more, but what will happen to Kulsum? Who is going to look out for her?

"We have unfinished business, Brother Kamal. That's why I came back. I've been searching for you for days. It's been difficult, but I found you. No one escapes me. When I was a professional, my jobs did everything to hide from me. But I found every one of them and collected their heads. Yes, no one escapes me, Brother Kamal."

I think about making a run. I have strong legs and I'm a good runner, but I don't. We come to a ridge. He stops.

"I'm giving you a second chance, Kamal. This time I can't go back empty handed. I really mean it. If you want to keep your Bihari, you have to do it. Do you follow me?"

He takes the machete out of the sack and places it in my hands. Then he lies on the ridge. Face up. His head arched back to provide me with a clear view of his throat. His throat is surprisingly smooth, like that of a young woman.

"Come on, Kamal. Let's see what you're made of. You're not just a chicken shit, are you? You're a motherfucking traitor, that's what you are. Come on, you ugly son-of-a-bitch, see if you got the balls. You want to do pimping for that Bihari whore? Yes, yes. I bet the Bihari vomits every time she looks at you, you motherfucking traitor."

He looks at me as if he is looking for himself in a mirror. I shake my head as if to say, You're not going to make a murderer out of me, Bosa. I refuse to do it. He looks at me, but his eyes have shed all the cruelty that used to frighten me. His eyes are pleading now, as if he's the destitute one, like Kulsum, who comes knocking at my door.

"Please, Brother Kamal. My life's work is done. The war gave me the chance to redeem myself. If I live after the war, I might go back to being a cutthroat again."

I look at him as if to say, So you want me to take your place. Be the new cutthroat?

"Let me remind you that it's your call, Kamal. If you don't do it, I will do your Bihari in. I really mean it. Yes, you will have her blood on your hands. Understand?"

I am still arching over him, but I don't move. He looks at me again like the destitute one. So much like Kulsum when she sought my protection. Suddenly he sits up and grabs my hands which are still holding on to the machete. He brings them down on his throat, the blade touching the skin over his jugular. And I don't resist him.

I press the machete with all of my strength and slide it forwards and back. Blood spurts into the hole of my mouth. He thrashes about for a while, then becomes still. I push him into the ditch at the bottom of the slope and bury him under mud. Allah bless your soul, Brother Bosa. I know you have been a genuine fella-who-loves-his-country. I will never forget that. Then I go down into the river. Closing my mouth with my right hand, I jump in. The water is cold, but I stay submerged for a long time. When I surface I hear the harsh cry of the osprey but I don't see it anywhere in the sky. It is just empty and blue.

CHAPTER 21

I get back in the late afternoon.

Legless has been looking out for me from the ghat. He swings his way down to the mud plain to greet me.

"Has the freedom fighter gone? What did he tell you, Elder Brother?" I walk head down, barely paying him any notice.

"He was a good man. Yes? He was very nice to me."

I nod without looking at him and continue to walk towards the hut.

"Why are you not wearing your shirt? Where did you leave it, Elder Brother?"

How can I make him understand what has happened? How can I tell him that I left it drowning in the river, because it had Bosa Khuni's blood all over it? I walk briskly, ignoring him. He follows me for a while and then swings away from me. I stop by the well and draw a bucket of water to wash myself.

Legless comes back with one of the merchant's long white shirts and a dhoti.

"Use these, Elder Brother," he says. "Now that the old master is not here, we can take his things. Yes?"

I stay rigid as though I haven't heard him.

"Don't be silly, Elder Brother. Everyone knows that clothes don't make you a master," he says, grinning.

I wish I could look at him, but I fear he will see a murderer in my eyes.

"What's wrong, Elder Brother? Has the freedom fighter said anything bad to you?"

I still don't look at him.

"I don't know what's going on, but it must be something bad. Since you left with the freedom fighter, your wife, I mean Bhabi, is also acting strange. I ask her many times, 'Shall I bring you coconut, Bhabi?' She doesn't answer me. She just plays with Joker and looks sad."

Legless looks away to allow me to change into the merchant's clothes. I am relieved to take off the lungi, because it is also smeared with Bosa Khuni's blood, which I have been trying to hide by folding its top several times around my waist. Before Legless has a chance to see the blood stains, I rumple the lungi into a wet ball and head for the hut. He follows me.

"I can wash it for you. It's no trouble for me, Elder Brother."

I give him an irritated grunt from the back of my throat. He stops, then he crawls away. Before the hut, I pause by the door. I can hear Joker's chattering and whining, but nothing from Kulsum. Now that I am a murderer, will she see me differently?

When I enter the hut, Kulsum lifts her head slightly, giving me a cursory glance. She bends her head again and strokes Joker's black, silky fur. She doesn't look at me, nor does she say anything as I drop the lungi in a corner and tidy the bed. When I begin sweeping the mud floor she gets up and takes the broom from my hand, but still she doesn't say anything or meet my eyes. As she sweeps, Joker follows her for a while, whimpering, then he curls up in a corner. I can smell his musk. It seems he has decided to leave the merchant's tin hut and make his new den here with us.

I'm squatting on the floor, looking out through the open door. In the evening sun the hayrick, which lies next to the forge, looks as though it's a dome inlaid with beaten gold. I hear the swish of her broom behind me, feel the agony of this wait, but am paralysed to do anything about it. Suddenly she comes to the front and blocks my view. She is continuing to sweep with her head down, but now her movements are brisk and agitated. Then she turns and looks me in the eye. She stands a stone figure, her eyes glazed, and seconds pass as long as eternity until she slumps on me, wailing. I hold her and together we cry and cry until Joker comes over and whistles piercingly.

"So, you did it then?" she says, drying her eyes.

I nod.

"He told me if you didn't do it he would come for me. I know he really meant it. I was prepared for it, you know. I didn't want you to do it. I didn't want you to become a killer for my sake."

Yes, yes I did it for you, I want to tell her, but I also did it for him. And for me too. He wanted me to release him from the terrible future that he dreaded. He didn't trust himself not to go back to being a cutthroat again after the war. He wanted to die while the belief that he was a liberation fighter was still with him. And I couldn't bear losing you again. Yes, I know I am a murderer. Yes, I have become him. Instead of communicating to her any of these thoughts, I look at her blankly.

"I don't like you wearing Hindu clothes," she says suddenly.

I tell her in gestures that I have nothing else to wear. My lungi is full of Bosa Khuni's blood.

"We will bury it tonight. If they find out that you killed one of their so-called freedom fighters, they will hang you as a traitor. You understand that?"

I nod. She gets up and wraps the lungi in one of the banana leaves I collected the previous day.

"Do you trust that boy?"

Yes, I gesture.

"Still, it is wise if he doesn't know anything about this."

I wonder what has happened to her during the months we've been separated. She seems to have changed a lot: her conduct is more grown up, more forceful and practical. I didn't want her to change. Why did she have to change? Why does everyone have to change? I wonder why she hasn't yet called me Ata Allah.

She comes and squats before me.

"Am I your wife? You know, really, really your wife?"

I take out the ledger and write, "Of course you are, Kulsum. I have been thinking of you all the time."

She examines the letters carefully.

"It's much better that you are writing on paper. I didn't like your slate. It seemed so childish."

She tries to flip the pages to see what else I have written, but I take it away from her. She makes an annoying little noise with her lips, but doesn't say anything. She is silent and seems to be deep in thought.

"It won't be easy for us. You do understand that? Apart from your condition, you have nothing. I have nothing either. Besides, in your land I will always be an enemy."

"I know that. But if we have each other and work hard we will survive," I write.

She gets up and closes the door before she sits on the bed.

"Soon we will have more than the two of us to think about."

Have I heard her correctly? I go to her. We look at each other again and break into crying. She wipes my tears with the corner of her sari.

"You're going to be a father, Ata Allah."

I am so happy that I don't know what to do. I hold her and she rests her head on my shoulder. I run my fingers through her hair, brush the skin of her nape with the back of my hand. She seems to be the old Kulsum again.

I tell her that I want to celebrate the news. She, Legless and myself.

"Is it wise to tell the boy?"

"Just like us, Legless has nothing. He's an untouchable Hindu."

"But still he might hate me as an enemy. Don't forget that I am a Bihari."

"Legless is like a younger brother to me. He will never hate you. Besides, it's not in his nature to hate anyone."

Kulsum doesn't look that convinced, but I go out to look for him. It's already night but not dark. A full moon is casting a bluish light. Everything looks soft, as though floating on a lagoon. The palm trees, the bamboo groves, the lines of huts. Crickets are out too, singing their sweet songs. I find him milking his cow before the ruin. He tells me that he is milking it for Kulsum.

"Bhabi needs to drink milk?" he says.

I make him understand that we are to have a baby. He gives me a broad smile.

"I am so happy, Elder Brother. Oh, I will have a little niece."

I show him that we don't know what it will be. It could be a boy.

"But I know. It will be a beautiful niece. We must make a feast, Elder Brother."

Legless dangles the milk pot from his neck and crawls ahead of me. In the hut he offers it to Kulsum and says, "Oh Bhabi, this is for you. May Mother Kali bless my little niece. She will be as pretty as the moon," he says.

All of us go out to the yard in front of our hut. Legless swings away and brings back gourds, beans, cabbages, okras, mangoes, and a large jackfruit.

"We need some fish, Elder Brother. We can't have feast without fish."

How do we catch fish? Joker doesn't respond to Legless's whistles; I haven't seen any suitable water around here for spear fishing, and we don't know how to use the fishermen's nets. Legless strokes Joker's fur and whispers something into his ears. Joker purrs like a cat and curls around him.

"He's a funny otter. Sometimes he thinks he's a dog, now he thinks he's a cat. But he will listen to me now, Elder Brother. I had a good talk with him."

Legless and Joker are ahead of us. Strange, how they look so similar, especially the way they move. We cross the mud plain and when we come within yards of the riverbank, Joker makes a dash for the water. He dives, he swims, he catches fish. Legless whistles and whistles but still he doesn't bring us any.

"He's a greedy sod. Shall I give him a good beating, Elder Brother?"

We watch him for a while in silence. He floats on his back as though trying to catch the moon on his cheeky little face. Suddenly, Kulsum begins whistling, and both Legless and I turn to look at her. We don't notice Joker diving under water, but when we see him next, he is climbing up the bank with a large carp. He drops it by Kulsum's feet and chatters.

"Joker is very naughty," says Legless. "He is too fond of women."

We dig a hole and light a fire in the yard outside our hut. Although we have good visibility under the full moon, Legless insists on bringing his hurricane lamps – all six of them – and spreads them in a circle around us. Soon numerous insects of the night are drawn into our circle, and they buzz and swirl around the lamps. Sometimes, in their mad rush to get to the light, they hit the glass, and then they drop dead on the ground.

We don't assign ourselves tasks. Instead, all three of us do anything and everything, and in two hours we complete the cooking. It's a feast of four different types of vegetables, and the carp cooked in two different ways – large pieces marinated with mustard and chilli paste and then steamed, wrapped in banana leaves, and smaller pieces curried in a light gravy with floating coriander leaves. Of course, we have cooked a large mound of rice to accompany the dishes. Legless and I can't get enough of the fish, but Kulsum – being a Bihari – is still not used to eating bony fish. She eats her rice with the vegetables. After the main meal we eat mangoes and jackfruit, then wrapping ourselves well with quilts we lie on the ground and look at the stars.

"Legless, do you know that I'm a Bihari?" asks Kulsum.

"What's that, Bhabi?"

"I don't belong to your people. Your people and my people are enemies."

Legless stays silent for a while.

"You talk in a funny accent, but I like you. You're my Bhabi and you are the mother of my niece. Yes?"

Legless puts his hurricane lamps out and we don't talk any more. We look at the stars and listen to the crickets until it's well past midnight.

For the following few days Kulsum and I try our best to live the life of a normal married couple, but there are things that come between us. I see her tense up every time she passes the Bangladeshi flag that flutters outside our door. She doesn't look at it, but hurries past it as if it is some kind of evil that she must avoid, or her very person might be contaminated by it. We don't speak about it, but I feel irritated by her conduct. I haven't told her about the foot out of which the flag now flies, either.

One morning I am sitting on the mound beside the flag and looking at the first rays of the sun breaking through the mist. I see Kulsum hurrying past to fetch water from the well. I clap my hands to draw her attention and then beckon her to come over. She lumbers towards me as though dragging her body and comes to where I am. I show her the iron foot and tell her that I have made it and that it is hers.

"So, you want to drive the flag through me now. I will never be a part of your country. You understand?" she says, and stomps away. Yes, yes I know that when I made Kulsum's foot I meant to welcome a stranger, but why do I feel angry when she rejects our flag? I'm still sitting on the mound when Legless approaches me.

"Are you sad because Bhabi doesn't like our flag?" He must have been hiding somewhere around and watching Kulsum and I. I nod in response to his question.

"You are silly, Elder Brother. She is she, yes? Bhabi doesn't have to like the flag to be nice to us."

I shrug my shoulders.

"I like our flag and I like Bhabi too. So, there is no problem. She is she, yes?"

How come everything is so clear to him? I wish I had his feelings and his wisdom. It is not that I haven't told myself some of these things, but it's one thing to say them and quite another to feel them. Acting on them is yet another. What is your secret Legless, would you teach it to me?

Kulsum and I avoid any talk of flags, of countries, of religion, but there are still things that come between us. I know she has her own dark memories, the nightmares that sometimes make her wake up screaming in the night. Although in those moments I hold her tight, she doesn't tell me what they are, nor am I prepared to hear them, because they are bound to be full of malicious accusations thrown at us – the heathens, the "impures". I, of course, have my own dark memories. Sometimes I try hard not to remember those who were slaughtered in the school yard, but not a single day passes without my hearing their voices. Every time I am caught unawares; before I know it they crawl up into my ears and buzz like the insects of the night. How can I forget Ata Banu, the teacher, Datla Nuri, Zomir Ali, Ducktor Malek, Ala Mullah, Sona Mia and the Majee brothers? Their eyes look at me with the same blankness, with the same destitution as Kulsum's had when she sought my protection. Should I not be there for them in the way that I am for Kulsum?

Something else comes between us. These days, especially in the silence of the night, I have the strange sensation that Bosa Khuni's face is imposing itself on mine. I'm sure he knew it would happen like this. Perhaps that's why he looked at me the way he did, the look that searched for his face in the mirror of mine. It's not always there, but there are moments, especially intimate moments, when I look at Kulsum and feel I am looking at her with his face, a murderer's face. I have the feeling that she senses that too. I know I have a hole for a face, but I would have that any time rather than the perfectly formed face of a murderer. How can I rid myself of that murderer's face when I look at Kulsum? Perhaps Legless can show me how to do it.

In a matter of days, winter has crept in on us. Cold winds now blow from the mud plain, which has been slowly turning into dust. All of us get along fine, but there is something between Kulsum and Legless that I find hard to fathom. Look at them now in our hut. I'm sitting on the bed and they are on the floor, and they seem so absorbed in each other that I feel as if I'm not even in the same hut with them. She and Legless play with Joker, stroke his fur as he whines and whimpers, nibbles at their fingers or curls onto their laps. I feel they have erased all the memories that tie us to our particular plots of earth – memories that make her a bloodthirsty Bihari beast and make him an impure stain in the land of the "pures". Perhaps that's why they seem to be merging into each other, and doing so with an ease that baffles me.

Suddenly Legless breaks the intimate circle.

"What are you thinking, Elder Brother?" he asks, but without expecting an answer. "When my niece is born I will carry her in a pouch dangling from my neck. Then I will take her to see the river. Yes?"

I nod with my eyes and Kulsum smiles and rubs his head.

"We don't know what it will be. If it's a girl she will love you to show her the river. A boy will love it too. They will call you Uncle," says Kulsum.

"I know it's a girl. Oh my Bhabi, what are you going to call her?"

Kulsum rolls her eyes as if she hasn't given it a thought. Then she looks at me.

"What are you going to call her, Elder Brother?" asks Legless.

I don't know why I act this way, but I take the ledger and write the name in it. Legless takes the ledger from my hand and gives it to Kulsum.

"What is the name? Tell me the name, Bhabi?"

Kulsum looks at it for a long time, then reads, "Moni Banu."

"Who is Moni Banu?" asks Legless and brings the ledger to me to write.

"It's long story," I write.

When night falls, after Legless has left us, Joker is curled up in his den, and Kulsum and I are tucked up under a quilt, she says, "How can we call our daughter Moni Banu? Didn't she send Bosa Khuni to cut my throat?"

I don't respond.

"What does she really mean to you?"

I get up, turn up the wick on the lamp, and open the ledger.

"I have told you already. She's a sister to me," I write.

"But she's not a real sister, is she? Sister Nuri told me things, you know."

"What did she tell you?"

"Many things. For instance, that Moni Banu's family used you as a servant. That you were her servant boy to play with."

"That's not true, Kulsum. Her family gave me life. And she has been more than a sister to me. She never saw me as a deformed creature with a hole for a mouth. She cared for me just the way I am."

"So, you think I don't care for you the way you are?"

"Of course you do, Kulsum. I know it and I feel it."

"If she is so accepting, then how come she sends her butcher to kill me?"

"I know Bosa Khuni was a butcher in the past, but people change. All of us have changed in this war. He became a freedom fighter."

"Did he? Well, what I think wouldn't make any difference now, would it? But what about Moni Banu?"

"She is a freedom fighter too. You know, she lost her parents, her husband and most of her villagers. She could have stayed in the refugee camp and felt sorry for herself. Instead, she fought to save our people. If it weren't for the likes of her, Biharis and Pakistanis would have butchered us all for being heathens and impures in their pure land of Islam. Do you understand this?"

"So, killing me would save your people?"

"No, it wouldn't, Kulsum."

Our discussion isn't going anywhere. So, I put away the ledger, lower the wick on the lamp, and try to fall asleep.

I can't, though. How are Kulsum and I to live with these things between us? I stay curled up, very still, but my mind is racing like dust in the wind. I get up to go outside. I know she is still awake, but she doesn't make a noise. She's no doubt upset with me, perhaps thinking some of the things that I am thinking.

Under the full moon, the sky is still bright. I make my way to the ruin. Legless is a light sleeper and always on the alert. He meets me outside the cluttered room from which the tunnel to his shelter begins.

"What is it, Elder Brother? What's troubling you?"

We go to his shelter. With only one dimly lit lamp it looks even more like a cave than it did before. I sit on a floor-stool and as far away from the mirror as possible. He lights the other lamps and comes to sit in front of me.

"What is it, Elder Brother?" he asks again.

I tell him in gestures that I killed Bosa Khuni. He seems to understand me clearly and shakes his head.

"Why did you have to kill him, Elder Brother? He was a freedom fighter. A good man, yes?"

I nod my head to say that he was indeed a freedom fighter.

"I don't understand. Why did you kill him then, Elder Brother?"

It is too complicated to explain how he himself wanted me to kill him, so I just tell him that if I hadn't killed him he would have killed Kulsum.

"Oh I see," he says. "You killed to save the mother of my niece, yes? I'd kill for her too."

I try to tell Legless that Kulsum is our enemy, that she doesn't like our flag, our country. I don't know how much Legless follows of what I try to communicate.

"You shouldn't worry too much about flags and country, Elder Brother. You are not a master, are you? Only masters worry too much about these things."

I've heard Legless say the same things before. I'm thinking that it's all very well for him to say these things, but he didn't kill a man and put on his face.

"We go now, yes?"

"Where?"

"We go to where you buried the freedom fighter. And we will do some nice things for him there. Yes?"

It is nearly dawn. The mist has descended on the island. We go across the mud plain to the river; Legless swings his way in front and I walk briskly behind. Bosa Khuni's dinghy remains moored where I tethered it. We climb into it; Legless sits on the stern-post and I in the stern. In the dense early morning mist I can't see him clearly.

"I wish I could give you my face, Elder Brother. It's a nice face, yes?"

I follow my hunches about where we are so as to paddle us across the river. Soon, we arrive at the ditch where I buried Bosa Khuni.

"Bring water, Elder Brother, yes?" says Legless.

I look at him, baffled, but run back over the mud plain to the dinghy. I take the calabash scooper out, fill it with water from the river and hurry back to the grave. Legless tells me to pour the water into the large hole next to it. I do as he says. It makes barely any difference: the dry, dusty mud in the hole sucks in all the water, leaving only a wet stain behind.

"We need more water, Elder Brother. You go and fetch some more. Hurry up."

I run back and fetch another calabash of water.

"We need to fill the hole, Elder Brother. It's not enough water. Be quick, yes?"

I go back and forth again and again over the mud plain to the bank to scoop water from the river and carry it to pour into the hole. I do this for hours and still the hole is only a quarter full. By now the mist has thinned and I can see the river waking up to an orange glow. I'm exhausted and sweating, despite the cold, but Legless doesn't want me to stop until the hole is full. Slowly, all the mist disappears and I can see the outline of the island across the river. I haven't stopped in all this time, and I'm barely able to walk now, so I crawl back with my next load.

My limbs give up on me and I lie face up on the ridge, but I can't open my eyes as the sun is now almost directly above the hole of my mouth.

"This is enough, Elder Brother," says Legless. "Get up. We have to build a large mound for the liberation fighter. Yes?"

I drag myself up, break off pieces of hardened mud and soften them with the water from the hole, then I paste them on Bosa Khuni's grave. Legless looks on but doesn't help me. The sun has long since drifted over me and I am still adding soft mud to the top of the grave. The mound is now several feet high. My nails are bleeding from all the digging that I have done with my bare hands, pulling out pieces of mud from the hard ground.

"You've done well, Elder Brother. You have built an impressive mound. People will see it until the next flood comes and will remember the liberation fighter. I bet this will make the liberation fighter very happy. Yes?"

I smooth the soft mud on the mound with my palms, then let myself fall sideways, my head on the ridge where Bosa Khuni's head had been. I can hear the cry of the osprey but I don't see him anywhere in the sky. My vision is blurred. Perhaps that's why I can't see it, but I do see Legless's face peering into mine. What is he looking at? I don't know, but he seems to be trying to reach me. Is he trying to give me his face? Are you trying to save me, Legless?

"Shall we go back to Bhabi now? She must be getting worried, yes?"

We return late in the afternoon. Legless draws a bucketful of water for me from the well and I wash myself. He pulls another bucketful of water.

"You are fine now, Elder Brother. Your face looks nice. Now you go to Bhabi. Yes?" he says and leaves me.

You are a great healer, Legless. I feel that you have chased the murderer away from me and helped me get back my own face. I know it is a face with a gaping hole in it, but it is mine.

I carry a bucketful of water towards our hut, but stop by the flag. Dust has gathered on Kulsum's foot. I don't know what possesses me, but I wash it and wash it, look at it again but I am still not sure I have cleaned off all the dust and the stains, so I wash it once more. Then I consider how I made it as a token of the feelings that stirred deep inside me; feelings that told me to welcome the stranger. It was for Kulsum, but when I made it, what she was never crossed my mind. It was just a foot without any memories, without any past.

Yes, I have been lucky to have so many wise teachers in my life, but none wiser than Datla Nuri when she said, If someone knocks on your door, you don't ask who it is. You even don't look at their face. You just do everything you can for them. Legless teaches me the same thing but in a different way. He doesn't need to say it with words; it is there in the way he looks at me or Kulsum; the way he accepts us without asking where we come from and who we are. I suppose I must have looked at Kulsum that way when I first saw her in the middle of that vast floodplain, covered by a veil and smeared with mud. I know I have done some terrible things since then, but Legless is so wise and kind, he gives me his face, he pulls me up like Moni Banu used to do until she got married. I mustn't lose that feeling again, the feeling that stirred inside me when I made the foot, and when I saw her for the first time as a stranger in a veil in the middle of that floodplain.

I go inside the hut. Kulsum has lit the lamp and is hunched over the vegetable cutter, chopping a gourd. I pick up the ledger and squat by her; she talks to me without looking up.

"Where have you been the whole day? I've been worried sick. Have you eaten anything?"

She lifts her head to look at me searchingly, then it changes into a tender gaze as though she has been affected by something in my eyes. Have I lost the murderer's face? I open the ledger and show her the first line I ever wrote in it: Kulsum, I'm missing you.

"You are my home, my gift from Allah," she says. "I'm not going anywhere. So, you don't have to miss me any more."

Legless joins us in the hut. After the meal, we wrap ourselves well, go out, and sit by the flag. Everything still looks bright and blue, as it did the previous night. I am no longer looking on from the outside; all three of us are playing with Joker. He jumps on my lap and nibbles at my fingers. He relates to me the way he has been relating to Kulsum and Legless. I am so absorbed in playing with Joker that I don't notice the approach of the boats, but Legless never lowers his guard.

"Look Elder Brother, look at the lights. There must be so many boats."

Legless doesn't want to take any chances, especially with Kulsum. On his insistence we follow him to his shelter. Both he and I know that those who are coming in those boats are not

316

Pakistani soldiers because they always travel in gunboats. Besides, we have no reason to doubt the news that they have left the swampland for good. It is over a month now since we heard any gunshots and bombardment. Although I can't be certain, my gut feelings tell me that the boats belong to the liberation fighters. Legless tells Kulsum not to leave the shelter no matter how long it takes us to return.

"Allah be with you," she says as Legless and I go out.

We run across the mud plain, reach the riverbank and see the boats, about twenty of them, edging towards the shore. Legless and I crawl our way nearer to where they are preparing to moor. We lie down flat on our bellies behind a muddy ridge, but not for long as it soon becomes clear that the boats indeed belong to the liberation fighters.

Legless is first to approach the group of fighters who have already come on the shore. Some of them seem to know him.

"Have you taken good care of the island?" they ask.

"Yes, very good. My elder brother and myself," says Legless.

Some of the fighters lift their lamps to take a good look at me, but they are not sure what to make of me.

"I didn't know you had an elder brother," says one of the fighters.

"He was away at the start of the war, but I waited for him. He travelled long and hard to get back to me. I'm happy we found each other again."

"Good for you, Legless," says the same fighter.

"We hear the war is over. Is that true?" asks Legless.

"Yes, it is true. We defeated them in the swampland months ago. Now the Pakistani army is about to surrender in Dhaka."

"We're already flying a Bangladeshi flag on the island. My elder brother has made a nice metal thing for the flagpole. It is beautiful."

Now many more freedom fighters from the boats behind the first row are coming onto the shore.

"My elder brother and I are very happy that you are coming to our island. We love liberation fighters, but what do you plan to do here?" asks Legless.

"Nothing much," says the liberation fighter. "Our commander

wants to visit the villages, just to see how you all are doing. We also want to clean the villages of collaborators. You know, in case any of them are still hiding."

"I know everything about this island. I can tell you that there is no collaborator, no enemy here. Only myself and my elder brother."

"I'm sure with you in charge," laughs the liberation fighter, "no collaborator, no enemy would dare come here."

More and more liberation fighters are landing now. My heart is pounding because if they make a search of the island, they might discover Kulsum. Perhaps they already know that she is here. I wonder who the commander is.

Then someone from a group that has just landed runs towards me.

"Kamal," screams Big Suban.

Liberation fighters make room for him to pass; his right hand is bandaged.

"Oh Allah I thought I wasn't going to see you again. Madam sent Bosa Khuni to look for you after you left the camp with your wife. He came back telling us that he couldn't find you," says Big Suban. "About a week ago he went off on his own looking for you. We haven't seen him since. He just disappeared. Madam was very worried, you know."

I smile with my eyes to tell him how happy I am to see him again.

"Where is the wife?"

I look at him blankly, but Legless swings to my side.

"My elder brother has no wife. On this island only he and I live."

Suddenly there is a commotion among the liberation fighters, then they separate into two groups and make files that run from the boats to the bank. I am standing behind one of the files. The commander, surrounded by six fighters – all heavily armed – comes to the shore. They walk briskly between the files. As she passes me, Moni Banu casts a brief glance in my direction, but doesn't pause as she climbs the bank. When she reaches the mud plain she stops and seems to say something to one of the fighters escorting her. He comes back and announces that they are to stay here for the night.

The liberation fighters, about a hundred and fifty of them,

break into groups and run towards the island. Moni Banu and her six armed guards are also heading inland, but at a much slower pace. Legless, Big Suban and I are behind them, but at some distance.

My heart is still pounding at the prospect of the liberation fighters finding Kulsum, but I don't want Big Suban to see my nervousness, so I point to his bandaged arm to ask what happened.

"Soon after I saw you in the camp I was hit. See," he shows me his arm. "Half of it had to be cut off. I am much better now, and it doesn't hurt any more. In a few days' time I will be able to take the bandage off."

"You're like me, freedom fighter. See," Legless says, and shows Big Suban his stumps.

Big Suban rubs Legless's head with his good hand. We have crossed the mud plain. I don't see any of the liberation fighters; I assume they must be searching the island to make sure that no collaborator or enemy has taken refuge here. Moni Banu and her escorts are walking between the nets towards the huts. Big Suban tells Legless to go ahead so that he can talk to me alone. Legless looks at me, and when I signal him with my eyes, he swings away from us.

"I'm so glad to see you, Kamal. Now that the war is over, what are we going to do?" he asks.

I touch him on the shoulder.

"In a few weeks' time our unit will be disbanded. We are all supposed to go home. Actually I can go home now as I am no longer part of the unit – since I lost my hand. Madam lets me stay because I have nowhere to go."

I look at him to say that I have nowhere to go either.

"Why, Kamal? You will go to the village. Madam is counting on you to help her. You know, to help her rebuild the homestead."

I don't look at him. We reach the well and I draw a bucket of water for him to wash himself.

"What am I to do, Kamal? Now that I've lost my hand I can't cut trees any more. What's going to happen to me?"

I touch him again.

"All I wanted was to go back to being a woodcutter. I know nothing else, Kamal." His voice almost breaks into a sob.

He washes himself with his good hand and seems much calmer afterwards.

"What's happened to your wife, Kamal? I heard rumours that she is a Bihari. Is that true? I told Madam, 'She couldn't be a Bihari. I have seen her myself, Madam. I was witness to their marriage. She is only a speechless girl, just like our Kamal.' I wasn't sure if Madam believed me."

I try to avoid Big Suban's eyes.

"We're still friends, no? In the war other fighters talked about their mothers or sisters, but I have only you, Kamal. I'll never let any harm come to your wife," he says.

It crosses my mind to ask him if he would still be my friend if he found out that Kulsum was a Bihari, and that I have been deceiving him about her, but I avoid his face again.

Some of the freedom fighters have gathered in the yard in front of the merchant's hut. We make our way through them and find Moni Banu sitting on a chair on the veranda, her guards standing around her. Legless is sitting on the floor talking to her.

"He's my elder brother. I look up to him," he introduces me.

"He's my elder brother too. I also look up to him," she says.

Legless looks at me, baffled, then he mumbles that he has to tend to his vegetable patch and swings away. Moni Banu looks at me and says, "Kamal."

I squat on the floor where Legless has been; Big Suban sits next to me. Moni Banu is busy as more and more liberation fighters come to the yard to report to her. They all say the same thing: apart from Legless and his elder brother, there is no one else on this island, Madam. When the last of the groups makes its report, Moni Banu stands up to speak. Her voice is self-assured and strong. She tells them to go back to their boats and stay there for the night. They get ready to go back, except the six guards.

"I want to talk to my brother," she tells them. "This island is safe. So, you also wait for me in the boat."

They leave her reluctantly. Now only Big Suban and I are with Moni Banu.

"So we have another brother now," she says.

I scratch my head. Moni Banu stands up and tells Big Suban to fetch his things from the boat as he is to remain with us on the island. She also asks him to look for Legless. As soon as he leaves, she and I go inside the merchant's hut.

"How are you, Kamal? I have been so worried for you. You see, Bosa Khuni went to look for you about a week ago, but we haven't heard from him since. I wonder what has happened to him. He didn't find you, did he?"

I don't look at her but shake my head to say that I haven't seen him.

"I hope the collaborators didn't get him. You know, some of them are still about and hiding. Anyway, you haven't yet told me how you are."

I nod to say that I am fine.

"We tried to find you before. When you left the camp I was really worried for you. So I sent Bosa Khuni to look for you. That time he came back without finding you. I feared that I had lost you, Kamal. You can't leave me all alone."

I look at her and take the ledger and the pen out.

"I don't know what for, but I have survived the war," I write. She looks carefully at my writing.

"So, you are writing on paper now. Good. It suits you better." I shrug my shoulders.

"For the last few days I have been visiting the villages in my charge. We want to reassure the people that they are safe now. Also to mop up any remaining collaborators. But I have also been looking for you. I have no one else left, Kamal. Except you."

"You are an important commander now. You don't need the likes of me," I write.

"War is over, Kamal. We will hand over to the new government and be disbanded in a few weeks' time. We all have to return to where we were at the beginning of the war. I don't want to go back to Zafar's homestead. I'm thinking of going back to our homestead. At least you will be there for me, won't you, Kamal?"

I look at her. She looks like the Moni Banu of old when she used to demand things of me with tearful eyes. And as then, I don't have the heart to refuse her. I'm wondering what to write when Big Suban and Legless come back and knock at the door. Big Suban has brought a transistor radio, along with a bundle containing his things. Legless has brought green coconuts for Moni Banu.

"You are Elder Brother's sister. Yes? So, you are my big sister."

"Yes, I am your sister. What should I call you?"

"I am Legless."

Legless cuts a coconut for Moni Banu. When he comes to give it to her, she smiles at him broadly and affectionately rubs his head before taking it.

"Now Legless, listen to me carefully. Have you seen anyone else on this island? Think before you answer me. It's very important."

Legless becomes very sombre, as though he is giving the matter some very serious thought.

"Only elder brother and myself. No one else."

Legless asks Moni Banu if she wants to eat anything for the night. She says she has already eaten before coming to the island.

"I want you and Kamal to go back to our village as soon as possible," she tells Big Suban. "You must wait for me there. Take Legless with you as well." She then turns to Legless and says, "You come and live with me, yes? I will look after you."

"I will go anywhere my elder brother takes me. I don't want to stay on this island and be a servant boy again. When the old master comes back he will make me a servant."

"So, that's settled then. We will be two brothers and a sister living together," says Moni Banu.

Legless looks worried. No doubt he is thinking of Kulsum.

"Take the freedom fighter with you. Can you find a place for him to sleep? He's a war hero, you know," Moni tells Legless. Then she turns to Big Suban.

"I will see you back in the village soon. There will be enough room for all of us in our homestead."

"Yes, Madam," Big Suban says meekly and leaves with Legless. I don't know where Legless is taking Big Suban, but I'm sure he will not take him to his shelter.

"Close the door. It's cold," says Moni Banu, wrapping a quilt around her.

I get up to close the door and come back to sit on the edge of the bed.

"I'm scared, Kamal. I wish the war would last for ever and ever, so that I don't have to think of what will happen to me afterwards.

I wish I were dead like so many other comrades, but for some reason the bullets just passed me by."

I look at her. Suddenly the imposing figure of the commander seems to have left her. She looks thin and dark. When I see her looking so scared I feel that I have to be there for her, no matter what the consequences. But what am I to do with Kulsum? I can't leave her. I have already made her my home.

"I'll be back in our homestead in few weeks' time. Promise me, Kamal, you'll wait for me. Baba would have wanted that for us. We, brother and sister, helping each other. We will build a new hut for you with tin roof and lots of room for books. Perhaps you can build a little library in the village. Besides, I have so many projects in mind. I want to turn our pond into a fishery. Introduce new farming methods on our land. We need to be a self-sufficient country. We need to feed ourselves. Otherwise, our independence will mean nothing. I want to bring modern healthcare to our village. Dig many more tube-wells. It's not right that our people should die drinking polluted water. We will build new dykes along the river. Yes, we can control the floods. We will go from homestead to homestead to teach people how to read and write. You will be good at that, Kamal. I have read quite a few books, but I am not as learned as you are. You can be an inspiration to our village. I have so many dreams, Kamal. But I can't do it all by myself. War is one thing, but who will listen to a woman on her own afterwards? I need you with me, Kamal. Promise me, you will go back to our village and wait for me."

I'd like to promise this, I'd like to promise anything to Moni Banu, but I stay still with my head down. After waiting for a while for me to write something or give her a sign, she hardens her face.

"Where is the Bihari woman that you married? We know that you left the camp with her. Where is she?"

"We were caught in a storm. She was swept away by the waves," I write.

"Look at me, Kamal," she commands, and I look at her.

"You know, you can never lie to me. Why are you lying to me? War is over, Kamal. No harm will come to that Bihari woman. I am sure she would want to be repatriated back to Pakistan. We can help her with that."

"She was taken by the waves. That's the truth of it, Moni," I write again.

She looks at me quizzically, not believing me, but unable to challenge me either. She asks me to escort her back to the boat. Although we still have enough moonlight to find our way, I carry a lamp. We walk in silence across the island, but once on the mud plain she opens her mouth.

"I wish Baba were here. He would have talked to us in a way that made sense to us all. He wasn't one to speak much, or express his feelings. But he loved you, Kamal. More than you know."

I touch her hand to say that I know that. It feels strange because it is the first time that I've touched her since she fed me rice pudding with her fingers on her wedding day. It's even stranger to feel that I am walking with her as we used to do, especially on that afternoon when we were returning from the fair and she became a woman. Then we listened to the crickets in the dark, as she lay resting her head on my thigh and I stroked her hair, and she asked me, "If I become a woman and you are already a man, then what am I to you?"

How I would love to go back to the way we were, but I know something is broken between us. Perhaps this is the last time I will see her. We walk in silence again, her steps much brisker, as if she wants to get away from me. I lag behind and don't make any attempt to catch up with her. Then she slows down to fall in next to me.

"So, this is how it ends, Kamal. You're casting me off with a lie."

What am I to say? I gurgle from the back of my throat and lift the lamp to my face. She looks into my eyes as though she never knew me. We can't separate like this. No, no I can't do that. So I use my eyes and gestures to tell her everything about Kulsum. She is in Legless's shelter, Moni, she is there hiding from you. I had to lie to you because I didn't know how else to protect Kulsum. You see, she is my home now. Forgive me, Moni, forgive me for betraying you.

"What is it, Kamal? What are you saying?"

She'd never said anything like this to me before, because she always understood whatever I wanted to tell her, no matter how feeble my hints had been. Sometimes she understood me long before I made use of any gestures.

"It's better that I don't understand you any more, Kamal. I really don't want to know what you have to say."

I don't know what else to do, so I make a clumsy attempt to hold one of her hands, but she yanks it away. Then she walks briskly towards the boats. I almost run to keep pace with her. Ahead, I see some of the liberation fighters; they are slowly approaching us. Suddenly Moni Banu stops.

"Beautiful One," she says, as though it is the beginning of something she wants to tell me. But that is all she says; then she walks in among the liberation fighters and disappears into the boats without looking back.

Back on the island I find Big Suban in my hut. He is sitting on a floor-stool, smoking the merchant's hookah. Legless has already retired to his shelter.

"Madam still has feelings for you, Kamal. Are you going back to the homestead with her?"

I shrug my shoulders.

"That's your homestead too, Kamal. You grew up there," he says, and then pauses, as though considering something serious. "I know Madam is strong, but after the war the village will be the village. It won't be easy for a young, single woman. You know what I am saying, Kamal? You can't leave her on her own."

I look at him to say that he will be there.

"I don't know, Kamal. I can't be a woodcutter any more. So, what will I do in the village? I know Madam means well, but I don't want to be a servant boy in her homestead. Doing odd jobs. Perhaps I should go to Dhaka. No one knows me there. So, it will not matter even if I clean latrines."

We lie on the bed, side by side.

"I'll never get a wife now. At least you were married. Where did you lose her? You shouldn't have lost her, Kamal. If I were married I wouldn't hesitate to kill to save my wife."

Big Suban doesn't say any more. I lie wondering how can I tell him that I haven't lost her and that she is hiding in Legless's shelter? He touches my hand and says, "I'm your friend, Kamal. I have been a witness to your marriage. I also have nothing – like you – but I will do anything for you."

I get up, and ask him to get up, too.

"Where are we going, Kamal?" he asks, but I don't tell him anything except that he should follow me.

Legless is as vigilant as ever. He meets us outside the ruin. I touch his head to communicate that he shouldn't worry about Big Suban, that I know what I am doing. He doesn't seem that reassured, but leads us to his shelter.

"Ah, my brother's wife," Big Suban screams, seeing Kulsum. "You're alive. I'm so glad to see you."

Kulsum comes up to him, her head lowered. She pauses for a while as though unsure whether to speak or play dumb as she did before with him. Then she lifts her head and looks straight into Big Suban's eyes.

"How are you Brother Big Suban? Thank you for being a witness to our marriage."

Big Suban looks at her as if he is looking at a stranger. He looks at me in the same way. He then sits on the floor-stool scratching his head, his mouth squeezed tight. I know he is fighting to contain the sounds that his throat is itching to spill out. No doubt something full of anger. Legless senses what is happening and crawls in front of him.

"Shall I bring you milk? Very nice milk."

It takes Big Suban a while to say no.

"Bhabi will call my niece Moni Banu. Very nice name, yes? She will grow up strong like Big Sister," says Legless.

Big Suban looks at Kulsum, then at me. Legless's words seem to have had a mellowing effect on him.

"Why were you keeping this from me, Kamal? Aren't we friends?"

I look at him to apologise.

"You took a Bihari wife! That's serious, Kamal."

"Bhabi is very nice. She is kind to me," says Legless.

Big Suban looks at Kulsum again, but doesn't say anything. I look at him as if to say: Now that you know, what are you going to do?

"I don't know what I would've done in the war. We do crazy things in wars, Kamal. No? But the war is over. Now she is my brother's wife. And also the mother of my niece. Nothing more, Kamal."

Big Suban is like that. He can't stay angry for long, especially with me.

"Can I call you Middle Brother?" Legless asks Big Suban.

Big Suban nods and Legless smiles.

"What are we going to do Kamal? You can't go to the village with her. Everyone will get to know who she is," says Big Suban.

I shrug my shoulders to say that I don't know what we are going to do.

"You can't stay here for long. The fishermen must be on their way back from the refugee camps. They will be here any day. Understand?" says Big Suban.

Early in the morning we go to the shore where the liberation fighters had moored their boats. It is hard to believe that they were here the previous night because they've gone without leaving any traces – as if they'd never come. For the following few days we listen to Big Suban's transistor radio. We hear that the Pakistani army has surrendered in all the areas of the country except Dhaka, which is about to be liberated. The freedom fighters and our Indian allies are already on the outskirts. We also hear that the refugees are streaming back from their camps in India. Feeling the urgency of leaving the island, it does not take Kulsum and I long to decide to join Big Suban and try our luck in Dhaka. Only a large, anonymous city like that can hide us, and offer us some sort of shelter. Legless will go wherever we go.

It is 15th December 1971. We decide that we will set off for Dhaka tomorrow. Big Suban is staying in Legless's shelter. Kulsum, Joker, and I are in our hut. Both Kulsum and Joker are sleeping; their breaths are in perfect harmony. I realise then that somehow Joker has escaped our thoughts – what should we do with him? We can't take him to Dhaka; it wouldn't suit him there. He is better off here in the swampland. Besides, he doesn't need us, he can fend for himself. Perhaps he will miss us for a while, then his nature will take over, and he will go back to being wild.

I go and lie beside Kulsum, turning my back to her. Still in her sleep she puts her arms around me. I can feel her stomach pressing against my back. I know Kulsum may not be carrying a girl, despite what Legless says. And yet, I feel that my daughter is trying to snuggle up to me through the skin of her mother.

Who knows what the future holds for you, my little Moni Banu, my daughter, but I hope you will have my luck. You see, people of my parentage and condition don't usually get a chance in life, but the teacher gave me a home, he educated me, and he treated me – at least I like to think so – as a son, but best of all, he gave me a sister, Moni Banu; I am glad that you will be carrying her name. Only a few days after she was born, when she looked at me for the very first time, her eyes opened wide, as though she was pouring out the light of joy into me. Yes, I am lucky. She always looked at me that way.

Despite what has happened I am lucky to have survived the war. Three million of our people were slaughtered in nine months by the Pakistanis and their collaborators, and yet I lived. Besides, it brought me your mother. Who would have married me if there hadn't been a war on? Some luck – no?

Above all, it is the thought that you will be coming into my world that makes me feel the luckiest. You see, I never even dared imagine that one day someone might call me Baba. Yes, I have been lucky, but it is you who will be needing all the luck in the world now. It won't be easy at the best of times to be the daughter of a mouthless one like me, but on top of it you have a mother who is a Bihari, who is condemned to live among her enemies.

I turn around and put my hand on Kulsum's stomach, but it is still early days to feel the baby. She moans and turns over and curls up tucking my hand between her breasts. You see, my little Moni Banu, you were conceived in the middle of the war by a couple who were supposed to be enemies. It was partly due to circumstances – and we had our own reasons – that we married each other, despite our separate memories, the horrors we had witnessed, and the flags that came between us. Yet, when I first looked at your mother I just saw a woman in a veil who needed me to be there for her. It didn't matter that I didn't hear her voice or see her face – I was just there for her the way your auntie Moni Banu was there for me. Your mother did some crazy things, too. While I was a prisoner in the military camp, she was safe among her people, and it would have been natural for her to forget all about me, but she kept vigil over me day and night, then risked everything by rescuing me and coming over to live among us –

her enemies. With my memories of the camp still raw I was harsh with her, and yet she nursed me back to life and made her home inside me. I am sure many people – from her side and mine – will think of us, your mother and I, as having betrayed something of what we were supposed to be. Perhaps they will be right, but out of these betrayals you will be born – the most beautiful thing. People will say: look at the miracle, look how a deformed creature and a Bihari whore have produced the most amazing thing. I bet they will be lost for words to describe your beauty. But I will need no words when you open your eyes and look at me, because I will be trembling the way I trembled when your auntie Moni Banu first opened her eyes on me. I don't know how, but in that moment the wind will bring me the song of our swampland:

> My Bengal of gold, I love you
> Forever your skies, your air set my heart in tune
>   as if it were a flute…
> And I will become the flute to play with the sky again.

CHAPTER 22

It is 16th December 1971.

I am knee-deep in the river. Kulsum, Big Suban and Legless are already on board. I clamber over the gunwale into the dinghy, then I use the punt-pole to propel it away from the shore. Before taking the paddle I pause and cast my eyes around. The others are doing the same; we are all wanting to catch a last glimpse of Joker. In the past, when we were travelling in the cargo boat, he always appeared just before we set off from one mooring point to the next.

We can hardly see anything beyond the dinghy. A dense mist has descended on the river. Kulsum whistles but there is no sign of Joker. I begin to paddle, then stop; Kulsum whistles again. Earlier, Joker came with us from the island and dived into the river as we were loading the dinghy. So he must be somewhere nearby.

"Joker doesn't like people making a fuss when they take their leave. It's better this way. Let's go, Kamal," says Big Suban.

I begin to paddle again and the dinghy moves slowly upstream through the mist. At this rate it will take us ages to get to Dhaka, but if we catch a favourable current downstream, especially when we reach the river Meghna, we can make it there in four or five days. It will be several hours before the mist lifts, but with Legless guiding me from the stern-post I have no difficulty following the right course. We go north for a while, then take the bend west. Wrapped in a quilt, Kulsum is sitting on the plank near the stern, just in front of me. Big Suban is in the middle. Suddenly Kulsum flings the quilt away and takes the other paddle. It takes us a while to get used to each other's timing, but once we get it we cut the water faster and smoother than I thought possible in such conditions. Sensing that we don't need his direction any more, Legless stops shouting and comes to sit next to Big Suban in the middle of the dinghy. Now we can only hear the splashes of water as we slide the paddles through it. We do it together, Kulsum and I, and do so in such harmony, as if merging into each other. Still enveloped in the mist, our dinghy makes me feel that its gunwales enclose us as if they are the boundaries of our own floating country – a country comprising only the four of us: Big Suban and Legless, Kulsum and I. And in the middle of us all, of course, is our little Moni Banu.

We reach the river Meghna and catch the downstream current. The mist has disappeared and the sun is shimmering on the water. Now there are so many boats on the river, passing either side of us. All of them are flying the Bangladeshi flag. Between the sky and the river they look like a green forest that has given its leaves to the bright red orb of the sun. The people passing us in their boats are a noisy lot: if not thumping their feet or clapping their hands or shouting or laughing or crying, they are singing because today is the day that Bangladesh is finally liberated. *Joi Bangla.*

We are now moving fast in the current. Kulsum and I are still paddling together. More than ever we are matching our strokes and drifting into each other. Somehow, Big Suban and Legless seem to have caught our rhythm and gone into a trance. Like Kulsum and I, they no longer hear the other boats passing us by. We are now hardly touching the water and the dinghy seems to be gliding on its own. Yes, we have become a country all by ourselves: Kulsum and I and Big Suban and Legless. Soon my daughter Moni Banu will join us. Perhaps she will be able to do without my luck. Because, born of a mouthless one and an enemy, she will be the song of our swampland.

The most beautiful one.

ABOUT THE AUTHOR

Syed Manzurul (Manzu) Islam was born in 1953 in a small northeastern town in East Pakistan, (later Bangladesh). He came to Britain in 1975. He studied philosophy and sociology and then literature at the University of Essex between 1978-86. He has a doctorate and recently retired as reader English at the University of Gloucestershire, specialising in postcolonial literature and creative writing.

His writing grows out of his memories of Bangladesh and the experience of working as a racial harassment officer in East London at the height of the National Front provoked epidemic of 'Paki-bashing' which terrorised the lives of many Bangladeshis and other Asians in the area. Experiences from these years fed into the stories in *The Mapmakers of Spitalfields*, and his novel, *Burrow*.

He is also the author of *The Ethics of Travel: from Marco Polo to Kafka* (Manchester University Press, 1996) which explores the question: how is it possible for us to encounter those who are different from us – racially, culturally and geographically – and what are the consequences of such encounters?

The Mapmakers of Spitalfields
ISBN: 9781900715089; pp: 144; pub. 1998; price: £7.99

'There are many who date the day he took to walking as the beginning of his madness. But others mark it as the beginning of that other walk when, patiently, and bit by bit, he began tracing the secret blueprint of a new city…'

He is Brothero-Man, one of the pioneer jumping-ship men, who landed in the East End and lived by bending the English language to the umpteenth degree. He, 'the invisible surveyor of the city' must complete his walk before the mad-catchers in white coats intercept him and take him away.

These stories, set in London's Banglatown and Bangladesh, bring startlingly fresh insights to the experiences of exile and settlement. Written between realism and fantasy, acerbic humour and delicate grace, they explore the lives of exiles and settlers, traders and holy men, transvestite hemp-smoking actors and the leather-jacketed, pool-playing youths who defended Brick Lane from skinhead incursion. In the title story, Islam makes dazzling use of the metaphor of map-making as Brothero-Man, 'galloping the veins of your city' becomes the collective consciousness of all the settlers inscribing their realities on the parts of Britain they are claiming as their own.

Chris Searle writes: 'a luminous collection, a work of rare empathy and moving insight into the minds and hopes of new Londoners.'

Debjani Chatterjee writes: '…there can be little doubt that they add a fresh and distinctive voice to the contemporary British short story scene. At his best, Islam is a talented writer who impresses with his skilled craftsmanship and poetic style.'

Burrow

ISBN: 9781900715904; pp. 320; pub. 2004; price: £9.99

Tapan Ali falls in love with England and a student life of pot-
smoking and philosophy. When the money to keep him runs out
there seems no option but to return to Bangladesh until Adela, a
fellow student, offers to marry him. But this marriage of conven-
ience collapses and Tapan finds himself thrust into another
England, the East London of Bangladeshi settlement and National Front violence.

   Now an 'illegal', Tapan becomes a deshi bhai, supported by a
network of friends like Sundar Mia, who becomes his guide, anti-
Nazi warrior Masuk Ali, wise Brother Josef K, and, sharing the
centre of the novel, his lover, Nilufar Mia, a community activist
who has broken with her family to live out her alternative destiny.
Tapan has to become a mole, able to smell danger and feel his way
through the dark passageways and safe houses where the Bangladeshi community has mapped its own secret city. He must evade
the informers like Poltu Khan, the 'rat' who sells illegals to the
Immigration. But being a mole has its costs, and Tapan cannot
burrow forever — at some moment he must emerge into the
light. But how can a mole fly?

   Manzu Islam has important things to say about immigration
and race, but his instincts are always those of a storyteller. Using
edgy realism, fantasy and humour to compulsively readable
effect, he tells a warm and enduring tale of journeys and secrets,
of love, family, memory, fear and betrayal.

Boyd Tonkin writes in *The Independent*:

This summer, the enterprising Peepal Tress Press has published
Burrow by Manzu Islam (£9.99). His enjoyably picaresque novel,
satirical and lyrical by turns, follows an illegal migrant's adventures in the Bangladeshi "underground" community through the
grim Paki-bashing years of the late 1970s. Much more so than
Monica Ali, Manzu Islam finds comedy in adversity. I relished
the plot to liberate the Koh-i-Noor diamond from the Tower, the

concoction of bizarre "Banglish" dishes in restaurant kitchens to satisfy barbarous English palates, and the finger-in-every-pie shenanigans of would-be community leader, "Dr" Karamat Ali.

In this urban palimpsest, the Bangladeshi stories lie just above older layers of memory and myth – a continuity symbolised by the hero Tapan Ali's elderly Jewish friend, "Brother Josef K".

OTHER TITLES YOU MIGHT LIKE

Shaukat Osman
The State Witness
ISBN: 9780948833588; pp. 112; pub. 1993; price: £7.99

Abandoned by her husband, Saburan leaves her village to work in town. She drifts into the employment of Alamin, a small cog in the business of exporting illegal migrants from Bangladesh to the Gulf States. When she is arrested as keeper of a brothel for women in transit, she becomes the State Witness in the trial of her employer. Though the Defence finds surprising grounds within the tenets of Islam for their acquittal, both Saburan and Alamin find that, as small fish, the sharks of the immigration racket are not easy to escape. Told through the narratives of Saburan and Alamin in their prison cells, and the drama of the court sessions, *The State Witness* is a powerful satire on corruption and religious hypocrisy.

In Osman Jamal's lively translation, English readers have, for the first time, the chance to appreciate a small part of the humanity and richness of Shaukat Osman's work.

'... the force of its human commitment and satirical brilliance is a timeless achievement.' - Chris Searle, *Morning Star*.

Mirza Sheikh I'tesamuddin
The Wonders of Vilayet
trans. Kaiser Haq
ISBN: 9781900715157; pp. 160; pub. 2002; price: £10.99

In 1765, Mirza Sheikh I'tesamuddin, a Bengali munchi employed by the East India Company, travelled on a mission to Britain to seek protection for the Mogul Emperor Shah Alam II. The mission was aborted by the greed and duplicity of Robert Clive, but it resulted in this remarkable account of the Mirza's travels in Britain and Europe.

Written in Persian, 'Shigurf Nama-e-Vilayet' or 'Wonderful Tales about Europe' is an entertaining, unique and culturally valuable document. The Mirza was in no sense a colonial subject, and whilst he wrote frankly about what he felt accounted for India's decline and Europe's contemporary ascendance, he was a highly educated, culturally self-confident observer with a sharp and quizzical curiosity about the alien cultures he encountered. His accounts of visits to the theatre, the circus, freakshows, the 'mardrassah of Oxford', Scotland, of the racial alarms his presence sometimes provoked and of his impressions of British moral codes (including the 'filthy habits of the firinghees') make for fascinating reading.

Kaiser Haq's scholarly, modern translation is the first to appear in English since the original 'abridged and flawed translation' which appeared in 1827. *The Wonders of Vilayet* is an important document, a salutary addition to Western accounts of the 'Otherness' of India, orientalism in reverse.